BULL
SHE COULD BE THE END OF ME

PENNY DEE

Bull
Kings of Mayhem MC Series Book 6

Penny Dee

This book is a work of fiction. Any references to real events, real people, and real places are used fictitiously. Other names, characters, places and incidents are products of the Author's imagination and any resemblance to persons, living or dead, actual events, organisations or places is entirely coincidental.

All rights are reserved. This book is intended for the purchaser of this book ONLY. No part of this book may be reproduced or transmitted in any form or by any means, graphic, electronic, or mechanical, including photocopying, recording, taping, or by any information storage retrieval system, without the express written permission of the Author. All songs, song titles and lyrics contained in this book are the property of the respective songwriters and copyright holders.

Disclaimer: The material in this book contains graphic language and sexual content and is intended for mature audiences, ages 18 and older.

ISBN: 979-8669786939

Copy Editing by Elaine York at Allusion Graphics
Proofreading by Stephanie Burdett
Book design by Swish Design & Editing
Cover design by Marisa at Cover Me Darling
Cover image by Wander Aguiar :: Photography
Cover model by Barett Stowers
Cover Image Copyright 2019

First Edition
Copyright © 2019 Penny Dee
All Rights Reserved

DEDICATION

For Laurie

I can still remember how excited you were when I told you about my idea for an MC story. How you read the prologue to book one and got super enthusiastic about it. When self-doubt set in, you were there, encouraging me to continue. As a result, the Kings of Mayhem were born. So I'd like to take this opportunity to thank you. Many years ago, you reached out to me on Facebook, and it changed my writing career because I was so inexperienced at the time, and you taught me so much about the indie book world. I am so grateful to you, my friend, and I hope the future is as sparkling and wonderful for you as you deserve it to be.

Much love,

Penny

PATH OF FAMILY

The Calley Family
Hutch Calley (deceased) married Sybil Stone
Griffin Calley
Garrett Calley (deceased)

Griffin Calley married Peggy Russell
Isaac Calley (deceased)
Abby Calley

Garrett Calley married Veronica Western
Chance Calley
Cade Calley
Caleb Calley
Chastity Calley

The Western Family
Michael 'Bull' Western
Veronica 'Ronnie' Western

KINGS OF MAYHEM MC

Bull (President)
Cade (VP)
Ruger (SAA)
Chance
Caleb
Davey
Vader
Joker
Cool Hand
Griffin
Matlock
Maverick
Animal
Yale
Tully
Nitro
Hawke
Ari
Picasso
Caveman
Reuben (honorary member)

Prospect 1
Prospect 2

Employees of the Kings
Red (Chef, clubhouse housekeeper)
Randy (Clubhouse barman)
Mrs Stephens (Bookkeeper, administration)

BULL
SHE COULD BE THE END OF ME
PENNY DEE

PROLOGUE

BULL
Eighteen Years Ago

My wife was going to kill me. I was due home more than an hour ago and I was only now walking out the door. I know she's cooked me dinner, because today she found out the sex of our baby and instead of telling me over the phone, she wanted to tell me face to face. And in typical Wendy style, she was going to make it a big deal. Because in reality, it was a big damn deal.

We were having a baby and I was beyond excited.

My cell phone rang.

Speak of the devil.

Wendy.

My gorgeous wife of three months.

The woman I couldn't get enough of.

The woman now four months pregnant with my baby.

I flicked open my phone. "Hey, babe."

"Please tell me you're on your way home."

"I'm out the door. I promise."

"Good, because dinner is almost ready and I want to celebratory-fuck my husband before we eat. So, you need to get your sexy ass home now."

I grinned. What my wife wanted, my wife would get. "Yes, ma'am."

"Did you get the wine?"

Fuck.

Her doctor told her she was allowed one glass of wine to celebrate. And in Wendy's words, she wanted to make it count with a bottle of Stags' Leap Viognier. It was her favorite. The same bottle we drank the night I asked her to marry me. Unfortunately, there was only one liquor store in town that sold it, and it was in the opposite direction of the clubhouse.

"I'll get it on the way home."

She growled but she wasn't angry. "The liquor store is in the opposite direction. I'll go. You just get your sexy ass home. I want you naked and ready when I get back."

It started to rain as I pulled out of the clubhouse parking lot. My Harley was being painted, so I was driving the club's van for the next two days. It was rush-hour traffic, and as my headlights cut into the late afternoon gloom, I made my way out of town toward the watermelon fields where Wendy and I lived in a renovated, sixties bungalow. Out here the traffic was lighter, but as I approached the water tower on the edge of town, the traffic crawled to a stop.

It was raining hard now. Impatiently, I tapped the steering wheel. It had been almost an hour since I'd told Wendy I'd be home. I took off my dark glasses to peer through the windshield. I had a rare form of color blindness. One that doesn't tolerate light. So, I had to wear dark glasses nearly all the time. It's also given me eyes the color of arctic ice. As a kid, I used to scare all the other kids with my unholy demon eyes. And as an adult, things weren't much different. You can see the dread on people's faces when I remove my glasses and they see my otherworldly irises. Oddly enough, it scares the men, but it attracts the ladies.

I wiped the fog from the windshield. Up ahead, red and blue lights cut into the bad weather. This stretch of road was notorious for accidents. Especially when it rained. And by the look of this one, we were going to be stuck for a while.

I reached for my phone and tried ringing Wendy to tell her I'd be late, but it went to voicemail. A second call did the same.

Bull

An ambulance raced past me on the side of the road, followed by a patrol car.

Slowly the minutes ticked by. I continued to thumb the steering wheel, knowing I was letting my wife down.

Again.

I'm working on it, baby. Don't give up on me. I love you so damn much.

The rain slowed to a gentle sprinkling, and as we inched toward the wreckage, I peered through the windshield to get a better look.

Two cars had collided head on. One had crossed onto the wrong side of the road and had a blanket covering the windshield. The driver obviously dead.

But the other car...

The one it had run into.

It took a moment to register.

The crumpled wreckage.

The license plate.

The shock of blonde hair trailing out the open window.

The blood.

Dread washed over me.

Wendy.

I ripped open the door.

Wendy.

My feet barely touched the ground.

Wendy.

My legs struggled to keep up with my desperation to reach her. I ran toward the wreck, pushing past people and calling her name. A police officer tried to stop me, but I shoved him out of the way. I could see Wendy trapped inside. Her eyes were open, her brow pulled in with pain. *She's alive. Dear God, thank you.* A paramedic was treating her through the smashed-out window. I launched at the broken remains of her car and dropped to my knees. Recognition lit up in her eyes.

"Baby, I'm here. I'm here."

Her eyes focused on me. And she smiled softly. "Michael..."

I reached for her hand.

Christ, there was so much blood.

"Yeah, baby, I'm here and I'm not going anywhere." I looked at the paramedic. *Please, save her. Please, save my wife.* I squeezed Wendy's fingers. They were stone cold. "You're going to be alright."

"I feel okay..." she said, sleepily. "I was going to get wine... he came out of nowhere... I want to go home."

"I know, sweetheart. They'll have you out of here soon, okay?"

"I'm cold..."

"It's raining."

"It is?" She looked around her, dazed.

"Don't move, baby."

Her eyes suddenly widened with terror, as if she only now realized what was happening. Panicking, she started to struggle.

"You're going to have to calm down, darlin'," the paramedic said as he tried to inject some kind of medication into her IV.

Wendy stared at me, her eyes round with fear.

"It's going to be okay, baby, I promise. But you need to let them work on you so they can get you out of here."

She started to cry but took a deep breath to fight back her tears. "The baby..."

My eyes dropped to her lap. There was so much blood.

I soothed her damp brow with my fingers, pushing back her wet and bloody hair. "You and our baby are coming home with me, do you hear me? You're both coming home with me."

She searched my face for reassurance. When she found it, she relaxed and her eyes softened. *She's going to be fine.* But when I glanced at the paramedic, the look on his face told me a completely different story.

"I'm so tired," Wendy said. Her lids were heavy. "Is our baby okay?"

"Our baby is fine. You're fine."

A small, weak smile softened her lips.

"I was so excited when I found out I was having your baby... I love you so much..."

"And I love you..."

"I wanted us to have a big family..."

Oh God, she's talking like it's not going to happen.

"And we will..."

"Promise?"

I nodded. I was crying. Because somewhere deep inside, I already knew things weren't going to work out that way.

"Michael…."

"Yeah, baby…?"

But she didn't answer.

She became very still.

I gently shook her, but she was like stone. And in that moment of pure agony, I watched the light go out of her eyes.

"No, no, no, no…!" Fear roared through me and my body started to shake. "Wendy…baby!" I turned to the paramedic. "Do something!"

But he just shook his head. "I'm sorry, sir. There's nothing we can do."

I turned back to my wife. Rain poured from the sky, hitting her soft white skin and mingling with her blood.

She was gone.

No!

A primal scream ripped from my body.

Wendy.

My life.

Gone.

I collapsed against the wreckage and my body heaved with the sudden grief, my brain tilting with the sheer agony of it all.

Someone pulled me away.

"I'm sorry, son." It was Deputy Buckman. I fought him and tried to get back to Wendy. I turned and tried to shake him free, but his grip on me was tight. And somehow, through the fog of panic, my mind was able to register the meaning of the blanket being draped over the window, and the agony that followed was excruciating.

My wife.

My knees weakened.

My baby.

I fell to the ground.

How was this possible?

Rain battered my skin as I fell back and screamed into the stormy sky.

And in that moment, I prayed for the heavens to erupt with lightning and take me out with one violent bolt.

Instead, strong hands pulled me to my feet, and through my pain I realized it was Garrett, the club's president. Where had he come from? Had Deputy Buckman called him? I fought him but I was numb, weakened by my devastation, and no match against his strength. He hauled me to his chest and held me there, his strong hand pressing into the nape of my neck.

"I've got you, brother. I've got you."

I shook against him as the shock sank into my bones. I couldn't think straight. Couldn't breathe.

All I could see were Wendy's vacant eyes.

All I could feel were her fingers going limp against mine.

All I could hear was the fall of the rain as the life I knew slipped away from me.

Seventeen Years Ago

Rain soaked the green grass of the cemetery as I stumbled my way down the muddy slope toward my wife's tombstone. Bourbon sloshed on my boots and fogged my brain.

I was a mess.

A fucking shell of a man.

I put the bottle of whiskey to my lips and bit back the burn as it made its way through my chest. I took another swig, hoping it would wash away the never-ending pain, and ran the back of my hand across my mouth.

I was in hell.

And I was done.

I stared at the gun in my hand.

I had tried. No one could say that I hadn't. For twelve fucking months I had dragged myself out of bed every single fucking day, existing only to put one foot in front of the other. I ate. I worked. I pushed my body to the extreme at the gym. And sometimes I even fucked just so I could feel something—anything but the pain of losing Wendy—hating myself more and more with every passing day without her. Because no matter how hard I tried to keep her alive, the love of my life was dead, and every day I could feel the memory of her pulling further and further away from me.

Yeah, I was done with this shit.

If there was a heaven, then heaven was where I wanted to be.

With her.

And if there was no heaven, if there was just darkness waiting on the other side, then that would be fine too.

Anything but this.

I gripped the handle of the gun and stared at Wendy's tombstone. *I'm coming, baby.* I raised my arm and pressed the gun to my temple.

"She'll kick your ass," came the voice behind me. "And then she'll kick it some more."

I knew without looking that it was Ruger. Wendy's younger brother.

"You know it's true. You know this isn't what she would want."

I closed my eyes and let the hand holding the gun drop to my side. "Go away, Ruger."

I felt him walk up behind me. "I can't do that, Bull."

Rain ran down my face. I opened my eyes and looked at Wendy's name carved into the marble tombstone, a renewed pain tightening around my heart. I raised the gun again and felt the cold, wet steel press into my skin.

"You really going to do this to me?" Ruger questioned.

Even through my mental agony, I realized it was a fucking weird thing for him to say. I turned my head but still didn't look at him. "What the fuck are you talking about?"

Through the corner of my eye I saw him walk around me to stand between me and his sister's grave.

"I'm only twenty-two fucking years old. My sister just died. You're really going to splatter my best friend's brains all over the ground in front of me. Christ, Bull...I'll end up a fucking basket case. And you know what, it'll all be your damn fault."

He crouched down so we were eye-level. And when I looked into his bright eyes, I saw his sister, and my face crumpled. I missed her. I missed our unborn baby. Bone-achingly so. And I wanted her back. Wanted them both back. I didn't want to feel like this anymore. He had to understand that.

I narrowed my eyes as the rain continued to fall, running in rivulets down my face. "Go home, Ruger."

But the fucker shook his head. "I can't do that, man, and you know it."

Too bad.

I had given him the option.

He wasn't my responsibility. I couldn't make him leave.

But he needed to look away.

Because I was ready.

Baby, I'm coming…

With a rush, I raised the gun to my temple and pulled the trigger.

Unfortunately, my motor skills were bourbon-soaked and unsteady, and no match for Ruger's lightning-fast reflexes. He wrestled the gun from my hand and knocked me to the ground.

I fought back, sort of, but Ruger pushed me down and put my drunk ass to sleep with his fist.

Unfortunately for me, it wasn't permanently.

CHAPTER 1

BULL
Present Day

Fuck!

My eyes snapped open.

I wasn't in my bed.

I had slept over.

Fuck!

I ripped the bed covers off and climbed out, walking naked across the room to where my clothes lay scattered across the floor. She had ripped them off of me the night before, piece by piece as we'd kissed ferociously on our way to her bedroom. The sex had been good. Good enough that I'd fallen into a contented asleep and ended up spending the night. *Which wasn't good.* That wasn't part of the deal. There were rules. *My rules.* We fucked. We talked. I left. It was a situation that suited us both fine. I couldn't afford to be with someone who wanted anything more than a good time between the sheets, and she couldn't afford to have anything more than a good time with a bad guy like me. The fact that my Harley had been parked in her driveway overnight was a mistake. For both of us.

I pulled on my jeans but left them unzipped as I searched for my t-shirt.

In a few weeks, her campaign for re-election as town mayor would begin, and I had no doubt our evenings in her bed would be over.

Which suited me just fine.

Because this was never going to be a long-term thing.

"You're so fucking hot, you know that?" she said.

I looked over at her on the bed. She was sprawled naked among the sheets, giving me a serious case of fuck-me eyes.

"You're not so bad yourself."

She grinned. She knew she was hot. Five years older than me, she took good care of herself. Firm thighs. Tight body. A few trips to the plastic surgeon.

And she fucked like it was an addiction.

I walked shirtless toward her and she crawled across the bed. "You know, I'm announcing my candidacy to re-run for mayor this week."

Well, there you go, that was sooner than I expected.

"I knew it was coming..." I said as she pulled me closer by the open zipper of my jeans.

"You know it means we won't be able to fuck in secret anymore, right?"

"Pity. The secrecy thing was hot."

"Exactly how I like it. But I can't afford to...well, you know what this town is like. They want me all wrapped up in a tidy package... Andrew Voight asked me out on a date the other night."

Voight was the principal of the elementary school. And a more suitable date for our town mayor than me.

"He did?"

"Yes."

For a politician, she was surprisingly honest. She didn't beat around the bush. She called it as she saw it. It was one of the things I admired about her.

"And what did you tell him?"

She reached into my jeans.

"I told him yes."

She started to stroke me.

"Sounds like a smart answer," I replied.

When I hardened in her hand, she licked her lips and heat flared in her eyes.

"I'm going to miss your cock," she said, as she released me from my jeans.

Bending her head, she wrapped her juicy lips around the thick shaft and sucked me into her tight, wet mouth, sending a shiver through me.

"And I'm going to miss your perfect mouth…" I replied, my breath ragged because this woman was extremely good with her mouth.

She pulled away and lay back on the bed, opening her legs. "What about my pussy, are you going to miss that too?"

I grinned down at her.

Our involvement had run its course. We would go our separate ways and move on to other people. There was no heartbreak. No disappointment. No pain. Just a finality.

But for now?

What the hell.

I climbed on the bed and took her in my arms, and kissing her fiercely, spent the next hour showing the mayor of Destiny exactly why they called me Bull, and why size really does matter.

CHAPTER 2

TAYLOR

Watery blood swirled at my toes before disappearing down the drain.

I cried, tears streaming down my face as my fear and grief spiraled through me like a tornado. I held my hands out in front of me, they were shaking and the shower water mingled with the blood coating my fingers.

I did it to make him happy.

I did it because I loved him and wanted him to love me back.

But I hated every second of it.

It hurt.

It hurt right through to my soul.

My eyes dropped to the sopping wet wig laying in a pool of water on the bathroom floor and the overturned stilettos scattered beside it, and my stomach churned violently until I had no choice but to release its contents into the drain.

Sitting up, I hit the tiled wall with the back of my head and bit back my agony, reminding myself to stop being a pussy. I had been raised to be stronger than this. And this was my life now. I had to suck it up if I was to survive.

The bathroom door burst open and he walked in. Fear gunned its way through my body and I started to shake again.

Bull

This was my life now and I had nowhere to run.
But one day... one day I would run far, far away.

I sat up with a rush. Sweat soaked my skin as fear thrummed through my veins. My lungs heaved and burned, desperate for more oxygen.

I glanced out the window. It was dark. *The middle of the night dark.* Outside, a streetlight glowed in the blackness giving me enough light to see my surroundings, and the familiarity of them grounded me, bringing me back to Earth.

It was just a dream, Taylor.

Just a dream.

Just a distant memory.

Those days are over now.

But...

Feeling the sudden rush of panic I always felt after the nightmares, I ripped off the bedcovers and tore down the hallway to Noah's room. Fear knotted in my throat and my knees buckled with dread as I pushed open the door, terrified I would find my younger brother was gone. But the relief was instant when I saw him sleeping soundly in his bed, hugging his pillow and lost in a sweet slumber. I gripped the door knob, the sudden absence of fear making me weak. Sagging against the door, I heaved out the breath I had been holding onto, sucking the cool night air into my lungs and willing my heart to stop racing.

See, it was just a dream.

Those days are over now.

For seven years we'd been running.

For seven years we'd been hiding in the shadows of one new town after another.

But soon we wouldn't have to run or hide anymore.

I looked at my eleven-year-old brother and my grip tightened on the door knob.

He was my world.

The only thing I had left.

And I would do anything to protect him.
Anything at all.

CHAPTER 3

BULL

"Is that a fucking hickey?" I asked, as I walked into chapel the next morning.

Davey, our giant, perverted teddy bear, grinned proudly. "Fucking A, it is. Haven't had one of these bad boys since I was in high school."

"That's because you're supposed to be a fucking grown up," Cool Hand said, throwing a beer bottle cap at him. "What are you, thirteen?"

But Davey couldn't care less as he sat back in his chair, and laced his fat hands across his fat belly, looking proud of himself. "What can I say? Tiffani could suck a golf ball through a garden hose."

"I can second that," Hawke agreed.

"Hell, that girl could suck the chrome off my exhaust pipes," Matlock added, ripping the cap off his beer and flicking it onto the table.

Ignoring them, I sat down. Already seated around the massive wooden slab of Carolina ash were nineteen Kings.

Nineteen mean-looking sonsofbitches who were everything to me. My brothers. My family. *My responsibility.*

We met in chapel once a week. More if things were happening.

And right now, *things were happening.*

Thanks to one piece of shit drug dealer.

Gimmel Martel.

The Kings of Mayhem number one arch nemesis.

He had arrived in our town under the guise of being a wine importer. But in reality, he had been a drug importer with a thriving cocaine business. I gave him a chance to leave quietly because this was *my town*, *my people*, *my county*, and I wasn't going to let him spill his poison into the well and destroy the people my club and I protected. But my offer fell on deaf ears. And instead, he decided to send me a message. He sent someone to intimidate my niece, and when that *someone* put his hands all over her, well, Martel had to learn who he was dealing with.

No one touched my family and got away with it.

To drive this point home, I burned his cocaine and his vineyards to the fucking ground.

In retaliation, Gimmel Martel ordered his men to shoot up my nephew's wedding, putting my sergeant-at-arms in the hospital with life-threatening wounds. He executed orders to inflict damage on my club. *My family.* But he was already gone before I could retaliate. He vanished into the bowels of a seedy underworld, his whereabouts cloaked by a dark network of criminals and organized crime.

I wanted revenge.

Hell, I wanted to tear him apart with my bare hands.

But the coward slid into the shadows like a scared little mouse because he knew I was coming for him.

I was a patient man. At some point, he would have to surface for air, and when he did, I would be waiting.

In the meantime, because I couldn't hurt the man, I destroyed the empire.

Piece by piece.

Alliance by alliance.

One deal at a fucking time.

I used different pieces of information I found in the ashes of his burned-out vineyard to pick at the threads of his business interests, to slowly unravel his entire fucking kingdom.

And he felt it too. Right where it hurt.

His pile of cash.

He needed to learn.

No one fucked with me and my club.

And no one, *fucking no one*, fucked with my family.

My anger and lust for revenge had grown into something unstoppable.

He could hide, but he couldn't hide forever.

I would wait.

I had time.

But time made me more dangerous.

And the longer he kept me waiting, the more dangerous I would become.

I would keep pulling at the loose string of his empire—his drug *distribution*—until it slowly unraveled everything that meant something to him.

I was going to smoke him out.

And then I was going to kill him.

After chapel, Ruger hung back.

"How's my niece?" I asked.

"She's as big as a whale," he said with a grin. When I gave him a filthy look, he held up his hands in surrender. "Hey, they're her words, not mine."

"But you tell her she's wrong, right?"

"Hell, brother, I'm no fool. I value my balls." His eyes glittered with happiness. I'd never seen Ruger look as happy as he was when he was with or talking about Chastity. "She's getting antsy for our boy to arrive."

"It's a boy?"

"Found out yesterday. Actually, that's what I want to talk to you about. She's on her way over here."

"What for?"

Before he could answer, Chastity walked into the club. Eight months pregnant and glowing, she looked beautiful. Pride swelled in my chest. But it was quickly followed by a surge of venom when I remembered what happened to her last summer. How one of Martel's thugs had pulled her over on the highway pretending to be a cop. How he had put his hands on her, threatened her. It was hard to forget because Chastity meant everything to me, and I felt a wildfire of hate in my brain every time I thought about it.

She was the daughter I'd never had, and I wouldn't think twice about putting someone in the ground for hurting her.

Her whole life, I'd been a little overprotective of her.

If having three older, biker brothers wasn't bad enough, then having a fiercely protective uncle was a nightmare. And she wasn't shy in telling me.

When I discovered my best friend was involved with her, I'd lost my shit. In my mind, no one was ever going to be good enough for her. Not even the man who'd stopped me from blowing my head off during the dark days following Wendy's death.

But Ruger had proved himself to be more than fucking worthy. He worshiped Chastity. Treated her like his queen. Took three bullets for her when he'd thrown himself in front of a gunman at Cassidy and Chance's wedding.

I couldn't ask for more than that. And now they were about to become parents.

"Hey, Uncle Bull," Chastity said, pressing a kiss to my cheek.

"Hey, sweet girl. You feeling okay?"

"Yeah, but the sooner this baby is out of me, the better. I'm tired of waddling like a duck and dry heaving every time I smell meat." She rubbed her huge belly. "Can we talk?"

"This sounds serious. Should I be concerned?"

In my family, pregnancy wasn't without risk. My mom almost died giving birth to my older sister, Veronica, and I was born by C-section after my mom's heart stopped during labor. Thankfully, she'd pulled through. But I was the last of her children, even though she'd wanted more.

And Veronica had problems giving birth to all four of her babies. After her eldest, Chance, was born, the doctor advised her not to have anymore. It was the same advice he gave her following Cade and

Caleb's birth. And it was advice she finally listened to following Chastity's harrowing birth.

I prayed that things went smoothly for my niece.

Her smile was beautiful. "No. Everything is fine. Perfect, actually."

I relaxed.

"Come on, we can talk in my office." I led her and Ruger out of the bar.

"I hope you don't mind but I asked Indy and Cade to join us," Chastity said.

No sooner had we walked into my office when the door opened, and Cade walked in with his very own mini-me on his shoulders. River was almost five, and the spitting image of his father.

Indy walked in behind them, carrying little Bella in her arms. As soon as she saw me, Bella reached out her chubby arms and wriggled against her mom as if to say, *give me to him*. Her adorable little face broke into a big smile the moment Indy handed her over and I secured her in my arms. The kid loved me, and I was fucking crazy about her.

Her name was an homage to Mirabella, the murdered wife of a now-deceased club member. Mirabella died when a psychopath executed a campaign of revenge against the club. The same man also kidnapped Indy, but fell short of killing her because Cade put two bullets in him.

"So, what is this all about?" I asked, sitting behind my desk with Bella on my lap.

"Well, we have a favor to ask," Chastity said, trying to get comfortable in the chair.

I gave her a nod. "Go on."

"We'd like you to be Will's godfather," she said. "And we'd like Cade and Indy to be his godparents too," she added, looking at her brother and his wife.

"If anything happened to us...we want our boy to be raised by family." Ruger placed his hand on his wife's belly. "By the people we know will raise him right."

Our world was unpredictable. Life could turn on a dime.

Godfather.

It was the closest I was going to get to being a father.

I was resigned to having no children of my own. I had the club. I had my nieces and nephews, and now my grand-nephews and nieces. And while there had always been a dull ache in my chest knowing I'd never hold my own kid, I gave up the dream.

After all, my chance died in a car wreck eighteen years earlier.

And I had never come close with anyone since. There had been no close calls, of course, because when I fucked, I fucked with protection.

A baby I would love.

A fucking STD, I wouldn't.

I smiled at my niece and my best friend. "Nothing would make me happier."

CHAPTER 4

BULL

I left the clubhouse and headed for home. As the wind whipped across my face, I thought about Indy and Cade, and how River looked just like his father, and how Bella was the cutest thing since fucking sliced bread. Then, I thought of Caleb and Honey, and how their kids crawled all over them, spreading their love and adoration over their parents like fairy dust. I thought of Cassidy and Chance, and precocious little Ava who had her daddy wrapped around her little finger like twine.

Then I thought of my best friend and my niece, about to start their very own family, and the small ache in my chest, the one that had been there for eighteen years, seeped into every nook and cranny of my dark heart.

I wasn't one to feel sorry for myself. It was a waste of fucking time.

And nobody liked a pity-party for one.

But something about today's meeting with my family had dragged some deeply buried shit to the surface.

I put it down to the apprehension I felt toward what I was going to do. Tomorrow was going to be ugly. I didn't enjoy a lot of the things I did as president, but some things needed to be done. Tomorrow was no different. It was probably why I was feeling so damn nostalgic.

I rode through the afternoon light, hoping the warm breeze coming in off the river would clear away the nostalgia. I wasn't a man who was a slave to his emotions. Like everything in my life, I kept them in check. But when I felt the slow creep of something dark entering my mind, taking a ride was the perfect fucking elixir. There was nothing like the wind whipping against your body and rushing past your face to clear your head and leave you feeling high.

As I pulled up to the set of lights near the elementary school, something out of the corner of my eye caught my attention. In the parking lot behind the bus stop, three older kids were pushing around a smaller kid. It was your typical middle school shoulder shoving stuff, but experience told me the smaller kid was way out of his league with these guys.

One thing I won't ever tolerate is an older punk picking on someone smaller than him. Let alone two on one.

Obviously, I belong to a motorcycle club. We thrive as a pack. But I'll tell you one thing, my club exists as a powerful union. Not a pack of fucking bullies. And you won't catch us crushing the little guy just because we can. It was a lesson my daddy taught me from an early age. And one I was about to teach these little punks right now.

Because I knew what it felt like to be picked on.

Knew what it was like to feel small and feeble.

When I was a small boy, I used to walk home from school by myself. I used to cut through the watermelon fields and wade through the shallows of the river toward our home near the railroad tracks. Jethro and Camryn Stuber were three years older than me…and mean as fuck. Their older brother, Waylon, was four years older, and even meaner. They thought it was fun to throw stones…and then rocks. Then they thought it was fun to hold me down in the mud and water until I couldn't breathe. One time, they thought it would be really fun to hold me down until I stopped fighting and became still in the murky water.

Four decades later, I could still feel my lungs burning and my brain crying for oxygen as my world slowly and excruciatingly turned to black. Veronica had found me in the shallows, barely alive. She told me later that she thanked God every single day for saving my life, that if she had come along a few minutes later, I might have died. But I did

Bull

die in those shallows. Because the boy who woke up from the terrible darkness was different. He knew how it felt to be helpless, how it felt to feel vulnerable and weak, and he promised himself that he wasn't ever going to feel that way again.

Roaring off the road, I startled all of them when I pulled up with a violent screech of tires.

Two of the punks were smart enough to look scared. They were twins. Identical. Both sharing the same look of panic at my arrival.

The third, a taller kid who was obviously the leader of the pack, looked impressed by me and my bike. He let go of the smaller kid's t-shirt and puffed out his chest.

"Nice bike, man," he said with a raise of his chin.

Flattery never got anyone anywhere with me.

"You know who I am, kid?"

"You're Bull. You're the president of the Kings of Mayhem."

"That's right. And do you know who the Kings of Mayhem are?"

The kid grinned. "They're bad motherfuckers."

I nodded. "Yes, we are, indeed, bad motherfuckers. And you know who the meanest, baddest motherfucker of them all is?"

His brow wrinkled. "You?"

"That's right. Me. And see that kid over there that you're roughing up—"

"I wasn't roughing him—"

"Now, don't go making a liar out of yourself, son. You lie and people get to knowing that they can't trust you. And in my world, that gets you in some pretty deep shit. Now, like I was saying, see that kid over there whose shirt you had in your fist when I pulled up?"

The kid nodded, his face slowly stiffening with fear.

"He's a friend of the Kings of Mayhem."

"He is?"

"Damn straight. And we don't like our friends being picked on by older kids."

"I...we didn't...know."

"I realize that, son. But now you do." I took off my glasses, bending down a little to get up close and personal, letting the little shits see my eyes in all their glory, and the kid almost wet himself. "Do I make myself clear? Or do you need me to spell it out for you?"

The kid looked over at his friends who were still staring at me, their eyes wide and mouths open. The smaller kid, the one whom they'd been picking on had backed away, but his big blue eyes were glued to me, watching on intently.

"I'm sorry...Bull."

"What's your name, kid?"

"It's Tommy."

"And Ren and Stimpy over there, who are they?"

"That's Jethro and Eli."

"Ok, Tommy. It ain't me you should be apologizing to, it's him." I nodded toward the little guy.

Tommy followed my line of sight to the kid who had shrunk back even farther.

"We're sorry..." he called over to him.

"You don't speak for your friends," I said. I turned to look at the twins. "You all do the crime, then you all do the time."

The twins hastily offered their apologies.

"It won't happen again," Tommy said.

I fixed my cold eyes on him. "No, it won't."

He shivered and ran his hand through his hair.

That's when I noticed the small tattoo on his thumb. It was crude and ugly, made by cutting the skin and rubbing ink into the wound.

I gestured to it. "You do that?"

He nodded.

"It doesn't make you tough, Tommy. When you're eighteen, come see us. We'll hook you up with some art. Now get the hell out of here."

The three kids scattered and ran off, leaving me alone with the little guy.

He didn't say anything, he just stared at me with those big eyes and took a step back.

CHAPTER 5

TAYLOR

"This has to be some kind of bad joke."

"I assure you it ain't no joke, *sweetheart*."

I looked at the bill in my hand. It was for three-thousand dollars.

"But I didn't do it. I wasn't anywhere near your car." I looked at Willy Breeze, my sleazy boss. We were in his office at *Slingers*, a place where men came to jerk off to women sliding up and down a pole, and where my dreams came to die.

Although I shouldn't complain. It paid the bills. And as far as strip joints, this wasn't the worst—and I'd worked in enough of them to be a good judge.

I looked at my watch. Very aware of the time.

My shift had finished five minutes ago, and I needed to pick up my younger brother from school. I didn't have time for Sleazy Breezy to get his panties in a twist about something I didn't do.

"I got CCTV footage of you taking out the trash, *sweetheart*. You brushed it up against the Camaro on the way to them bins and scratched the paintwork."

"I've never taken the trash out, Willy."

"Then how come I got it on camera?"

I folded my arms across my chest. "Oh yeah, if you got it on camera, then let's see this footage."

"I can't. On account I have already given it to my lawyer."

"Your lawyer?" I raised an eyebrow at him. I knew a shakedown when I saw it.

"He says I got a case for compensation from you."

"I'm sure he does."

"Says you pay the bill and we're square."

I shook my head. "Just so we're clear, I'm not paying you one penny."

"Then I'll have no choice but to sue you."

"Go ahead."

"And fire you."

I shot him a filthy look. "You really are an asshole, Willy."

"Of course, I don't want it to get to that. Lawyers can be such leeches. Now, if you're willing, I'm open to negotiations."

The look on his face made the hair on the back of my neck curl.

"How about I throw you a bone?" he said lasciviously, his voice lowering and taking on a sickly, syrupy cadence as he took a step closer to me. "Since I'm a nice guy, I'll let you work it off in *other* ways. What do you think, *sweetheart*?"

I think if you call me sweetheart one more time, I'm going to set fire to your face.

I took a step away from him.

"Let me get this straight? You're trying to blame me for scratching your car, which I didn't do, and now you're offering me a chance to work off the money I apparently owe you by climbing on your dick?"

He grinned. "That's it, baby. You got it in a nutshell."

"This is bullshit," I said scrunching the bill up and throwing it at him. "If you think I'm paying that, then you're delusional. And if you think I'm going anywhere near that pathetic dick of yours, then you're even crazier than they say."

I threw my bag over my shoulder and turned to leave. I should've been gone ten minutes ago. Noah's school let out in five minutes, and I still had a fifteen-minute car ride across town to get there.

But as I went to walk out, Willy grabbed my arm and yanked me back to him. "Listen to me, you stuck-up little bitch, you gonna pay for

Bull

what you did to my car. And if you don't, then I'm just going to take it from you, with interest. And I don't mean out of your wages. You feel me?"

He reached between us and forced my hand onto the bulge in the front of his pants. Feeling his erection against my palm, my reflexes kicked in and I shoved a sharp knee into his groin.

When he keeled over with a groan, I stood over him. "Yeah, I felt that loud and clear, Willy. And I gotta say, it really wasn't that impressive."

"You fucking bitch… you gonna pay…" He spat, clutching his balls.

"So you keep saying." I crouched down beside him and leaned closer so only he could hear me. "Just so we're clear. If you ever try to put your hands on me again, I'll fucking kill you."

Rising to my feet, I pushed open the front door and burst into the mid-afternoon sun, making a sprint to my beat-up car parked in the alley behind the club. I hated being late to pick up Noah. We'd only been in Destiny for three months, and he really hadn't made any friends in that time. He wasn't a confident kid, no matter what I did to try and boost his self-confidence.

I sped across town, arriving twenty minutes late, panic flaring in me when Noah wasn't waiting in his usual spot under the maple tree in front of the administration office.

I sent a text message to his phone. *Where are you?* Then checked the playground, the parking lot, and finally the bus shelter.

That was when I saw him.

With a stranger.

A stranger with tattoos up and down his arms.

A stranger in a Kings of Mayhem cut.

CHAPTER 6

BULL

"Where's your mama, kid."

The kid was watching me intently, and I had a feeling those eyes of his didn't miss a thing.

"I don't have a mom. Just my sister, and she's late picking me up." He looked around the empty lot, and his gaze landed on the three punks watching us from up the street.

"They do that often?" I asked.

When he didn't reply, I took a step toward him and he looked at me.

"They pick on you a lot, kid?" The look on his face told me I was right. "You spoken to your sister about it?"

He looked away and nodded. "But she calls the school and tells them, and that makes them meaner."

"I see." I drew in a deep breath as I thought about it for a moment. When I crouched down so I was eye-level with him, he looked up. "You wanna know what I do when someone is mean to me?"

He nodded.

"I defend myself. If I can't talk my way out of shit—*I mean, a situation*—then I make sure I can fight my way out."

I glanced at the kids up the street. Tommy was lighting a cigarette and started to cough. When the twins laughed at him, he shoved one of them in the shoulder.

Yeah, I wasn't leaving this kid alone on the street with those little punks watching. Sure, they said it wouldn't happen again, but I knew how kids were prone to temptation.

"Want me to show you how you can protect yourself while we wait for your sister to show up?"

The kid's eyes lit up and he grinned. But it faded quickly. "She says I can't talk to strangers."

"Your sister sounds like a real smart lady. And she's right, you shouldn't. You got a name?"

"Noah."

"That's a pretty cool name, dude. You can call me Bull."

"Your name is cooler than mine." He glanced over at the kids still lurking at the end of the street. By the looks of it, the twins were trying to get Tommy to leave, but he wasn't having any of it. He leaned against a streetlight, watching. Noah looked nervous. "I suppose we ain't strangers no more."

I smiled. "I guess not. That mean you want me to show you how to stop them if they try bullying you again?"

He nodded shyly.

I walked him through some simple block moves, and was surprised at how quick he picked it up. It was almost like he already knew some of them.

So, I showed him one or two moves you wouldn't find in any martial arts handbook. *Thug moves.* Because when you needed to protect yourself against a thug, you needed to know how a thug moved.

After showing him the quickest way to get someone's hand off you, I glanced up. The kids up the street were still watching us. *Good.* Let them see what this kid was about to learn. Maybe then they'd stop bullying him. The little fuckers.

But just as I was about to show him something else, I heard a feminine voice call out. I glanced up. A woman was storming across the parking lot toward us. And for God knows what reason, but in that moment the first thing that squirreled its way into my head was how fucking hot she was. Good body. Long legs in the shortest, tightest Daisy Dukes. An ample rack barely contained behind a black tank top. A thick ponytail trailing behind her.

When she reached us, I was taken back by the fire in her big brown eyes.

She looked like she was ready to kill me.

She looked like she was ready to kill me, over and over.

Yet I couldn't suppress my smile.

This woman was a firecracker.

And I didn't know it yet.

But this was the very moment my world flipped on its ass, and nothing would ever be the same again.

CHAPTER 7

TAYLOR

"Who are you?" I demanded, protectively pulling my brother to me. I glanced at the Harley beside us, and then to the biker standing in front of me. The patch on the front of his leather vest read *President*. "And what the hell are you doing with my brother?"

"It's okay, sweetheart," he said with a smooth, Southern drawl. "I was just helping the kid out."

"It didn't look like you were trying to help him. It looked like you were trying to hit him."

The biker looked at me casually, his brow creased. "You've got it all wrong, sweetheart."

I glared at him. "Then explain it to me."

"The kid was having some issues with his friends. I was riding past when I saw what was happening, so I stopped."

I looked around us, but the parking lot was empty.

"Friends?" I held Noah at arm's length so he could read my lips because I could already see he had taken his hearing aids out. "Did Tommy Albright and the Lewis twins do something to you?"

My brother's downcast eyes and reluctant shrug confirmed my fears, and my heart broke. I had spoken to the school. I had even spoken to the parents. And for a while things had improved. But for some reason, when the three troublemakers got bored, they entertained themselves by picking on Noah.

Because he was different.

And because they were assholes.

I pulled him back into my arms, but he wriggled free.

Don't treat me like a baby, he signed. *I'm not a freak.*

Another crack split into my heart.

No, you're not, I signed back to him. *No one here thinks that.*

He will, he signed angrily, aiming his thumb at the biker who was watching us intently.

"He's deaf?" the biker asked.

I gave him a sharp look. "Not completely. He usually wears hearing aids, but he takes them off because the kids pick on him."

His brow furrowed, and it was a ridiculously sexy look.

"I was just talking to him and he seemed to understand me," he said.

"He can read lips," I explained, trying not to notice how smoky and delicious his deeply masculine voice was.

Noah tugged my arm. *Stop talking about me like I'm not here.*

I'm sorry, I signed back.

The biker stepped forward. He was big. With broad shoulders and arms that were all muscle. From afar he had been impressive. But up close, he was spectacular. Inky black hair. Strong jaw with the right amount of scruff. Full lips. His good looks were savage. I couldn't see his eyes because he was wearing dark glasses. But I was pretty sure they would be just as spectacular as the rest of him.

"Listen, sweetheart—" he started.

But I cut him off. Because I had reached my quota for nicknames today.

"While I'm sure women get all hot and tingly whenever you call them sweetheart, I assure you, I am no sweetheart, especially when it comes to strangers talking to my kid brother. I'm also not impressed, or am I appreciative or interested in who you are, what you do, and how fantastic you think you are."

Just then the biker took off his glasses and dear God, his eyes really were as spectacular as the rest of him. More so. Like sapphires fused with the brightest white light.

"What about *hot and tingly*?" he asked with a heated, sweeping gaze up and down my body.

My eyes narrowed despite goose bumps prickling along my skin. "Just stay away from me and my brother."

"But Taylor..." Noah protested.

I ignored him, momentarily locked in battle with the biker. I knew I was being slightly over the top. But I was still frazzled from my run-in with Sleazy Breezy. Not to mention, now even more worried about the bullying.

And when Noah wasn't where he was supposed to be...

The biker stepped forward, one perfect, dark eyebrow arched, his voice low and smoky.

"The kid needed someone to help him. That someone was me. You're welcome." He swung one long leg over the Harley, and with a flick of a switch, brought it to life. He slid his glasses back on.

"Remember what I said, kid. The best way to avoid a fight is to talk your way out of it. But when that doesn't work, think about those moves I showed you, okay?" He nodded at Noah, then pointed those dark glasses in my direction, a small smile tugging at his lips. "Catch you later ... *sweetheart*."

With a roar he was gone.

And I was left standing there reeling.

I was always going to meet the president of the Kings of Mayhem motorcycle club.

I just never imagined it would happen like this.

We were both silent during the ride home.

Noah, because he was angry at me and my overreaction.

And me, because try as I might, I couldn't get the biker out of my head.

I was irritated with myself for giving him a moment's thought. The man was too self-assured for his own good.

Not to mention, confident and charming.

A dangerous combination.

I gripped the steering wheel. I had been ambushed by his charisma. I hadn't expected him to radiate so much... *maleness*. Or for my body to react so voraciously to being so close to his.

He was the kind of guy who made all the panties drop with one flash of that perfectly wicked smile. But I didn't plan on dropping mine. I didn't care how delicious he looked.

My life was complicated enough without fantasizing about those big hands and how they could make me... nope, nope, nope. I wasn't going there.

I didn't care how long it'd been since I'd felt a man's touch.

If he thought he could just flash that amazing smile at me and think I was going to turn to putty, then he had another thing coming.

Christ. There goes my body again, pulsing in all the right places because of that stupid smile.

But he was the president of the Kings of Mayhem motorcycle club.

And I had no business thinking about him that way.

Besides, I had more concerning matters to think about. Like the assholes who thought it was okay to bully my kid brother because he was hard of hearing, and the ignorant fools who thought they were better than him.

I pulled into the driveway and killed the engine. When Noah went to climb out, I stopped him.

"I know you're angry at me. But why don't you let *me* teach you some more moves? It might be fun. Like old times."

Growing up, I did martial arts for eight years, and when Noah was a lot smaller, I had taught him the basics. Because even before the bullying, I wanted him to know how to protect himself.

Because of my past.

Because of who I was.

Because someday, he might need to know how to fight.

To survive.

"How about *I* take you through some Krav Maga like I used to when we were living in Charleston?"

"Because I liked him and I wanted *him* to show me," he said angrily.

"But we don't know him."

"I do. I know him! And he was nice to me."

When he looked away, I gently turned his chin to face me and was gutted to see the disappointment in his big blue eyes. "You know better than to talk to strangers."

"He stopped Tommy Albright from kicking my ass."

"Hey…!" I reprimanded him. But my face softened. "We don't talk to strangers because not everyone is a good guy."

"He was!"

"He was a biker, Noah."

"So?" My brother's face was tight with anger. "If he was so bad, why did he help me? You weren't there. He was!"

Again, I felt guilty for not being there when he needed me.

"We don't know him."

"I don't care." He frowned at me. "You want me to make friends, but then stop me from being friends with who I want to be friends with."

"You need friends your own age." I knew it was hard on him. He was a shy kid. He was also self-conscious because he wore hearing aids. I sighed. "Will you let me walk you through Krav Maga again?"

Anger was bright in his eyes at the suggestion.

"Why is it always just you and me? Why can't we be like the rest of the kids in school who have a mom and a dad?" Noah climbed out of the car and slammed the door behind him, then yelled at me through the open window. "Why can't we have a normal family?"

He threw his bag over his shoulder and stormed away, while his words rippled over me like a violent gust of wind.

Wow! Okay.

That was a new argument.

He'd never said anything like that to me before, and I wasn't going to lie, it stung like a slap to the face.

I knew our situation wasn't ideal, but it was better than the alternative.

To keep the sudden surge of emotion at bay, I sucked in a deep breath and slowly exhaled, remembering the things from my past that kept us running. That kept us living in our own little bubble. That kept us from making any real attachments to people. Hoping that someday, we would be free from living life on the run, and that Noah would be safe *and* happy.

Fighting the guilt, I turned back to the window and watched him stalk across the driveway to the front door and disappear inside the house. He deserved better than this. But unfortunately, this was how it had to be for now.

I'm sorry, bud. But one day it'll all be over. I promise.

CHAPTER 8

BULL

It was early morning dark when I met Cade and Ruger at the clubhouse. Sitting in my office, we went over the plan. This morning's business was going to be gruesome. But it was necessary and unavoidable, and it would send another clear message to Gimmel Martel.

I'm coming for you.

It needed my focus. Because at the end of the day, we didn't know what we were about to see. Yet somehow, sitting there with my brothers, my mind wandered back to my encounter with the kid and his big sister the day before.

I'd be lying if I said it was the first time I'd thought about her.

Because it wasn't.

In fact, there wasn't an hour since I'd met her that I hadn't thought about her.

And it was no secret why.

She was wildly beautiful, with eyes as dark as black stone and hair the color of redwood tumbling down her back in a thick ponytail. And that mouth on her. *Jesus.* She wasn't afraid of me. Hell, I didn't think she'd be afraid of anything. She was a strong woman, and just as fiery as her blazing hair. I admit, seeing the passion in her eyes as she yelled at me had made me hard. And seeing those perky nipples pressing against the soft fabric of her black tank top had almost driven me insane with lust.

Now I couldn't get her out of my damned head.

But she was much younger than me. At least by a decade and a half. And I wasn't into young ones.

Hell, wasn't that one of the arguments I'd had with Ruger when he'd fallen in love with Chastity? He was sixteen years older than her, and I thought that was too much of an age gap.

And yet, here I was fantasizing about a woman who was at least that much younger than me, like a hypocritical asshole.

I told myself it was because I hadn't been laid in weeks. That the mayor and I were done, and without the regular release I found in her bed, my body was sending crazy messages to my brain.

But I needed to focus.

Needed to keep my head on straight.

Draining my coffee, I forced her out of my mind, telling myself that later, when I was alone, I would fuck her out of my head with my hand. Because I didn't need any distractions. The club had put a lot of effort in tracking down Martel's associates, the ones who continued to help him as he marinated in perverted bliss during his exile, and I couldn't afford to be distracted by a woman.

Even if that woman was a five-foot-seven redhead with wild eyes and a killer body.

"Are we ready to do this?" I looked at my sergeant-at-arms and VP.

Cade and Ruger nodded. "We do what we gotta do," Ruger said as we left the clubhouse and headed for our bikes.

We rode through the gray dawn to the seedy motel outside of town. It was a lonely place where the scum of society moved about in blatant sordidness, marinating in bad choices, and festering in their resentment for the hand life had dealt them. Here they robbed, lied, cheated, and scammed, passing their misfortune and disease onto whoever had the bad luck to cross paths with them.

Long ago, back when Nixon was president, the motel was the jewel in the crown of a thriving motel chain. It was clean and well-kept, a popular place for families to vacation, for respectable traveling businessmen to stop on their travels, and for respectable young women to lie by the pool in their modest bathing suits and big, floppy hats.

But those days were long gone.

The decay began when the highway bypass was built back in the early eighties, cutting traffic past the motel by more than eighty percent. Eventually, the families stopped coming, the pool turned green, and the respectable traveling businessmen only dropped in to bring their mistresses or paid-by-the-hour hookers.

The emptiness and little traffic also attracted the kind of people who liked to live in the shadows so no one could see what they were doing. They wanted the seclusion. The quiet. The anonymity. It was a melting pot of drug dealers, black market concierges, and killers.

When Ruger, Cade, and I pulled onto the gravel driveway, the only noise was the crackle of stone beneath the tires, and the tired hum of a neon sign that blinked, T E PINES M TEL.

We entered through the side door, slipped into the office and met with the manager who was waiting for us. No words were exchanged, only the three promised Benjamin Franklin notes I had agreed to when he'd contacted me the night before. I passed over the cash and he passed me the key.

Room 17.

It was on the second floor.

We crept up the concrete stairs, and the stench of piss and puke violated my senses. You could see the nicotine stains on the walls and feel the depravity hanging in the air. Nothing good ever happened here.

My disgust registered in my brain. I would put a bullet in my head before I lived a life that led me here.

Outside room 17 we paused. From inside, we could hear the distinct grunting and panting of emotionless fucking. Apparently, we had caught Scud Boney in the middle of getting rid of his morning glory.

I looked at Ruger and Cade. They were as ready as I was to make this shit stain pay.

For a brief moment I thought about Scud Boney and what I knew about him. We had never met. Never spoken a word to each other. And until I'd walked through the ashes of Eagle's Nest, I had never known what he had done.

To them.

Six women in six videos.

The evil was mind-blowing.

When we had ransacked the ruins of Eagle's Nest, Maverick had found the metal box of flash drives in the burned-out study, tucked away in a small floor safe that had been partially breached by the fire.

They had been hard to watch.

Hard to stomach.

I was the president of a motorcycle club, and I had seen some sick shit over the years. Bad shit. Crazy shit. Shit that made the hair on the back of your neck stand up and your eyes bleed.

But I'd never seen the type of depravity like what I saw in those videos.

What Scud had done to them made my stomach turn. He was a sadist.

And Gimmel was a sadist for purchasing the videos from him.

As I continued to unravel his business interests, I was learning more and more about the sick fuck I knew as Gimmel Martel. He thought he'd covered up his sick, twisted pastime, but he was wrong. He liked to watch pain. Specifically, he liked to watch pain being inflicted during sex. And even though I tried not to imagine it, I knew he'd sat in front of these videos and pulled his grubby little cock out as he got off on them.

Scud had been careful to wear a mask. To disguise his voice. But after months of investigating the videos, we finally had the full picture of who was involved and what the arrangement was...and now we were here to make them pay.

Gimmel had met Scud at a sex club in Jackson, and was delighted to hear about the amateur filmmaker's lust for homemade pornography. But Scud's movies weren't your everyday porn, they were *dark porn*, the darkest, where the most deviant of minds reigned, and every dark fantasy was possible. It wasn't long before the two sickos struck up an

Bull

agreement for Scud to make videos customized to Martel's vile fantasies. For Scud, it killed two birds with one stone. Martel was giving him the cash he needed to get high, and at the same time, he got to play out his own fantasies in real life, and make bank because of it.

Before I burned down Eagle's Nest and he fled underground, Martel had received six videos, each containing an unfortunate woman enduring Scud Boney's disgusting acts.

The first five women were still alive.

But the last woman was dead.

Her name was Annie Stonebrook. She was a prostitute and heroin addict, who plied her trade at the truck stops along the I-55. But she was also a mother. A sister. And a daughter.

One fateful spring evening, she climbed into Scud's car, and he had driven her to his very own night of horrors.

After abusing her during sex, both physically and psychologically, Scud had given her a hot shot of heroin before filming her dying of her overdose. The visual was horrendous; the audio even worse.

That video earned him ten-thousand dollars of Martel's money, and sent Scud on a trajectory that needed to be quelled. Because Scud had found a lucrative forte. His gravy train. *Snuff films.* And it wouldn't be long before he was going to be paid to make another one.

Ready to kick in the door, I could taste the disgust in my mouth as I recalled Annie's video.

I had no doubt, once Martel was settled in his hidey hole like the predatory spider he was, he would want to indulge in his fantasies again, and he would make contact with Scud.

I was here for two reasons. To stop Scud from hurting any more women. And to make sure Gimmel never got to enjoy another one of his sick videos again.

With a powerful kick fueled by my lust for revenge, and revulsion for everything that was Scud Boney, I burst into his room, taking him by surprise, mid-climax. He leaped up from the bed, his cock swaying like a sticky little tree branch in the wind.

He went for his gun, but I had mine rammed into his shoulder before he could reach it.

"You don't want to do that," I warned him, my voice was deep and dark, a direct reflection of how this guy made me feel. "Now, drop your hand to the side and stand up real slow, you understand me?"

"Who the fuck are you?" he yelled.

Resisting the urge to put a bullet in his brain, I took a step toward him and fixed my eyes to his. He shook with a dangerous mix of agitation and fear. Any second now, this stupid fuck was going to think he could reach for a second gun or weapon he had somewhere in this room.

"I'm the guy who's going to kill you."

His eyes widened. "W-what...the...f-fuck?"

The girl on the bed who was now quivering in the corner, started to scream.

Ruger pointed at her. "Get dressed and get the fuck out of here."

With a terrified whimper, she grabbed a dirty t-shirt off the floor and fled out into the early morning. She wouldn't raise the alarm. She would run back to whatever flea-bitten hellhole she'd come from and hide until this was over. And from the look of the track marks and scabs all over her skin, the heroin she enjoyed would take her out within the year.

I looked around the room. It smelled sour, like rotting garbage, rancid sheets, and old sex. Cigarette butts floated in near-empty beer bottles, and discarded needles and dope baggies were scattered across the floor. Most likely leftovers from previous occupants...or just from Scud, because I was starting to think that room 17 was his permanent address. Either way, I could guarantee you that cleanliness was not part of the hourly rate at this establishment.

In front of the closet, looking very out of place in the derelict room, was an expensive camera set up on a tripod.

"What do you w-want from me, m-man?" Scud blubbered.

But I ignored the question. "Where is he?"

"Who? I don't know what is happening...who the fuck are you t-talking about?"

The image of a dying Annie Stonebrook swung before me.

"Your perverted buddy, Gimmel Martel."

"I don't know anyone by that name—"

I shoved my gun under his chin. "Don't waste my time lying. Tell me, and I won't kill you. Now, one last time. Where the fuck is Gimmel Martel?"

"I-I don't—"

My knee collected with his now flaccid cock, and he doubled over with a cry.

"Let's try that again. Where the fuck is Martel hiding?"

"I don't know, man…all I know is he's coming to town because he has a shipment arriving."

I looked at Cade and Ruger.

The motherfucker was still trying to use our untapped interstates for his drug haul. We always knew he would try again. But so far, our intel hadn't found anything to suggest he had managed to set up his distribution arm again.

Until now.

"What kind of shipment?" Ruger asked.

"I-I don't know. Coke, maybe? Please, don't hurt me."

"When is the shipment due?" I asked.

"I-I don't know…" Scud was shaking and wouldn't look me in the eye.

I glanced to the camera on the tripod. Above the pillows, two metal shackles hung from chains nailed into the filthy wall.

"You making him another movie, Scud?"

He finally looked at me, surprised that I knew about his gruesome pastime. "What?"

"I've seen your handiwork, Scud. I've seen the sick shit you do. Did Martel order another one? Is that what you had planned for Heroin Harriet, that poor girl you were just balls deep in? You going to do psycho shit to her and then snuff her like you snuffed out Annie Stonebrook?"

"I don't know what y-you're talkin' about—"

I put my gun against his temple. "Lie to me again. I dare you."

"Okay, okay!" He put his hands up in surrender and squeezed his eyes shut. "He ordered one…"

His confirmation was like a nail being dragged down my spine, and I had to bite back my disgust. Every nerve in my body fizzled with anger and repulsion.

"Where were you supposed to deliver it to him?" I turned his chin with the barrel of my gun to make him look at me. "You don't send something like that to a post office box. Where is the drop-off point?"

"He didn't tell me!" His eyes slid away from me again, and I pressed my gun deeper into his jaw so he would look at me. "I-I swear...he said to have it ready by the fourteenth, and he would contact me."

"How?"

"By p-phone!"

Ruger stepped behind him, careful to avoid touching anything, and picked up Scud's phone from the nightstand. He took a quick look through it.

"There's no number for Gimmel Martel," he said.

Scud winced when I pressed my gun deeper into his skin. "He told me to store any contact with him under the n-name Caligula."

I gave him a pointed look. "Seriously?"

Caligula was a Roman Emperor known for his cruelty and sexual perversion.

Ruger scrolled through the contacts and then nodded at me. "There's a Caligula in his contacts." He started looking through the conversation and his face screwed up. "Oh, you sick fuck. You really going to do this to someone?"

"What does it say?" I asked.

"I ain't repeating this shit. Finish up here and you can read it yourself." Ruger said as he closed the phone and tucked it into his cut. "I'm gonna need to wash my own mouth out with soap if I read that shit out loud."

"Hell, I think I might just do that anyway after standing in this shithole," Cade said.

I turned my attention back to Scud. "Are there more?"

"More?"

"Videos." He shook his head but winced again when my gun burrowed into his jawbone this time. "Come on, Scud, a talented guy like you? I can't imagine you went all this time without making more of your filthy shows."

"No, I-I didn't."

He was lying. I gestured for Cade to look through the closet, and I

Bull

could tell by the fear on Scud's face that we were going to find something he didn't want us to find. Within seconds, I heard Cade groan.

"Oh, hell no," he said, stepping back, his gloved hands clasped around a stack of Polaroids. He handed them to Ruger. "You are not going to believe this shit."

Scud's eyes closed. He knew this wasn't going to end well for him. Whatever was on those Polaroids was going to seal his fate.

"This just ain't right," Ruger said, showing me two of the photographs.

My stomach tightened with disgust. Scud was a sick fuck, and I would never unsee what was in those pictures.

"You s-said you w-weren't going to k-kill me!" he stammered.

I looked him in the eye and thought of Annie Stonebrook dying of an overdose. Her last moments painful, undignified, and all caught on camera and broadcast for the perverts of the world to see, because men like Martel got off on watching it.

I thought of the images on the Polaroids. Of the other girls in the videos, the ones who survived but who would have to live with what he'd done to them for the rest of their lives.

And then I thought of the ones he had yet to meet and break.

"Oh, I'm not killing you." I leaned in. "Not here, anyway."

Ruger shoved his gun into his spine. "We're going for a little drive."

Leaving the cesspit that was his obvious home, we slipped into the dawn light and took him to the abandoned drive-in theater a few miles out of town. On the empty lot, there was an old building we liked to use for *club business*. It was a good location. No one could hear the screams out there.

Waiting for us was a scary motherfucker we only knew as Blowtorch. He liked to inflict pain, and we always got our money's worth whenever we used him. He was capable of things not many human beings could stomach, and it was exactly what Scud deserved.

Because he was about to dish up a hot serving of karma to Scud with his blowtorch.

Ruger, Cade, and I stood on and watched, disconnected from the pain and suffering we were witnessing because we had seen what

Scud had done to those innocent women on those videos. We'd seen how he'd ignored his victims' cries for mercy as he'd brutally raped them. We'd heard them *begging him* to stop as he tortured them.

Now it was his turn to beg.

When he finally passed out from the pain, I nodded to Blowtorch, and he killed the flame. Walking over to the unconscious Scud, I slapped him awake until he finally looked up at me through glazed eyes and a sweaty brow, his slack mouth drooling blood, spit, and puke.

I pressed my gun to his chest. "This is for all the nasty shit you did to those women."

And I shot him.

I shot him right through his miserable, black heart.

As I rose to my feet, I looked over at Cade and Ruger, who both remained expressionless.

The job was done.

Scud Boney was just one more thread in Gimmel Martel's dark web of perversion that I had picked apart and destroyed.

No one would miss him, and the world would be better off without him.

CHAPTER 9

TAYLOR

I was having one of those days. The type that starts with your alarm not going off because of a power outage overnight, and usually ends with you drowning your sorrows in a bottle of wine and a bag of Doritos as you contemplate life and where the fuck it all went wrong.

Unfortunately, I wasn't at the wine and Doritos part yet.

It wasn't even lunch time.

And who was I kidding, I couldn't even afford a bag of Doritos.

I walked to my car feeling the hot sting of embarrassment on my cheeks. I'd just come from my first job interview since losing my job at *Slingers*. But it had been a nightmare, to say the least. I'd been completely unprepared. I thought it was a simple bar job, slinging beers in another dive bar. But when the guy who was interviewing me—an overweight guy in his fifties with a cigar propped between his yellow teeth and beer stains down the front of his white polo shirt—told me to take my top off, I was a little taken aback. When I refused, *because hey, I didn't realize I was applying for a topless waitress position, given they never mentioned it in the ad or the phone call inviting me in for an interview*, he started yelling at me to get out and to stop wasting his time.

He didn't have to ask twice.

Now, I sat slumped in the driver's seat of my car with my head against the headrest, contemplating my next move.

It wasn't easy getting a job in this town, when the first question they asked was, "Why did you leave your last job?"

Because, *I kneed my sleazy boss in the balls,* didn't make me an attractive candidate to any potential boss.

The only other option was a waitressing job at an upmarket bar over in Humphrey, the kind where you could purchase a little more than a drink from the waitress if you had the right amount of cash.

And I wasn't willing to do that.

I groaned.

Now I was back to square one.

Stone-cold broke.

But we're safe.

I thought about my brother and what he'd said to me in the car after our encounter with the biker. He was still angry at me. And clearly, he was struggling with it being just the two of us. The thought killed me. As a little boy, he'd never asked about our parents, or the man he'd known briefly as his godfather, but as he got older, he grew more insistent on knowing more. *Wanting more.*

And that terrified me.

As I pulled out of the parking lot, I blew out a puff of air and rolled down the window. It was a warm summer day, and the lack of air conditioning in my car had me hot and sticky. I wasn't one to dwell on what I didn't have, I always tried to make the best of things, but today was pushing every one of my damn buttons.

Although, no matter how bad my day could get, it was infinitely better than what we'd left behind.

We came to Destiny for a fresh start. It wasn't a hard decision. Moving here put a bigger gap between us and our past, and promised us a chance for freedom.

When Credence Clearwater Revival's, "Feeling Blue" came on the radio, I leaned forward to turn it up. I was distracted for a nanosecond. A blink of an eye. But it was enough for me not to see the van in front of me stop at the light, and for me to slam into the back of him.

Fuck. Fuck. Fuckity. Fuck.

Bull

After the jolt of the impact rattled through me, I took a moment to press my forehead to the steering wheel because I wasn't sure my day could get any worse.

I raised my head in time to see the driver of the van climb out. He was a knockout gorgeous biker in a Kings of Mayhem vest, with bright blue eyes and tattoos covering two very muscular arms. He took one look at my car that had rammed into the back of his van and his eyebrows rose.

"Damn," he said, surveying the damage.

I climbed out, ready to grovel. I didn't have the money for repairs. And insurance was for people who weren't stone-cold broke.

"I'm so sorry. I didn't see you. I looked away for a split second and—" I stopped when a second biker appeared from the passenger side. A biker with inky black hair and a voice I hadn't been able to get out of my head for the last two days. My shoulders sagged. *Day meet worse.* "You've got to be kidding me!"

A smile tugged at his lips.

"Of course, it has to be you," I said, folding my arms across my chest as if I was protecting myself against some unknown force. Because apparently, fate was having a fun time fucking with me.

"You say that like *I* was the one who ran up *your* ass," he said wryly, lifting up his sunglasses and squinting in the sunshine.

My cheeks grew hot. I was flustered. And it had nothing to do with the way he was looking at me.

Because today has been a really shitty day, that is all.

"Well, if I'd known it was you in the car, I'd probably have driven a little faster," I mumbled.

I couldn't help myself. Being caught between a rock and a hard place made me a smartass.

"And I'd expect nothing less, *sweetheart.*"

The other biker looked at me, then to his passenger, then back to me.

"Wait. You two know each other?" he asked.

We answered simultaneously. But with completely different answers.

"No," I said.

"Yes," he said.

The biker who wasn't the arrogant ass raised an eyebrow. "Right."

"I wouldn't exactly say we know each other," I said.

"It was a brief but *memorable* encounter," said the man who was torturing me with those broad shoulders and big biceps.

"For you, maybe."

He grinned to reveal a mouth full of perfect, straight white teeth.

Of course.

The other biker watched on, intrigued. "I see. Well, as much as I'd love to stand here and watch whatever this is, we should get these off the road." He pointed to the van and my now-damaged car. "The van looks okay, but we'll have to get the prospects to tow the Honda back to the clubhouse."

"You really don't have to do that," I said, trying desperately to ignore Mr. Arrogant Ass. I could feel the heat of his piercing gaze sliding over me like a warm caress.

"I think we kinda do," said the man I was now calling Mr. AA. "Unless your plan was to cause traffic chaos this afternoon."

I rolled my eyes at him, but he just gave me a ridiculously sexy grin.

Because he was an ass.

"Bull's right. It's almost rush hour," the nice biker said. "We need to get the Honda back to the clubhouse."

Bull.

Nope.

Mr. AA suited him better.

I turned to the nice one. "I appreciate your help. Thanks."

He smiled and reached into his vest for his phone. When he stepped away to make a call, Mr. AA stepped forward.

"I didn't get the chance to introduce myself the other day." He offered me a hand. A big hand. "Name's Michael, but people call me Bull."

I shook it. "Taylor."

Our handshake lingered, and a warm rush swept through me. "Nice to meet you, *Taylor.*"

The way he said my name sent a ripple through me. Our eyes locked onto one another in a tense standoff.

Bull

"The pleasure is all mine," I said sarcastically.

His eyes gleamed. "Not yet. But I can guarantee you that it will be."

Which earned him an eye roll.

The *nice* biker reappeared. "The prospects are on their way." He looked at me. "Come on, you can ride up-front with us. It can get a bit rough in the back."

But Bull didn't let go of my hand or remove his eyes from mine. "Don't worry, Caleb…I don't think this one minds it rough."

I flashed him a dark look, trying to ignore the warmth of his fingers still wrapped around mine.

Finally, I pulled my hand away and raised an eyebrow at him. "You have no idea."

Bull and Caleb drove me to their clubhouse, while two bikers with the word *Prospect* written across their vests took care of my car and followed us. There was only minor damage, one of them assured me, and they could have it fixed in no time.

By the time I'd reached the hallowed halls of the Kings of Mayhem clubhouse, I'd managed to calm my nerves.

And somewhere during the five-minute drive, Mr. AA had managed to lose a little of his arrogance and assholery. We stood in his office, his massive timber desk between us.

"How's the kid?" he asked.

His concern seemed genuine, and it was enough to lower my guard.

"Mad as hell at me for the other day." I slid my hands into my back pockets. "I'm sorry about that. I'm just a bit protective of him. He's had a rough time lately, but I really shouldn't have taken it out on you."

Whether or not he accepted my apology, he didn't acknowledge it.

"Has he had any more problems with the bullies?" he asked.

"Are you kidding me? Apparently, the encounter with you the other day lifted him to legendary status. It's been all around the school that he's friends with you."

His beautiful lips pulled with a hint of a smile.

"Thank you," I added. "I don't think you realize what you've done.

It's helped him with his confidence, and I can't tell you what a relief that is. He's been struggling for a while and needs someone besides his annoying older sister in his corner."

He frowned but then his eyes found mine and his face smoothed. "Has he been deaf since birth?"

"No. It's recent."

"You mind me asking what happened?"

His courtesy was surprising, and caught me off guard. I exhaled deeply. When it came to my brother, I tended to be a bit of a mama bear, ready to sharpen my claws on anyone or anything who threatened his wellbeing.

"He had meningitis a couple of years ago and it left him with significant hearing loss."

I watched as Bull absorbed the information. "Can the doctors do anything?"

"They did enough when they failed to diagnose him," I snapped before I could stop myself.

The experience had been a traumatic one, and it was still raw, and even though I taught Noah to move on and focus on the future, sometimes it was a little hard to swallow my own advice. Especially when I thought about how close I'd come to losing him.

"Sorry. It's been a rough journey." I gave Bull a wry smile. "And I think we've already established that I can be a little overprotective."

I continued and told him about Noah falling sick and how the overworked ER doctors had discharged him twice, one telling me that it was a virus, and the other suggesting he had behavioral issues and was struggling with the symptoms of a migraine. I also told him how I'd shown up a third time and almost gotten myself arrested because I wasn't leaving until someone did something to help my brother.

"By then he was so sick he almost died." I thought of Noah lying in that hospital bed, and my blood still chilled in my veins. "But he's a tough kid."

"And he lost his hearing because of the infection."

"Not completely. He can hear better with his hearing aids, but he takes them off because the kids pick on him." Kids could be assholes because they didn't realize the impact their bullying could have on someone's self-esteem. "He started to take them out when he went to school, but his schoolwork started to suffer, so the school contacted me. After we had a long talk, he promised he would keep them in. I didn't realize he was still taking them out."

"But he signs."

"At one stage he was almost completely deaf from the infection. We didn't know how significant the loss would be, so we learned how to sign. His hearing improved enough for him to wear hearing aids, but he still likes to sign sometimes."

He nodded and moved around the desk to stand in front of me. And damn, it was as if his aura was molten lava and wrapped its heat around me. I felt my face flush and my heart kick in my chest.

There was something a little fascinating about him.

"Where is he now?" he asked, leaning against the lip of his desk.

"Our neighbor babysits him for me sometimes."

"I bet he hates that."

I chuckled. "She's a seventeen-year-old blonde cheerleader with big boobs and legs for miles. He's an eleven-year-old kid discovering girls. I'm sure he hates it."

He smiled, and dear God, I almost fell over. His smile was breathtaking.

"Sounds like hell."

A sudden pang of longing assaulted me and I had to draw in a deep breath. How long had it been since a man had made me feel that with just a damn smile?

In all honesty, it had been easier to take care of things myself.

I'd been so damn preoccupied with keeping Noah safe and spending as much time with him as possible, there was no time to make that connection with someone.

I cleared my throat. And now most definitely wasn't the time to start.

Yet, when Bull turned around and asked me out to dinner, my first inclination was to say yes.

"You're seriously asking me out to dinner?"

"I am."

I folded my arms. "Let me get this straight. I yell at you for showing my brother how to protect himself, then crash into the back of your van because I wasn't paying attention, and now you're asking me out for dinner?"

"Yes."

What was this guy up to?

"Fine," I said.

"Fine?"

"Yes, I accept your invitation."

"Great, let's go."

My arms fell to my sides, surprised he'd called my bluff.

"You mean right now?"

"Is there ever a better time?"

Again, his smile lit up parts of me that had been dormant for years.

"I can't believe this. Shouldn't I be buying you dinner so you don't sue me?"

He grinned as he handed me a helmet. "Who said you weren't. I hope you've got money, because I'm ordering the biggest fucking lobster on the menu, and I'm definitely not a cheap date."

CHAPTER 10

BULL

Despite what I'd said earlier, she wasn't paying for dinner.

And I wasn't eating lobster either.

I was fucking allergic to seafood.

I was also allergic to being a jerk.

Despite my shortcomings—and let's face it, I had a fucking ton of them—I still knew how to be a gentleman.

I took her to a small Italian restaurant where they had little candles and baskets of breadsticks on the tables.

"You like Italian food?" I asked.

"I love it," she replied, flicking her long hair over her shoulders as she got settled in her chair.

I liked how she did that.

I also like the way she bit her bottom lip as she looked over the menu.

"Funny, I don't see any lobster on the menu," she said with a twinkle in her big brown eyes.

"What a shame," I replied, trying not to notice the cute dimples flickering on either side of her bee-stung lips. "Maybe next time."

"You're confident there'll be a next time."

"I'm a pretty confident guy."

She smiled. "So I can see."

The waiter came to take our order.

"I think I'll have the *tagliatelle al ragù*," she said, handing him the menu.

Her pronunciation was perfect.

"Make that two," I said. "And a bottle of the *Fontodi Vigna del Sorbo*."

When he left, she leaned her arms on the table, and her beautiful eyes shone across at me. "You've been here before."

"What gave it away?"

"I didn't see a hundred-and fifty-dollar bottle of chianti listed on the menu. It tells me you know they have it."

"You're very observant."

"I have to be," she said, ambiguously. But before I had a chance to ask her why, she grinned mischievously. "Tell me, do you bring all your first dates here?"

"It might surprise you to know this, but I don't date."

One eyebrow jumped up. "I call bullshit."

Of course, she did. Because she was a straight shooter and I liked that.

"Tell me, how do you know your bottles of wine and how much they cost?" I asked, changing the subject.

She sat back and shrugged. "I was raised in an Italian household."

"You're Italian?"

"No. When my parents died, Noah and I were raised by a man I called my godfather, Alex. He's from a big Italian family. Food and wine were a big deal in our household." She smiled softly. "Alex's nonna spent hours teaching me how to make pasta and biscotti."

I noticed how her face softened when she spoke about the nonna, and, *Christ*, she was beautiful when she smiled.

"I'm sorry about your parents."

"I never knew either of them." She tried to appear unaffected by it, but changed the subject quickly. "Tell me, why do they call you Bull?"

I smiled at the memory.

Garrett Calley had given me the nickname a long time ago.

It was just after he'd became president of the Kings of Mayhem. At the time I was a prospect. *Young, dumb, and full of cum.* During his inauguration party, he'd walked in on me getting a blowjob from the pretty, blonde Harley Davidson sales rep from Humphrey. He'd taken one look at my junk, and his eyes had bugged. Then the sonofabitch went and told the entire club I was hung like a horse. But since Horse and Moose were already club members in other chapters, he decided I deserved the title of Bull.

But Taylor wasn't getting that version.

Yeah, I was hung. But I didn't fucking need to brag about it.

If I had my way, she would find out for herself.

"It's been so long, I can't even remember," I lied.

Judging by the look on her face, and the small tilt of her head as she studied me, she knew I was lying. But she smiled anyway. A smile that I felt all the way along my dick.

"So what do I call you? Michael or Bull?"

"Darlin', you can call me whatever you want."

She thought for a moment, then smiled. "I like Bull."

She picked up a breadstick from the basket on the table and put it between her lips. Immediately, my dick throbbed. She was sexy without even trying. And my body was reacting to everything she did with acute enthusiasm. I'd already noticed the hair and the beautiful face. Not to mention, the shiny pink lips, and her flawless slender throat. And don't get me started on her curves, or the way her beautiful breasts gleamed under the muted restaurant lights.

When the waiter came over with the bottle of wine, I tasted it and nodded for him to pour two glasses.

"*Salute*," I said, clinking my glass to hers.

"*Cin cin*." She took a sip of her wine, and I was momentarily spellbound by the look of rapture on her face. "That's incredible."

"I'm pleased you like it."

She took another sip, and I couldn't tear my eyes from the way her plush lips slid over the rim of the glass and drew the wine into her mouth. When she sat back, she licked the sheen of wine from her lips.

Christ, I wanted to do the exact thing to her. I wanted to taste the sweetness of her mouth and lick the wine from her lips.

Thankfully, the waiter returned with our meals, distracting me before I did something stupid, like clear the table and devour her in the goddamn restaurant.

"So what brought you to Destiny?" I asked.

She thought for a moment and I noticed how the gleam in her big brown eyes darkened slightly. Like she was recalling something she'd rather forget. But then she smiled. "After Noah's illness, we needed a change. A different pace. Somewhere we could live simply and quietly." She looked around the room and chuckled. "Although, I'm not sure having dinner with the president of the Kings of Mayhem is conducive to a quiet life."

"I'm harmless, really."

"Harmless? I don't think so." She slid her tongue across her lips as she looked around the room. "Why do I feel like me having dinner with you is going to be burning up the small-town grapevine by the time the check arrives?"

I drank a mouthful of wine. "I don't think anyone really cares."

"Oh, they care alright." She leaned forward on her arms as if she was going to share a secret with me. "See that table of four women over there? They've been glancing over at us since we sat down. And the one with the blonde ponytail, she's reapplied her lip gloss three times in the hope that you'll notice." She grinned and I had an overwhelming urge to kiss her. "And the lady over there in the red dress? She's passed by us no less than four times on her way to the bathroom trying to get your attention."

I had noticed the lady in red. But only because Taylor was right. She *had* passed by our table several times, and each time she had made eye contact, offering me an unmistakable invitation.

I brushed it off. "They recognize me, that's all."

"No, they want to fuck you," she said, leaning back with a sexy smile on her lips. "And apparently, they don't care if you're having dinner with another woman or not. Who knows, the more the merrier if they can get you into bed with them, I suppose."

Her forthrightness was a turn-on. I was hard as fuck now.

"Tell me, what do you do when you're not yelling at bikers and ramming their vehicles with your car?" I asked, changing the subject.

Her cheeks flushed. "Sorry about that."

Bull

"Don't be. You're passionate, I like it."

She toyed with the stem of her wine glass. "I was angry that first day we met because I'd just lost my job."

She told me how her boss had tried billing her for a custom paint job to his Camaro. He accused her of scratching it when she was taking out the trash. She said she was nowhere near his car. He said he had CCTV footage of it, but when she demanded to see it, whaddya know, he didn't have it.

When she told me she'd been working at *Slingers*, a seedy strip club just out of town, it made sense. The owner, a greasy cretin called Willy Breeze, was as slimy as they came.

"He fired you because of that?" I asked, taking another drink of wine.

"No, he fired me because I kneed him in the groin when he said I could pay off my debt by bouncing on his balls three afternoons a week."

My wine almost came out of my nose.

"Sounds fair enough," I said, putting the glass down on the table.

"Which one, his offer, or the ball busting?"

"Definitely the ball busting." This woman had fire, and it was getting me more and more turned on by it. "There's plenty of women in this town who'd line up to shake your hand."

"Yeah, well, it felt good at the time. But I'm not so sure it was a good decision. Despite being a cesspit of broken dreams, with way too much DNA sticking to the floor, it was still a good job. Doing the lunchtime shift meant I finished in time to pick up Noah from school, and there were less cockroaches who came out to frequent the establishment in the daylight."

I'd been to *Slingers* once, purely for business, and didn't touch a thing while I was there. Even the glass our drinks came in looked suspect.

"And you haven't had any luck finding a new one?"

"Not yet." She shrugged.

"And you're not completely opposed to slinging beers to drunken, crude men who use words that'd make your mama cry?"

Her eyebrow went up. "Why, do you have somewhere in mind?"

"As a matter of fact, darlin', I do. One of our bar girls is moving out of town. The job is yours, if you want it."

She suddenly straightened in her chair. "You're giving me a job?"

"Sounds like you need one."

If her last smile seduced my dick, then the next one slayed me. She was so damn beautiful, and I couldn't help but fuck her ten different ways till next Sunday in my head.

"You're kidding! I mean, are you sure?"

"I assure you, darlin', I rarely joke about business, and I never make an offer I can't back up. If you're interested, come by the clubhouse on Monday at 12:30 and I'll introduce you to our bar manager, Randy."

She sat back, and her dark eyes twinkled with mischief. "And here I thought I'd end this day getting laid. Not with a job."

Part of me fell in love with her, right then and there.

"Why not both?" I suggested, a smile playing on my lips.

She shook her head. "I've mixed business with pleasure before," she said. "It doesn't work."

"Sounds like you have a story."

She shrugged and toyed with the stem of her wine glass. "Not much of a story. I drank too much at an after-work party and went home with one of the male strippers from the club I used to work at. He read more into it than there was, and when it became obvious I wasn't interested in a repeat performance, he became a petulant child. He was difficult and intolerable. He tried picking arguments with me. Started complaining to others about me. When our boss caught wind of it, he hauled us into his office and told us to sort our shit out. Slick said either I left, or he did. He was a big draw on Ladies' Night, so I suddenly found myself with less and less shifts."

"I can't imagine you taking that lying down."

"You're right, I didn't. I was ready to take it further. But Noah was about to start school, and working nights was going to interfere with our time together. So instead of wasting my energy fighting for a job that wasn't worth it anymore, I moved on. Lesson learned."

I thought about what she said for a moment.

"We're not all big bags of dicks," I said.

"No." Her eyes grew serious. "I can see that."

Bull

Something crackled in the air around us, and we both knew it. Our eyes lingered, and a hot longing took up residence in my veins.

But Taylor broke the spell. "I should probably get back to Noah."

After I paid the bill, I took us the long way back to the clubhouse, enjoying the feel of her arms around my waist as we rode through the sultry summer night. They were warm and comforting, and I felt myself relax, feeling my soul at ease as the wind whipped past my face.

Taylor was relaxed too. Her warm body softened against mine, and her fingers spread across the hard plane of my abs, making me ache to feel them all over the rest of my body. I felt tight with need, turned on by the closeness, and hard as fuck because this woman was somethin' else.

Despite taking my time, the ride was still over too soon, and we arrived back at the clubhouse. I pulled up next to her car. The prospects had done a good job repairing the damage, no doubt with the help of Hawke who was a genius when it came to minor panel repairs.

"Thanks again for dinner...and for the job," she said, climbing off. She undid the helmet and handed it to me. "And for fixing my car. You'll have to let me know how much I owe you."

I shook my head. "Consider it a *Welcome to Destiny* gift."

She gave me a soft smile, and in the muted glow she looked like every man's dream, and I was about done holding back. I was dying for a taste, and if I wasn't mistaken, so was she.

I was going to kiss her.

Then I was going to take her into the clubhouse and do things to that beautiful body of hers until we were both breathless.

I stepped closer so there was no space between us.

"That's not a good idea," she said when my hands slid around her jaw.

Good idea or not, I was aching to make her moan.

"I'm not interested in a one-night stand," she added.

"Who said anything about one night?"

She gave me a doubtful look. "What are you saying?"

"I'm saying I want to fuck you. *A lot.* And judging by the heat in your eyes and the way your pulse is throbbing against your throat, I think you want to fuck me too."

"Are you always this straight to the point?"

"No point wasting time."

A small smile touched her perfect lips. "Like I said, I don't mix business with pleasure."

"The business hasn't started yet, sweetheart."

She licked her lips and, *fuck me,* I was salivating for a taste.

Her eyes narrowed slightly and she lifted her chin. "Say you're right—"

"I usually am."

"—and I *do* want to fuck you—"

"I'm fucking praying that you do."

"—then what happens when you're done coming? I'll lose my job."

I let my hand drop.

"I may be a lot of things, *honey,* but a fucking douchebag ain't one of them. Your job will always be safe. You have my word."

"Excuse me if that doesn't reassure me. I don't even know you."

"If I'm not mistaken, I'm trying to change that."

"Don't kid yourself, you're not trying to get to know me. You're trying to get me into bed."

"Bed, floor, up against the wall…tell me your preference, and I'm all yours. I'm an adventurous guy."

"And not in the least bit arrogant." A ghost of a smile softened on her lips. "I'll tell you my preference. Tonight, it's a cold shower before climbing into my bed…*alone.*"

"Why go to bed alone when you could go to bed with me? Believe me, I have a million different ways to make you come. Why would you deny yourself?"

"Oh, I'm not denying myself. I'm going to go home and take care of myself with my vibrator." Her eyes flashed up at me. "Probably more than once."

I bit back a groan. The idea of her getting herself off had me so hard, I knew I was going to come tonight, either with her or with my hand. Preferably with her.

"I don't suppose you'll be thinking of me," I said.

"I don't suppose I will."

Bull

I couldn't help but smile. She was an absolute firecracker.

But then I knew that the moment I met her.

I grimaced, already feeling the onset of blue balls.

But I wasn't going to push her. It wasn't my style. Besides, Taylor didn't strike me as someone who could be won over so easily, and that was part of the attraction.

Plus, I was no Willy Breeze. I didn't pressure women. And I sure as fuck didn't beg.

No, when this happened, it was going to be Taylor's choice of the time and the place. When that would be, I had no fucking idea. But what I did know was that Taylor was going to be writhing beneath me, scratching her nails down my back, and coming on my cock, and when she did, it was going to be worth the wait.

I watched her walk to her car and climb in. She looked over and gave me another wicked smile before closing the door and driving away.

The challenge was on.

And I was never one to back down from a challenge.

CHAPTER 11

TAYLOR

"Things are finally looking up, kiddo," I told Noah over breakfast the next morning.

He looked at me and then dropped his eyes.

"I don't know why we had to move here in the first place," he grumbled over his cereal.

I sat down at the table as he raised his chin to look at me, and it killed me to see the sadness in those big brown eyes. "It's a new start for us, buddy."

"But I liked our old place."

"I know. But this is a better place for us to be. We'll be safe here."

As soon as I said it, I regretted it.

Noah didn't know anything about our past.

Or why we were running.

Hell, he didn't even know we *were* running.

He was so young when we left.

"What do you mean? What do we need to be safe from?" he asked, a frown creasing his sweet face.

Fuck.

To protect him, I had never told him anything. About our parents. About our godfather. About the horrors of days long gone. None of it.

Bull

And I didn't plan to either, because the less he knew, the better.

"I mean, it's a safe town, and we live in a nice neighborhood, with good neighbors." I gave him a reassuring smile and ruffled his hair. "Speaking of which, I'd better fix Pickles his breakfast while you get ready for school."

Mr. Gino Piccoli, or, *Pickles,* as he was nicknamed by his comrades in Vietnam, was our neighbor. He lived across the pathway from us in an apartment that mirrored ours. He lived alone, and was frail and elderly. Yet when we first arrived in Destiny, he'd hauled himself up onto his unsteady feet and offered to help us unload the U-Haul.

He was a kind man. With a kind, toothless grin and laughing eyes.

He also knew how to sign.

His only son had been deaf following a bad case of the mumps.

But all of his family was gone now—his son in a car accident when he was nineteen, and his wife from cancer almost twenty years ago, and in the first few weeks of living here, I realized he had no visitors. No one to call on him. No one to make sure he was alright.

My heart broke for him. Some days I would see him sitting out on the porch as the sun set, just staring out at the world and thinking about days gone by. A lonely old man in the last years of his life with no one to talk to.

One day, when he saw me arrive home with bagels, he told me about living in New York with his wife just after the war, and how they would wake up early and wait outside in the dark for their favorite bakery to open, just so they could buy their bagels fresh out of the oven.

The following day, I brought bagels from a cupcake bakery in town, and every morning since, I dropped a fresh cup of coffee and bagel to him as I was leaving to take Noah to school. No matter how broke we were, I made sure he had a visitor and a bagel.

Some days, we would sit with him while he ate his breakfast. Other days, Noah would pop over after school and watch TV with him, or talk with Pickles about what life was like when he was a young man.

Today, Pickles was sitting in his chair by the front door, dressed in his pressed slacks and button-up shirt, his feet in a pair of plaid slippers.

When he saw us walk across the path, his face lit up.

"Bella!" he said cheerfully. His eyes gleamed in the pale morning light. "And my favorite bambino, Noah!"

He held up his hand for Noah to high five, while I leaned down and pressed a kiss to his cheek. "Morning, Pickles."

He accepted his coffee and bagel with appreciative delight. "You spoil me!"

"Well, you're worth spoiling. How are you feeling today?"

"If I were any healthier, I'd be dangerous!" He laughed, then turned to Noah and started to sign. *"Are you feeling happy today?"*

There was no need to sign. Noah was wearing his hearing aids. But signing was a part of their bond. A magical language between them. A tie to his own son who was gone.

"I'm okay."

Pickles knew about the bullying.

"Have you chosen the next film yet?"

Noah and Pickles were both crazy about westerns. It was one of the many things they bonded over. On a Saturday night, you could find them wrist deep in popcorn with their eyes glued to the TV. But they were running out of DVDs because we had borrowed everything available at the local library over the past couple of months.

"The store has a copy of Shane *in the bargain bin. But Taylor says we need to save our money."* Noah replied.

I felt momentarily horrified. "Only until I get paid."

Pickles reached into his ironed slacks and pulled out his wallet, removing a ten-dollar bill. With a shaky hand, he held it up to me.

"You put that away, Pickles."

"Let me buy the kid the DVD," he said.

Pickles was on a pension. His house was sparse. His belongings few. Yesterday was pension day. His money had a long way to go. Advanced lung disease wasn't only a bitch, it was expensive.

"You don't let me pay you for the bagels, it's the least I can do," he said.

"And you watch Noah for me all the time without letting me pay you," I countered. "Besides, I have ten dollars set aside to buy the DVD this afternoon."

Noah's face lit up. "*You do?*"

Not really. Things were tight. I had enough for some groceries and gas. A DVD, even if it was in the bargain bin, was not in the budget. But damn it, I was going to make it work so my two favorite people could watch their movie.

"Sure, I do. Thought I might get a pizza, too, and we could celebrate my new job tonight." I already knew Trader Joe's had them on special. I turned to Pickles. "You want to join us?"

"You got a new job?" He looked delighted. "Where?"

"The Kings of Mayhem clubhouse. They need help behind the bar."

Pickles eyes rounded and then sparkled with amusement. "The Kings of Mayhem…well, I'll be damned."

Everyone in town knew the Kings of Mayhem. But I wasn't sure if Pickles knew much about them.

"You know them?"

"Know them! *Cara mia*, I got in a bar fight with their president back in the sixties." He chuckled. "He clocked me right on the jaw, almost took all my teeth out."

"Why?"

"Because of a sassy redhead named Sybil Stone." He chuckled again, and shook his head. "Boy, she was a wild one back then. Great lady. This was well before my lovely Annabelle came along, of course. I was young and dumb. Just about to be shipped out. Took my chance on a striking redhead serving drinks behind the bar at the roadhouse out near the railroad tracks. It's long gone now, just a pile of bricks and dust, but it was the place to be back in sixty-nine. And Sybil Stone sure was a beautiful woman."

"You hit on the president's girl?"

"Didn't know she was his girl. But when he told me, I had a belly full of beer and a head full of worry. I was going to war. I didn't know if I was coming back. That gets you a little crazy when you've had more than your share of liquor. He told me she was spoken for, and I guess it just made me a little stupid. But like I said…I was a dumb kid about to head off to war."

"What happened?"

"We brawled. Broke a few chairs. Smashed a few bottles. I got a few punches in, but I was no match for Hutch Calley. He was a strong sonofabitch!" He glanced over at Noah. "Sorry, *cucciolo*."

Noah grinned, while I was intrigued.

"How did it end?"

"My friend, a young Marine called Vinnie, said something about us being shipped out. It stopped Hutch mid-throw. He was back from Vietnam going on two years. He grabbed me by my shirt collar and he told me to live every moment I had like it was my last. Because we were about to fly into hell, he said, and when we came back nothing would look, smell, or taste the same. Then he shook my hand and brought me a beer." His eyes drifted off for a moment, then he came back. "We saw each other around town, every now and again. And he was right, you know. I survived the war, but nothing was the same again."

I smiled. I loved Pickles' stories.

"The people of this town love the Kings of Mayhem. You could do a lot worse than working for them."

I had done a lot worse. My whole life.

"Thanks, Pickles."

The clock on the small table next to him suddenly buzzed, making us all jump.

"Damn thing. The visiting nurse set it to go off when I need my medication. Damn near gives me a heart attack every time."

After I got Pickles his meds, I picked up Noah's bag. "Come on, time to get you to school."

We left Pickles with a promise to pick up pizza for dinner while we watched the movie, and made our way outside.

As we reached the set of stairs leading down to the road, I noticed a black Cadillac parked down the street and I stopped walking. It was out of place in this neighborhood, and I felt my gut tighten. I couldn't see inside, but I was sure it was the same car I had seen a few days ago outside the store. Fear tickled at the base of my spine.

I turned to Noah. "I think I left my purse on the kitchen counter." I handed him the house keys. "Would you mind running and getting it for me?"

I waited until he was out of sight before making my way down the

Bull

front steps, my eyes firmly set on the Caddy parked twenty yards away. Despite the tightening in my chest and the tingle of fear in my bones, I was going to face whoever was behind the wheel and ask them why they were following me. But as soon as I opened the front gate to the apartment complex, the car pulled away from the curb, the driver keeping his face ahead as he drove past me. He was wearing a baseball cap and sunglasses so I didn't recognize him. But I wasn't dumb. I was being watched.

A chill ran through me as I stood on the curb and watched the Caddy disappear down the street and out of view.

Then, like a firecracker went off under me, I ran back through the gate and up the steps, only slowing down when I reached the front door to my apartment. I took a moment to suck in a couple of deep breaths to calm my nerves before stepping inside because I didn't want Noah to see me in a panic.

When I found him in the kitchen, my face brightened. "Sorry, babe. I just realized I left it in my bedroom. Wait here for me."

I hurried to my room, careful to close the door behind me, and rushed to the closet. Reaching into the shadows of the top shelf, I felt around until my hand brushed against the cold steel box. Pulling it down, I punched in the sequence of numbers in the keypad to unlock it, and then lifted the lid.

Inside was a Beretta pistol.

A Beretta 98A1, to be exact.

A tactical pistol.

.21mm caliber.

125mm of impressive firepower.

I lifted it out and held it in my hand, feeling a familiar comfort as my fingers wound around the grip.

This would keep us safe.

I would make sure it did.

# CHAPTER 12

TAYLOR
Ten Years Ago

"Where are we going?" I asked my godfather, Alex.

We were in the backseat of his shiny black SUV while his driver, Serge, drove.

"I have a surprise for you."

My face lit up.

"You do?" Alex was too good to me. Always surprising me with gifts. Always lavishing me with nice things. Last week he'd bought me a brand-new Porsche for my birthday. He wasn't really my godfather. But it's what he wanted me to call him. *"What is it?"*

His hand slid over mine. "You'll see soon enough."

Excited, I peered out the window and wondered what he had done for me this time, watching as we left the affluent suburb of Lincoln Park behind us. As the miles rolled by, the landscape slowly changed from the kind of comfortable suburbia, where soccer moms drove Range Rovers and packed their kids nice lunches for school, to the slums of my old neighborhood, where moms were passed out on their heroin highs, while their kids were neglected, malnourished, and left to be unwitting prey to whoever was lurking about.

I felt my throat tighten, and I struggled to swallow the sudden excess of spit in my mouth.

I hadn't been back to this part of town since I'd fled ten years earlier. When my junkie father tried selling me to one of his dealers for his next high. I shifted uncomfortably against the plush leather seat and glanced at Alex. He was watching me, trying to gauge my reaction.

We never spoke about this place. And I never told him of the horrors of living on the streets for the three years before he found me. About the hunger. About the cold—the type that sank into your bones and froze you right down to your very core. About the sleepless nights and the fear. About the rape. But he knew, I knew he did. Because it was like he'd been trying to make it up to me ever since he'd found me starving and cold, and huddled under a cardboard box in a part of town that no fifteen-year-old should ever call home.

When we pulled up in front of the dilapidated little house with grimy windows and weeds growing as high as the porch steps, my stomach began to churn.

"Alex?" I asked, shakily.

Again, his big, warm hand covered mine. "It's going to be fine. I promise."

He gave me a familiar look of affection. The kind that I craved so badly from him. I wanted to believe him. But as much as I loved Alex, and as much as I wanted his attention and his love, he could be unpredictable. And sometimes that frightened me.

He came around to my side of the car and opened my door for me, extending his hand. "You can trust me, my darling goddaughter."

I climbed out and followed him along the pathway of broken concrete to the front door. The door was slightly ajar, and inside, a kid was crying.

"Goddamnit, will you shut the fuck up!" Screamed a woman.

I started to shake. I knew that voice.

It was my mom.

My hateful, junkie mother.

Alex pushed open the door and I followed him inside, and immediately, the sour stench of garbage and stale weed hit me, curling in my nostrils and taking me back to a life I wanted to forget. It was dark inside because the shades were drawn, but it was easy to see the chaos and filth. A dirty couch lined a wall mottled by yellow stains, while cigarette butts spilled from an ashtray on a coffee table littered with frozen dinner plates and drug paraphernalia. I glanced around us, absorbing the house I had grown up in. The putrid green carpet. The dishes piled high in the kitchen, and garbage gathering maggots in the corner. The sickly stench of desperation, frustration, and neglect.

The room was empty, but as we stood there looking around us, the sound of a crying child grew louder until he suddenly appeared in the hallway. He couldn't have been more than eighteen months old, and he was filthy. He wore nothing but a diaper and judging by the state of it, it hadn't been changed in a while. When he saw us, he stopped and wobbled unsteadily on his little feet. He was distressed, his face slimy with tears and snot.

My instinct was to go to him. To scoop him up in my arms and take him from this terrible, terrible place.

But then she appeared. My mom. Or, as I called her, Maggie. Because I had stopped calling her mom the moment I realized she wasn't much of one.

At first, she didn't notice us standing in her living room, and yelled at the little boy again. But then she saw us, and her face paled with recognition and her eyes narrowed. Slowly, she removed a cigarette from her lips with two dirty, nicotine-stained fingers.

"Well, look what the cat dragged in," she drawled, blowing out a puff of smoke.

More spit formed in my mouth as the bad memories I'd long since buried raced through my mind. The abuse. The yelling. The inappropriate touching. The yearning for something better. The need to escape this pisshole.

"Maggie," Alex said her name coolly. "Do you know who I am?"

Her hollow eyes focused on him. "Of course, I do. You bring the gear? Playboy told me you were bringing the gear."

I remembered Playboy. He was my parents' dealer. The one they tried selling my virginity to when I was twelve.

Ignoring the little boy, she sat down on the couch and squashed her cigarette onto a discarded dinner plate before lighting another one.

I could only stare at her, and she noticed. "You got something to say to me, girl? Or you just going to keep standing there staring?" I was afraid to open my mouth. I was barely keeping down the vomit collecting in my stomach. "What's wrong with you? The cat got your tongue?"

"Is he my brother?" I finally managed.

She rolled her eyes and sighed, as if my first words to her in ten years were a disappointment. "Of course, he is, why else would I put up with his hollering all day if it wasn't because he was my son."

"And where is my father?"

Her face hardened. "Dead. Going on three months now. Stupid junkie fuck. Got himself caught up in some bad shit, and ended up with a bullet in his gut. Didn't think about me and Noah before he went and got himself involved in all that gang shit. Now I'm left holding the bratty kid."

Noah.

My brother's name was Noah.

She looked up at Alex. "Where's the gear?"

"You're still using?" I asked.

"Is the Pope catholic? What the fuck does it look like to you." She shoved her arms out. They were covered in scabs. Ugly track marks, both old and new. "Also got some real nice ones on my feet, you wanna see them too?"

When Noah started to cry again, she yelled at him. "Shut the fuck up, you little shit."

"He needs cleaning up," I said, barely containing my anger. The rage was coming back to me. The darkness of my past. "He needs his diaper changed."

"Well, why don't you go buy him some, then. Look around you, Miss Hoity-Toity, does it look like I got money for diapers laying around here?"

My eyes narrowed with disgust. "But you've got enough for your next fix, I'm sure."

She glared at me. "Don't you judge me."

I shrank back, remembering the tone in her voice and the beating that usually followed. I turned to Alex.

"We can't leave him here," I said desperately. "Please, Alex. We have to take him with us."

I didn't know how, but I knew Alex could make anything happen.

Maggie looked up at him from the filthy couch. "Where's the money? Where's my drugs?"

Confused, I watched as Alex pulled a fat envelope from the breast pocket of his Armani suit and dropped it onto the coffee table in front of her.

"There's ten-thousand dollars," he said. Then he leaned down and placed a plastic bag full of white powder on top of it. "Consider this a thank you gift. I trust we won't be hearing from you in the future."

But Maggie was already too preoccupied by the bag of drugs to answer. I watched, disgusted as she stuck her finger in her festering mouth and then shoved it, wet and slimy, into the white powder. Running it across her rotted teeth, she moaned.

"Alex, please...we can't leave my brother here with her."

"I know. That's why we're here. That's why I set this up." He fixed his dark eyes to mine. "But if I do this for you, Taylor, you have to promise to do something for me."

I didn't know what he wanted me to do. But if it meant saving my brother from this life, then I'd agree to anything.

"Yes. I promise. Whatever you need me to do, I'll do it."

And in that moment, my fate was sealed.

CHAPTER 13

TAYLOR

On the Monday following my dinner date with Bull, I started working at the Kings of Mayhem clubhouse.

Driving into the compound, I couldn't help but wonder if I was jumping from the frying pan into the fire. By all accounts, this job was less stable and more dangerous.

But then I thought about Noah and why I was doing this. The job was a lifeline, and I meant it when I told Bull I was grateful.

I looked at the picture of my brother hanging on the rearview mirror. Whatever he needed, I would do it.

Climbing out of my car, I crossed the large parking lot, heading toward the clubhouse and walked inside, entering the world of the Kings of Mayhem motorcycle club for the very first time.

The clubhouse was enormous, with a huge bar to the right, a row of red-vinyl booths hugging one wall, a small stage set up next to an old jukebox, three pool tables, and a mix of couches scattered throughout the rest of the room. It was a masculine place. All timber and galvanized iron, with a polished concrete floor and a high ceiling.

Across the room, a massive Kings of Mayhem MC logo was laser cut into a slab of iron, and backlit by hidden LED lights. And over the bar was a huge medieval chandelier of rusted chains and iron, lit up by industrial lightbulbs.

As I walked in, The Marshall Tucker Band's, "Can't You See," filled the room from a surround-sound system.

Leaning up against the gleaming bar top were two bikers. One looked like Jason Momoa, and the other was a head taller, bald, and looked like he'd walked right out of a commando movie. They were talking to the girl behind the bar who was busy drying the inside of a beer glass. When I walked in, they all turned to look.

"You must be Taylor," the girl said, setting down the glass and walking over. She was tiny, with a head of dark brown hair and big green eyes. She wore well-worn Daisy Dukes, and a faded Metallica shirt tied in a knot over her flat stomach. "Bull told me I could expect you. Randy was supposed to be here today to show you the ropes, but his mama has taken ill, so you're stuck with me the rest of the week." Her hand was cool and firm as she shook mine. "I'm Cherry. Nice to meet you."

"Nice to meet you, too."

She let go of my hand and nodded to the bikers still leaning against the bar. "And these two big lugs are Maverick and Ari."

They were both big. Not as big as Bull, but still *big*. They nodded their hellos, but said nothing, their cool gazes suddenly making me wonder if I'd made a big mistake accepting this job. I mean, sure, the establishment was a lot cleaner than *Slingers* and there was probably a lot less semen on the floor, but the clientele was a lot bigger, and by the looks of it, a hell of a lot more dangerous.

But I was low on options, so I'd have to suck it up if I wanted Noah and me to have a roof over our head.

"I have to admit, when Bull told me he'd already found someone to replace me, I was surprised. I only told him that I was moving out of town a few days ago."

"You're leaving?"

"My boys and I are moving down to Florida."

"For business or pleasure?"

"A fresh start." The twinkle left her wide eyes, and with the light suddenly gone, they looked haunted.

I gave her a self-conscious smile. "I'm sorry, I only met you two

Bull

minutes ago and here I am already prying."

But she waved it off. "Don't be silly. You'll know my story soon enough. You can't keep anything quiet around here, you'll learn that real quick." She smiled brightly. "Come on, let me show you around."

The clubhouse was massive. The bar was just one small portion of the ginormous building. Just past the jukebox was a corridor leading to a huge kitchen, some kind of hall, and a couple of restrooms. Off the main corridor was a second smaller one.

"That's where the bedrooms are," Cherry explained. "Every King gets one."

There must've been a lot of bedrooms, because the hallway descended out of view and into darkness. "And that over there is Bull's office." She pointed to a closed door with PRESIDENT burned into the timber. My eyes lingered, wondering if Bull was in there, and my tummy did a strange little dance.

As if she could read my mind, Cherry added, "He's not here. He and Ruger are out somewhere, and I'm not sure when they'll be back."

An odd disappointment dampened the excitement in my stomach.

"And this over here," she said, leading me around the corner, "is the Showcase. The Kings of Mayhem pride and joy."

"Wow," I said, taking in the huge glass case running the length of the wall. Behind the glass was an eclectic collection of old biker belongings, framed photographs, letters, helmets, dog tags, and other personal items. It was fascinating. And in the center of it all was an old chopper pilot helmet with the name HUTCH scratched into the brow. On the wall behind it was an enlarged black-and-white photo of a very handsome young man. He was sitting in the cockpit of a helicopter, wearing Army greens and the helmet. I leaned in closer to read the description written in the corner. "Hutch Calley. Vietnam, 1966."

This was the man Pickles had spoken about. The man he'd brawled with at the roadhouse all those years ago.

"Hutch started the Kings of Mayhem when he came back from Vietnam. He was the original president," Cherry said.

"Was?"

"He died some years back. Way before my time. He was my husband's granddaddy."

"Your husband is a biker?"

Her eyes softened. "He was."

Across from the showcase was a wall of framed photographs. She pointed to one, it was of a gorgeous blond man with twinkling blue eyes and a cute, dimpled smile.

"That was taken about six months before he was killed."

"Oh, Cherry, I'm so sorry."

She smiled but it was closed-lipped and full of sadness. "He's been gone a few years now. The world has moved on. It's time for me and my boys to move on, too."

"Is that why you're leaving?" I asked softly.

"I need a fresh start. My sister moved to Jacksonville about six months ago and I really miss her. And as much as I love it here, I can't seem to move forward as long as I'm walking these halls. I miss him too much, you know?"

I looked at the faces in the other photos. "Who are these people?"

"This is the Wall of Fallen Family. Any King or his Queen who have died are up there."

"You mean, all these people have died?"

She nodded and I was taken aback. There were so many of them.

"Who is that?" I asked, pointing to a photograph of a beautiful young woman with shiny, caramel-colored hair and skin the color of toffee.

"That's Mirabella. She was murdered by the same man who killed my husband." She pointed to three other photos. "He killed all of them as well. It was a revenge thing. But the psychopath got his just desserts. He's rotting in a jail cell up at Parchman Farm."

Parchman Farm was a maximum-security prison over in Sunflower County, about seventy-five miles from here.

She pointed to a photograph of another biker. His face was hidden by a full beard and shaggy, shoulder-length hair, but I could see he had kind eyes.

"His name was Jacob. He was married to Mirabella. He couldn't cope with her death, so he laid his bike down in front of a truck."

Bull

I squeezed my eyes shut. When I opened them, I was again struck by the number of faces looking down at me from the wall.

And quite a few of them were women.

"The MC world can be exciting. And to me, it's family. But it's also dangerous and definitely not for the faint-hearted." She gave me a warm smile. "You look real sweet, and the boys are going to lose their shit over you, but if I can give you one bit of advice?"

"Sure," I shrugged.

"Don't give your heart to a biker." She toyed with a crown pendant around her neck. "Because you'll never get it back again."

CHAPTER 14

TAYLOR

Working at the clubhouse was a lot easier than working at *Slingers*. No handsy men with bourbon spilled down the front of their shirts, and a hard dick in their pants, as they made a grab for my ass.

And I really liked Cherry. She was friendly and sweet, and took the time to fill me in on the club members as they slowly spilled into the clubhouse.

"See them there? Those three honeys with the killer baby blues and all those muscles, they're the Calley brothers. Cade, Chance, and Caleb." I recognized Caleb from the day I ran into the back of the van. "They're Bull's nephews. And the lady talking to them, that's Ronnie, their mom. She's Bull's older sister. She's fierce, too. A word of advice, don't get on the wrong side of her. She's an amazing woman, but man, she's terrifying when she's pissed about something."

Ronnie looked like Cher in the movie *Mask*.

Cherry nodded toward the corner of the room where four bikers were playing pool.

"That's Cool Hand, Tully, Davey, and Hawke. Davey can be a bit of an old perv, but he's harmless. Just let him know straight up that he can't get away with anything around you, and you'll be fine."

Two girls in very tight jeans and tops that revealed a lot of skin, lingered at the table.

"Are they their girlfriends?" I asked Cherry.

"No, they're club girls." An amused grin spread across her lips. "You'll get used to them. They're here for the guys. Some of them are hoping to become old ladies, but most of them just want to suck club cock."

My eyes darted from the girls to Cherry, a little surprised.

I thought about Bull and wondered if he indulged in any of the club girls.

Before I could say anything, she added, "But a lot of the Kings ignore them, like the Calley brothers, and my Isaac. He wasn't into club pussy. And Bull never goes there. He tolerates them, but he's not into them." She smiled to herself. "Listen to me, I'm probably saying more than I should."

"No, I really appreciate the insight."

She walked over to a case of beer sitting on the bar and started refilling the refrigerator. "A few of the guys aren't here because they've gone to pick up Nitro. He's been doing a stint inside for arson, but he gets out today. They'll all be in later, I'm sure. Although, Nitro's probably going to spend most of the night at *The Den*."

"*The Den*?"

"Yeah, it's the brothel the Kings own. Really classy joint."

"They own a brothel?"

"Among other things."

"Like?"

"They own *Spank Daddy's* on the other side of town. It's a strip joint. I've been there once, it's a little dark and dirty, but it's a lot better than the *Slip N Slide*, and a trillion times better than *Slingers*." She straightened. "Sorry, Bull mentioned you worked there."

"I did and you're right. Anything would be a trillion times better than that dump."

She gave me a nod and started refilling the shelves again.

"They also own Head Quarters, it's a production company that specializes in movies for people with particular tastes, if you get my drift." She shrugged as she said it. "Nothing too over the top. Just your typical, everyday porn."

I smiled. "So they like porn and prostitution, huh?"

Cherry grinned. "Oh, honey. This is the MC world. It's all about money and pussy."

Cherry said she was going to hang around until she was sure I had the hang of it, but by the end of my first shift she came over to me and started to laugh.

"What?" I asked.

She leaned a hip against the bar and folded her arms. "Honey, I could leave today and you'd be fine. I've never seen anyone handle those boys like you do."

"Are you kidding me? They're nothing but big teddy bears."

The Kings were loud and brash, and Bull was right, they used language that would make your mama cry. They also looked mean, some of them murderous, but there was something about them, something simmering beneath the surface of the brotherhood that made me feel like I was at the safest place on Earth. They were a family built on bond not blood, and somehow it seemed stronger because it was all about choice.

And I couldn't complain about how they treated me.

At first, I was like a shiny new toy appearing underneath the Christmas tree. But by the end of the week, I was firmly rooted in the friend zone. They were bikers and they were full of testosterone and bravado, but they treated me with the respect they would show their little sisters.

On Thursday, I met Randy, the bar manager and we hit it off like we had known each other our whole lives. Randy looked like a surfer with sun-kissed skin, bright white teeth, and a mop of unruly blond curls. He'd lost his arm in a motorcycle accident years earlier, but was one of the fastest liquor slingers I'd ever met. He was also a lot of fun, and I had a feeling we were going to be close friends.

By Friday, I hadn't seen much of Bull, and I was beginning to wonder if I'd imagined the crazy attraction between us. Whenever he came into the clubhouse, he was flanked by bikers, or busy talking on his phone, and he would walk past me and give me an occasional wink that would heat my face and send a throb to my traitorous clit. Other

Bull

days, there was barely any acknowledgment from him, making me feel as if I was a part of the furniture. At first, I thought it was just because he was busy and preoccupied because everybody, it seemed, wanted a piece of him. But when it continued, I realized it wasn't because he was busy, it was because he was an asshole.

It made me think back to our date and made me grateful that I hadn't given into my urges that night and slept with him.

Because now I appeared to be invisible.

I didn't like it.

And for some stupid reason, I didn't like it...*a lot.*

I mean, he was my boss and I shouldn't see him as anything more than the man who signed my paycheck.

Yet it didn't stop me from thinking about him. *Fantasizing about him.* Like when he walked past the bar with Ruger and Maverick this afternoon, and I couldn't stop staring at him just because he was wearing a white t-shirt under his cut, and I had never seen him in a white t-shirt before.

And because, dear God, Bull in a white t-shirt was pure porn for warm-blooded females.

My thoughts got the better of me and I couldn't help but wonder about how his body looked beneath that white t-shirt, his Kings of Mayhem cut, and black slacks.

I couldn't help but wonder how it moved.

How it flexed.

How it fucked.

On the other side of the bar, Cherry cleared her throat, and I almost dropped the beer bottle I was opening as I tore my eyes off my boss to look at her.

She raised an eyebrow at me and gave me a knowing smile.

"What?" I shrugged, trying to hide my embarrassment. "So, shoot me, I'm a sucker for a guy in a white t-shirt."

She shook her head. "Dear God, it's only taken you a week."

"For what?"

"For you to fall under the spell of our enigmatic leader." She grinned. "But, honey, you gotta get in line. And there's a lot of women in front of you."

I shook my head. "Hell, Cherry, he's my boss, and I've got no intention of getting hung up on him or anyone. But just because I'm on a diet, doesn't mean I can't look at the menu."

She laughed as she walked off. "Sure, just keep telling yourself that."

But I was serious.

Deadly serious.

Later that afternoon, I was drying glasses fresh from the steamer, while Vader and Joker debated some facts about *Star Wars*.

"George Lucas didn't know Darth Vader was going to be Luke Skywalker's father when he wrote *Star Wars*," Vader said matter-of-factly. "That didn't come out until he wrote the script for *Empire Strikes Back*."

"He must've known, though, because Vader means father in Dutch," Joker replied.

"Pure coincidence," Vader said, peeling the label from his beer bottle and letting it drop onto the shiny wood.

Joker didn't look convinced. "A pretty big coincidence."

"The proof is in the movie. Remember the conversation between Obi-Wan and Skywalker, when Obi-Wan explains to him that Darth Vader killed his father? If Lucas knew Darth Vader was Luke's father during *Star Wars* then that conversation really doesn't make any sense."

"Lucas did that on purpose. It was a lead up to the twist," Joker insisted.

"No, no, no. Lucas turned it into the twist when he wrote *Empire Strikes Back*."

"I don't believe you," Joker said, taking a swig from his beer bottle.

Vader brushed him off. "I think I would know."

"Why? Because you wear a *Star Wars* shirt under your cut? You're full of shit."

Any second now, this was going to get out of hand.

"I don't want to play favorites here, boys," I said, leaning down on the bar in front of them. "But Vader is right. George Lucas didn't plan on Luke Skywalker being Darth Vader's son when they made *Star Wars*. He didn't work that out until *Empire Strikes Back*."

Both bikers turned to look at me.

"You know *Star Wars*?" Vader asked.

I stood up straight and grinned. "Three-time Comic-Con Princess Leia, at your service."

Both bikers continued to stare at me.

"Is it strange that I have an overwhelming urge to kiss you?" Vader asked.

"*I'd just as soon kiss a Wookiee*," I said with a wink, quoting a line from the movie.

Vader looked like he'd just seen heaven. "That's it, I'm going to marry you. Today."

"How about you just do me a favor and stop peeling beer labels all over the bar instead?" I swiped the pile of torn paper into my palm and walking over to the trashcan.

"I think Vader just fell in love with you," came a deep, masculine voice.

I looked up from dumping the pile of torn paper in the trashcan, straight into a pair of bright blue eyes.

Bull.

I hadn't noticed him walk in. Hadn't seen him take up a spot under a giant picture of Peter Fonda in *Easy Rider*.

And just like that, my crazy pulse took off.

"Is it true?" he asked.

"Is what true?" I asked, trying to calm the craziness going off in my chest.

I glanced over to where Vader and Joker had been sitting, but now they were gone.

"You really dress up as Princess Leia and go to Comic-Con?"

I couldn't help but grin. Even though I didn't want to. Because a part of me, *the immature and childish part*, was angry at him for ignoring me the past week.

But I smiled anyway. Because Bull had that effect on you.

"Guilty as charged." When he didn't say anything, I stopped what I was doing and looked at him. The expression on his face making me hot and bothered. "You got something to say about that?"

A sexy-as-sin smile touched his lips. "I'm just picturing you dressed as Princess Leia. You still got your costume?"

"As a matter of fact, I do."

The bright light of his eyes sent a searing heat through me.

"You might have to show me some time," he said.

"I didn't think the Kings of Mayhem were into costume parties."

"I was thinking more along the lines of a private party…for two."

His eyes fused to mine. My pulse roared in my ears. His look was pure sin. His words even more sinful. And the light in his eyes, it was predatory and so damn hot, I could feel the prickle of goose bumps on my skin as his gaze swept over me.

"And here I was thinking I was invisible to you."

"Is that a fact?" he replied casually. "Why would you think that?"

"I guess since I've been working here all week, and this is the first time you've stopped and spoken to me." I sounded more needy than I intended to and hated myself for it. So I busied myself with wiping down the bar, looking as if I didn't have a care in the world. When he didn't say anything, I looked up and saw the amusement tug at the corner of his full lips.

"You think I didn't notice you every time I walked in?" he asked.

I shrugged. "Didn't look that way to me."

His eyebrow went up as he leaned in. "You think I didn't notice how sexy you looked when you tipped your head back and laughed every time one of my brothers said something crazy to you?" He leaned in closer, his voice smooth and dangerous. "You think I didn't get hard when I saw you bending over in those little shorts you wear?" I licked my lips and his voice dropped. "You think I haven't fantasized about making you come a hundred different ways, just standing here now?"

His words had me rooted to the spot, and the dark carnal gleam in his mesmerizing eyes sent a quiver down my spine.

"Don't think for one moment that I'm not wanting you," he said huskily. "I have a ridiculously good poker face, but inside I'm dying to touch you."

My throat went dry at the bluntness of his words, and I struggled to swallow as a pink flush spread over me.

A small smile twitched at the corner of his ludicrously beautiful mouth. He knew he was affecting me. And I hated that he did.

I needed to change the subject. And I needed to change it quick.

I raised an eyebrow. "Do I need to remind you that you're my boss."

His smile was cocky. "Your shift ended three minutes ago. You're off the clock."

I glanced at my watch. "Well, I'd better get going, then."

He reached for my arm as I walked past him. His smile gone. His eyes serious. "I stay away for you. Not for me. But if you don't want me to…you only need to say it."

His hand was large, his touch warm and enticing, and looking into his eyes, I told myself I should run as far away from this man as possible.

Instead, I gave him a smile. "Don't hold your breath waiting."

And I walked away under the heat of his enticing gaze, the thrill of his words still quaking through my body.

Later, when Noah and I sat at the breakfast counter doing his homework, I thought about Bull and the things he said to me. The way he looked at me. The way he made me feel. The warmth. The attraction. *The craving*. In the future, I would have to be careful not to get caught under his spell. He knew I wanted him just as much as he wanted me.

He just didn't know the real reason why I couldn't give into it.

CHAPTER 15

TAYLOR

While my first week introduced me to all the Kings of Mayhem club members, the party they held on the weekend, introduced me to the *Queens* of Mayhem.

The party was for Nitro, the biker who was recently released from prison. Randy had already warned me the party could get sloppy.

The queens arrived late and sat at a booth across the room. Five strikingly attractive women who walked with confidence and a swagger in their hips that came with self-assurance. There was an air of untouchability about them. Something a little fascinating.

There were two blondes, two brunettes, and one with a halo of bright red curls. As soon as they took a seat, the bikers I knew as the Calley brothers, plus Ruger and Maverick, descended on the booth.

As the night wore one, I noticed how the club girls stayed away from them. There seemed to be a distinct difference between the two groups.

While the club girls favored scant clothing that left little to the imagination, the queens were sexy as fuck, without revealing too much skin. Although, their clothes were tight, sexy, and complete biker chic.

The first queen I met was Chastity, the baby sister to Cade, Caleb,

Bull

and Chance, and wife to the formidable sergeant-at-arms, Ruger.

We hit it off the moment she approached the bar and ordered a round of beers.

"Hi there, you must be Taylor. I'm Chastity." Her eyes twinkled and her smile was warm and genuine. "Ruger said Bull had hired a new bar girl. Welcome to crazy town."

She was sweet and I immediately felt at ease with her.

"Thank you. What can I get you?"

"Four beers for my girls, and a Coke for me, please." She rubbed her huge belly as she eased herself down onto the bar stool.

"When are you due?" I asked, flipping the tops off four beers.

"Not for another month, can you believe it? I'm already as big as a whale. Can you imagine how huge I will be in another four weeks?" She smiled as she fanned herself. "Ruger warned me that his mama had big babies, and her mama before her. I should've known this one was going to be big, too. Although, it kinda feels like this one is going to come out with a beard and be ready for college."

Chuckling, I placed the four beer bottles on the tray in front of her. "You look gorgeous."

She smiled. "You're sweet, thank you. So, tell me, how was your first week? Has old Davey tried to cop a feel yet? I mean, he's harmless but you have to let that big ol' teddy bear know he can't get away with being handsy."

"Cherry warned me. And no, he hasn't. Actually, they've all been really respectful."

"That's because my uncle warned them to keep their hands off you, or they'd have him to deal with."

"He did?" The idea of Bull warning a room full of bikers to keep their hands of me made my skin flush and my belly tighten.

"I probably shouldn't have told you that. Oh well, I can always chalk it up to pregnancy brain if he finds out."

"Your secret is safe with me; I won't tell anyone." I gave her a wink and she rewarded me with a huge smile.

"You're nice, I like you. I think we're going to be good friends."

"Thank you."

"See...pregnancy brain. I just think something and it falls right out of my mouth."

Grinning, I scooped ice into a highball and filled it with Coke and a piece of lime. I added it to the tray. "Want me to carry that for you?"

"Oh, hell no. Ever since he knocked me up, my husband treats me like a porcelain doll. Like I'm going to break if I show any signs of exertion. Carrying a tray of drinks is going to be a novelty for—"

Before she could finish, Ruger walked up behind her and took the tray from her. "Here, baby, let me take that for you."

Chastity gave me a pointed look.

"See?" She shook her head. "It was nice to meet you, Taylor. When you get a break, come over and meet the girls, okay?"

Not long after Chastity walked away, a blonde in a barely there pink dress and sparkly diamond choker that spelled TIFFANI came over.

"You're new," she said, leaning two elbows on the bar.

"I started a few days ago," I said, looking up from pulling two beers from the refrigerator.

"Wow, Bull really threw you in the deep end making you do a clubhouse party so quick." She pulled a packet of cigarettes out of her handbag. "Speaking of which, I saw you talking to him earlier. How do you two know each other?"

Her eyes glittered across at me. Studying me. She was trying to work out how much competition I was.

"He offered me this job," I said, uncapping two beer bottles and passing them to one of the band's roadies.

"So, you're his latest?"

"That depends on what you mean," I said, laying out two shots glasses and pouring bourbon into each of them. "If you're asking if I'm his latest bartender, then yes. Anything else, then no."

The shots of bourbon went to a second passing roadie.

"That'll change. A pretty young thing like you..."

I cocked an eyebrow at her. "You're pretty forward, aren't you?"

She shrugged, unaffected. "What's the point of beating around the bush? You'll get used to me. I'm like a permanent fixture around here. The boys like to keep me around, if you know what I mean." She winked, then put a cigarette between her glossy pink lips and lit it. "So, you really aren't riding the Big Man's pony?"

I presumed she meant Bull.

"He's my boss. That's all. I have no interest in him other than that."

Which was a lie because I'd been undressing him with my eyes all night.

"Hmmph, that's a shame. He must still be schtooping our lady mayor," she said, looking around the room for him.

Ignoring her comment, I walked over to her. "What can I get you?"

"Oh, I'll have a shot of vodka." She took a drag of her cigarette. "That'll pass."

"What will pass?" I asked, placing a shot glass in front of her and pouring her vodka. She threw it back like it was water.

"Him and the mayor. He never sticks with his fuck buddies for very long." She tilted her head to the side, her heavily made-up eyes narrowing. "He'll never settle down."

Tiffani was a mean girl. I could spot one from a mile away. She came over here for two reasons. To see if I was a threat. And to stir trouble.

"Sounds like there is a story there," I said, uncapping another beer and sliding it across to one of the pole dancers at the end of the bar.

"You mean, you don't know?" She laughed lightly. "You must be the only woman on planet Earth who doesn't know about Bull's wife."

Until the W-word got flung across the bar at me, I hadn't really been paying much mind to what she was saying.

Now I looked at her. "He's married?"

"Was. She died some years back in a car wreck. He never got over her. Now he just fucks and runs. Well, he *eventually* runs. He's not like the rest of the Kings who want you gone from their bed by sunrise." She sighed.

"You've kept him company before?"

I couldn't deny the thrum of disappointment I felt at the thought. Because this girl was toxic, and if Bull was into that type of women, then I had him pegged all wrong.

"I'm currently working on it." She cocked an eyebrow like she couldn't believe he hadn't fallen for her charms yet. "He doesn't usually indulge in club girls, but I come with some very strong recommendations, if you know what I mean."

"You're not an Old Lady?"

"Oh, hell no." Her words came out harsh, but her shrug hinted of remorse. "Old ladies are nothing but drags. When the Kings want a good time, they leave their old ladies at home and come and see me."

She gave me a wink.

Right.

So that's how it works.

It was kind of disappointing. I wasn't one to judge because of the whole *people in glass houses* thing, but to think these guys cheated on their women with this club girl was a real bummer.

Although, when I glanced over at the queen's booth and saw Caleb being so affectionate with his wife, I couldn't imagine he was one to indulge. Or Cade and Chance, for that matter. They all seemed pretty happy with their wives.

And Ruger.

Well, I knew a pussy-whipped guy when I saw him.

He only had eyes for his wife. I doubt he'd even notice this girl if she fell onto his lap naked.

"By the way, the name's Tiffani." She extended a hand, and as I shook it, I noticed the tattoos creeping up her wrist but couldn't make out what they were. "Have you met everyone yet?"

"Some of them. Can I get you another drink?"

She pointed to the shot glass. "And I'll take a white wine, too."

As I poured a second shot, Tiffani decided to tell me about everyone and who they were in the club. She spoke of the men like they belonged to her. But when she came to the queens, she was less enthusiastic.

"Indy, she's the queen of queens," she explained. "Cade's been so messed up in love with her his whole life, he really never stood a chance with anyone else." She drew on her cigarette. "Honey is sweet. Although, I didn't pick her to be Caleb's type. He's always gone for women a little, how do I put this delicately? Let's say, *less curvaceous*. I guess it figures, on account that she owns a bakery in town."

I had seen Honey walk in, and that girl had curves to die for. I wondered how many times Caleb had turned Tiffani down.

"Cassidy is okay, I guess. Has a voice like an angel, if you like that kind of thing. Got pregnant with their daughter real quick. Too quick, if you ask me. Unless, of course, that was what she planned all along. Mind you, if I hid from my psychopathic brother in a cabin with Chance for weeks on end, I'd leave there knocked up, too. That man has a body I could eat with a spoon."

Chance definitely turned her down at least once, too.

"The one with the crazy red hair is Autumn. She and Maverick are getting married soon. Such a shame." She looked disappointed as she glanced over her shoulder to Maverick, who had his big arms wrapped around his fiancée. "He's a lot of fun. Can't believe he's slapping on a ball and chain. I thought he liked to have a good time."

"With you?"

She grinned wickedly. "Not yet."

"He's about to be married."

She shrugged. "That doesn't matter."

"I'm sure it matters to Autumn."

Tiffani waved it off as she took a long draw on her cigarette.

"And you've met Chastity…she's the club princess. Daughter of the dead president, niece to the current one. Ruger must have a huge set of balls on him to take her on. Especially with their age difference." Her eyes sparkled across at me. She was having a good time. "Most of the other wives don't really hang out here too much. For some of the boys, this is their chance to get away from their ball and chain. That's when they come and see me."

I didn't like the vibe this girl was giving off, and I wanted her to go away.

But she wasn't finished yet.

"A word of advice?" she said, turning her cigarette packet between her fingers.

"I didn't know I needed any."

She smiled, but it wasn't sweet. "If you're going to drop your panties for any of them, you'd better make sure you make it memorable so they'll want to keep you around."

I put her white wine down in front of her. "Anything else?"

Tiffani's nice girl mask finally slipped. "You're not one of us. This place, the Kings, me—we're family. If you have any intentions of going after Bull—"

Yep, this bitch felt threatened by me.

If only she knew.

I leaned against the bar in front of her. "Honey, the only reason I want them to keep me around is so I get paid every week for doing my job." I started to walk away but paused. "And just so you know, if I did drop my panties for anyone, you'd better believe I'd be fucking anyone else they've had right out of their heads. Including anyone who comes very highly recommended. *If you know what I mean.*"

If looks could kill, then I was dead a hundred times over. Tiffani's eyes narrowed and a smirk spread across her glossy lips. But she didn't say anything, she simply stubbed out her cigarette and walked off.

"Girl, you're a badass!" Randy said as he walked up to me. "I knew I was right about you."

"About what?"

"Matlock bet me you wouldn't last the week. Said you looked too sweet to last in a place like this. Said if the boys didn't get to you first, then the good-time girls would eat you alive. And he's a tight motherfucker, too." He grinned. "Boy, I'm going to relish the look on his face when I tell him he just lost twenty bucks."

"Don't start celebrating yet," I said, throwing three empty beer bottles into the recycle bin. "My first week isn't over yet, and if anyone else comes at me like that, Bull will probably fire my ass when I pour some Miller High Life all over their heads."

He tipped his head back and laughed. "Oh, baby doll, you have so much to learn. This is an MC clubhouse. Hollering back and tipping beer over heads won't get you fired, it'll get you a fucking pay raise."

CHAPTER 16

BULL

I deliberately hung back and watched her from the shadows of a booth across the room. I wanted to see how she handled her first clubhouse party. And I'd be lying if I said I couldn't help but glance over more than I should. There was something fascinating about her. Something intriguing. But also, something else. Something I couldn't put my finger on. Something scratching at the back of my brain, wanting my attention, but not fully revealing itself.

So, I settled for what I did know.

I wanted her.

I wanted to taste her.

I wanted to feel her.

I wanted to see those succulent lips part with the deepest moans as I did so many things to that luscious body of hers.

I had from the moment she confronted me in the parking lot behind the school.

Then for reasons I couldn't fathom, I'd offered her a job, making the task almost impossible.

There was a small part of me that wondered if the job offer had come from a place of desperation. Because she wasn't easily impressed by me. She didn't care who I was, or what I looked like, or what bike I rode. The cut wasn't a turn-on for her, and she didn't care how many other women wanted my attention.

Part of me knew that if I'd let her walk away that night, I'd probably never see her again. Sure, she said she thought she was getting laid. But by that stage, I'd already offered her the job. Besides, she had been joking. Because something told me it was going to take a lot more than an expensive bottle of wine and some good food to get her under me.

I looked across the bar at my brothers celebrating Nitro's return. He'd done a stint in prison for arson after an insurance job went wrong. It was the type of shit I warned the guys about. Poorly vetted side jobs could get you time. Or worse, dead. Thankfully, there was no blowback on the club, and our razor-sharp lawyer had gotten him a light sentence.

While the band set up in the corner of the clubhouse, Led Zeppelin's "Rock and Roll" blared from the speakers, and the energy in the room was high. It was a full house tonight. All the boys were here, and most of the old ladies, too. A few of the girls from *The Den*, *Head Quarters*, and *Spank Daddy's* had also turned up, including Matlock's movie star girlfriend, Danni Deepthroat.

As I watched everyone having a good time, I tried to absorb their enjoyment and their enthusiasm, but the truth was, I couldn't seem to muster the excitement for club parties anymore. It wasn't a recent thing. It was something I'd grown more aware of ever since I'd watched my niece and nephews grow up and find happiness away from the partying and club life. And it wasn't just my family moving on. It seemed everyone was.

But me? I was fucking frozen in time.

Trapped with a memory.

Chained to it by guilt.

Or so it felt.

I shook my head to dislodge the depressing thoughts, and took a swig of the beer I'd been nursing for the last hour.

I knew what they thought about me. My brothers. They thought I was cold. Ruthless. That my heart dried up and scattered like confetti when my wife died. That I was incapable of feeling anything. They thought I was some kind of sociopath who didn't feel the consequences of his actions or the weight of every choice I made as club president.

But the truth was, I felt it all.

Every single decision.

Every choice.

Every death.

Every damn consequence of the MC world.

I absentmindedly touched my hip where six dark lines were inked into my skin.

Some days I didn't just feel it, some days I was fucking *haunted* by it.

But I did what I needed to do. Then I compartmentalized it. Tucked it away in the dark corners of my mind and hoped my subconscious did a good job processing it so it made some kind of righteous sense. Because I was the president, and that was my fucking job.

But there were moments where I craved the love of a woman. For someone to go home to at the end of the day. Someone who would wrap her arms around me after I'd brutally slayed a psychopathic murdering rapist, and remind me that I was still human. That I could love. That I was deserving.

Some days I thought I wanted it all. The wife. The kids. Even the damned picket fence. But I had spent far too long believing that I didn't deserve to move on. Because if I had put Wendy first that night, if I had picked up the wine like I said I would, she wouldn't have died in that car wreck.

I deserved to be alone.

It was my sentence for being a shitty husband.

For my wife and my unborn baby dying in the rain.

And I had rules to ensure I never forgot.

It was why I fucked with no attachment.

It was why I avoided any involvement with a woman that included feelings or commitment. Or love.

It was what kept my heart a barren wasteland and my bed cold.

It was my choice.

My penance.

But it wasn't without its own consequences, because some days I was fucking lonely.

Like now.

Like last week.

And the week before that.

Not that there was any shortage of available women. Especially in the clubhouse.

But I didn't indulge in club girls, and they had given up trying.

Except Tiffani.

Tiffani would never give up.

"Hey there, baby."

Speak of the devil.

Tiffani slid into the booth across from me.

I gave her a nod and she grinned, tipping her head to look at me through her heavy lashes. "You look lonely. Feel like some company?"

"Not tonight, darlin'."

She saw me glance over at the bar and her mood shifted. "You know, your new girl is a real bitch."

My eyes darted to hers. "Why do you say that?"

She looked over at Taylor pouring Tully and Cool Hand shots at the bar, and her eyes narrowed. "Thinks a lot of herself, that one. Got a mouth on her too. She's a bad seed, I'm telling you. You watch out for her, baby. I don't trust her."

I usually avoided Tiffani. If she wasn't so popular with some of my brothers, I'd have her gone from the clubhouse permanently.

She was a troublemaker.

And she could turn crazy on and off like a goddamn faucet.

When she looked back at me, her demeanor changed dramatically and she smiled sweetly. "But let's not waste time talking about some bar girl."

"You bought her up," I reminded her.

She scoffed, but waved it off and batted her long lashes. Looking coy, she licked her already glossy lips and curved one bare shoulder toward me. "When are you going to put me out of my misery, Bull? What does a girl need to do to get your attention?" She ran a long nail along my forearm. "No need for you to sit here looking so lonely. Let's go to your room where I can make you feel real good."

I pulled my arm away. "It's not going to happen, Tiffani."

She pouted at the rejection. But didn't take the hint. Instead, she upped her efforts. She leaned in closer. "You've got my panties soaked right through." She let out a little whimper. Her eyes hooded. Her teeth biting into her lip. "Give me half an hour with that beautiful cock of yours, and I promise, you won't regret it."

How she knew I had a *beautiful* cock was beyond me. I had never, and never would, touch Tiffani.

I was just about to tell her to leave me alone, when my attention was dragged away by some random cheering across the room. As I looked up, I noticed Sheriff Buckman walking into the clubhouse. Normally, when the cops arrive at a clubhouse, they're not walking in, they're storming in. But things were different here in Destiny. We had a good relationship with the sheriff, thanks to a long-standing agreement between him and the last three presidents, as well as a nice fat retainer at the end of each month.

So, seeing him walk into the chaos of a biker homecoming celebration was hardly a concern, and no one really paid him much mind. Except a couple of club girls who made a flirtatious show of saying hello to him. He awkwardly untangled himself from them and made his way over to me.

Tiffani took one look and screwed up her face. She didn't like Bucky. Not since he'd arrested her for being drunk and disorderly at a roadhouse on the interstate toward Humphrey. She stood up and snatched her purse from the table. Out of courtesy, he lifted his hat and gave her a polite nod. But she was still furious at him. She scowled and brushed past him without a word before making her way over to the pool tables.

"You got a minute?" he asked me.

"All the time in the world, Bucky."

I nodded when he gestured to sit down.

"I want to talk to you about that incident out near the railroad tracks on the edge of town," he said, placing his hat on the table in front of him.

"Incident?"

"Yeah, someone called the sheriff's office to report a body."

"They did?"

I was playing dumb, and Bucky knew it.

"Yeah. Found it in a ditch with a bullet in his chest and some burns that the medical examiner said was done with a blowtorch."

I let out a whistle. "Brutal. Anyone we know?"

"A real sleaze bucket called Scud Boney. You know him?"

"Can't say that I do."

"Yeah, well, he had his slimy fingers into a lot of terrible shit. Some of the Polaroids we found back at his motel room made one of our forensic guys puke his breakfast all over the goddamn parking lot."

"Sounds like someone did the world a favor."

"I guess they did." Bucky's knowing eyes shone across at me. "I just hope that *someone* got rid of the gun they used so it can't be traced."

"I reckon whoever did what you said they did probably took care of it already. The Mississippi is a damn big river."

Bucky nodded, absentmindedly curling the brim of his hat with his hands as he thought for a moment.

"You know, if this *someone* had called my department before they took the law into their own hands, we could've taken care of it, and they wouldn't be looking down the barrel of a murder charge if they are caught."

I looked unaffected at the suggestion. "Maybe that *someone* thought that the world was a better place without him. Sounds to me like he is better off rotting in hell than in some jail cell."

"Yeah, well, hopefully next time I'll get a chance to do *my* job."

"Don't sweat the small stuff, Bucky," I said. "The bad guys are like weeds. One dies and another one sprouts up to take his place. I'm sure if you dig further into Scud Boney, you'll find plenty of other *sleaze buckets* to collar."

He didn't look convinced, but nodded as he rose to his feet. "I take it there won't be any more Scud Boneys floating to the surface anytime soon."

I gave him a blank look. "Some of the best advice I ever received was to never say never."

"Well, here's some more advice for you to contemplate. I know

Bull

you're hellbent on revenge, son. I just hope you know what you're doing. Because you know what they say…before you start on a journey of revenge, best you dig two graves." He looked uncomfortable as he placed his hat back on his head. "Just something for you to consider."

As he walked away, I took a long pull on my beer.

I didn't want to think about Scud Boney or the cesspit of a motel room I'd found him in. He was in hell now, right where he belonged, and the moment he hit the floor dead, I had started to forget about him.

CHAPTER 17

TAYLOR

"Hey, T. You interested in more shifts?"

I had just walked into the clubhouse to start my first Wednesday shift when Randy approached me.

"Are you kidding me? Sure, I'm interested. What do you have available?"

"Chrissy's shifts."

"Who is Chrissy, and what are her shifts?"

"She works the weekends and all the other shifts you don't work. But she works to six o'clock some nights. Can you do that?"

I chewed the inside of my mouth. I would have to make sure Pickles was fine with watching Noah.

"You could always bring Noah back to the clubhouse after school. Hawke and Vader's kids sometimes hang out and do their homework when their mama's have to work."

"They hang out here?" I asked surprised.

"This place is PG until five p.m."

Just as he said it, Nitro and Caveman walked in dropping the F-bomb as they talked about pussy.

"Yeah, real PG," I replied wryly.

Randy threw the dish towel over his shoulder.

Bull

"Come on, kids hear worse than that on Netflix."

I appreciated the offer. But I was determined to keep my personal life separate from my professional life.

"I'll work something out. I have a neighbor, Pickles, he usually watches Noah. And when he's not available, there's always Mindy the cheerleader. She lives on the other side of the unit complex."

Randy leaned a hip against the bar. "You know, Vader's kid, Luke, is Noah's age. It might be a chance for Noah to make some more friends."

The thought was more than appealing.

But my reason for keeping them separate was by necessity, not by choice.

"Let me think about that some more."

I didn't need to think about it.

Noah wasn't going to hang out at the clubhouse.

"Great." He straightened. "Oh, and while I think about it, are you free to work Maverick's bachelor party?"

"I'll make sure I am. When is it?"

"Last Saturday of this month." He raised an eyebrow. "But I have to warn you, it won't be as tame as Nitro's coming home party."

"I think I can handle it."

He tipped his head back and laughed. "We'll see, T. We'll see."

Needing to pee, I ran to the bathroom before I started my shift. But as I headed back toward the bar, a sound stopped me in my tracks.

Standing still, my skin prickled with goose bumps as I listened, trying to work out what it was and where it was coming from.

It was a purely raw, masculine sound, a heavy, rhythmic pant that ignited a flare of excitement in my stomach, and sent a torturous throb to the muscles between my legs.

Grunting.

And it was coming from Bull's office.

I told myself to keep walking. To ignore the erotic, primal sounds coming from inside the other side of the door marked PRESIDENT.

But while my mind said one thing, my feet did another.

The door was slightly ajar, and it was too much of a temptation. Curiosity got the better of me and I crept toward it.

I didn't know what I expected to see.

Was he with a woman?

Did he have her bent over his desk?

I couldn't hear a female. No soft moan. No feminine gasp. Just a thick, rhythmic grunting that ignited every sexual urge in me.

Was he jacking off?

Would he even do that here?

I knew I should walk away, but I couldn't help myself. I felt drawn toward the gap in the door.

At first, I didn't see him. But when I dropped my gaze to the floor, there he was, shirtless and doing push-ups.

Jesus, Mary, and Joseph.

My lips parted with longing because a shirtless Bull doing push-ups was something else. Even better than white t-shirt Bull.

I was riveted to the spot by the big round shoulders. By his massive arms as they pushed and pulled. By his torso, thick with slabs of muscle. By the up and down motion of his pelvis as he lowered himself toward the floor, only to thrust upward again.

I couldn't look away.

Dear God, this visual was going straight to the spank bank.

I knew I was being a creeper. But I didn't care. This was mesmerizing and nothing was going to drag my eyes away.

When he stopped, it was almost disappointing. But I didn't dare move, I was afraid if I did he would see me, watching him like a stalker from the gap in the door. Holding my breath, I watched him climb to his feet, his broad torso gleaming with a sheen of sweat, a deeply carved V disappearing behind the belt of his black pants. I tried to swallow, but my throat felt thick, and I had to force down the saliva that had pooled in my mouth.

Turning his back to me, he grabbed a gym towel from his desk, and I drank in the wide shoulders and the broad back tapering down to a thick waist. On his back was a massive Kings of Mayhem tattoo with the words *For Life* inked in black beneath it.

He wiped the thin mist of sweat from his heavily tattooed arms and across his broad chest, his muscles flexing and clenching with every movement.

Bull

"Are you going to come in?" His voice cut into the air between us. "Or were you planning on standing there all afternoon?"

Fuck.

I was busted.

I let out a shaky exhale.

"I'm sorry," I said awkwardly, taking a cautious step into his office.

"For what?"

He turned around, and for a moment I was distracted by his chiseled six-pack and all that damn muscle.

A small grin played on his lips. "Taylor…?"

You're being ridiculous, I told myself.

I lifted my chin. "I heard a noise."

"And?"

"I thought you might…need…*assistance?*"

Wow.

He raised an eyebrow. "Assistance?"

"I thought I should check to make sure you were okay."

I shrugged like it was nothing.

Because it was nothing.

It wasn't like I was standing there with soaked panties and a thumping heartbeat.

Okay, *I was standing there with soaked panties and a thumping heartbeat,* but the important thing was he didn't know it.

Or did he?

Fuck, he did.

It was written all over his ridiculously handsome face.

He took a step toward me, bringing with him an aura of heat and pure manliness. "And you thought you could save me from whatever it was that was happening in here?"

I stepped back. Because I could feel the pull of his orbit, and it was powerful. "I thought I should at least try."

For every step I took backward, he took one forward. *Predatorily.*

"And what if I was in here with a woman. Would you have saved me from her? Or would you have…joined us?"

It was my turn to raise an eyebrow. "Seriously?"

He grinned. He was fucking with me.

I shook my head, deciding this whole encounter was stupid.

"I'm sorry. I should've respected your privacy."

He stepped past me, his deeply carved chest only inches from my body as he reached for a shirt hanging on the door behind me.

"Don't be," he said, his voice low and seductive. "I like it when you watch me."

A shiver rippled through me. His words excited me. And the raw scent of him hit me like a drug.

He slid his t-shirt over his head and down his body, but didn't make an attempt to move away. "Can I help you with anything else?"

"No," I said under his warm gaze.

And with legs as steady as Jell-O, I walked out of his office.

CHAPTER 18

TAYLOR

I settled into life at the clubhouse with ease.

But it was an MC clubhouse. It was an unpredictable world. Anything could happen at a moment's notice. Peace and quiet couldn't be taken for granted, because a peaceful afternoon could easily be spun on a dime, and I could find myself with my guard down, exposing a little bit more of myself than I would like.

Like this afternoon, when I was startled by the sudden *bang bang* of shots being fired. My eyes darted to Randy, who looked more annoyed than concerned. We were alone in the clubhouse. I followed him outside into the midday sun where we found Tully, Nitro, Vader, and Cool Hand in the parking lot. Cool Hand was standing as straight as an arrow with a gun in his hand, aimed at a wall of sandbags. He let another round of shots ring out across the compound.

"Have you guys lost your minds?" Randy said, walking over to them. "You almost gave our new girl a fucking heart attack."

Tully, Nitro, Vader, and Cool Hand glanced over at me.

"That might be a bit of an exaggeration—" I mumbled, feeling a little embarrassed. I hadn't been scared. I'd been startled. There was a big difference. I was no scaredy cat. And the last thing I wanted was these guys treating me like I was a little porcelain doll who jumped at the sight of her own shadow, or the *bang bang* of a handgun. I wasn't that kind of girl. Never had been. Never would be.

"Sorry, sweetheart, but it ain't nothing to be scared of. Just Cool Hand getting a feel for his new Beretta," Nitro said.

I thought of my Beretta in my purse.

"You got a new one?" Randy asked with a raised eyebrow.

"Check it out, brother." Cool Hand gave him the gun, and after admiring the sleek-looking firearm, Randy fired three shots into the target on the sandbag. He was an awful shot. All three bullets landed outside the painted lines.

"She's beautiful," Randy said, admiring the weapon. "Nice and smooth. Little kick back."

Cool Hand glanced over at me. "You want to try?"

Nope. I didn't want to try. I didn't like guns. They were an unfortunate necessity in my life because of my past, so standing there and shooting at a wall of sandbags for fun was about as appealing to me as a root canal with a pair of pliers.

"It's okay if you've never fired a handgun before," Cool Hand added, a little condescendingly.

I folded my arms across my chest.

"Dude, does she look like she's ever fired any kind of gun before?" Nitro asked.

Which grated at my nerves.

"Good point," Cool Hand replied.

I didn't like being shoved in a box by someone's assumption.

I let my arms drop to my side.

Fine.

I would shoot the damn gun.

"Nothin' to be afraid of, darlin'. No one gets it perfect the first time," Cool Hand said as Randy handed me the Beretta. "I'll walk you through it."

But before Cool Hand had the chance to show me anything, I had the safety off, my feet stepped apart, my back straightened, and I was firing five rapid shots into the target on the sandbag with an eagle-eyed precision no one saw coming.

In seconds, I had blown the center target to pieces.

Bull

Because I don't like people making assumptions about me.

When the echo of the last shot faded into the sunny afternoon, you could hear a pin drop. I stood for a moment, watching the waterfall of sand spill from the sandbag onto the concrete before taking a look around me. Chins had dropped. Mouths were open.

I handed Cool Hand his gun. "How'd I do?"

But he couldn't find the words.

Feeling a little smug, I walked away and made my way toward the clubhouse, smiling when I overheard Vader say, "That's fucking it. First *Star Wars*, and now this. If Bull doesn't make his move, then I'm going to sweep her off her goddamn feet and marry her."

Randy followed me inside. "Want to tell me what the fuck that was all about?"

I shrugged. "Nothing to tell."

"Uh-uh. What you did out there was not beginner's luck. Now spill. How'd you learn to shoot a firearm like that?"

Brushing him off wasn't going to work here, so I looked him square in the eye and I told him the truth.

"Once upon a time, someone made me a victim. Afterward, I decided it would never happen again."

CHAPTER 19

TAYLOR

The following Monday, after dropping Noah at school, I stopped into the gas station to fill up.

"Your card has been declined," the attendant said when I went to pay.

"Are you sure?" I felt the sudden flood of heat run through me. I knew we were running low on money, but I was sure I had enough for gas. "Can you try it again?"

The attendant looked put out as he retried my card. "Declined."

"But that's impossible."

"Not according to the machine it's not."

"Can you try it once more?" I asked, praying for it to be a mistake.

This time the attendant sighed dramatically as he put my card through. But just like the previous two times, it was declined.

"That'll be twenty-three dollars...cash."

I swallowed back my embarrassment. I didn't have twenty-three dollars. Hell, I didn't have ten dollars.

I felt the lady behind me shift on her feet impatiently, and the person behind her huffed out their frustration at having to wait for me to pay. I looked over my shoulder and saw it was a man in a dark blue, pinstriped suit, looking very exasperated.

I swung back to the attendant. "Look, I'm sorry, I don't have the cash. But today is payday—"

"Sure, it is," he said, his apathy astounding. "Listen, I don't care if today is payday, your birthday, or freaking Hanukah, or Christmas day...you gotta pay twenty-three dollars, right now, or I'm calling the cops."

The cops were the last people I needed to be called.

"What's the hold up?" The man in the pinstriped suit called out peevishly.

"Her card is declined, and she doesn't have any money to pay," the attendant announced to the store.

I glared at him. *Jerk.*

The large lady behind me sighed. When I looked over my shoulder at her, she looked me up and down, and shook her head with pure, uninhibited judgment.

"Oh, for heaven's sake!" The man in the pinstriped suit pushed past her to get to the counter and handed the attendant his card. "Put hers with mine, will you, and let's get this fucking done. Some of us don't have all day to stand around."

"You don't need to do that," I said, wishing the floor would open up and swallow me whole.

"Excuse me, but from where I'm standing, it looks like I do," he snapped, looking at me with the arrogance of a person who had never seen skid row, or felt the grip of hunger pains because money was tight and you had to pay for your kid brother's school excursion.

I stood as still as a mouse as we all waited for the transaction to go through, my body aching with mortification. When the attendant handed him the receipt, he shoved it into his wallet and gave me a contemptuous look.

I followed him out, grateful for his generosity, even if he was being an asshole about it.

"Thank you," I said, sincerely. "That was really nice of you. If you give me your number, I can call you and arrange to give you your money back this afternoon. Like I said, today's payday."

Pinstripe just looked at me with his conceited, gray eyes. "Give *you* my number? You're kidding me, right?"

I was taken aback but managed to hide it. "How else am I going to get you your money?"

He scoffed. "It's twenty-three dollars. Hardly worth the irritation of having to give you my number."

Okay, this guy was an absolute jerk.

But still, he had helped me out of a tight spot.

And just because I wanted to punch him in his egotistical mouth for the way he was talking to me, didn't mean I should show it.

"Well, thanks again," I said.

"I don't need your thanks, lady. Just get out of my fucking way. I've got somewhere important to be, and you've already made me late." He brushed past me abruptly, and I watched him stride across the parking lot and get into his Porsche. With a violent rev of the engine, he sped off into the morning.

Feeling the hot sting of humiliation, I climbed into my car and made a deal with myself that if I didn't cry, I could blow ten dollars out of my paycheck on a big juicy bottle of wine tonight.

And maybe some ice cream. Not the cheap kind either. No, it was going to be the good stuff, thick and rich, and so damn sugary you could feel the calories thickening your waistline.

Feeling hopeless, I looked at the picture of Noah swinging from the rearview mirror and felt a renewed strength harden in my bones.

I refused to cry. And by the time I got to the clubhouse for my shift, I had found my resolve.

Because sometimes it was easier to do things when you were doing them for someone else.

It was a quiet day in the clubhouse with a lot of the Kings in town helping set up for the Fourth of July celebrations on the weekend, so it gave me a chance to get to know Red, the Kings of Mayhem cook, a little better.

Toward the end of my shift, he helped me carry stacks of glasses from the dishwasher in the kitchen and out to the bar, and as we stood drying them, he filled me in on how he came to be a part of the MC's inner realm.

"The first time I met Bull, he put a gun in my face," he said with an amused chuckle. "Damn near scared the skin right off my body...*fuck*!"

Red had Tourette's, and despite his medication controlling it, his tick often peppered his conversation with curse words.

"I was running with a bad crowd. Really found myself at the bottom of the barrel hanging out with the pond scum. They were a rival MC. They stirred up some real shit with the Kings. Roughed up some girls. Stole something from Bull. I knew they didn't see me as one of them. Didn't treat me none too good neither. But I had nowhere else to go, so I stayed. You know, better the devil you know. *Motherfucker!*"

"What happened?" I asked.

"Bull came looking for payback. Rode right up to the door and stormed in. I was the first he saw. He put a gun to my head and told everyone he was going to start shooting unless the president gave him back what he stole."

"And did he give Bull back what he stole?"

"Yeah. Bull can be an intimidating motherfucker."

I could imagine. Every time he walked into a room, he dragged in a powerful energy with him.

"What was it?" I asked him.

"What was what?"

"What did Bull take back from your president?"

Red chuckled. "Oh, it was his dog."

"A dog?"

"Yeah, his dog, Max. He fucking loved that girl. That's one thing about Bull everyone knows. You don't fuck with what he loves, or he'll rain down some heavy shit on you. He was ready to start a war over that dog."

I had already heard things about him.

That he was ruthless.

Hard.

Unforgiving.

But the more I heard about him from the people he spent time with, the more I realized he was passionate rather than cold-hearted.

Charming rather than cruel.

And sexy as fuck.

"How did you end up staying with him? Once he got his dog back, didn't he take his gun out of your face?"

"He had me carry Max out to his car, and in a crazy, panicked moment, I begged him to take me with him."

"Really? Why?"

"Like I said, they were a bad crowd. *Fuck. Fuck.* Real bottom feeders. It was only a matter of time before they killed me. I wasn't one of them. They kept me 'round to do the dirty shit no one else wanted to do. Clean toilets. Mop up puke. But they thought I was a joke. Treated me like I was entertainment. Laughed at me."

He did a good job in hiding it, but I could still see the hurt in his eyes.

People could be real assholes when someone was different.

He grinned. "If Bull hadn't come along when he did, I reckon I'd be dead." He glanced over at Matlock, Cool Hand, Davey, and Nitro playing pool across the room. "They're my family now, and that's how they treat me. They might look big and mean, but they're good men. They've had my back ever since."

Across the room, I noticed Tiffani and Hawke enter the room from the corridor leading down to the bedrooms. While Hawke joined his friends without giving her a backward glance, Tiffani sauntered toward us looking like the cat that licked the cream. *A mouthful of it.*

She threw her little purse onto the bar and took a seat on one of the stools. Throwing her blonde hair over her bare shoulder, she looked at Red.

"I'll have a coffee," she said dismissively. "And make it strong."

Red and I exchanged a look, and it seemed to irritate her.

"Hey, Stuttering Stanley, are you deaf?" She snapped.

I crossed the bar until I was standing opposite her. "What the fuck did you just say to him?"

She was lucky there was a bar between us.

"Oh, settle down, Shorty, he knows I'm only kidding, don't you, Red Bear?" She gave him a flirtatious wink, followed by a sweet smile. "And make it extra sweet, will you, baby."

Bull

"Don't do that," I said.

She looked at me blankly. "Do what?"

"Don't talk to him that way."

She rolled her eyes and pulled her pack of cigarettes out of her purse. "No need to get your panties in a twist. Red doesn't care."

"Well, I do. You don't treat people like that. Not in front me."

She paused before lighting her smoke. "Here's an idea, why don't you mind your own damn business."

"It becomes my business when you do it in front of me."

Again, she rolled her eyes and then lit her cigarette. "He probably gets off on it. A pretty girl paying him attention. *Fucking freak.*"

This woman was a rude bitch, and she needed to know that I wasn't going to put up with it. She might have the Kings fooled, or maybe they just kept her around because she gave out blowjobs like candy, but whatever. She wasn't getting away with the bullshit on my watch.

And no one—and I mean no one—was going to pick on someone in front of me because they might be a little different and expect me to say nothing.

I wasn't a *sit back and watch* kind of gal.

I was reactive. Probably too reactive. And if she ran her mouth off one more time, she was going to experience a mammoth reaction, so it was a good idea if she left.

"Get the fuck out," I said.

Tiffani turned her attention back to me, and I watched her phony mask slip and her eyes harden. "Excuse me?"

"You heard me. I said, get the fuck out."

She slowly removed the cigarette from between her lips, her eyes fixed firmly on mine. "And exactly who the fuck do you think you are?"

I murdered her with my eyes. "I'm the bitch who is going to teach you some fucking manners if you don't get the fuck out of my face."

Her gaze narrowed. "Is that right?"

"That's right. You don't get to treat people like that, so take your shitty attitude and get the fuck out of here."

She sighed dramatically. "I wonder what the boys would say about that? Should we ask them?"

"I'm confident they'll see my point of view."

Her face darkened. "You think they'll pick *you* over *me*?"

"That's not what this is about."

"Oh, don't kid yourself. That's exactly what it's about."

"No, this is about you treating people like something you stepped in."

She made a *tsk-tsk* noise followed by a condescending shake of her head. "You poor thing. You really think you mean something to them, don't you? Well, let me tell you something, *girlfriend*. You mean nothing to them. The boys. Bull. *Especially Bull*. In fact, you're his little pity project. A lost little mouse who needed a job because she couldn't find one on her own." She pulled a sad face. But then it hardened and her eyes narrowed. "He's not attracted to you. He feels sorry for you! Oh, you might think he wants to fuck you. But, honey, you're not his type." Her eyes glittered over my hair, while her fingers raked through her blonde tresses. "Everyone knows he prefers blondes. Look at his wife. The woman he compares every other woman to. She was blonde and beautiful, while you're so...well, you're nothing like her." She leaned closer and whispered. "And, honey, you reek of desperation."

I slowly leaned down on the bar, somehow managing to keep my cool, my voice low and unsafe. "And you reek of contaminated pussy and bad manners, you ridiculous bitch. Now get. The fuck. Out."

She stood and picked up her purse, a nasty smirk spreading across her lips. "I'll be back. But in the meantime, just remember this. While your panties are getting all wet for Bull, he doesn't see you as anyone other than someone who needs fixing. He feels sorry for you, *desperado*." She wiggled her fingers at me. "See you later."

Laughing, she walked away and I felt my chest tighten with anger.

You're his little pity project.

He feels sorry for you.

Her words lingered in me.

The strong and rational part of me told me she was wrong. That Tiffani was nothing but poison.

But the other part of me—*the place where my pride and self-respect existed*—burned with a sudden questioning.

Was she right?

Bull

Is that what Bull thought of me?

Did he see me as someone who needed fixing?

Was this crazy sexual attraction all in my head, and he saw me as nothing more than a pity project?

Someone to toy with?

Hot on the tail of this morning's encounter at the gas station, the humiliation spread through me like a firestorm, and I reacted before I had the sense to stop myself.

Feeling hot with hurt pride, I stormed out of the bar and into his office.

He was sitting at his desk and he looked up when I burst in.

"I'm not some pathetic project," I blurted out.

I was uncharacteristically worked up, and the words tumbled out of my mouth with embarrassing ease. I stormed over to his desk and thrust a pointed finger onto his desktop. "I'm not some little bird with a broken wing that needs you to fix her!"

I didn't know why I was so worked up. This shouldn't matter to me, because at the end of the day, we were nothing. He was just some guy who'd given me a job. And as long as I did that well, what did it matter what he thought of me?

Yet for reasons beyond my understanding, the thought of *him* seeing me as nothing more than a pet project was painfully humiliating.

I wasn't a damn project.

I wasn't broken.

He didn't know who the fuck he was dealing with.

I watched as he slowly removed his dark glasses and rose to his feet with a dangerous calmness.

His gaze slid over me, his face chiseled and full of heat.

When he rounded his desk and came toward me, I trembled beneath his magnetic eyes. They were wild and bright, and full of warning. And suddenly, my boiling emotion left me, and I felt myself being pulled toward that mesmerizing gaze.

I backed away until I felt timber touch my back.

"Is that what you really believe?" he asked, coming closer.

I was pressed up against the door with nowhere to go, and he was coming toward me wearing an expression of danger and barely restrained need.

I wasn't scared.

I was fucking turned on.

And it made me wild with anger.

He didn't stop when he reached me. Instead, he leaned over me and pressed his elbows against the closed door above me, caging me in with his big arms and the hard wall of muscle that was his body.

"Is that what you think, *little bird*?" He growled in my ear.

His warmth, his scent, his fucking *everything* washed over me like warm water, softening my fight and making me want to give in to the lust pumping through my veins.

"You think I want you here because I want to fix you?" He brushed his cheek against mine, and a violent shiver rolled through me. "I don't want to fix you, *little bird*. I want to fuck you."

His words both appalled and excited me.

"And I think you want to fuck me, too," he growled.

He was right. I wanted him to touch me. Christ, I wanted him to touch me so bad.

But my mouth said otherwise. "And like I told you, I don't mix business with pleasure."

I felt flushed with anger and…*desire*.

His body was so close, I could feel the brush of his cut against my breasts, and the sweet whisper of his breath against my cheek.

"Are you sure about that?" His voice was deep and rough.

And challenging enough that I got ready to fight back.

"This is my job," I said thickly. "I can't afford to throw it away by giving into my urges like some stupid schoolgirl."

He exhaled roughly in my ear. "But giving in is so much more fun."

"I mean it, Bull."

"Tell me you don't want me." His lips were close. So close. And I could smell the rich scent of his skin, and it was driving me crazy with need. And he knew it. "Tell me you don't want me to kiss you." The tip of his nose brushed mine. "Tell me you don't want me to touch you."

I was seconds from shattering my resolve and giving in. Because he was too much to resist, and my attraction to him was too damn potent

Bull

to fight anymore. It had been forever since I'd been touched, and my body ached and throbbed with need, demanding I give in to him.

"I don't," I breathed. But it was a lie, and the word snagged in my throat.

"Tell me you want me as much as I want you," he whispered, pressing his big body against me so I was utterly pinned to the door.

"I...I..."

But he ignored me and pressed his face to mine, and my heart sped up, kicking wildly in my chest.

"It's alright, *little bird,* I can wait," he whispered, and I felt him breathe in deeply as if he were absorbing a part of me into him. "Because I know sooner or later you'll give in to those urges, and you'll be screaming my name when I make you come."

Placing my palms flat on his chest, I pushed him back. "Seriously?" His arrogance was beyond words. "You really are the most arrogant man."

He grinned, but it was dark and wicked. "You say arrogant, I say confident."

"No, I say, *Fuck you, Bull.*" I pushed him in his stupid rock-hard chest. "I'm not some club girl who'll drop her panties because you're so ridiculously hot. So, give it up."

I stormed out, angrier than when I first stormed in.

Thankfully, the bar was empty now, so I didn't have to hide my anger and frustration, *and my arousal*, as I got back to work and tried to forget about my feelings for the man who signed my paychecks.

CHAPTER 20

BULL

She's a fucking firecracker.

Storming into my office and pointing her finger at me.

Fixing me with those big dark eyes full of wildfire.

Fuck. The moment she slammed her finger into my chest, I was turned on and fucking hard...just like that.

I didn't usually come on strong like I did with her yesterday. But something about this woman brought out a need in me. A need to be close. A need to touch.

A need to have her up against the wall of my office.

I'd spent a lifetime resisting women by building a wall so high, no one was ever getting over it. Yet somehow, this woman, *this siren*, was getting under my skin by simply pointing her goddamn finger at me and telling me off.

It was a first for me, and I had no idea what to make of it.

So I forced her out of my head. Forced myself to think about club business and revenge. I needed to keep my head pointed in the right direction. Because we were getting more and more intel on Gimmel Martel every day, and I had to keep on top of it all. It was like the fat rising to the surface from the bowels of the criminal underbelly of our county. It meant I had to focus. Meant I would be away from the

Bull

clubhouse and *a certain distraction* while I investigated them.

Every lead had to be followed up.

Every nook needed to be checked.

Every rock turned over.

But damn if I couldn't get *her* out of my mind.

Deciding I needed a distraction, I kicked back from my desk and grabbed my bike keys from the desk. Taking the Harley out to the backroads and letting her fly was a good way to clear the fog from my mind and rattle the sexual tension from my body.

But when I left my office, I walked straight into the one person I was trying to get off my mind.

She was in the showcase corridor, standing in front of the Wall of Fallen Family. Her hands shoved into the back pockets of her tight denim shorts, her perfect tits pressed tight against a shirt that was open just enough to get a tease of what was underneath.

She licked her lips, and my body reacted accordingly.

Fuck.

As I walked up behind her, visions of spending the afternoon making her moan hit me in the cock.

"I didn't know about your wife," she said without looking away from the photographs that lined the wall.

Her words brought my carnal thoughts to an abrupt standstill, and the lust moving through me ground to a sudden halt.

I looked up at the picture of Wendy smiling back at me, and braced myself for the familiar ache to knot in my chest.

"That was taken a week before she died," I said, my voice suddenly craggy

This was a conversation I wasn't expecting.

"I'm sorry," she whispered.

I swallowed thickly. "Me too."

She turned around, and I could see by the look on her face that she knew how it felt to lose someone you loved.

"I know how hard it is," she said.

"Your parents?"

She looked away. "And others."

"Want to talk about it?" I gently lifted her chin with a finger so she would look at me.

But she was a tough little heart, and she was going to take some time to crack. Instead, she raised a challenging eyebrow at me. "Do you?"

Our gazes fused, and that familiar urge to kiss her washed through me.

But despite the recent heated looks from across the room, the coy smiles and raw lust lighting up her eyes whenever we were around each other, she wasn't ready to give in to her own urges yet. And I'd given her my word, I was going to wait until she was ready.

"You're right. Let's change the subject." I stepped away from her, my plans for an afternoon ride vanishing like smoke. "Come on, I'm in the mood for shooting some pool. Do you play?"

"We'll soon see."

"I promise I'll be gentle."

She gave me a wicked look. "No need. I like it a little rough, remember?"

I bit back a groan.

My desire for this woman...I had a feeling it was going to be the death of me.

CHAPTER 21

TAYLOR

"You and I should talk."

Bull looked up from his desk. "This is twice in two days that you've burst into my office. I'm sensing a pattern."

"I think we should lay our cards on the table."

He leaned back in his chair. "Go on."

"You're right. I *am* attracted to you, and it's damn distracting. But I need you to know that I can't afford for it to go any further."

"It sounds like this might be up for negotiations."

"Really? Because I'm pretty sure what I said meant the complete opposite."

He rose to his feet, his mesmerizing gaze warming my skin from across the room. "What's it going to take to get you to give in to me?"

Despite myself, I smiled at his arrogance. "A lobotomy."

His lips twitched. "Give me one night and I'll change your mind."

"I told you, I don't do one-night stands."

"And I told you I don't date," he said, walking over to stand in front of me.

"Neither do I."

"So, we're on the same page."

I pressed my palm against his rock-hard chest. "No, we're on very different pages."

"How so?"

"You want to fuck me until you've had your fill. And I don't want to sleep with my boss."

His eyes were full of heat. "Oh, darlin', I promise you, there'll be no sleeping involved."

I raised an eyebrow at his cockiness. "And *I* promise you, there'll be no fucking involved, either."

I moved away from him. Because being that close to him was dangerous.

"It could be uncomplicated and mutually enjoyable for both of us." He was completely at ease as he leaned against his desk, his big fingers gripping the edge, and his silver wallet chain dangling against his black pants.

"So I've heard."

A hint of a smile touched his lips, and a lustful shiver ran through me when I let myself imagine the way they would feel moving over mine.

"I didn't think gossip would be your thing," he said.

"It's not. But working here, I see a lot. I hear what they say about you...see the lust in their eyes. You're powerful. Women fall all over themselves to get close to you. Every club girl out there wants your attention. Hell, every soccer mom wants to drop their good-girl panties and ride you in the backseat of their SUVs. And why not? You're fucking hot. You're the king of kings."

"I'm also fucking great in bed."

My eyes narrowed. "Is that why you're trying so hard with me? I don't want you, so I'm a challenge?"

He started to laugh.

"What's so funny?"

He stood up and walked over to me, towering above me. "Darlin', you want me, you're just not ready to admit it yet."

His arrogance was astounding.

And kind of sexy.

Not that I'd ever admit it.

Bull

I folded my arms across my chest. "Is that so?"

"It's written all over your face."

His smile disappeared, replaced by heat and seduction as his eyes glittered all over me.

"You think you keep your cards close to your chest, but you don't. Your body tells me everything I need to know."

When his fingers found the curve of my jaw, my hands fell to my side and I trembled beneath his tenderness.

His gaze was searing.

His touch merciless in its pleasure.

His voice luxuriously dark and seductive.

"Like the way you clench your teeth so hard your jaw ticks because you know you're fighting a losing battle."

His fingertips whispered across my cheek, until his thumb found my mouth and glided over the delicate skin of my lower lip.

"The way you bite down on your lip when you know you shouldn't want something but *you can't help it*, because you want it so bad you can taste it."

I had to resist drawing him into my mouth, because the way he was looking at me had me spellbound.

But before I could part my lips, his fingers trailed down the curve of my throat and over the slope of my collarbone toward the swell of my breast.

And Christ, I wanted him to touch me there.

Every cell of my being screamed for him to push my tank top down and secure those glorious lips over my tight, aching nipples.

My lips parted with want.

My pulse raged in my neck.

I had to squeeze my legs together to quell the aching throb.

I wanted him to take my breasts in his big hands.

I wanted him to torturously suck each nipple.

But he didn't.

Instead, he pressed his palm to the spot over my heart and secured his eyes to mine. "The way your heart beats faster whenever we're close."

I tried to swallow, but my mouth was dry. I looked away but he lifted my chin so I had no choice but to meet his gaze, and in that moment, I was a goner. I felt my cheeks flush. He was going to kiss me and I wanted him to.

"Tell me you don't want this," he said hoarsely. "And I'll show you how your body is telling me you're lying."

Without thinking, I bit down on my lip and he groaned. It was all he needed. With a growl, he sank his lips to mine and kissed me with a searing passion. Shock and excitement took a backseat to the pleasure of his mouth moving luxuriously over mine, and I whimpered. His lips were soft and luscious, his tongue confident and commanding, both of them driving me toward a dizzying mindlessness.

With a moan, I melted against him, powerless to stop, and when he felt my surrender, he took the kiss deeper, dragging his fingers through my hair and tilting my head back.

His lips dropped to my jaw, and slid along my arched throat, and I gasped at the sensation. It was like I was drunk and high, and every touch was amplified with primal pleasure.

"I want you, *little bird*," he groaned against my throat. "And it's driving me insane."

He had me crushed against him, the full length of his powerful body pressed hard into mine, and I could feel every wonderful inch of him. It was exciting. Intoxicating. And so damn delicious, it made me hungry for more. I was breathless and wet, my clit wildly throbbing in time with my racing heart, begging for more. Ravenous for more.

"I'm trying to resist you," I moaned.

"Well, stop," he growled.

His lips crashed to mine again, and they were warm and delicious, and so fucking irresistible, and I was ready to give into every fantasy and let him take me there on his desk.

But just as I was about to submit everything to him, there was a knock on the door.

It was a short, sharp knock. One he must've recognized because he sank against me, disappointed.

Exhaling with frustration, he took a step back and adjusted himself before replying. "Come in."

Bull

The door opened, and Mrs. Stephens walked in carrying a clipboard.

She had worked for the Kings of Mayhem for years. Somewhere in her late forties or early fifties, she looked more like a boarding school matron than a personal assistant to the president of a motorcycle club. Tweed skirts. High-cut silk shirts. Modest heels. Horn-rimmed glasses. Brown hair tied into a tight bun at the nape of her neck. A face bare of makeup.

She looked like she belonged at the opposite end of the social spectrum to a bunch of booze swilling bikers who grew pot and talked about pussy.

But she was responsible for organizing all the events for the club, including the booking of jelly wrestlers and the purchase of blow up dolls for the occasional bachelor party. Tasks she did without batting an eyelash.

"I hope I'm not interrupting," she said, making eye contact with me. I blushed, certain she knew *exactly* what she was interrupting.

Bull signaled for her to come in.

Embarrassed, I stepped farther away from him and straightened my tank top as subtly as possible. But if Mrs. Stephens realized, then she didn't show it. Forever the professional, she would never allow her emotions to show in her job.

I, on the other hand, was just about to give it up to my boss on his desk.

"These need your signature so I can organize the deliveries for this week," she said, handing Bull the clipboard of papers.

"I'll leave you to it," I said, backing out of the room.

Bull fixed me with those bright, otherworldly eyes, and his expression told me that this wasn't over.

But he was wrong.

It would never happen again.

CHAPTER 22

BULL

My house was in a quiet part of town, a converted three-bedroom terrace overlooking the river. Ten years ago, I'd finally moved out of the little house Wendy and I had bought shortly before our wedding because I needed a respite from the memory of her lingering in every damn room. I lived alone and never invited anyone over. I had never taken a woman in my bed. Never touched a woman within these walls. My home was my privacy. My sanctuary from a world that could weigh heavily on your soul.

The clubhouse was for fucking, but I rarely indulged in it there either. If sex happened, then it happened in someone else's home, or for privacy reasons, in a motel out of town.

But never here.

Never in my bed.

But now, as I lie awake and alone, my mind scratching over the events of the day, I longed for the warmth of a body next to me. For someone to touch. For the pleasure of skin on skin. To lose myself in the heat and the comfort of lovemaking. My body was tight with longing, to the point of pain. The mayor and I were well and truly over, and since her there had been no one. Hell, I hadn't even taken care of the morning woods or random hard-ons in weeks because I had been

Bull

so preoccupied by my lust for revenge.

As a result, now I was hard as fuck and completely at the mercy of my body screaming for me to do something about it.

I needed a woman.

No. I needed Taylor.

Beneath me.

Moaning.

My thoughts drifted back to today's encounter in my office. The way she walked in and demanded we talk. The way my body had come alive the moment she set foot in the room.

The way my chest lit up with warmth the moment she opened her beautiful mouth.

I was aching to take her, so much so it was to the point of distraction.

But there was something else to it. I told myself it was just sex. Yet somewhere inside, I knew I was fucking lying.

She was much younger than me. Maybe too young. Even though she acted a lot older than what she was, there was still a significant age gap. Although, seeing how happy Chastity and Ruger were with their sixteen-year difference made the age-gap thing less of an issue.

I groaned and rolled onto my side, tormented.

Anyway. She'd made it clear that casual sex wasn't an option. And I didn't do relationships. Or commitment.

Frustrated, I rolled onto my other side.

Yet, I couldn't shake her out of my head. Couldn't help but notice her every time we were in the same room. The subtle moves of her body. The rich scent of her hair. The way her eyes shone and her lips broke into that beautiful smile whenever one of my brothers entertained her.

I wasn't afraid of much, but something told me I should be terrified of her.

Before I could stop myself, I started to imagine her naked and tangled in my sheets. And then I couldn't stop imagining her. Her creamy, lithe body, her pink, luscious nipples, her thighs parted just enough to tantalize. Those dark, black eyes heavy with lust and gleaming with a wicked light. *Fuck, I was getting even more turned on.*

I closed my eyes, and couldn't help but think of her sweet body writhing beneath me on my bed, moaning my name and clawing the sheets as I made her come, again and again.

I punched my pillow and shifted into a different position, ignoring my hard cock and the brief sensation of pleasure shooting along the shaft when it brushed against the mattress.

Don't do it, I warned myself. Don't think about those long legs and the way those Daisy Dukes hug her sweet ass so tight and firm.

Groaning, I rolled onto my back.

Forget the way her perfect breasts press against her t-shirt.

And the way her thick hair falls around the smooth slope of her slender neck.

Or how tight and wet her pussy would be wrapped around every throbbing inch of me.

Fuck.

Now I had my hand on my dick and I was stroking it. I don't even know when I started. But somewhere between thinking about her tight pussy, and the feel of her luscious lips against mine, I had reached down and clamped a hand around the thick shaft. *Christ, I was hard.* And now that I was stroking it, there was no stopping. The tension was already building in my belly, and I wasn't stopping until I jerked her out of my head.

I gripped the base and jacked it slowly, releasing the tension after a few pumps to slide my fingers up to the head where I was slippery with semen.

I wiped my thumb pad across the milky liquid and trembled, a thrill running through me from my head to my toes.

I closed my eyes and bit down on my lip, thinking of Taylor's beautiful face and the swell of her tits, and I started pumping again. Slowly. *Teasingly.* My hand firm around the shaft as I pictured her sinking her perfect ass onto me.

The swell was rising. My balls tightened and I could feel the wave coming. My hips took up the rhythm, subtly rising to meet every stroke of my hand as a shiver of anticipation quaked through me.

I thought of her captivating smile and her mesmerizing, smoky voice.

Bull

I thought about the scent of her skin and the warmth of her body as I had her pressed against the wall in my office, and I groaned, wanting her, wanting to feel her beneath me, wanting to feel her pussy milking my cock as I made her come.

"*Fuck.*" I thrust my head back into the pillows. I was so damn hard. So damn needy for her. I wanted her, goddamnit. I wanted her to drop to her knees in front of me and wrap those luscious bee-stung lips around me.

I wanted to hear her moan, and know it was because of me and what I was doing to her.

I wanted her to want this just as much as I did.

My lips parted as my breath hitched from my mouth.

I slowed my hand, but dragged it all the way up to the engorged head, needing to come, but holding back, torturing myself with slow, leisurely tugs until the dam finally broke in me with an untamable force.

A choked cry ripped from my chest, and I arched my back, digging my toes into the mattress as I started to come.

Taylor.

The strangled growl filled the room as cum roared from my body in thick, hot streams, and hit the rock-hard flesh of my abs. And it kept coming, and I kept moaning and pumping until there was nothing left in me, nothing left but the need for a woman I so desperately wanted beneath me.

CHAPTER 23

TAYLOR

I stared at the sign hanging between the two oak trees that read, 'Destiny Middle School Cookout,' and mentally groaned.

Apparently, the cookout was a big deal on the school calendar. The whole town participated, with local businesses setting up food booths to help raise money for much-needed school resources.

Noah was already inside having opted to go earlier with one of his new friends from class. He was slowly getting more confident and making new friends, spending more time at sleepovers and at friends' houses.

"Let the torture begin," I sighed to myself, climbing out of my car and grabbing the tray of cupcakes from the backseat.

As soon as I entered the gates, I saw them.

Three familiar, big-haired trolls making their way through the crowd of students and their families.

The Destiny Middle School PTA.

Otherwise known as Hell's Sisters.

In my mind, anyway.

I had a few other apt descriptions, but they were less appropriate.

They walked through the school grounds like homecoming queens, flicking their hair and ignoring the stares of the *unpopular* people as they passed by.

It was like fucking high school. They were the plastics, and the rest of us were fodder for them to pick on.

It was typical *us* and *them* bullshit.

But they ruled the PTA. And as a result, they ruled over every middle school event, from fairs and school dances, to picnics, carnivals, and today's cookout

The leader of the pack was Audrey Scotsdale, a bone-thin bully who was a gazillion inches tall in her Louboutin stilettos, with big blue eyes and frosty pink lips. She had an air of friendliness about her, when she wanted you to think she was nice. But in reality, her smile was fake, her eyes cold, and her tongue was as mean as a cut snake.

The first day we met, she decided she didn't like me. She'd cast an arrogant look over my Avenged Sevenfold t-shirt and denim shorts, her over-made-up eyes sweeping up and down with pure disdain as she shamelessly put me in the category of *them*.

Her two subordinates, who were never far from her side, were vapid clones who never reached her dizzying heights of Queen Bitch. They were two tight-faced women who had peaked in high school, and now followed Audrey's lead so they could be a part of the cool kids.

Normally, I didn't worry about women like that. After all, I was all about *you do you, boo*, and all that.

But some days they fell on the wrong side of my badassery.

Like today.

"Oh, you brought cupcakes to the cookout," Audrey said, looking at the tray of chocolate cupcakes like they were frosted grenades.

"It's not a dessert event," Malory said, like I'd broken the cardinal rule of cookouts.

"It's a barbecue…" Mary-Lynn added, offering no value to their argument whatsoever.

If this was a teen movie, she was the simple one.

Audrey gave me a condescending look. "I probably should've put it in the newsletter that we don't encourage desserts at the cookout."

Yes, you probably should have.

"We frown upon sugary foods, you understand. Given that my Henry is a dentist and we like to promote dental prosperity," she added matter-of-factly.

I didn't know who Henry was, but I felt sorry for him.

And what the hell was dental prosperity?

"Well, they're from Honey Bee Cupcakes in town, if that makes any difference," I said brightly.

"Are they sugar free?" Mary-Lynn asked.

"Gluten free?" Asked Malory.

"Nope, just good ol' cupcakes. Oh, but Honey made them especially for the cookout."

"Honey made these for *you*?" Malory asked.

"Well, she made them for the cookout, but as a favor to me, yeah."

"Why would she do that?" Mary-Lynn asked.

I gave her a strange look. Because like I said...*the simple one.* "I guess because we're friends."

Audrey looked at me in disbelief. "You're friends with Honey?"

"Yeah, why is that so weird? I work at the clubhouse…"

Three pairs of heavily mascaraed eyes lit up.

"As in, the Kings of Mayhem clubhouse?" Audrey scoffed.

I narrowed my eyes at her obvious disbelief. "Is there another clubhouse I don't know about?"

I felt the energy shift around us. Suddenly, Malory and Mary-Lynn were like my best friends.

Malory slipped an arm through mine. "Let's sit down and have one of these delicious cupcakes you brought, and you can fill us in on what it's like to work for the Kings of Mayhem."

"Oooh, yes, I've always wanted to see inside of the clubhouse," Mary-Lynn added.

I freed my arm from Malory's grasp.

These women were something else. It was like I was suddenly in a different conversation with different people. People who hadn't treated me like I was a piece of toilet paper stuck to their heels for the past three months.

Apparently, the Kings of Mayhem were a clique these women wanted desperately into, and I was their golden ticket.

"Wait!" Audrey said, putting a hand up. Her smile slipped, but she quickly restored it. "You expect us to believe that *you* work at the clubhouse? Next you'll be telling me you know the president personally."

"If you mean the president of the Kings of Mayhem, then yeah. If you mean the president of the United States of America, then no."

Her eyebrow went up and she folded her arms. "I don't believe you."

Another sweep of her cruel eyes rattled my last nerve, and the hair on the back of my neck bristled. "I don't care if you do or you don't."

"Well, I guess if you're such good friends, then you won't mind showing us."

A smugness twisted in her frosted pink lips as she jutted her chin to something over my shoulder. I swung around and felt my stomach knot when my eyes collided with Bull. He was standing with Ronnie and Roberta at the Kings of Mayhem booth where Red and Maverick were serving up lettuce cups full of blue crab.

"Well?" Audrey prompted.

I turned back to her. "Well, what?"

"Go over there and say hello…I mean, if you're *such good friends*…"

I wanted to go over there like I wanted a bullet in my brain. The last time I'd spoken to Bull, he'd put his tongue down my throat.

And I'd let him.

Now my body acted appropriately, *or inappropriately*, at the memory.

Should I go over there like Audrey dared me?

Normally, I wouldn't bother reacting to a challenge from someone I couldn't care less about. But there was that small part of me that wanted to prove these frozen, mean girls wrong.

"Whatever…" I turned and walked away, taking my black sheep cupcakes with me.

The moment Bull saw me, a small smile curled on his stupidly perfect lips.

"I didn't pick you for a barbecue kinda girl," he said.

"And I didn't expect to see the Kings of Mayhem president hanging around a middle school cookout." I raised an eyebrow. "Or are you stalking me?"

"It's all part of our community service, darlin'."

"Sure, it is. I think the stalking scenario is more likely."

I liked the way his smile pressed two dimples on either side of his perfect lips.

"We do it every year. We might work outside of the law sometimes, *little bird*, but we're very much involved with our town."

"Next you'll be trying to tell me you go to church each week."

"I do go to church every week, except, we call it chapel."

"Hmmmm …"

"What does hmmmmm mean?"

"I was just wondering…"

"What?"

"Other motorcycle clubs refer to it as church."

He looked mildly surprised. "Sounds like you've done your research."

He was right. I had researched them.

And him.

"Why do the Kings call it chapel?"

He gave me a grin that was merciless as it slayed me. "Well, darlin, that's because the Kings of Mayhem aren't like any other club in the world."

For a moment I lost myself in his beautiful face. He was too much. Too big. Too potent. *Too tempting.*

Stepping away from his magnetic pull, I reminded myself why I was over here.

"Do me a favor. Without being obvious, you see those women over there?"

"The ones who look like they're about to star in an '80s country music video…?"

"Yeah, they're part of the PTA, and I have a feeling they're big fans of yours."

"Is that a fact?"

"And they really aren't the nicest of ladies. Well, to me, anyway."

"You want me to go over there and—"

"No, I don't want you to go over there. Hell, they'd eat you alive."

"Now I'm intrigued."

"They seem to think I'm not good enough for anything in this town.

Bull

Including working at the Kings' clubhouse."

For a moment his face darkened and his eyebrows pulled in. But in a second it was gone. "Now why would they think something like that?"

"Because they're mean girls." I glanced over at them. They were watching us. Audrey had her arms folded and her narrow eyes sharpened in my direction. "And the only thing mean girls respond to is a taste of their own medicine. Normally I wouldn't care but...people like that shouldn't think they can treat people like they're worthless and get away with it."

"Agreed. But I'm trying to work out where I fit into all of this."

"They think I'm making it up when I say that I know you. And I know it's ridiculous that I'm actually over here proving them wrong, when really I should've just told them to go to hell but—"

"You want me to kiss you, again?"

His words stepped on my tongue, stopping the verbal vomit.

"A simple hello would suffice," I said, suddenly shy, my heart taking up a violent drumbeat in my chest.

Amusement twitched on his lips. He leaned in. "Or perhaps you'd prefer if I went over there and told them how much I want you in my bed? How I lie in bed at night fantasizing about you." He leaned even closer; his face close, his breath tickling my cheek. "About making you scream."

I almost dropped the tray of cupcakes in my hand.

He stepped back and grinned. "Too much?"

"Yes." My voice was tiny. I had to get away from this man before I made a huge mistake. Because every nerve and fiber was screaming at me to give in to him, and I was afraid if I moved an inch, I'd reach for him and slam my mouth to his. *Take that, Audrey Scotsdale.* I cleared my throat, my mouth dry. "I have to put these cupcakes in the refrigerator."

I walked away, desperate to escape. But he followed me into the home economics kitchen, which was only a few yards away.

"I see I was correct about the stalking scenario," I said, placing the tray of cupcakes on one of the countertops.

"I didn't realize we'd finished talking."

"I think Audrey and her two cronies got the picture."

I had expected the kitchen to be busy. But there were only two other people inside, and once they'd finished filling a pitcher with orange juice, they disappeared outside, leaving me alone with Bull.

"You expect me to believe you came over to me to make a point?" His eyebrow was raised. "So the fact that you went as red as a beet and speechless as a stone has nothing to do with liking what I said, and everything to do with you wanting to show those women that they were wrong."

"Yes, I was only using you to get back at those bitches. It means nothing."

His brilliant blue eyes sparkled with amusement. "I see."

But he knew better. I could see it on his face. The slight raise of his eyebrow. The flash of knowing in those magnetic eyes. The hint of a smile tugging at his lips. He fucking knew I was barely holding onto my fight. That I was hanging off the cliff, my fingertips bleeding as they held onto the last of my resistance.

I turned away because I was seconds away from crashing my lips to his. Because I knew how they tasted. How soft yet commanding they were. How it felt when his tongue slid up against mine.

I busied myself with repositioning the cupcakes on the plate.

But he came up behind me and caged me between the hardness of his body and the counter, his breath whispering along the nape of my neck.

"This. *You and me.* It's going to happen. Whenever you're ready. I'm a patient man. And I'm tenacious as fuck. But you need to accept that you've already lost the fight, darlin'." His lips brushed my ear. "And it's only a matter of time before you lose the war."

His words sent an exhilarating thrill down my spine and I shivered against him. Wanting him. Craving him. *So fucking ready for him.*

I turned in his arms to face him. He was right. I had lost the fight the moment I'd accepted this job. But what he wanted, I couldn't give him. I had to think about Noah.

The war raged within me.

Because being this close and feeling the heat of all that muscle surrounding me was making me dizzy with lust. All and everything

Bull

outside of this moment was forgotten. I couldn't think straight. My pulse roared in my ears, and my heart was pounding so hard I thought it'd break free and burst from my chest. When my mouth parted, Bull's brilliant blue gaze dropped to it, a look of raw hunger taking over his face as I dragged my tongue along my lips.

Hell yeah, I had lost the fight and was about to raise the white flag in surrender just to feel everything this man had to offer.

Everything else be damned.

I wanted this.

Fucking needed this.

But in that moment, Noah's teacher walked into the kitchen with two of her students, and the spell was broken. I quickly moved away from Bull, immediately feeling the loss of heat from his body. Goose bumps tightened along my skin and the cold ache of disappointment swelled in my chest.

Damn, that was close.

I would have to be smarter in the future.

Because my attraction to Bull was off the charts, and I was quickly losing power over it.

I would have to pretend.

Pretend I didn't want to touch him as much as I did.

Pretend I wasn't yearning to give in to a longing I couldn't shake.

And I knew I could do it if I had to.

Because I was really good at faking it.

Ten Years Ago

For as long as I could remember, I had enjoyed dressing up. For me, there was a fascination about slipping into a fairy princess dress or a costume pulled from a dress-up box, because putting them on allowed me to escape from the real world. It was how I coped with my childhood. How I dealt with the truth about my parents and who they were. It was my escapism. A skill I would call upon, time and time again, when I needed to get through another day of neglect.

I never dreamed it would become my profession. That when Alex called on me, I would become whoever he needed me to be. All it took was a wig, a certain style of clothing and a whole lot of play acting.

Tonight, I was a blonde. With red lips and false eyelashes. My dress was black, tight to show off my curves, and matched with a pair of five-inch heels. Later I would slip on a long-sleeve jacket and a pair of Hermes gloves, and I would walk with phony confidence toward another night of memories I'd rather forget.

I stared at my reflection in the mirror, feeling the disgust already rolling through my stomach.

"Are you ready?" Alex asked, walking up behind me.

I looked at him in the mirror and nodded.

I wasn't ready. I didn't like doing what he wanted me to do. The men were always so gross. Some were old, some were young, some were even good looking, but they were all vile and they made my skin crawl.

"He is waiting for you," he said, cupping his hands over my shoulders. "Serge is downstairs ready to drive you."

In the back of the limousine, I looked at the bright lights of the city moving past the window. I was calm, despite the repulsiveness I felt for what I was about to do. Tonight, I was meeting Luciano, the Lamb, Bianchion, a well-known underworld figure known for his love of good wine, good food, and for inflicting pain. He also had a penchant for blonde women with long legs and red lips, and often indulged in all of his desires in one night.

According to Alex, one of Luciano's dates ended up losing an ear when he bit it off during sex. Another suffered internal bleeding when he took her virginity with a police baton.

His nickname was ironic. Because he was anything but a lamb. No matter who you were. Family. Business associate. Lover. Streetwalker. High-class call girl. If the urge possessed him, he could be brutal on a whim.

"Keep your wits about you, my darling, and you'll be fine," Alex had said. "This one is worth a lot of money."

I found Luciano at his usual hangout, a nightclub he owned called Sin in the City, where the town's rich and coked-up twenty-somethings liked to party. It was a dark and sophisticated bar where you could get away

Bull

with just about anything in the shadowy corners. A place where coke was currency, human decency was optional, and a good time was everything.

He was waiting at the bar, a man in his early sixties with white hair and jowls, nursing a tumbler of whiskey. When I approached him, his gaze swept up and down the length of me, a lascivious gleam in his watery eyes.

He bought me a drink, which I accepted but didn't touch.

We flirted and did the dance two people do when sex is in the cards.

I laughed at his embellished stories and looked at him through heavy lashes when the conversation became suggestive, while he got hard behind his Armani slacks.

I played the part I was expected to play.

I became the person I had to be to get the job done.

I ignored the bile rising in my stomach as his clammy, fat hand slid along my thigh.

"Are you wearing any panties beneath that dress?"

I held back the vomit I needed to hold back as I slightly parted my legs. "Want to take a look for yourself?"

It wasn't long before he was leading me out of the club and into a waiting limousine. We were on our way to his penthouse where he was about to have his mind blown, and I was about to make more unpleasant memories.

CHAPTER 24

BULL

"This has got to stop, Bull."

Tito's whiny voice broke through a pounding headache as he stood in front of me, his hand on his hip, his comb-over sticking to his forehead beaded with sweat.

He ran our production company, Head Quarters, and was brilliant at what he did. Granted, he was a little weird. And I really didn't want to think about what he got up to behind his closed office doors. But he knew porn and he knew what sold, and he had made us a lot of money.

He was also terrified of Sybil.

The original queen of mayhem, who was nearing eighty and was as fiery as her bright red hair, was a force to be reckoned with. She wasn't afraid to tell Tito when she thought he was overstepping the line with movie names. She didn't like him fucking with the classics. And she would stir him up when she told him so.

"Cade is in charge of Head Quarters, Tito. Speak to him about it."

"I can't talk to Cade about this. She's his grandmother... you're the president, can't you do something about her?"

I rubbed my temples. Between Tito's whining and the sexual tension tearing at my body *day after day*, I was going to have a fucking stroke.

Bull

"She's a seventy-something old woman. Speak to her yourself," I said.

"Hello, have you met Sybil?"

Point taken.

"Fine. Tell me exactly what I am confronting this *elderly* lady about?" I asked wearily.

"It seems every other week she's yelling at me about something. Can't you ban her from Head Quarters?"

There was a conversation I didn't want to have. I'd rather spoon my eyeballs out of my sockets with a fucking fork, than tell Sybil she couldn't do *anything.*

"I am not banning Sybil from Head Quarters."

"Why not?"

"Because I value my balls, Tito."

Plus, Garrett Calley had already banned any queens from stepping foot in Head Quarters, following the day Sybil tore through the production set of *Some Like It Hard* because she was pissed about it dishonoring Marilyn Monroe's memory. I pinched the bridge of my nose. I had never upheld the rule because it was ridiculous. "Let me talk to Cade, see if he can make her see sense."

"You need to do something, Bull, because I don't know how much more of her I can take."

"I'll handle it," I said.

After Tito left, I planted my face on the desk.

Some days being president was a headfuck. Give me something tactile like war and revenge, something I could make sense of, not a problem between a control freak in a fucking safari suit, and the original first lady of the club.

A sudden ruckus coming from the clubhouse lifted my head off my desk. The female cry that followed had me off my chair and out of my office within seconds, tearing down the hallway.

In the bar, I found Taylor on the floor clutching her arm, with Randy crouching over her.

"What happened?" I asked.

"She was standing on the bar changing one of the lightbulbs—"

I glared at him. "Why the fuck did you let her do that?"

"I wasn't here. I walked in just in time to see her fall."

"Goddamnit!" Taylor winced.

I dropped down next to her.

"Where does it hurt?"

She was shivering. "My shoulder."

I took a closer look. Her shoulder was grotesquely warped, clearly dislocated.

"Want me to call an ambulance?" Randy asked.

"It feels like I've been hit by a truck," Taylor moaned, her beautiful face showing her pain.

"Fuck the ambulance," I said, scooping her up into my arms. "It'll take too long."

It was a fifteen-minute drive to the hospital. We made it in nine. If we'd called an ambulance, we'd still be waiting.

I glanced over at Taylor leaning her head against the door as I drove. She had gone pale, and I could see the pain in her eyes, but she barely made a noise.

"You ain't gonna pass out on me, are you?"

Her eyes shifted to mine. "And miss out on your awesome driving skills?"

I smiled at her sarcasm. "That's my girl."

When we pulled up, Indy was waiting for us because Randy had called ahead. "What happened?"

"She was trying to impress me with her acrobatics."

Fighting back pain, Taylor was still able to give me a sarcastic laugh. "You're hilarious."

Indy took a quick look. "You've dislocated your shoulder. Let's get you inside. Do you need me to help you walk?"

"I got her," I said, protectively placing my hand at the small of Taylor's back.

Indy's eyes narrowed slightly as she looked at me. But as quick as a flash, her questioning look was gone, and she led us out of the sun and into the hospital.

"I'll order some pain medication, then see about fixing your shoulder back into place," she said, directing us into a cubicle where I helped Taylor onto the hospital bed. I took her hand in mine as Indy

Bull

prepared a syringe. "This is going to sting a little, but I promise, it's going to help."

Indy gave her an injection, and immediately Taylor's big eyes grew hooded. She relaxed and sagged back into the bed, a drunk grin spreading across her lips.

"I'll let that take effect and be back in five, okay?" Indy said and Taylor nodded dreamily.

"Looks like it's gone straight to her head already," I said. "A few more minutes, and she'll be singing karaoke."

Indy gave her wink. "I gave her the good stuff."

"How do you feel?" I asked when Indy left.

Her docile smile grew wider. "High as a kite."

"You feel any pain?"

"Only the one sitting next to me."

I grinned. "Now who's the comedian?"

Her eyelids flickered and then closed.

"I feel great," she said.

I couldn't help but chuckle. I'd never seen Taylor under the influence of anything. And she was fucking adorable.

I couldn't help myself.

"Be honest, was this an attention thing?" I asked with a cocked eyebrow.

Her eyes opened.

"Are you asking if I dive-bombed off the bar onto the floor to get your attention?" She chuckled. "My God, you are so arrogant."

And then she started to murder Carly Simon's, "You're So Vain," slurring it as she weaved in and out of lucidness.

"Again, you say arrogant, I say confident."

She reached out and pushed a bendy finger into my bicep. "And I say, *fuck you*."

Her head fell back and she floated away on her medicated delirium.

"I'll give you a tip." I leaned forward. "If you want my attention, all you need to do is creep past my office and watch me do push-ups again."

Her luscious lips pulled into another drunk smile. "Oh God…I was so turned on watching you…"

As her words fell away, my body tightened with a strange excitement.

"You were?"

She opened her eyes. "What?"

"You were?"

"I was *what*?"

Okay, she was really high now.

I shook my head. "Never mind."

Indy stepped into the cubicle. "How's the patient? Those pain meds kicking in?"

Taylor opened her eyes and her head lolled about on her neck. "I think so."

"Good. Let's get this shoulder back in place, shall we?"

Taylor looked up at her. Her usual sass was gone, and she looked soft and gentle. "Is it going to hurt?"

"I'm not going to lie. It doesn't tickle. But don't worry," Indy gave her a wink. "I've done this before."

Despite the reassurance, Taylor still looked worried, and I was overcome with a need to take her in my arms and kiss the concern from her face.

Which, I'll be honest, I was ready to overthink.

And I would have, if it wasn't for Indy maneuvering Taylor's arm into position, and then yanking it into place.

"Sweet mother of Christ!" Taylor cried out.

I felt my fists tighten, then relax.

"Feel better?" Indy asked.

Taylor exhaled heavily. "Wow. Yes. That…feels so much better." Her eyes sparkled with the heady combination of relief and drugs. "Thank you."

Indy put her arm in a sling. "You'll need to wear this for the next few days. And try to keep it as immobilized as possible, okay?"

Taylor nodded. "Sure."

"I'll leave you to rest up. The drugs should wear off in the next hour or two. Until then, you can wait it out here."

"Thanks, Indy," she slurred.

While Taylor fell back into her drug-induced nap, I waited beside her. I had shit to do. A fucking ton of it. But none of it seemed more important than sitting right there.

Suddenly, Taylor's eyes flicked open and she sat up.

"Noah!" She looked at her watch. "I have to pick him up from school."

I reached for my phone in the breast pocket of my cut. "I'll organize someone to pick him up from school. He can hang out at the clubhouse."

"No!" she frowned, struggling with the haziness. "I mean...he'll freak out."

"Relax. He'll be okay."

"I should call our neighbor Pickles." She wilted against the bed. "I forgot. He has a doctor's appointment in Humphrey today. He won't be home until late. And Mindy has cheer practice..."

I frowned. "Why don't you want Noah at the clubhouse?"

Taylor's head rolled to the side so she could look at me. Her eyes were still glazed, but she seemed to be coming down from her high. "Because I'm trying to keep my personal life separate from my professional life."

"You don't want Noah hanging around us?"

"Not in the way you're making it sound."

"Then tell me because I'm trying to work you out." My tone was tight.

She struggled to sit up. "Remember when I told you about Slick, the stripper, and how mixing work and my personal life got me less shifts at work?" When I nodded, she continued. "I'm afraid if I bring Noah into the clubhouse..." She struggled through her delirium to find the right words. "If he gets close to you, to the club...what happens if this doesn't work out? I'm a package deal, Bull. I can't afford for him to have his heart broken."

Before I could stop myself, I reached for her face and tenderly brushed my fingertips across her cheek. "No one's heart is going to get broken."

She smiled, but it was weak and she didn't look convinced.

But it was a start.

"Let me get him being picked up from school. Let me do this for you."

She thought for a moment and then gave in, nodding as she reclined back on the bed. I pulled out my phone and she spoke to the school. When she handed the phone back to me, her glazed eyes lingered on me.

"Thank you for today," she said with a gentle smile.

She reached for my hand and pressed her sweet lips to my fingers.

And that was the moment I knew I was in trouble.

CHAPTER 25

TAYLOR

Bull drove us back to the clubhouse. The drugs had worn off, but I was still feeling foggy in the head, and when I walked into the clubhouse and saw Noah sitting in a booth with Maverick, *signing*, I thought I was still high.

I turned to Bull. "Maverick knows how to sign?"

He nodded. "His youngest sister was born deaf."

I watched from the doorway, my heart hitching in my throat as I watched my brother laughing and signing with Maverick.

Quietly bonding over their shared knowledge of a silent language.

He looks so happy.

From what I could see, they were telling each other jokes, and then laughing so hard their palms were pressed flat to their chests and their eyes were squeezed shut. Warmth poured through me. I hadn't seen Noah laugh that much in years.

And you tried keeping him away from this, a little voice in my head reminded me.

Bull and I walked over to them, and as soon as Noah saw us, his face lit up and he ran over to me, throwing his arms around my waist. "Are you okay?"

"I'm fine. You look like you're having fun."

"Mav picked me up from school and we came back here. Red made me some chili and Randy gave me a Coke. This place is cool. Wait till the other kids at school hear about it."

I hadn't seen this much excitement from him since…well, ever.

"Vader said his kids are coming here after school tomorrow. Can I come and hang out, too?" he asked, almost pleading.

I glanced around me, swallowing uncomfortably. I was fighting a losing battle.

It was days like today that made it easy to forget why I was here.

But it was moments like these that weakened my resolve and made me give in.

Perhaps having Noah at the clubhouse would be a good thing for him after all.

"Sure," I said, lighting fire to my resolve and burning it all down. "Why not."

And that was how my professional life became complicatedly entwined with my private life.

Soon after my shoulder dislocation, Noah visiting the clubhouse became a regular thing. Some days he'd sit at one of the booths and do his homework by himself while he waited for me to finish my shift.

Other days, Vader's ex-wife, Roberta, would drop Luke and Shelby off, and they would sit in the booth and talk and play. Luke was the same age as Noah, while Shelby was two years younger, and it wasn't long before the three of them were as thick as thieves.

Roberta was cool. I met her the first day she dropped her kids off. Some nights she worked the late shift at the hospital and had to leave them there until Vader was ready to take them home.

"I think my ex-husband has a crush on you," she said with kind, twinkling eyes.

"He has a crush on what I know about *Star Wars*."

She smiled warmly. "That'll do it."

We looked over at Noah teaching Luke and Shelby how to sign.

"Looks like they're going to be good friends," I said, feeling relieved.

Bull

Noah needed more friends. And this was a very good start.

Roberta put a gentle hand on my shoulder as she was leaving. "Anytime you need me to watch him, you just give me a call, okay?"

An uncharacteristic surge of emotion moved through me and I wanted to hug her. Instead, we shared a smile as I thanked her.

While hanging out at the clubhouse after school, Noah also struck up an unusual friendship with Maverick, and they would often have lengthy conversations that involved a lot of laughter and the occasional signing.

"I hope Maverick isn't teaching him swear words," I said to Bull one afternoon as we stood in the bar watching them.

"I hate to break it to you, darlin', but I think he already knows them," he replied with a wink.

But as much as he loved Maverick, it was Bull who Noah took to the most. I could see it in the way he looked at him. The way his face lit up whenever Bull walked into the room. How his eyes shone with admiration. Bull was someone he could look up to. A positive male influence. Noah talked to him about motorcycles and cars, and, I suspect, girls. Once a week Bull took him through self-defense training, and sometimes Maverick and Caleb would join in. And when Noah put Tommy Albright on his ass for picking on a fourth grader, despite my reprimands, I'm pretty sure Bull and Noah shared a secretive high five.

They got close. And it was as terrifying as it was heart-warming.

One day I was stopped in my tracks when I walked in and found them sitting in the booth together, both concentrating as Noah taught him how to sign. I was struck by what a contradiction Bull was. There was a dangerousness to him. A darkness. Yet, I couldn't shake the feeling that he wasn't the big, growly alpha dog everyone made him out to be.

If I was a betting girl, I'd bet my life there was something gentle shimmering just beneath the tough exterior of tattoos and hard muscle.

And I'd be a liar if I said I wasn't drawn to it.

I knew I was getting slightly carried away by letting my private life blend with my work life.

Penny Dee

It was dangerous.
People would get hurt if we had to skip town.
But the risk was worth it just to see Noah this happy.

CHAPTER 26

BULL

The morning of Maverick's bachelor party, I was surprised to see Ronnie waiting in the clubhouse bar for me. "Listen, can you do me a favor? Can you drop in to see Sybil? She's checked into the hospital, but needs something dropped off to her."

"Is she okay? Which hospital is she in?"

"Greenwood Psychiatric."

I looked at my sister, surprised. "Sybil finally lose her marbles?"

Ronnie shook her head, her mass of dark curls falling around her face and tumbling down her back.

"Are you kidding? While we're all losing our minds, she'll still be as sharp as a tack. No, she had hip surgery, and when she couldn't get a private suite at the other two hospitals, she somehow managed to talk Greenwood into giving her one. Probably the best place for the crazy old coot."

My sister and her mother-in-law had always butted heads. Theirs was a love-hate relationship. But I had a feeling that if it came down to it, both would give their life for the other. Thirty years of trying to outdo each other had created a weird, but volatile, bond between them.

"Sure, what do you need me to drop off?"

Ronnie handed me a joint. "This."

"And Caleb couldn't do it?"

"He's the one who gave it to me. You know he's busy with the crop harvest."

"And you don't want to go because…"

"Because she asked for my little brother to drop it off," she said with a wink, walking away.

Great. I had been summoned by the mighty Sybil Calley.

"You happen to get two of these?" I asked, holding up the joint. "Because I think I'm going to need one afterward."

My sister smiled wickedly. "What? You afraid of a little old lady?"

"Just this one." I raised an eyebrow at her. "Just as anyone in their right mind should be."

Greenwood Psychiatric Hospital had once been known in town as an asylum. But now it was an exclusive medical facility renowned for its drug and alcohol rehabilitation programs, as well as its treatment and care for dementia patients.

Sybil was in an exclusive wing where rich celebrities often came to dry out.

Propped up in bed, the original Kings of Mayhem first lady was just as glamorous as always. Bright red hair brushed and set perfectly. Red lipstick. Painted eyes. A glittering caftan of turquoise blue. A vision of color among too many pillows, reading a copy of the *Kama Sutra.*

Of course.

When she heard me, she looked up from the book and her face lit up.

"Well, to what do I owe this pleasure?" She gasped, as if she hadn't orchestrated the whole thing.

She put down her book and held out her arms. As she wriggled her fingers, rings of gold and precious gems glimmered in the artificial light.

I leaned down to give her a hug, and was immediately engulfed in her signature perfume. *Chanel No.5.* She made sure we all knew the name of it. Every single one of the Kings of Mayhem. Because the way she saw it, if everyone knew what she liked, then they'd buy it for her on her birthday, or Christmas, and she'd never have to fork out for a bottle ever again.

Sybil was cunning.

Mischievous.

And as sharp as the pointy end of a fucking knife.

She took one look at me and started in straight away. "Well, don't you look happy. Got anything to do with a pretty young thing working at the clubhouse?"

I gave her a wry look. "Boy, the MC grapevine must be working overtime."

She looked proud. "I have my spies."

"I don't doubt that."

She patted the side of her bed. "It's time you and I had a talk."

"I can't stay long. Just bringing you this." I held up the joint and Sybil's eyes lit up.

"Well, don't just be standing there, son, light her up."

I lit the joint with the Zippo I kept in my cut. When I handed it to her, Sybil took a big toke, then lay back, satisfied. "Sweet mother of God, that is good."

I wondered how long it would be before the staff caught a whiff of the sweet scent of weed.

Not that Sybil would care.

She was the original rule breaker.

The wild rebel who walked to the beat of her own drum.

Only now, she could bat her fake eyelashes and blame it on her age.

Sybil rarely saw problems, only opportunities.

"So, tell me about the new girl. She must be special if she's got you looking as goofy-eyed as a teenage boy on his first date," she said, taking another toke on the sweet-smelling joint.

"There's nothing to tell." I raised an eyebrow. "And just for the record, I'm not fucking goofy-eyed. You're just stoned."

"Don't lie to me, son. I might be one step closer to the bucket, but I haven't kicked it yet. I see what's going on."

"Nothing is going on."

"Then there's something terribly wrong if a strapping young man like you isn't getting any tail."

"I do okay."

"Come on, Bull, even I'm getting more than you, and I'm almost eighty years old."

You never knew what was going to come out of Sybil's mouth. Ever.

Despite myself, I chuckled. "Thanks, Sybil."

"Well, it's true." Again, she patted the bed next to her. But I opted for the arm of the visitor's chair. "It's been a while since you and I have talked."

Shortly after Wendy's death, Sybil and I had gotten close. I was a grieving young man, and she was a tough-as-nails first lady. She took me under her wing. Lent me an ear. Gave me a shoulder. Helped me put one foot in front of the other until getting through the day wasn't agony, and I could sort of start to live again.

She was intimidating as fuck. Then *and* now.

But she was also capable of great compassion and empathy.

"You know, I've watched you struggle with this for years. Now, I've never said anything because it wasn't my place. But now…well, I'm old, and I don't care much for what I should or shouldn't do. I could check out for good tomorrow, and as far as I see it, that gives me a free pass to say whatever I damn well want."

"Okay, let's hear it, then," I said, humoring her.

"You have to get over it, Bull. It wasn't your fault."

When she didn't say anything else, I gave her a wry look. "That's it?"

"That's the short version, yes."

"Okay," I said, bracing myself for the longer version.

"I know what it's like to lose a great love. But life is for the living, Bull."

Just then, a familiar song floated down from the speaker in the ceiling, catching my attention. "Blue Bayou." *Wendy's favorite song.* But I pushed the sting away, which was easier to do these days. The moment the cold trickle of guilt or grief entered my veins, a flood of warmth was close behind it, surging forward to overpower it.

Bull

Things were changing.

I was changing.

Even if I didn't want to admit it.

"My point is, life is a gift. And a life with someone special is a precious gift. Don't waste any more time living it alone."

I appreciated what she was saying.

But it was pre-emptive. Nothing was happening. And nothing was going to happen.

I had my rules, and they were non-negotiable.

If anything happened with Taylor, then it would be purely physical.

"Duly noted," I said, leaning forward and pressing a goodbye kiss to her forehead.

After I left Sybil's room, I noticed an elderly lady sitting on a chair farther down the hall.

She was humming "Blue Bayou."

Obviously remnants from what had been playing on the overhead speakers still in her mind.

I gave her a polite nod, but as I walked past her, she reached out and grabbed my hands with her bony fingers. "It's a lovely song, don't you think? She sings it all the time, you know."

The hairs on the back of my neck stood up. "Who?"

The old lady's watery eyes grew very round. "The lady in the floppy yellow hat."

I pulled my hands away as if she had burned me. "What did you say?"

"She's got a message for you."

I started to back away from her.

"She said that it's okay."

I kept walking backward until my ass hit the door. "I don't know what you're talking about."

She smiled dreamily, lost in whatever delirium she was having. "She said that it's about time." She giggled. "She's laughing, you know, saying she doesn't know why it took you so long."

Frowning, I pushed through the doors and crashed into the afternoon sunlight, feeling uncharacteristically shaken.

By an old lady.

What the fuck was wrong with me?

It was the mention of the floppy yellow hat that did it. Wendy was damn obsessed with her sunhat and wore it whenever she had the chance. I could still see her gripping onto the edges of it as she twirled around in the sunshine, laughing and smiling like she never had a care in the world.

Oddly, the memory didn't bring the searing pain it would have a few weeks ago.

I frowned as I walked to my bike, trying to work out what that meant. Come to think of it, I hadn't felt the agonizing pain of loss for some time.

For weeks now, things had been changing.

I didn't wake up aching.

I didn't feel that hollowness in my chest.

Somewhere inside me, buried deep beneath years of grieving, a light had begun to shine, and the heaviness had started to lift.

I climbed onto my bike but took a moment, feeling fucking rattled.

She said it's okay.

That it's about time.

Is that really what the old lady had said?

And had she really been humming "Blue Bayou," or was I one more sleepless night away from losing my goddamn mind?

Deciding my lack of sleep was fucking with me, I pushed the incident to the back of my mind where I buried all the other shit I couldn't afford to think about. And during the ride back to the clubhouse, I refocused. When I pulled into the compound, I was surprised to see Taylor's car wasn't in its usual parking space.

I found Randy at the bar. "Where's Taylor?"

"She called in sick. Said some old dude died, and they had to wait for the medical examiner."

"Died?" She must mean her neighbor. The one Noah was close to. *Fuck.*

I was out the door and on my bike within a minute. When I pulled up to Taylor's apartment complex, the medical examiner was removing a body from the apartment across from hers.

Bull

Taylor was inside her apartment, sitting on the couch comforting her brother. When I walked in, she looked up and her face broke. I went to her and she stood up, falling into my arms, and burying her face in my chest.

"I'm sorry," I said softly, smoothing down her hair and pressing my lips to the crown of her head. "Wanna tell me what happened?"

She nodded, and I felt her soften against me with a sigh. Stepping back, she wiped her wet cheeks.

"He was going to watch Noah while I was at work. He was in his chair. I thought he was asleep. He looked so peaceful..." Her chin quivered. But she was trying to remain strong for Noah, so she straightened and inhaled sharply. "They said he died in his sleep..."

Noah sobbed, and I crouched down in front of him. "It's okay, buddy. Going in your sleep is the best way. He wasn't in any pain that way."

He nodded and fought his tears, trying to be strong. "We were going to watch *The Magnificent Seven*."

I glanced over at Taylor, surprised by the movie choice.

"He loves westerns," she said.

"So far we've watched *Shane*, *Once Upon a Time in the West*, and *The Good, the Bad and the Ugly*. Pickles said *The Magnificent Seven* was his favorite, and Taylor found it in the bargain bin at the store."

The poor kid looked crushed.

When a deputy from the sheriff's department appeared at the door, his face crumpled again.

"Ma'am, we're done," he said.

While Taylor stepped outside to talk with the deputy, I distracted Noah.

"I haven't seen *The Magnificent Seven* since I was a kid. You feel like watching it with me?"

For a moment his face lit up, but then dropped again, and he had to squeeze his lips to stop himself crying.

"You think Pickles would mind if you watched it with someone else?"

He thought about it for a moment, then shook his head. "No. I think he'd like that."

I knew I was no replacement for his friend. But perhaps if I was here while he grieved, maybe this kid would find some kind of comfort tonight, even if it was only briefly.

And to be honest, I wanted to stay for Taylor, too.

She was a strong woman. Feisty and resilient. But even the toughest of hearts needed to be held up occasionally.

I told myself that was all it was.

I was someone to lean on tonight.

Nothing more.

But when Taylor stepped back into the doorway, and the late sun cast a golden aura around her, something unlocked inside of me. She looked like a goddess. A beautiful, broken-hearted goddess whom I had a sudden urge to take in my arms and kiss until she was breathless and I was drunk on the taste of her lips.

But I pushed the sudden longing into the dark pit of my brain where all the other craziness lived.

"You okay?" I asked. She smiled as she nodded, but it was fake. "Want to talk about it?"

She glanced at Noah and then back to me, shaking her head.

"I promised the kid we'd watch the movie. Is that okay?"

"Don't you have a bachelor party you need to get to?"

I took a step closer to her, resisting the urge to take her hands in mine. "I'm in the mood for some Steve McQueen and pizza. Besides, Maverick won't even know I'm missing."

"Somehow I don't think that's true." She gave me a reassuring smile. "You don't need to stay. We're fine, really. Go to your party. Tell Randy I'm sorry about tonight. But I'll help clean up tomorrow morning."

I put my hands on her arms. "I'm not leaving."

Our eyes remained locked in battle until she finally relaxed and gave in. A small smile played on her lips. "Fine, I'll call for pizza. But just so we're clear, you don't need to stay. Especially while there is a clubhouse party happening. Aren't you the least bit curious what chaos they'll sow in the absence of their king?"

"They'll get up to plenty. And I don't want to see any of it." I grinned. "Believe me, I ain't missing out on anything."

Bull

I gave her a wink.
I had been to a million fucking clubhouse parties.
And I was already where I wanted to be.

CHAPTER 27

TAYLOR

He stayed.

Until midnight.

Gave up Maverick's bachelor party to stay with us.

But he didn't try anything.

No kiss.

No sexual innuendo.

In fact, a lot of the night was spent watching TV in comfortable, easy silence. We ate pizza. Watched movies. The three of us sitting together on the couch. It all seemed so natural. Even when Bull reached for my ankles and dragged them over his lap, it felt easy.

Despite losing Pickles, Noah seemed content and calm, and I had no doubt it was because Bull was here and he felt safe and comforted.

Finally, he'd fallen asleep during the last movie, and Bull had lifted him off the couch like he weighed no more than a feather and carried him to his room.

Watching him, I was taken aback by the sudden flood of emotion in me, and when he set Noah down in his bed, I had to draw in a sharp breath because I felt something inside me let go.

"Thank you for tonight," I said when we returned to the family room.

Bull

Bull took a step toward me, cupping my face. "Promise me you'll call me next time something like this happens."

The intense look on his face made me want to soften against him and lose myself in his arms. I was tired of fighting this.

But instead, I simply nodded. "I will."

For a moment our eyes lingered, before the smallest smile played on his lips and he pulled away. "I'd better go."

Disappointment weaved its way through me. I had wanted him to kiss me, and now he was leaving.

I followed him to the door. A little disappointed when he pushed the screen door open to leave. "What, no sexual comments? Not even an attempt to kiss me?"

I made out like it was a joke. But the truth was, I didn't want him to go. I was ready to give Bull what he wanted. *What I wanted.*

"Your kid brother is in the next room." He leaned forward to kiss me goodbye on the cheek, but not before I saw the wicked gleam in his eye. "But tomorrow, when you're not busy being a big sister, I'm coming for you, *little bird*."

And with that, he disappeared out the door.

The next morning, I arrived at the clubhouse early to help clean up, and was stunned by the aftermath of Maverick's bachelor party.

Two prospects and a couple of old ladies were already attempting to clean up around the sleeping bodies lying scattered throughout the wreckage of the clubhouse. The air was thick with stale alcohol and weed.

To my surprise, Bull was already there. He was leaning up against the bar drinking a cup of coffee and talking to Red. He winked when he saw me, and I felt a sudden thrill zip along my spine.

"Hey, Taylor." Red greeted me cheerily. He didn't drink alcohol, so he didn't have a hangover. "Can I get you a coffee?"

"That would be awesome, thank you." When Red disappeared into the kitchen, I stood next to Bull and looked around the room. It was in shambles. "Looks like it was a wild night."

"This is nothin'. An hour ago it looked like hell."

"You mean it looked worse than this?" I asked, just as Davey—who was lying at the base of the stripper pole— suddenly sat up and vomited on the floor between his parted legs. "Exactly how bad are we talking?"

"Think of your worst-case scenario...and then pump it full of steroids."

"Wow."

"And then there was Hawke's threesome."

"A threesome...?"

He nodded toward one of the couches up against the far wall. "I found Hawke passed out and buck naked, still entwined with two naked girls. My eyes are still bleeding."

I laughed. But as our gazes met, something zipped between us. An electrical charge. A chemical reaction. The air snapped with tension. Our gazes lingered. Heat burned beneath my skin.

Tomorrow, when you're not busy being a big sister, I'm coming for you, little bird.

Remembering his words, a flash of excitement rippled through me.

"What are you doing here so early?" I asked. "I didn't think I'd see you until later."

Before he could answer, a stunning blonde walked in from the hallway. Dressed in a tight blue dress with her heels in her hands and some serious *I've-been-fucked-big-time* hair, she stopped walking and scanned the room, a smile spreading across her face when her gaze landed on Bull.

My stomach dropped.

We made eye contact, and she smiled sweetly as she walked over to us.

"I had a great time last night, thanks," she said to Bull, her voice velvety and seductive. She winked at him. "I've made your bed."

Disappointment soared through me. She spent the night. And she spent it in Bull's bed.

"Nice," I murmured, taking a step away from him.

Bull looked at the blonde walking out the door and then back at me. "I think you and I should talk before you go and put two and two together and come up with five."

"Is that right?"

"Let's talk in my office."

"No need. I think I've got this figured out all by myself."

But Bull fixed me with a pointed stare that told me the conversation in his office was happening whether I liked it or not.

"Fine," I replied, my face stiff.

I followed him out of the bar and down the hallway, hating the uneasiness tingling at the base of my spine as my head started to boil with images of him and the blonde girl.

Once inside his office, he leaned against his desk. "It's not what you think."

I shrugged. The best thing I could do was show him that it didn't matter to me if he'd been balls deep in the blonde. Then go home and smack myself for being so stupid.

"You don't owe me any explanation."

"But you want one."

"Not in the slightest."

"You're not jealous?"

"Hardly."

He stood up and slowly walked toward me. "So it wouldn't bother you if I said I spent the night with her?"

My teeth snapped together and my jaw ticked. Going by the sudden flush of heat washing over my body, it appeared I would mind.

I would mind very, very much.

But before I had the chance to deny it, Bull closed the gap between us. "That's what I thought."

He pulled me to him and crashed his lips to mine, stealing my breath and making me see stars. His kiss was hot and demanding, his lips deliciously sweet, his tongue just as masterful as I remembered it.

But I pushed him away.

Jerk.

"Don't think for a second that you get to spend all night with her, and then get to kiss me like that."

His eyes gleamed predatorily as he pulled me back to his powerful body. "You know I didn't fuck her," he said, his voice smoky and dangerous. "And you know I didn't spend the night with her." When I tried to pull away from him, he held me tighter. "That the only woman I'm interested in fucking is the one I'm about to."

I resisted him. The nerve of him. The arrogance.

"Then who is she, and why is she making your bed?"

Amusement tugged at his lips.

"Her name is Melanie. She's Hawke's sister. She drank a little too much and stayed in my room."

"With you?"

"After I left your place last night I went home, jerked off while fantasizing about your beautiful body, and with your name on my lips when I came. So, no. Not with me."

My eyes narrowed, despite the thrill of excitement his words sent through me.

"You know, for someone who isn't jealous, you're pretty aggressive."

"And you're an arrogant—" His mouth sealed over mine again. I resisted at first, but his kiss was demanding and warm, and the way he moved his lips over mine was too inviting to fight.

When he pulled away, his eyes roamed over my face, searching, looking for a sign of hesitation. When he found none, he pulled me back to him and tangled his fingers through my hair, tilting my head back to seal his mouth over mine again. I had surrendered. I wasn't strong enough to fight it anymore. I wanted him. I wanted him so bad I could barely stand it.

"Tell me, dammit," he demanded huskily. And when I didn't reply, he tangled his fingers tighter into my hair. "Tell me you want me."

I moaned, feeling the delicious tension in my scalp. "Yes...yes...I want you."

He groaned and kissed me again, getting me high on his sweet lips and the deep licks of his tongue into my mouth.

He walked us backward, feverishly kissing me, and when he dropped into his luxurious desk chair, I climbed onto his lap and spread my thighs on either side of him, the move placing my aching clit right onto the erection growing behind his zipper.

Bull

He growled when I started to grind against him, shamelessly rubbing against him as we kissed desperately.

I had weeks of pent-up sexual craving aching to get out. Weeks of wanting him. My body so ready for whatever he could give me.

I kissed him fiercely, *hungrily*, losing myself in the tension building in me. His cock was hard, and I was throbbing as I moved against it.

God, I'm going to come.

The thought both excited and mortified me, but I had no intention of stopping. It was too late. His groans, the sounds of us kissing, the thick erection behind his zipper...it was all making me crazy. I started to whimper.

When he saw that I was going to unravel on top of him, Bull grabbed the back of my thighs and held me against the rigid outline of his erection, the move forcing my panties to rub harder against it. He started to move, little thrusts of his hips, which pushed me over the edge.

"Bull..." I moaned his name as I started to come. I pressed my palms into the thick muscle of his shoulders and trembled, my eyes losing focus as I fell to the mercy of an exquisite ecstasy, after months of wanting him, craving him, fucking *needing* him. My head fell back and my breath left me in a rasp, my eyes closing as I was rocked to my very core by my shattering climax. I trembled against him and Bull groaned, latching his lips to my throat as I came floating back down to Earth.

"You look fucking amazing when you come," he rasped.

Still trembling, I slumped against him. My heart pounding. My body throbbing. My breath panting.

I found his lips and kissed him again. My orgasm had been mind-blowing. But it wasn't enough. Especially when I could still feel the thick, hard outline of him pressing into my soaked panties.

"Fuck me on your desk," I whispered against his lips.

He chuckled, and with a delicious groan, lifted me up in his powerful arms and placed me onto the desk. Without a word, he parted my thighs and pushed my dress up to my waist, my face flushing with heat as he slid my panties down my legs.

He stood above me, his eyes dark, his face a mask of raw need. As he reached for his belt buckle, his gaze burned into me. "Are you ready for me, *little bird*?"

CHAPTER 28

BULL

I've never fucked anyone in my office.

No pussy was going to break the sanctity of the president's office while it was mine. Unlike the presidents before me, it was a rule I'd remained steadfast to for the past ten years.

But now, *fuck me*, I was going to blow that rule to smithereens.

She had gotten me so hard rubbing herself against me, so fucking turned on that wild horses couldn't stop this from happening. After weeks of wanting her, of fantasizing about her, hell, I'd almost lost it myself and come undone beneath all that grinding.

But now I was going to savor the moment. Temper the urgency.

I slid her ass across the desk and lowered my mouth to kiss her, while she reached between us, opening my zipper and springing me free. I groaned into her kiss, my heart almost pounding out of my chest.

Jesus, just the touch of her palm against my flesh sizzled and brought me close.

I was desperate to be inside her, and she was desperate for me to be there. But I wanted to take my time with her. We had been leading up to this moment ever since we'd met outside of Noah's school, and I wanted to soak in every sensation.

My hands slid up her thighs until I found the slick flesh and it suckled at my fingers. She groaned against my mouth as my thumb found the sensitive nub of nerves, and she trembled, her gasp falling between us as I teased her, rolling my thumb in circles until she was quaking with need.

She said my name into my mouth, but my mind was already gone, lost in the warmth and sensation of my fingers sliding into her, and her hand rolling up and down the hard length of me.

She ripped her mouth from mine and looked up at me with heavy eyes, her face ravaged with lust. "I need you inside me."

The feeling was mutual.

I had a condom in my wallet. I ripped it open with my teeth, and once sheathed with that important layer of latex, I pressed the head of my aching cock into the soft, dewy lips of her pussy.

"Look at me," I growled, and she did, just as I slowly pushed my rigid length into her, inch by fucking inch.

Her face shimmered and her hooded eyes darkened as every hard inch of me filled her. She bit down on her lip, and it drove me crazy. I started to rock into her, slow strokes so we could hear how wet she was. She widened her legs, and we both watched, fascinated and on the brink, as I slid in and out of her body, her pussy sucking my cock, the noise and sensation driving us both wild.

Wrapping my hand around the base of my cock, I eased out and rubbed the thick head through the lush, velvety skin. I found her clit again, and began to torture it with tight little circles, bringing her to the edge, but pulling away from the swollen nub before she could fall.

"Please..." she begged. "I need to come."

My smile was wicked. "You're so greedy."

Her fingers pressed into the muscles of my shoulder. "Fuck me, goddammit."

Only too happy to oblige, I plunged into her, and she cried out at the sudden intrusion. At my size. At the way I thrust deep and hard into her, making her gasp, making her claw desperately at the wooden desk beneath her. Grinding my pelvic bone against hers, I pressed harder, my hips straining to be as deep as I could ever be, while rubbing against the sensitive bud of nerves.

Bull

"Oh God..." She arched her back and her head dropped back, exposing her milky throat. "This is too good..."

I leaned in and trailed my tongue along the smooth slope. She clenched me hard, moaning loudly when my tongue found the soft, sensitive spot below her ear. "Oh God, I'm going to..."

She released a long, drawn-out moan and fell back onto her palms, and I could feel the tight little clenches of her pussy as she started to come.

I groaned. Overpowered by the sensation. Her moans. The tight fluttering of muscles against my cock. They pushed me over the cliff into oblivion, and my orgasm slammed into me with ferocious force. We came together, wild and uninhibited, our moans like a chorus as I pumped my release against her throbbing pussy, and she unraveled in ecstasy on my desk.

Breathless, I fell onto my palms and panted into her mouth. I could feel her heartbeat pounding in time with mine as we caught our breath and slowly floated down from the high we'd just experienced.

I flinched inside her, my cock sensitive and tender, and she licked her lips with a groan.

Chuckling softly, she leaned up and whispered in my ear. "Now I know why they call you Bull."

CHAPTER 29

TAYLOR

I told myself it was nothing to panic about.
It was just a one off.
We were both turned on.
Both attracted to each other.
Both needing to come.
And it was amazing.
I hadn't come with a man in a long, long time. But it was nothing more than that.
Really.
The sexual tension between us had been crazy. Who could blame us?
But it was done now.
Although…
When I left Bull, he said he would call me later. Then he kissed me, and something in that kiss told me I was in trouble.
Not because of him.
Because of me.
You like this guy.
I couldn't deny my attraction to Bull. And I couldn't control it. Yet I *could* control if I acted on it. Well, in theory anyway. Apparently, the

Bull

moment he got close to me, I was ready to drop my panties and climb onto his dick.

Fuck me on your desk.

I raked my fingers down my face at the memory and sat down on my bed, shaking my head as if I could shake my thoughts out of my brain. The closet door was open, and my gaze lifted to the suitcases tucked away on the top shelf.

We could leave.

Noah and I.

We could just pack up and go.

I knew Noah would be upset, but he would get over it. Bull couldn't become anyone to him—I'd already fucked up by letting the two of them get close.

I was panicking. Rushing to fix a situation I'd let get out of control.

I needed to calm the fuck down.

I couldn't leave. Not now.

My head fell to my hands.

I had let this go too far, but it had been so long since….

Since what, Taylor?

Since you felt something for a man, other than wanting to ride his cock?

Since you wanted to lose hours kissing a pair of deliciously demanding lips?

Since you wanted to get lost in the heat of a powerful body as it gave you multiple mind-blowing orgasms?

I stood up, pushing my fingers through my hair.

I felt torn.

But maybe I was being too hard on myself. Maybe I was overthinking it. Because realistically, since when did me fucking someone ever involve emotions? Bull had made it very clear he wasn't emotionally available. It was purely a physical thing. And I had always been really good at distancing my emotions from a situation.

Perhaps we could do the no-strings-attached thing?

But even as I thought it, I knew it wasn't true.

I could fuck without emotion, for sure. When had I fucked for anything else?

But I doubted that would last very long with someone like Bull. He was too addicting. Too fucking irresistible. Every delicious inch of him.

With a groan, I fell back on the bed and thought about the man who'd given me multiple, earth-shattering orgasms on his desk this afternoon, and my body came alive with need. And I knew, *just knew*, I was going to have a hard time keeping my hands off him. It was crazy. I should be wary of him. After all, I'd heard stories about him. Stories that painted him as a merciless man.

Cold-hearted with cold eyes.

Ruthless.

Bad.

But that was the problem.

I always did have a thing for the bad boys.

The next day I was in the clubhouse bar with Matlock and Randy. It had been a quiet shift because a lot of the Kings were out on club business. Matlock had just come back from Head Quarters. He was dating one of the actresses known as Danni Deepthroat. She was famous for the "Danni Deepthroat Does…" movies, including *Danni Deepthroat Does Dick* and *Danni Deepthroat Does It Down Under*.

He was wasting time at the bar, drinking beer, and from what I could tell, watching her latest movie.

"That right here is the girl of my dreams," Matlock groaned, handing Randy the iPad he'd been glued to for the past ten minutes. "I'm going to marry her."

Randy looked at the video on the screen and his eyes bugged. "Jesus! What the hell is this one called?"

"*Danni Deepthroat Does It Again*," Matlock said proudly.

Randy tilted the screen my way. I didn't particularly want to look, but once my eyes caught what was happening, I couldn't look away. It was like watching a car accident. It wasn't something you wanted to see, but once it was happening, it was hard to turn your head. "Wow, she really doesn't have any gag reflexes," I said, amazed by her technique.

Bull

"No, she doesn't." Matlock grinned with pride.

"And it doesn't bother you...you know...her doing that with other men?" I asked naïvely.

"She's an actress. It means nothing." He lifted an eyebrow as he gave me a wicked smile. "But with me, those moans mean something."

I grimaced at him. "TMI, dude. TMI."

I turned away and busied myself with dirty glasses.

Despite feeling a little weird about discussing Matlock's girlfriend's blowjob skills, I felt tingly and a little flushed. I thought about Bull. Thought about his thick, throbbing cock. Thought about how it felt when he pushed all of it into me yesterday and how full it made me feel.

So, when he walked into the bar from his office a few minutes later, my body lit up like the Fourth of July.

We had done the dance all day. The heated looks. The seductive smiles. The delicious lick of lips. By the time he asked me to follow him to his office so he could "*go over the liquor inventory,*" we barely made it inside his office before he had me pressed up against the door.

He kissed me deep and hard, and all previous convictions of this never happening again turned to ash and died. His growl was deliciously deep and desperate as I dragged my hands down to his hips so I could hold him tighter to me. I loved the feeling of him grinding into me, feeling him getting hard and knowing it was because of me.

We kissed like we couldn't get enough, and I drank him in, savoring the sweet flavor of his lips and the luscious licks of his tongue into my mouth.

"I've been dying to have you all day," he breathed heavily against my parted lips. "I want you on my desk again."

In that moment, I thought about Danni Deepthroat and felt a sudden rush of inspiration surge through me.

Without a word, I sank to my knees and my name slipped from his lips when I released his belt buckle and undid his zipper.

Reaching inside his black pants, my body flared with desire when I felt the heaviness of him against my palm. I licked my lips. This was the first time I was seeing his cock up close, and it was like the rest of him. Big and powerful. He grew harder in my hand as I marveled at the thickly veined shaft that looked primal and monstrous, yet somehow felt silky smooth against my skin.

I bent my head, and a rough moan rumbled from his throat as I slid my wet tongue across the wide head before sucking him deep into my mouth. When the heavy head of his cock hit the back of my throat, he groaned and I felt a tremor slide through his body. I drew back along the throbbing length and slid my lips over the thick crown, hollowing my cheeks and engulfing it with a tight warmth.

He inhaled with a hiss.

"Goddamn!"

Inspired by his moans, I drew him back in again, sucking him down to the root. I was aroused. Wet. Throbbing. Loving the taste of him and getting off on the act of driving him wild with my lips and tongue. His hands lifted and tangled in my hair, his fingers gripping the roots as his pleasure grew.

His cock thickened even more in my mouth. Heavy with weight and salty with semen. I licked and suckled greedily, losing myself in the act, drinking him in and getting off on the desperate groans falling from his lips.

He was at my mercy, weak at the knees and completely under my spell. With one hand grasping the base, the other slid under the warmth of his balls and began to massage them.

A tremor quaked through him. "Oh *fuck*..."

His head fell back, and I tasted more saltiness on my tongue.

"I'm going to come," he breathed desperately. He was giving me time to release him, but when I didn't, he moaned urgently, "Taylor..."

I felt his cock pulse. Felt his fingers tighten in my hair. Felt his knees go weak and tasted the briny tang of his release in my mouth.

When he stopped pulsing against my tongue, I gently released him, sending a sensitive tremor rolling through his body. He let go of my hair and gripped the edge of the desk to steady himself.

"Where the fuck did you come from," he rasped, taking a breath and zipping up his pants. He drew me to my feet. "How did I get so fucking lucky?"

He didn't wait for my response, instead, he kissed me slow and deep.

"I'm pleased you liked it," I replied, grinning.

He chuckled wickedly against my lips. "Oh, yeah I liked it. I liked it very much."

"Yeah?"

"And now I'm going to show you just how much."

Taking me by surprise, he ripped open my tank top and yanked down my Daisy Dukes. Lust sparkled in his eyes when he saw my black lacy thong. "Nice." But he ripped it off me too, until I stood there completely naked in his office.

His eyes darkened with carnal need.

"Now get on my desk so I can eat you for lunch."

CHAPTER 30

TAYLOR

So that was an epic failure, I thought as I climbed down from his desk, my legs shaky from my orgasm.

Completely ignoring my own rules, I had dropped my panties for Bull at the first damn opportunity.

Now, those panties were torn and discarded on the floor, and I would have to go commando for the rest of the day.

I pulled up my shorts and Bull gave me a spare t-shirt to wear. It was too big, so I tied it into a knot at the front.

When I went to walk out, he stopped me. "Hey."

It was weird. But the gentleness in his voice made me suddenly shy. Which was crazy considering I had just come on his desk with his face buried between my thighs.

When I hesitated, amusement tugged at his lips and he pulled me to him. "Don't be getting all coy on me, *little bird*." His kiss was warm and deep. "You ever want to come in here and do that again, you consider my door always open."

I smiled.

Did I want it to happen again?

Hell, yes.

Would it happen again?

Hell, no.

But then he kissed me, a searing kiss, as if he was promising me something. Something I couldn't see coming, but knew with infinite knowledge that it was going to happen.

He touched me tenderly on the cheek.

"I like this," he said, the warmth from his fingers seeping into my skin.

My teeth sank into my lower lip. "Me too."

"I think we need to renegotiate our terms."

"You do?"

"I want to keep doing this. You and me."

"But you don't date, and I won't share you."

"You won't be sharing me. I have no desire to be inside anyone else."

I gave him a wry look. "Isn't that breaking your rules?"

His fingers cupped my jaw as his spellbinding eyes found mine "Fuck the rules. You make me want to break every damn one of them."

"Is that a fact?"

"A hundred percent." A small smile tugged at his lips but then faded. "But you need to know that I'm not the marrying kind. And I won't fall in love. But I'm loyal and a fucking great lover. I'm proposing we make this exclusive. No sharing. No fucking games. Just fucking hot sex." He licked his lips. "Now that I've had a taste, I want more and more of you. But for it to work, we need to be on the same page. I don't want a girlfriend. I want a lover. And I've never asked anyone for exclusivity, but I'm asking you for it."

His change in attitude had me curious. "Why?"

His hands slid down my waist to my hips. "Because the thought of another man putting his hands on this beautiful body drives me insane."

I thought about it for a moment. "So, it's just sex?"

"Fucking hot sex. Just you and me."

I wasn't too stubborn to acknowledge how much I wanted him.

Fucking him once...yeah, that wasn't enough.

Dropping to my knees and making him come with my mouth, just the one time...definitely wasn't enough.

Him pushing me back on his desk and making me come with his tongue, just once … Wasn't. Enough.

He was addictive.

And even though I knew it was a big mistake to let it happen again, I knew without a doubt that it would. I wasn't tough enough to keep my own urges at bay any longer. I'd spent years denying myself, and I didn't want to do that anymore. I wanted this arrangement.

And as long as emotions didn't get involved, everything would be okay.

Right?

CHAPTER 31

TAYLOR

With the new terms in place, there was no stopping us. He was like my own private addiction. I couldn't get enough of him, and he couldn't get enough of me. We kept it simple. Didn't label it. Didn't complicate it. Didn't talk about it.

Instead, we let our desires reign.

In my bed.

In my bath.

Pressed against the tiles in my shower.

On my knees in his office.

Bent over his desk, his chair, his couch, and up against the wall in his office.

Sex with Bull was different every single time. He was wildly experimental, deeply passionate, and delectably virile, with a stamina that was out of this world. He possessed a big sex drive, and when he was fucking everything other than him out of my mind, he took control of me, both body and my mind.

It was wild. Passionate. *Addictive.*

We kept things quiet. We had to. I mean, when we didn't know what we were, how could we explain it to anyone else?

It only added to the excitement.

Bull was a busy man, and people were always wanting a piece of him for one reason or another. His phone was always ringing. People were always looking for him. So, we made every moment alone together count. And when it was just the two of us, he gave me all of his attention, and it was like I was the only person who existed in the world.

We made love a disproportionate amount of times. So much that we made it through a gigantic box of condoms in the first week, and I was sore from the sheer size of him.

I knew I was walking a tight rope with him. Our involvement had an expiration date. But it was easy to push it to the back of my mind when he would kiss me so hard it left me breathless and aching for more.

I wasn't naïve. I knew how easily the lines could get blurred. Silent expectations could sneak in, and someone's feelings could grow.

But by realizing them, we could pull back, I rationalized. Or so I thought.

Because sometimes they weren't so easy to stop.

Because sometimes you blindly took a step toward it being something more.

Like tonight when he reached for the condoms in the nightstand but I stopped him.

"I've never been with a man without one," I said, looking up into his handsome, strong face, knowing I was getting carried away, but unable to stop.

His brow pulled in, but then softened when he realized what I was saying. "And it's been almost twenty years since I was with a woman without protection."

Our eyes remained locked as I said, "Then we should be fine, don't you think?"

He searched my face, his lips slightly parted. Then his breath left him in a rush as he bent his head and kissed me hard. I felt him, thick and hard against my entrance, and he groaned deeply into my mouth when he felt how wet I was. His kisses became wild then, his hips hard and torturous as they rolled into mine, rubbing the slick shaft against the most sensitive part of me, but not entering. He seemed set on torturing me, making me wet, making me want him so bad I was a trembling, achy mess.

I was so desperate for him, I was ready to beg.

"Please..." I moaned.

He dragged the head of his cock through my slippery folds of flesh. He paused above me. "Are you sure?"

When I nodded, he took himself in his hand and pushed into me...every thick inch of him naked and powerful.

He cursed under his breath, his brows drawn in, his eyes closed. "Oh fuck..."

He licked his lips and they gleamed in the dim light. He slowly pulled back, dragging his big cock out of me until only the wide head remained. His face rippled with raw, uninhibited desire as I clenched around him, my internal muscles massaging the thick, bulbous head. His gaze dropped to my lips, his eyes unfocused and unseeing with pleasure, his breath craggy and tortured as he slowly pushed back into me.

Sensations cartwheeled through me like a scattering of fireworks, and I arched my back with a moan. He was thick, hard, and almost too good to bear.

"I love being inside you," he groaned, rolling his hips into me, every beautiful inch of him driving me toward unimaginable pleasure. "How the fuck am I going to last when it feels this fucking good?"

"Come in me," I panted, my mind dizzy and drunk on him. I wanted all of him. Every delicious part of him inside me. I wanted to feel the pulse of his masterful cock as he ejaculated into me, filling me with the most intimate part of him. I knew I was getting carried away, but I didn't care, because in that moment all I knew was him. All I wanted...was him.

In response, he thrust my arms above my head and growled when I wrapped my legs tighter around his waist, pulling him in deeper into me.

"Fuck...Taylor..." He moaned, kissing me hungrily, his body thrusting into me. "I'm going to—"

A primal roar ripped from his chest, his throat straining, the veins on his neck bulging as his orgasm overpowered him. He thrust into me one last time, and I felt the throbbing of his cock as he filled me.

Breathlessly, I let go, aroused not just by what he did to me physically, but aroused beyond belief at what was happening, and I came with him, my body tightening around his orgasm as pleasure claimed every cell and fiber of my being.

I shuddered beneath him, my nails pressing into the hard muscle of his shoulders as I got lost in my ecstasy, my mind blinded in a sweet haze. When I finally melted beneath him, he covered me with his rock-hard chest and buried his face in my throat, his teeth grazing my slick skin.

"You're fucking amazing," he murmured.

I could feel the warmth of his breath and the gentle *thump thump* of his heart against mine, and emotion like nothing I'd ever known bloomed in my chest. I closed my eyes, sinking further into my contentment, intoxicated with it.

I'm falling for him.

My eyes flicked open.

Wait. No. What the fuck am I doing?

I shifted beneath him and he rolled off me with a satisfied sigh.

But with the heat of our passion gone, the stark cold winter of my reality slipped in, bringing all the bad, uneasy feelings with it.

Needing a moment, I slipped from the bed and made my way to the bathroom, Bull's cum now sticky on my thighs.

After taking care of business, I stood at the sink and stared at myself in the mirror and asked myself again…what the fuck was I doing?

CHAPTER 32

BULL

With Taylor finally in my bed, the sexual tension and pent-up frustration was gone. Replaced with the most amazing sex of my life. It also gave me a brief but blissful reprieve in the relentless pursuit for my arch nemesis.

The latest intel on Gimmel Martel suggested he had set up a secret distribution vein for a new supply of cocaine. It was possible he had found a new supplier while hiding in the murky depths of his exile. Anything was possible when you had cash. That was another good reason to dry up each and every one of his income streams.

According to our source, Martel had a truck passing through our county once a month, heading to various locations throughout the country.

We found one of the trucks on a quiet stretch of road between Destiny and Humphrey, heading toward the I-55 highway.

At first the driver took a little convincing to stop. Riding in front of him and forcing him to slow wasn't going to work. He showed us that when he nudged the back of Cool Hand's bike and almost sent him off the road into a ditch.

Same with Tully and Hawke when they tried the same maneuver.

He was prepared to rundown anyone who got in his way.

Which told me he didn't want us getting our hands on that truck at any cost.

So Yale and I pulled over to the side of the road, and Yale climbed on my bike before we took off in a plume of dust and rocks to catch up to the others.

We roared past the other Kings until we were lined up beside the passenger door. I had no fucking idea if this was going to work. And if I was a betting man, I would probably hate our odds. But Yale was crazy enough to try, and because I was more determined than ever to stop that fucking truck, I was willing to let him.

The trick was to get my bike close enough to the truck and keep it there. Of course, the driver tried swerving us off the road a few times, but he had so many Kings buzzing around him on their bikes, he spread himself too thin trying to keep us all away from him.

While he was preoccupied with Cade and Ruger on the other side, I lined us up and a seven-foot Yale was able to grip onto the door handle and get himself onto the step.

Once he was inside the truck, the driver didn't stand a chance, and the truck came to a shaky, screeching halt.

I pulled up behind it and unlatched the back doors, swinging them open with the help of Maverick. Inside, there were crates stacked from floor to ceiling with the words Coffee Beans stamped on the outside. I hauled myself up, and using a tire iron I found secured to the wall, cracked open one of the crates. They were jammed full of plastic bags. Taking my knife from the sheath on my hip, I stabbed several of them open, and watched little brown coffee beans spill from the wounds.

Fuck!

The last time we hijacked one of Martel's trucks, he'd hidden his coke in a secret compartment of the crate. But a thorough search of these crates revealed nothing.

Motherfucker!

I carved my hand through my hair and thought about our next move. There was something on this truck. There had to be.

Ruger joined me in the back and we started to unload the crates, handing them to the others.

"Let's get every one of these crates out and split them open. There's something in here, and we're going to tear this truck apart until we find it."

It turned out we didn't need to search for long. We were only a few crates in when we saw it.

The black abyss behind the wall-to-ceiling crates of coffee.

"Fucking hell." I looked over at Ruger. "You better call Bucky."

There were sixteen of them chained to the walls, their ages ranging from early teens to mid-twenties. They were dirty, dehydrated and very, very frightened. A few were unconscious, passed out from exhaustion and starvation. I knelt down next to one of them, a girl who couldn't have been any more than sixteen. Her skin was bruised and scratched, her wrists and ankles purple and green from being bound for God knows how long. *Christ, what has happened to these girls?* She woke up and stiffened with fear when she saw me.

"It's okay, sweetheart," I tried to reassure her, but the fear in her eyes told me it would be years before she believed it. "Whatever hell you've been through, it's over now."

When I pulled out the knife on my hip she started to cry.

"I'm not going to hurt you," I said, cutting the zip-tie that held her bound wrists to the metal shackle above her head. Her arms went loose, and with a whimper she collapsed onto me.

"You're safe, I promise." She clung to me. "But I need to help your friends, okay?"

After freeing the other women from their shackles, I stormed to the end of the truck and jumped off. Cade had the driver at gunpoint. "You better call Bucky and tell him to get his ass over here fast. And tell him he's going to need back up and some ambulances." I indicated to the driver. "But get him out of here. Tell Bucky he ran off. He knows more than what he's saying and I'm going to get it out of him."

We took him to the abandoned drive-in theater where Scud Boney had lived out his final moments only a few weeks earlier.

At first, he was a tough guy. A real smart ass. But by the end of it, he cried like a baby and told us everything. His job was to pick up the *cargo* from a warehouse in Oregon and bring it here. He'd been with the girls for days, denying them food and water, and indulging in his own perversions with his choice of them whenever the opportunity arose. Apparently, he had a thing for the younger ones.

"But so what..." He spluttered, blood and mucus spilling from nose and mouth. "I'm not the worst they've seen. And not the worst they're going to see."

That bullshit deserved another up-close-and-personal moment with my fist. Repeatedly, until he was unconscious. Now it was my turn to *indulge.* In payback.

Some may have called me *psychopath* and *sick motherfucker* in the past, but I don't enjoy other people's pain. I actually thrive in peace. But I want what's best for my family. My club. And to ensure order reigned in my town, sometimes I needed to inflict a bit of chaos on someone's ass.

I didn't get a hard-on over hurting someone.

Even when that person was a child trafficking, raping piece of shit. I didn't enjoy the karma I was dishing up to his face.

It was a necessity.

My job as president.

Eventually, Ruger stepped in. "He's done."

With my chest heaving, I stepped away. "Take care of him."

I looked down at my bloody knuckles. They didn't hurt, but later they would hurt like a bitch.

I walked away and climbed on my bike. I was desperate to feel Taylor beneath me. To feel her tenderness calm the raging darkness in me. But I was going to take my rage for a ride and let it dissipate in the wind before seeing her. Because I wasn't going to touch that beautiful body of hers while my mind was black with so much rage and hate, and lusting for revenge.

CHAPTER 33

TAYLOR
Ten Years Ago

"My cock is so big you'll taste it in your mouth while I'm fucking your pussy."

Bradley Anstead, legendary corporate bad boy, leaned forward and planted a kiss on my bare shoulder. His dark eyes sparkled with cocaine and the lascivious thoughts crawling around inside his liquor-soaked brain.

He was going to fuck me. And he was going to fuck me good.

Or so he kept telling me.

"And you better believe I'm going to fuck you hard, pretty girl." He grabbed his groin. "And I'm going to fuck you deep."

Fighting back the urge to gag, I faked a smile and took a mouthful of champagne from my glass. It was good champagne. Cristal or Dom Pérignon. And the glass, too. It was some stupidly overpriced crystal from Europe. It was worth squillions. Or so Bradley had told me. Same with the Basquiat hanging over the fireplace, and the Louis the XV chaise by the window overlooking Central Park. They were all opulent belongings. All ridiculously over the top. All his.

Bradley Anstead was a mascot for young, corporate success.

Rich. Good looking. Successful.

Cruel.

He also had a thing for girls in knee-high boots. Like the ones I was wearing.

But he also had a lust for something he wasn't ready to admit.

Something he knew would cause his cold-hearted and emotionally vacant father to look at him with that air of disappointment he always seemed to have saved for him.

Bradley had a reputation for ruthlessness in the business world, and as a ladies' man in his circle of wealthy, successful friends. He was a corporate megastar. And his sexual escapades with women were legendary.

But he also had a secret.

A secret urge he couldn't control.

A secret urge he hated himself for.

Because it was an urge he couldn't resist. A secret desire. A need. An overpowering lust. And it frustrated him that he wanted something so badly, something his family and friends would never accept.

It was something he couldn't face up to, and it made him angry that he wanted it so bad.

His lack of self-acceptance was frustrating. It made him mean, more aggravated. More cruel. The first night he indulged, it was with a nineteen-year-old, wide-eyed cowboy who was new in town. He brought the naïve young man home and dazzled him with his magnificent Manhattan apartment and expensive things.

I suspected it started off intimate. I imagined he poured him a glass of Cristal or a Dom Pérignon, just like he had with me. Or perhaps it was something a little more unexpected, like a glass of rare Cognac or a drop of ridiculously priced Absinthe.

It might've started off nice. But the night ended terribly for the naïve, small-town cowboy. By the time the sun broke over the city the next morning, he was tied to Bradley's bed, spread-eagled and beaten, and very much dead.

The following evening, his broken body was found next to a sewer grate in a rain-soaked alley in Brooklyn.

Yeah, I knew Bradley's secrets.

Alex always vetted the men I'd be spending time with.

Bull

It was important to know what turned him on.

And it was vital to know what he was capable of in case I had to protect myself.

I'd spent time with a few bad men.

I drained my glass.

But I had a feeling Bradley Anstead was going to be one of the worst.

I sat up with a rush, my heart pounding and beads of sweat coating my skin. I glanced around me and tried to catch my breath, my body trembling, my mind racing with fear. It was dark. Shadows crawled through the room, the only light being a slant of moonlight coming in through the window. I was desperate for daylight, for the sunshine to chase the shadows away. But the clock on the bedside table read 3:08. The sun wouldn't be up for another two hours.

I looked at Bull sleeping soundly beside me, his big body relaxed among the sheets, his beautiful face soft with sleep. Naked, his skin radiated a warmth like I'd never known. Even in the coolness of the morning, it filled the space beside me with heat.

I wanted to wake him. Desperate to feel those strong arms wrap around me. To protect me from the past and my fear of the future. Because if I were a betting woman, I would bet everything I owned that my past was about to destroy us.

Feeling haunted, I pulled back the bed covers and walked to the window, the cool morning air giving me goose bumps as I padded barefoot across the wooden floors. Outside in the silvery night, a waxing moon looked lonely in the clear sky, making me feel nostalgic. Making me feel regretful.

The sob left me before I could stop it. It came out of nowhere, and worried I would wake up Bull, I slapped my palm across my lips. I couldn't let him see me this way. Because if he asked me now, I would tell him everything.

Everything.

And I would lose him.

I wiped my tears away and stood as still as a statue in the moonlight.

I had to face my past and fix this.

But how?

How did I face it and still protect Noah?

How did I fix this without destroying Bull?

When he came up behind me, I was immediately engulfed in his heat. He said nothing. Instead, he reached out and touched me, his fingers whispering across the nape of my neck and across my shoulders. I shivered beneath his touch as it pulled me further away from the echoes of my dream, grounding me with its familiarity and comfort. I softened against him, then moaned when his lips found the tender slope of my neck.

Strong hands came around me and pulled me against his powerful body, and I sagged into him, my lips parting with a moan, my body aching to feel him inside me.

I turned in his arms to meet his lips with mine, and the kiss was warm and needy. I needed this. I needed the physical contact to keep the phantoms of my dreams at bay.

With a growl, he lifted me up and carried me to the bed. Lying me down gently, he crawled over me and without a word, thrust deep into me.

Light and pleasure lit up behind my eyes. The sudden intrusion was all and everything I needed. The hardness. The length. The girth that stretched and filled me with so much man. The thrust of every inch into me. They pulled me further away from myself, and further into him.

He kissed me with so much passion and loved me with so much more. When I struggled to come, he slowed his pace, his pelvis grinding, his thick beautiful cock stroking into me with exquisite slowness. He took his time, knew what I needed, and he stoked that fire until I came beneath him with absolute abandonment.

But he didn't wait for me to come down from my high. Instead, he hooked my leg over his powerful shoulder and held me closer to him by my ass, so he was as deep into me as he could possibly get. The change of position put my clit in direct contact with the root of his pelvic bone, and it only took a small amount of friction before I was coming again.

He stole my cry of pleasure with a demanding kiss.

"That's it, *little bird*..." He moaned against my lips. "Hearing you come makes me so fucking hard."

I shook against him. Trembling and high, my body throbbing with pleasure. I wasn't sure how much more I could take. But Bull showed no signs of stopping. He had stamina. The strength to keep going for as long as it took. And it was like he knew that I needed this. Knew that the only thing he could do was fuck my fear out of me.

So that was what he gave me.

And I surrendered my everything to him.

Gave him full reign of my body. And he kept loving me like that until the sunlight breached the tree line outside, and I couldn't take any more. Until I was spent. My bones liquid. My body soft.

When he knew I was done, he came with a deep, smoky moan, his eyes closed and his face wrapped in a mask of pure ecstasy. And I watched from the pillows, spellbound, as he kept pumping his release into me, his body trembling, his beautiful cock filling me with all of him.

Afterward, he wrapped his body around me protectively, and I fell into the deep, warm abyss of sleep.

Whether he knew it or not, he had exorcized the demons from both my body and mind until all I knew was him.

CHAPTER 34

TAYLOR

Autumn said she didn't want a bachelorette party. That strippers weren't her thing and penis straws were creepy because they were thin little plastic sheaths with balls.

But Chastity decided she was having one whether she wanted to or not, and went right on ahead and organized a tamer, daytime version for her. "If that girl thinks she's missing out on penis straws, then she's got another thing coming."

She and Honey planned it right down to the last penis balloon. There was going to be all the cheesy elements of a bachelorette party, like a sash and a tiara, and penis paraphernalia that defied the imagination. There was also going to be cake and margaritas, and games like Pin the Junk on the Hunk, and Adult Pictionary.

I promised Chastity I would help her set up, and when I arrived early, I found her already knee deep in decorations.

We were at the home she shared with Ruger. The back deck overlooking the pool was festooned with rose gold and white decorations, including balloons, paper streamers, and a giant foil balloon in the shape of a big pink penis.

"Wow, she's going to love it," I said, walking up the steps and taking

Bull

in all the decorations. "How does Ruger feel about all the penises on his deck?"

"Who do you think hung the balloon for me?" She smiled and rubbed her big belly.

"It looks like you've almost got it all done."

"No way, there's still so much to do. Would you mind setting up the table while I try to untangle these party lights?"

She looked pale.

"Are you okay?"

She smiled brightly. "Just a bit tired. I'm not sleeping well."

"Are you sure that's all it is?" I knew she was holding something back. "Is everything okay with the baby?"

She sighed and sat down. "I had a routine doctor's appointment this morning. The baby is breach, and it doesn't look like he's going to turn. But that's not all. Apparently, I still have placenta previa."

"Placenta previa?"

"It means the placenta is over the cervix. I knew a while ago, but it usually rights itself as your baby grows. But in my case, it hasn't." She gave me a resigned shake of her head. "He's scheduled surgery for me."

"For when?"

"Next week. When I'll be thirty-nine weeks."

"You're going to become a mom next week?" My face lit up, and I couldn't keep the excitement from my voice. "Congratulations. Have you told Ruger?"

"Are you kidding? He'd have me in the hospital right this minute. Just in case something happened."

"He's head over heels in love with you. It's nice."

"It is, but he's driving me nuts. Don't get me wrong, he is the most amazing husband in the world. But sometimes he treats me like I'm a fragile doll."

"He loves you. I've seen the way he looks at you."

She smiled wickedly. "Like the way my uncle looks at you?"

My eyes widened. "What?"

"Don't bother denying it." She raised an eyebrow. "You only need to stand in the same room as you both to see there's enough electricity between the two of you to light up the entire state of Mississippi."

Heat went to my cheeks. I thought we'd been discreet.

"Don't worry, your secret is safe with me," she said with a big smile. "So, do you love him?"

"Love him?" I balked. I mean, there was no way. "This is just a casual thing."

"Sure, it is."

"We haven't really talked about it. You know, defined it. Only that we're…exclusive."

Okay, exclusive made it sound more serious than it was. And it fed right into what Chastity already believed, that Bull and I were more than casual.

She nodded her head knowingly, her eyes wide with glee. "A-ha."

"Do others know?"

"Not yet. But it won't be long before others notice the chemistry between the two of you." She thought for a moment. "You know, a lot of people think he's still hung up over Wendy. That she was *it* for him. But that's not the case. I know my uncle, almost as well as my husband—*his best friend*—does. It's not her he can't get over. It's the guilt he feels. He feels responsible for her and their unborn baby dying. It haunts him."

"But it wasn't his fault."

"I know, but he refuses to believe it. It's almost as if he feels like he doesn't deserve to move on. But…"

Her words trailed away.

"But what?"

"It's probably not my place to say this…but in the last few weeks, he's changed. There's something lighter about him."

"Lighter?"

"Not so dark. Not so weighed down with the guilt." Her eyes found mine. Her face grew serious. "You're good for him."

Warmth spread through my chest.

"It's just casual, Chastity."

She waved her hand in front of her beautiful face. "So you say. But while you two are telling each other that, I can see that neither of you really believe it."

Bull

"He told me it can't be anything more than sex. And I told him I wasn't interested in anything else."

"And I can see you're both lying."

I blew out a deep breath.

Was I?

Were we?

"Come on, we've got some penis balloons to blow up," I said, deliberately changing the subject. But as I set the table with napkins, paper plates, margarita glasses, and of course, penis straws, my mind replayed Chastity's words.

Had Bull and I slipped past *casual* and veered straight into *something*?

A sudden crash behind me made me jump, and I spun around. Chastity had dropped a tray of glasses and was standing very still, her brows drawn in. She didn't look so good. Something wasn't right.

"Are you okay?"

Her eyes shifted to mine. "I don't know..."

I guided her toward a chair and helped her sit down, then picked my cell phone off the table. "I'm going to call an ambulance."

"Oh no, I'll be fine."

As I rang 9-1-1, I kept my eye on her. All the color had left her face.

Suddenly, she let out a cry and bent over. Reaching for the edge of the table, she cried out again.

Terror swept through me as a bright red stain spread across the fabric of her white dress.

She looked at me with terrified eyes. She was going to pass out. I lunged and caught her as she rolled off the chair, her body going limp, her eyes rolling back in her head.

Cradling her in my arms, I told her she was going to be okay and prayed help would arrive in time.

CHAPTER 35

BULL

While Taylor was at Autumn's bachelorette party, Ruger and I met with Sheriff Buckman in his office.

"What happened to the girls?" I asked.

"They spent the last few nights in St. Vincent's. Some of them were beat up pretty bad and dehydrated. Nothing life threatening. But I can't imagine it's something they'll get over real quick." He shook his head and looked sick. He had three teenage daughters at home. "The hospital will hand them over to the bureau tomorrow morning."

I nodded. "You find Martel? Or information about where he is?"

"We're working on it. But you know these things take time." He gave me a knowing look. "We also haven't found the driver. Seems he disappeared off the face of the planet."

"Odd," I said, without looking him in the eye.

There was nothing odd about it. He was finally doing something good by fertilizing a patch of earth just out of town.

Bucky's knowing eyes gleamed across at me. "Yeah, I'm sure he just ran off."

Well, he *had* tried to run off.

Bull

But then I had caught up with him and it didn't work out so well for him.

"He's probably resting in some hole in the wall somewhere waiting for the dust to settle," I said with a reassuring smile.

But Bucky looked weary. "You gotta let me do my job, Bull."

My smile faded real quick. "If I let you do your job, there would be sixteen girls still being traded and raped, and God knows how many others shoved into the back of an airless truck breezing its way across the delta."

Ruger's phone rang and I noticed his brow wrinkle. "I gotta take this," he said, leaving the room.

Bucky walked to the window and looked out.

"The FBI are involved now. But then, I figured this was part of whatever plan you have to get your revenge on Martel." He looked over at me. "To save you time hoodwinking me any further, you got someone in the bureau you want made aware of this, as well as the swarm of FBI agents already descending on this town?"

Bucky was right. There *was* someone I wanted involved. But to get him involved, it needed to happen through official channels. Like the sheriff's department.

"Special Agent Guy Everett. This will be below his pay level, but if you make him aware, he'll step in."

Bucky shook his head in a '*I should've known*' kind of way.

He sighed. "You got this guy in your pocket, too?"

Before I could reply, the door to Bucky's office slammed open, and a panicked Ruger appeared in the doorway.

"That was Ronnie, we've got to get over to St. Vincent's right away. An ambulance is taking Chastity there now."

Fear exploded through me.

"What the fuck happened?"

"She collapsed. They think she's losing the baby."

Terrified for my niece, we bolted out of Bucky's office and took off for the hospital.

CHAPTER 36

TAYLOR

My heart pounded with fear as we waited for Bull and Ruger to get to the hospital. I sat with Honey and Autumn in a stiff, panicked silence, my skin chilled to the bone, my jaw shivering in the coolness of the air conditioning.

When sitting became too much, I got up and paced the linoleum floor, wanting to crawl out of my skin, heart sick that Chastity and her baby might die.

There had been so much blood.

By the time the ambulance arrived, her dress had been soaked in red, the blood seeping onto the floor beneath her.

It seemed like hours ago. *Where were Bull and Ruger?* I chewed at my thumbnail, watching the room fill up with worried family and friends, praying Bull and Ruger weren't far away.

When they finally arrived, Ruger was ushered through the heavy doors leading into the emergency room, while Bull checked on his sister. Ronnie was a strong woman. There were no tears. No emotional outbursts. She remained calm and stoic, but her face was tight and pale with unspoken fear. Bull took her hands in his, there were no words. A silent understanding passed between them. *Chastity was in good hands. She was going to get through this.*

Bull

Releasing her, Bull turned and scanned the room until his burning gaze found me. He crossed the room so quickly; he was almost a blur. "What happened?"

I told him and he pulled me into his hard chest, one strong arm around me, the other hand tangled in my hair. I could feel the chaotic thud of his heart syncopated to my own. He was a tower of strength and muscle, but his heart belied his tough exterior. He was terrified.

When the doors to the ER opened and Indy appeared, we crossed the room, and I could see the fear on his face as he braced himself for bad news.

As we listened to Indy, he reached for my hand and his fingers tightened around mine. And he didn't let it go. Even as Indy told us that both mother and baby were doing fine. Even as she said the threat had passed, his fingers remained tangled with mine. It wasn't until he was absolutely certain that his niece was going to be okay that he released them. With a deep exhale, he pulled me into him and buried his face into my neck, groaning his relief against my throat.

"Where's Noah?"

"A sleepover."

"Let me come home with you," he murmured quietly. "I need you."

We went back to my apartment, and after we showered, we slipped into bed, naked.

"Just let me hold you," he rasped, pulling me into his warm body and wrapping himself around me. He was in pain. Tonight, had scared him. He held me to him, and I curled my hands around his thick forearms, gently caressing his warm skin until I felt his breathing ease and his heartbeat calm to a slow thud as he drifted off to sleep.

I awoke a few hours later to the tender caress of his fingers down my back. I sighed; my body aroused. I was on my stomach, my hands curled under my chin. I felt his lips on my skin, felt the tender way he worked me up until I was creamy and ready. He gently raised my hips off the mattress slightly and nudged my thighs apart. He rubbed his cock against me, moaning at my readiness, pressing the slick head through damp skin to pause at my entrance. And then he was inside me and I gasped at the sudden fullness.

"You feel so goddamn good," he moaned quietly. "So good, baby."

He rocked into me, his massive body blanketing me, his big arms caging my head as he whispered into my ear the things my body was doing to him, telling me his deepest needs, begging me to be his little bird, wanting me, driving me head first into a slow, torturous climax.

"That's it, baby, come for me," he moaned. Then his hips suddenly stilled, and I felt him tense, felt him shudder as he released a deep, masculine rasp, his cock thumping violently against my inner muscles as he came. His head dropped to the nape of my neck. He was panting, and I could feel the emotion wrapped around us as he tried to calm his breathing.

He pulled out from my body, and I felt the sudden loss of his thickness, felt some of the warm liquid leave my body with him, as he rolled onto his back. He dragged me over to him and nuzzled his face into my neck.

"I need you, *little bird*," he whispered into the darkness.

I curled into his warmth and pressed my cheek to his chest. "You have me."

And he did.

He had all of me.

He just didn't know it.

CHAPTER 37

BULL

Today wasn't a day for revenge.

Not even one that was as venomous as mine.

Today was for family.

For forgetting.

"So, what do you think?" Chastity asked.

"I think he's fucking perfect," I replied, looking down at my grand-nephew secured in my arms. He was a big baby. Healthy. *Fucking cute.*

Chastity grinned at me. She was propped up against the pillows, her cheeks pink, her eyes sparkling.

"How do you feel?" I asked.

"Better." She nodded. "Yesterday is kind of a blur."

"You gave us all a scare."

"I know. Thank God, Taylor was there. You should've seen her, Uncle Bull, she was so calm. So…I dunno…like she switched on some kind of amazing autopilot. It was almost as if she became someone else."

"She's a good person to have around in an emergency," I said. "I'm just so grateful you and Will are safe."

When I was leaving the hospital, I got a text from Taylor.

Meet me at Catfish Cove. 7pm.

I met her at seven. She was waiting for me by the No Trespassing sign, a blanket under one arm, and a basket in the other.

"What's this?" I asked, looking at the bottle of wine and glasses inside the basket.

"After yesterday, I think you deserve a night of fun."

We walked down to the lake. The moon was full and bathed the shore in bright light. She took my hand, curling her fingers around mine and leading me toward the water.

In the moonlight, her deep brown eyes were like onyx, and I could see the affection gleaming in them.

And the mischievousness.

"What are you up to?" I asked suspiciously.

"Whatever do you mean?" she asked playfully, stepping back and raising an eyebrow. Her fingers started undoing the buttons of her dress. When it slipped from her body she was completely naked underneath.

Instant heat flooded my veins.

This woman was perfect.

And I was hard as fuck.

"You want this?" she asked, her voice teasingly hoarse and throaty. Her hands sweeping up and down her curves.

"Want it?" I stepped toward her. "Baby, what I'm about to do to you is going to answer that question tenfold."

"Is that right?"

I reached for her and her skin was like silk.

"You can count on it."

I went to kiss her, but she turned her lips away. "What *are* you going to do to me?"

She looked up at me through her lashes, her eyes full of heat.

The challenge was on. Amusement tugged at my lips as I looked into her beautiful face and thought about all the wicked things I was about to do to her body. "I'm going to make you quiver beneath me."

One eyebrow went up. "Tell me more…"

"I'm going to part those firm thighs of yours and bury my tongue

Bull

so deep into your pussy, you'll lose your mind."

She reached up and her lips lapped at mine, teasingly. "Sounds like torture."

"It will be desperate torture," I said, teasing hers right back. "I'm going to make you come on my face."

"I like the sound of that…"

"And when I finally push my hard cock inside you, you'll be so damn needy for me, it'll make you come again…but this time it will come from deep within you…. And it will make you cry out my name."

"You're very creative…" Her hand found the hard outline of my cock and started to rub. "And so big…"

I couldn't help but smile, loving the heat in my *little bird's* song.

Fueled by her hand rubbing against me, I continued. "You think you've come before. It ain't nothing like what you're about to experience. And when you think you've had enough, then I'm going to make you come again and again until you beg me to stop."

"I'm going to hold you to that…"

My hand slid between her thighs and found the slickness in the warm, velvety skin. I hissed in a deep breath, my body tightening, my cock getting even harder because she was so damn wet.

"You're soaking," I breathed out.

"Because my man is about to blow my mind." She licked her lips and gave my erection an enticing squeeze. "There's just one thing…"

She pulled her mouth from mine and stepped away.

"Oh, yeah? What's that?"

She gave me a wicked grin. "You'll have to catch me first."

Turning, she ran to the edge of the water and crashed through the shallows of the lake, diving into the moonlit water. When she resurfaced, water burst upward and danced in the air like diamonds.

"You want it, you come and get it," she called into the indigo light.

She didn't need to ask twice. I ripped off my clothes until I was standing there buck naked and armed with a raging erection. It was heavy and tapped my belly as I entered the lake and dove into the water.

When I found her, she came to me and curled her silkiness around me.

We kissed like teenagers and she wound her arms around my neck, getting as close to me as she could. When I entered her, her lips trembled against mine as I held her by her thighs and took control of the motion. She panted into my mouth with every wet kiss until her body quaked, and she cried her pleasure into the dark wilderness. When she came down, I walked her to the shore and placed her down on the sand.

"What are you doing?" she asked as I trailed wet kisses down her soft belly.

I opened her legs and looked up at her from between her thighs.

"I meant what I said. I'm going to do things to this beautiful body of yours that will blow your mind."

And burying my face into the soft warmth of her pussy, I did exactly as I had promised.

Later, when our mutual moans rippled in the moonlit night and then disappeared like smoke, we took another swim in the lake. She'd made me come twice, and I'd made her come so many times she was left spent and as supple as a ragdoll in the sand.

Now we swam together, looking at each other across the milky ribbon of light on the water.

She was so beautiful it hurt. Creamy skin glittering with water. Big full lips. Hair cascading down her flawless body like satin. Eyes gleaming like precious stones.

Walls had plummeted. Pieces of armor had broken off and fallen away. And in the bright moonlight, I felt my heart open for the first time in years.

In our time together, she'd only mentioned Wendy to me once, and I had deflected it. But now... *now* I wanted to share things with her. Let her know who I was. What I had lost. That I wasn't emotionally dead. That it was the guilt that erected the walls around my heart. Walls that no one but her had managed to break down.

I told her that it was my fault.

That my wife and unborn child died because I put the club first.

Bull

That I had never known a pain like it, and having felt it, promised myself I would never feel it again.

That it was guilt that kept me holding on.

That for years I didn't think I deserved more.

But now she had come along…and maybe I was wrong…

I told her about begging the medical examiner to know the sex of my unborn baby. About how he'd told me it was a girl. *My daughter.* A beautiful angel who would never feel the warmth of the sun on her face or the love of her father's embrace.

Then I pulled her to me and slid my palms across her wet cheeks, and felt the connection between us strengthen.

I didn't declare my love for her.

Didn't look her in her big, beautiful dark eyes and whisper sweet nothings to her.

But I did open up my heart to her, and when I kissed her, I made sure she felt it too.

CHAPTER 38

BULL

After the lake, we spent the night at her apartment. But the following morning, I had to leave early.

I didn't want to leave.

I wanted to spend the morning worshipping her body.

But I had to meet with Spider, our slimy but reliable informant in the seedy underbelly of our county.

He had important information about Gimmel Martel.

Important information that couldn't wait.

The *Slip N' Slide* was a seedy strip joint just past the Last Horizon trailer park. It was a place where women twirled on slippery poles as men with nowhere better to be drank watered-down booze, and stuffed crumpled dollar bills into thong bikini bottoms before heading off to the bathroom to jerk off. I pulled up in an alley behind the club and walked inside through the back door. Immediately, the stench of stale smoke and spilled liquor ground into my nostrils. It was also dark, so I took my glasses off. Here in the shadows there was no pain. I looked around, taking a moment for my eyes to adjust.

The place smelled of desperation and sleaze.

It looked even worse.

Across the room, a girl with dead eyes and a blank face slid up and

Bull

down a pole in front of an audience of three.

Spider, the owner, was sitting at the bar. Dressed in a plaid suit, he rose from his seat when he saw me and indicated for me to follow him. I knew the way to his office and headed for it, passing a patron indiscreetly jerking off in the shadows to a girl humping the stage in front of him.

"You okay with that?" I asked as I reached the doorway to his office.

Spider glanced over at the man ferociously jerking at his cock.

"Oh, for fuck's sake!" He whipped out his phone from his pocket and punched in a number. "Goddamnit, Bruno, do your fucking job. We got a fucker whacking off near stage three. Stop fucking around and throw him out. And tell the bastard that it's his one and only warning. Next time, he's out for good. Now get your fat ass over there before he blows his load all over my velour couch."

He thrust his phone back into his pocket. "Sorry about that. Not sure what's in the water, but that's the fourth guy we've caught with his hands dancing in his pants this week. Fucking degenerates." He gestured for me to step into his office. "Come in."

He closed the door behind me.

"So what is so important it couldn't wait?" I asked, deliberately not taking a seat. Spider was unsavory at the best of times. He was a good informant. But I could only imagine what went on in this office.

His sweaty brow furrowed. "A reliable source tells me Gimmel Martel has put a hit out on you."

I remained unfazed. Poker-faced. Calm. My body language relaxed. But hearing that you had a hit out on you didn't tickle the funny bone. No matter who you were. It meant things would have to immediately change. *My life* would have to change. Certain precautions were needed, not just for me, but for those I loved.

Including the one in my bed.

"You a hundred percent certain this information is reliable?" I asked.

Spider nodded. "It came from two people, Bull. People I trust."

I nodded. The hit on me was to be expected.

Although, why pay for a hit when he could send one of his thugs to do the job?

I could only assume Martel planned to rise from his exile and didn't want to be associated with my murder. The Kings of Mayhem were heavily connected. If he wanted to rise like a phoenix and rebuild his empire, then it was best not to burn any more bridges.

"Has anyone accepted the job?"

Spider nodded. "Apparently."

"Any idea who?"

"No, idea. None of the favorites. They wouldn't touch this hit with a hazmat suit. They know the consequences."

"But someone has definitely accepted?"

"According to my sources. But I can't confirm who accepted it. I'll keep digging around."

I nodded and clasped my hand on his shoulder. "If you hear anything else, let me know."

"Will do."

Outside, the bad weather had cleared, and bright sunlight stabbed my eyes. I slid on my glasses and climbed onto my bike. I didn't want to go back to the clubhouse and call chapel. I thought about Taylor and a warm glow filled my chest. I wanted to see her. Wanted to look at her and know that the beautiful smile on her face was for me.

But things had changed since I'd left her this morning.

I had a contract on my life now and I couldn't risk her or Noah getting caught up in this.

Every part of me screamed to stay away, and it was a warning I knew I should heed.

The best thing I could do for her was to walk away.

I wasn't good for her.

Not now.

But how could I walk away knowing what I would be leaving behind?

The idea of a world without Taylor suddenly seemed cold and miserable.

No, giving her up wasn't an option.

It wasn't an option at all.

I called chapel, and within the hour, I had brought the Kings up to speed. Except Ruger. I told him to take time off to look after his wife and kid.

"Fuck!" Yale pounded his big fist onto the wooden table.

A dark, unease rippled through the room.

"We can step up security," Chance said.

"And reach out to the other chapters, see what they can find out," Cade added.

"Or we can just put a bullet in Martel's goddamn head," Matlock said.

"Won't stop the hit from playing out," Joker said grimly.

Putting a bullet in Martel was more than appealing. And it was definitely something I was going to make happen. But Joker was right. It wouldn't put me in the clear. Once a hit was in play, it was almost impossible to stop. Even if the person paying for it was dead and buried.

"I'm not convinced Spider is right," I said. "A hired gun isn't Martel's style. He has his own men for it."

"But we can't take that for granted," Chance replied.

"You're right. We'll handle this how we handled it before. We'll reach out and see if we can find out who accepted the hit, and I'll arrange additional security for the clubhouse. But it's business as usual, you hear me? I refuse to let that fucker have any influence over the Kings and how we conduct business moving forward." I brought down the gavel, and the snap of wood against wood vibrated through the room.

As our brothers slowly dispersed and made their way out to the bar, Cade put his hand on my shoulder to stop me. "You know you're going to have to take some necessary steps here."

"Relax, this isn't the first time I've had a hit out on me. I know the drill."

"And I know you. The last time you didn't take this seriously."

He's right. The last time involved a backwater crime family and a hillbilly mobster-wannabe. To teach them a lesson, we'd destroyed their moonshine racket until it was nothing but a steaming pile of ash, while the would-be assassin was fermenting in the mosquito-ridden soil of Crawdad Bayou, just a few miles over the border.

"You have to admit, it was hard to take any of them seriously," I said.

"But you have to take this seriously, Bull. This is Gimmel Martel we're talking about. Not some hillbilly moonshine cartel." He fixed his bright blue eyes on me. "You'll have to tell Taylor."

My eyes shot to his. "You know about that?"

He raised an eyebrow. "About you and Taylor? You're kidding me, right? I'm sure they know about it in fucking Australia."

"It's not public knowledge."

"Yeah, that's where you're wrong." His mild amusement vanished and he looked serious. "She deserves to know what she's getting herself into."

Fuck.

"No, not until I know what I'm dealing with."

I didn't want to scare her.

Hell, I didn't want her to run away.

I knew it was fucking selfish of me. But I wasn't ready to destroy the best thing to happen to me in years based on second-hand information.

Informants got things wrong.

Hell, Spider got things wrong.

And I wasn't going to lose Taylor because he got fed incorrect information.

Cade shook his head. "Martel has a hit out on you, Bull. I don't need to tell you that you're going to have to make some changes. At least until we get this figured out."

"I already have this figured out."

"Yeah? What are you planning?"

"I'm going to find out who the assassin is and I'm going to kill him."

"How you figure on doing that?"

"I'm going to go straight to the horse's mouth."

Bull

"You're going to ask Martel?"

"Yes. Right before I put a bullet between his eyes."

CHAPTER 39

BULL

Later that afternoon, I headed north to Sunflower County to meet my contact at the FBI, Special Agent Guy Everett.

Everett was your quintessential special agent. Black suit. Crisp shirt. Tidy hair and cleanly shaven. Somewhere in his early forties, he looked like he'd stepped out of the pages of a goddamn fashion magazine.

Surprisingly, after twenty years chasing down the bad guys, he wasn't jaded. Because Special Agent Guy Everett made his own rules. He bent the law only to the point of not actually breaking it.

From time to time, that was where I came in.

Over the years we'd helped each other out. If something I needed fell into his jurisdiction, he fed me intel on it, and nine times out of ten, the result meant his case ended before he had the responsibility of closing it.

Other times, if I had information that was valuable to him, I shared it. But only if it was in my best interests, of course.

We met just out of Coldwater, on a roadside next to a sweeping field of corn crops.

"We have eyes and ears on the ground in Chicago," he said, unwrapping a stick of gum and bending it into his mouth.

"Chicago?"

"That's where Martel's been hiding out."

"*Been* hiding out?"

"As of two days ago, he's holed up in a small town just out of Jackson." He reached into his breast pocket. "It will require a quiet visit. Not ten Harley Davidsons riding into town, do you understand me?"

He handed me a piece of paper with an address on it.

I raised an eyebrow. "You're giving him to me?"

"I'm giving you *time*. What you do with that is up to you." Everett couldn't come out and say it. I had to read between the lines. "We have to secure a warrant first."

"But you're hoping I'll get to him first?"

"Would save a lot of paperwork."

I nodded. "How long have I got?"

"I'll wait to file for the warrant this afternoon. You've got twenty-four hours."

As soon as I left him, I called chapel and filled in the rest of the club. We spent a couple of hours formulating a plan. As we were finishing up, I was surprised to see Ruger walk in. I'd told him to take some time off with Chastity and his son.

After the room emptied, he hung back.

"What are you doing here?" I asked.

"Chance called me to bring me up to speed."

"Why aren't you at the hospital with Chastity?"

"Because my wife and I both agree that I need to be here."

"Why?"

"Because you're making mistakes and we're both worried it's going to get you killed."

I looked at him. "What the fuck are you talking about?"

"Why did you visit Everett without me?"

"Relax, the risk was low."

"Don't tell me to fucking relax. It makes me nervous when you go rogue on me."

"Meeting up with an informant is not going rogue. You're overreacting." I headed for the door. "You were at the hospital, where you should fucking be right now."

"You've got a hit out on you. Or has your girlfriend got you so fucking distracted you've forgotten?"

I stopped walking and looked at my sergeant-at-arms. *Did everyone know about Taylor and me?* "What the fuck is that supposed to mean?"

"It means, I think you're distracted and that makes me nervous." His eyes hardened. "You're taking stupid risks."

Beneath my skin, a sudden anger began to simmer. I didn't like the way he was talking, suggesting that I was not capable of making the right decisions based on the intel sitting in front of me.

My whole fucking life had been spent evaluating risks.

I knew what I was doing.

"I'm not distracted." I glared at him.

"Well, I fucking beg to differ. Martel has a fucking hitman waiting to put a slug in your fucking ass, and you're out there on your own without any back up."

My anger was scratching to get out. Ruger was overreacting.

The truth was, I doubted Martel had a hit on me. If he did, something would've happened by now. I bit back my temper because I knew Ruger was only looking out for me.

When I went to walk out, he stood between me and the door.

"What the fuck are you doing?"

"No more risks."

"The only person taking risks is you, right now. Get out of my way."

I responded with the coldest, darkest look I have ever given Ruger. It was one I usually saved for the likes of Behemoth or Churchill, or any of my rivals.

Not my sergeant-at-arms.

Or my best friend.

But right now, he was pushing my last button.

Without another word, he stepped away.

"Get back to the hospital. You should be with your wife and kid."

I brushed past him and walked through the clubhouse to my bike. I climbed on and lit her up with a flick of my wrist and roared out of the compound. I was pissed at Ruger, but at the end of the day I knew he was right.

Bull

I was distracted by Taylor.
I just didn't want to hear it.

The address Everett gave me for Martel's hideout was a two-hour drive out of Destiny. A small town built around a vast area of wetlands and mosquito-ridden swamp. It was a nothing town. Barely on the map. But it was close to the highways and connecting arterials, making it the perfect place to control his new drug distribution business.

He was holed up in a spacious log cabin surrounded by Carolina ash and pond cypress. A two-story mansion with a shingle roof and a wide porch. The perfect lair for an exiled crime lord.

We descended at twilight when the shadows were long and the tall trees were silhouetted against a dying sky. Seven Kings of Mayhem moving stealthily through the darkness, armed and ready to lay claim to Martel's death. Despite knowing I was about to finally face my nemesis and end his days on this Earth, I was calm. I was steady. I was clearheaded. Everything I needed to be until this was done. And I wouldn't be anything else until I was burying Martel in the damp soil of this *blink-and-you'd-miss-it* town.

There was a light on inside. A soft glow of a lamp against the darkness of the windows. With military position we surrounded the cabin so there was nowhere for Martel to escape if he should try.

Once we were all in place, I stepped toward the door and reached for the doorknob.

To my surprise, it was unlocked.

It should've been my first red flag.

Martel was in hiding.

No one in hiding left their front door unlocked.

There also seemed to be a complete lack of bodyguards.

Although, he would probably only have two or three and they would be inside.

Yet, there was no movement. No sounds. The evening was quiet except for the occasional splash of a waterfowl scurrying across the pond.

Something wasn't right.

I signaled for Cade and Chance to hang back as I entered the silent cabin.

It was empty. Settled and still. I glanced around, and that was when I saw it. The photo stuck into the wall with a knife. A photo of me. With the blade piercing my forehead.

Martel knew we were coming.

But how?

The thought hit me like a bolt out of the blue.

This is a set up.

"Everyone, get back!" I yelled as I raced for the door. "This is a trap—"

In seconds, the night went from silence to chaos as an explosion ripped the cabin apart and blew me across the porch and into the thick scrub where I landed with a heavy thud. The impact momentarily stunned me, and I saw a universe of stars as I struggled to get up. Embers and heat rained down me, but I couldn't move. My brain was rattled, my lungs still vibrating with the shockwave. It was Chance and Cade who dragged me away from the roaring flames and heat.

"What the fuck is going on?" Caleb panted as he ran up to us with Animal and Yale close behind.

"Where's Nitro?" I asked as Cade and Chance hauled me to my feet.

"I'm here," he replied, running toward us.

All seven of us were okay.

"What happened in there?" Cade asked.

I told them about the picture stuck into the wall with the knife.

"Martel knew we were coming." I drew in a deep breath and felt my lungs rattle. Coughing, I let my rage come to the surface as the dark emotions thumped through me. If I hadn't gotten out of there when I did, I'd be dead. "This was a fucking set up."

"You think Martel got to Everett?" Caleb asked.

"I'd bet my fucking life on it."

"How?" Yale asked.

"Everett would've gotten to him after we found the girls in the truck. We already know Everett can be bought. And Martel certainly has the money to buy him."

"Motherfucker," Animal growled.

"You want to pay him a visit?" Chance asked.

"He's a federal agent. We're not going to touch him." But I had things on him that the FBI would be very interested in receiving. Things that spanned years. Classified information. Secret recordings. *A handwritten note with this goddamn address on it!*

Let the FBI unravel Special Agent Guy Everett for now.

Because one day when he least expected it, I would be waiting for him.

And he would pay for his betrayal.

When the sound of approaching sirens cut into the night, we disappeared into the shadows once again, moving through the darkness until we reached our van parked a mile down the road.

Inside, I tried to calm my temper. But it was futile.

My lust for revenge was hotter than ever before.

Not only had I almost been killed tonight.

I had been betrayed, and that was almost as bad.

CHAPTER 40

TAYLOR

The moment he walked through the door, I knew something bad had happened, and one look at the scrapes and bruises on his skin confirmed it. He was frustrated. *Angry.* Wherever he had been he had showered since because he smelled of soap and the delectable scent that was him. When he saw me, he kissed me, crushing me to his rock-hard chest.

But his energy was off. It was hard. Primal. Lacking in warmth.

I broke off the kiss and pushed him back. "What happened?"

But Bull brushed me off. "I don't want to talk about it."

Instead, he yanked the belt of my robe and groaned when he saw the silky camisole I was wearing underneath. Without a word, he lifted me off my feet and slid me across the kitchen counter.

"Wait..." I said.

But he wasn't interested in waiting, he stepped between my legs and held me against him, reaching between us to undo his belt.

"Bull..."

He pushed my legs farther apart, despite my resistance, and kissed me hard as he went to undo his zipper.

I shoved him back. "I said stop!"

Bull

Exasperated, he stepped back and ran a hand through his damp hair. "Goddammit..."

I slid off the counter and pulled my robe around me. "Noah is in bed and I don't want him to walk in on this. Plus, something is wrong, and if you don't want to tell me what it is, then that's okay. But you don't get to walk in here and take whatever it is out on me."

"I'm not discussing club business with you."

"Then maybe you should leave and come back when you're ready to fuck me nice."

His eyes blazed across at me and his jaw was tight. "Forgive me for thinking my girlfriend might be a little more understanding than this."

His use of the word *girlfriend* jolted through me like a barreling freight train.

He turned and stalked toward the door as if he was going to walk right through the glass, but stopped abruptly when he reached it. He paused and exhaled harshly, his shoulders sagging, his energy shifting.

With a deep breath, his resistance broke.

"You know I don't always work within the law." His deep voice cut into the tight air between us.

When he turned around, I saw the vibrant anger burning in his eyes and I tightened my robe across my chest. "Yes, I know."

There was a pause before he spoke again.

"There's a hit out on me."

His words sent a cold shiver through me. "What do you mean?"

"I mean, someone wants me dead, and they're paying someone else to make sure it happens."

"A hitman?"

"Apparently."

Goose bumps prickled my skin. "Are you sure?"

"I have reliable informants. They haven't let me down yet."

I struggled to swallow, the blood in my veins running cold. The moment was too surreal. My brain scurried to make sense of it.

"Are you okay?" I went to him, my mouth dry, my throat thick. "Who would do this?"

"Last year I made a pretty big enemy when a piece of shit drug dealer moved into our town. I told him he wasn't welcome. When he didn't take the warning seriously, we showed him what a mistake that was. But he retaliated and it got bloody." He ran his hand over his head and turned away from me. "He disappeared before I could put a bullet in his head. But this morning we received some information about him. Good information. About where I could find him. And I thought that this was fucking finally it. I was going to end this motherfucker's life and…" With his back still to me, he shook his head. "Somehow, the sonofabitch is always one step ahead."

"Who is this man?" I asked, shakily.

"I've already told you too much."

"Why won't you tell me who he is?"

"Because I want to protect you from this."

"But you can't," I said calmly despite my racing pulse. I stepped toward him and put a gentle hand on his shoulder, and he calmed a little beneath my touch. "If you can't tell me who he is, then tell me what he did. Why do you want to find him so bad?"

He swung around and my breath snagged in my throat when I saw the glowing hate in his eyes, and the simmering rage on his face. It was terrifying.

Just thinking about his nemesis had the power to ignite his dark anger.

"Because that sonofabitch doesn't deserve to breathe the same air that we do," he seethed. "He is poison. A scourge. He's a fucking parasite! And someone needs to take him out before he can inflict anymore damage."

"But why does it have to be you? Look at what it's doing to you."

"Because that reptilian fuck came after me and my club. He went after Chastity. And goddammit, if anyone comes after my family, I'll fucking destroy them!"

I took a step back, alarm spreading through me like fire. "He hurt Chastity?"

Bull explained how this man had sent one of his men to scare Chastity. He pretended to be a cop and pulled her over on an empty highway. He put his hands on her. Threatened her. Said he had a

Bull

message to pass on to her uncle. But Chastity was a ballsy girl, she'd kneed him in the groin and handcuffed him to the stolen patrol car before he could do her anymore harm.

"He fucked with my family. So I burned his cocaine empire to the fucking ground."

He went on to tell me how this man ordered his men to storm Chance and Cassidy's wedding, and how Ruger had been seriously wounded protecting Chastity. How he'd died in surgery but miraculously survived against the odds.

"He won't ever stop." Bull's lust for revenge radiated from him. "Unless I make him."

I thought about Chastity, my friend, being caught alone on a deserted highway with a thug pretending to be a cop, and my blood began to boil. Then I thought about Ruger lying in a hospital bed on life support with three bullets in him, and how this mystery man had ordered his men to wreak havoc on the club, not caring who got hurt in the process, and I felt shaken.

I didn't know.

I didn't know any of this.

I went to Bull and wrapped my fingers around his big hands. Without words, I dragged them to my lips and pressed a kiss to his knuckles. His eyes softened as they searched mine. When he kissed me, it was tender and giving, *intimate*, with no rushed agitation, no desperate need to use sex as a way to release his anger.

His kiss became so much more. His touch purposeful and loving. He moved his lips to my jaw, lighting fires in me as he dragged them lower to my throat, his tongue sliding along the curve, the heat of his breath leaving me warm and flush. He held me by the arms, holding me to him, so close that I could feel the wild thunder of his heart.

"God, I need you," he moaned, lifting his hands to cup my jaw. "I need you so goddamn much."

The desperation in his voice turned me on, making the pulse between my legs grow to an almost excruciating need.

"Then have me," I whispered, aching to feel him inside me.

With a growl, he lifted me up in his arms, and I wrapped my legs around his muscular body, enjoying the friction of his jeans rubbing against the flimsy fabric of my camisole as he walked us to my bedroom.

When he lowered me to my feet, his forehead dropped to mine. "What are you doing to me?" He breathed desperately. He pulled back to look me in the eye, and I saw the *need* in his. The need for me. The need for something other than his lust for revenge. "I don't have a single rule left when it comes to you."

My fingers laced around the nape of his neck. "Forget about him for tonight. Forget about everything."

I stepped out of my camisole, loving the flare of heat in his eyes as he drank me in.

"Just be here with me," I whispered, lovingly removing his clothes and feeling the excitement as his big body shivered against my touch.

Climbing onto the bed, I pulled him down to me and spent the rest of the night replacing his frustration and anger with ecstasy and pleasure.

CHAPTER 41

TAYLOR

I didn't see him for days. Since the cabin explosion, a somber mood had settled across the clubhouse. Something was brewing. Something *big*. But no one was saying anything.

Bull was gone from the clubhouse, a lot. He was nearly always out when I arrived for my shift, and usually didn't return before I finished.

Away from him, I spent time with Noah, but he was rarely at home, preferring to hang with Luke and Shelby at Roberta's. It left me with a lot of spare time to think over the things Bull had confessed to me the night of the explosion.

About the hit.

About the man who had ordered Chastity's assault.

It made me feel sick.

Scared.

It made me want to tell him about my past.

About who I had been.

What I was running from.

Because he had let another wall down by opening up to me, and I felt like I should do the same.

But I couldn't bring myself to do it.

There was too much at stake.

I could lose Noah if I did.

When Bull finally rode his Harley into my driveway, I had missed him so much, I was ready to pounce. After days of not seeing him or being able to touch him, my body was tight with need, my head desperate for the distraction only he could give me.

"Fuck, I've missed how you feel," he moaned, after I'd launched myself at him as he walked through the front door.

"I need you naked and in my bed," I rasped against his lips.

He kissed me fiercely in response, but then broke away.

"Little bird, I'm dying to be in that tight little pussy of yours, but I desperately need a shower."

I led him through the apartment to the bathroom attached to my bedroom. "Make it quick."

I waited for him on the bed, my body tense and needy, my stomach knotted with excitement. I heard the shower turn off. Heard the glass door open and then close. Felt the warm flush of anticipation creep along my skin and an achy throb take up between my naked thighs. It had been days.

He appeared in the doorway. Naked and gleaming, his inky black hair damp.

I hungrily watched him approach the bed.

Bull dressed in his black clothes and wearing a cut was spectacular.

But Bull completely naked was something else altogether.

He was *magnificent*.

I raked my eyes up his body. It was thick with muscle and without an ounce of excess weight anywhere. Shoulders were wide. His chest was broad and cut like a sculpture. Abdominal muscles were deep grooves in his belly as he moved.

And his cock. Even soft, it was heavy and thick, and it swung as he came toward me.

My ravenous eyes swept over the flawless flesh and the tattoos that covered his arms and chest.

As he came closer, I noticed the notches tattooed over his hip bone. They seemed out of place in comparison to the intricate artwork of his other tattoos. They were darker, almost crude and amateurish. I swiped my thumb across them. One looked fresher than the others. I

Bull

counted them. There were six in total.

"These are different than your other tattoos," I said, my fingers brushing over his warm skin.

"Yes."

"What do they represent?" I asked, fascinated by them.

But Bull pulled me to my feet so he could kiss me, in an attempt to draw my attention away from them.

"Things you don't want to know about."

But my inquisitive mind couldn't let go. My fingertips skated down to them, my gaze following. Between us, he was growing hard.

"Are they people you lost?" My eyes slid up to his. "Or people you made disappear."

A shadow darkened in his eyes as he searched my face, looking for a sign. Trying to gauge my reaction. "They're a reminder," he said.

"Of what?"

"Of who I am."

He trembled beneath my touch as my thumb slid across the inked lines. When I lifted my eyes, I saw he was looking at me intently.

He was very still. "Is that okay?"

I held his burning gaze. "You never have to ask me that. I know who you are."

With a groan, he took me swiftly. Flipping me over onto my knees and taking me from behind.

I gripped my pillows, losing myself in his powerful thrusts and the thickness of him as he filled me. I thought about the tattoos on his hip. *The notches.* I thought about the hit. I thought about the night of the cabin explosion, and the crazy world I was falling further and further into.

Mental chaos and physical pleasure collided in me, and I clenched his cock with an impending orgasm.

But before I could let go, he pulled out and guided me onto my back, his thick cock glistening in his hand as he positioned me on the bed.

"I want to see your face when you come," he breathed, biting back his orgasm. "I want to hear and see my name scream from your lips."

He pressed himself to me, teasing me, making me shiver, before thrusting his heavy length back into me. And I gave him what he wanted, crying out his name as my orgasm shook me. Feeling me clench violently around him tipped him over the edge, and he let go with a mindless cry, the veins in his neck as thick as rope as he lost himself in ecstasy, and then collapsed onto me.

I barely got my breath back, and he was still inside me when he finally spoke.

"Be my date," he said, panting against my lips, his heart still pounding fiercely from coming.

"Date?"

His use of the D-word caught me off guard.

"Yeah," he said. "Be my plus one."

My heart was a drum beat in my ears because Bull had just given me multiple orgasms and was now asking me on a fucking date.

He wasn't just blurring the lines.

He was pouring gasoline all over them and setting them on fire.

"Where?"

"Maverick and Autumn's wedding."

"I'm already going."

"I know. But I'm asking you to go with me."

I didn't know what to say.

Date.

The word held a lot of connotations.

And it would be a silent announcement to everyone who knew us. So far, Chastity was the only one who knew about us. And probably Ruger.

Me arriving on his arm was going to raise eyebrows.

I moved slightly, and his cock flinched inside me.

"Why?" I asked.

He grinned. "I should've known you were going to take some convincing."

I couldn't help but smile back. "I'm pleased I didn't disappoint."

He started to move into me again, slowly.

"I don't usually take a plus one," he said.

"So why now?" I asked.

"Because I want to know I'm taking home the hottest woman there."

Bull

I raised an eyebrow up at him. "I think Maverick gets to do that."

He flinched inside me again, and I gripped him tighter with my inner muscles in return, making him groan.

"Be my date." He traced his tongue up my throat to the sweet spot beneath my ear. "Don't you want to come with me?"

I felt him grow harder.

"I'll never pass up an opportunity to *come* with you. But a date?"

He grinned back. He was fully erect now, and the shallow motion of his hips grew deeper.

"Then don't think of it as a date. Think of it as the prequel to amazing sex. Foreplay, if you will."

Despite my reservations, I smiled. "People will talk."

"I hope so."

"That doesn't bother you?"

His hips rolled into mine. "Do I look like a man who's bothered?"

"No. But you're the boss and—"

He brushed his lips against mine. "What will it take for you to say yes?"

He found my clit and started to grind against it, making me gasp, causing my toes to curl into the mattress as warm pleasure began to move through me.

"If I keep doing that, will you come with me?"

I moaned and my answer came out in a puff of breath. "Yes…"

More grinding.

More friction against my clit.

"I'm sorry… I can't hear you…"

Oh God, if he kept doing that I was going to come again.

"Or would you prefer I stopped?"

He paused, and the sudden loss of friction was devastating to my building orgasm. I shifted restlessly, searching for him, my clit needing the contact, my body craving the pressure rubbing up against it.

"Yes, yes, I'll go with you," I cried desperately.

Heat darkened in his eyes. "That's more like it."

He thrust into me then, and I saw stars. *Actual fucking stars behind my eyes.*

I gripped the sheet beneath me. *"Oh God…"*

I started to move beneath him, in sync with the leisurely strokes of his cock, knowing he was taking his time, knowing he was stoking the fire. He was so self-assured and confident. He knew it would only be a matter of minutes before I was a writhing mess beneath him, coming and calling his name as I scratched my nails down the length of his back tattoo.

And he was right.

Barely moving his upper body, and without his eyes leaving my face, he let his pelvis and cock do all the work until I came undone beneath him with a heady, drawn-out climax. Blinded by ecstasy, my nails bit into his skin and drew blood down his back, making him come with a primal roar and a fierce tremor.

He collapsed against me, his face buried in my shoulder so I could feel the violent pounding of his heart against my chest. Our skin was slick and sticky, our minds drunk with pleasure. I felt him pull out of me. Felt the immediate loss of heat as he rolled onto his back.

Pulling me into his chest, he wrapped his arms around me and I relaxed against him, too spent and lost in the afterglow to think of anything but him.

Being his plus one was a bad idea.

But he was my addiction.

And I wasn't ready to get clean.

CHAPTER 42

BULL

"You know there's still time to run," Joker said, giving Maverick a pat on the shoulder.

"*Ha ha*, motherfucker. You're so fucking funny," Maverick growled, giving Joker a dark look. He tried to look tough but failed. Looking a little green, he was moments away from bringing up the three shots of whiskey he'd just downed.

"Just letting you know your options, buddy."

"I didn't propose to Autumn seven fucking times to suddenly decide five minutes before the wedding that I don't want to marry her." He straightened the cufflink on his jacket sleeve. "Plus, the woman owns a shotgun and knows how to use it. She'd shoot my balls off and use them as earrings."

Joker shook his head with a grin. "You're so pussy-whipped."

"Don't think she wouldn't shoot off yours for encouraging me to ditch her at the altar."

I watched the exchange between the groom and best man from the couch where I sat with Cade and Caleb.

We were on the River Queen, a nineteenth-century paddle wheeler that cruised up and down the Mississippi hosting weddings and other celebrations. She was a tame old girl now, but once upon a time she was the queen of the river. Her colorful past was steeped in debauchery and intrigue, including a stint as a floating brothel during the turn of the last century, and an illegal floating casino during the prohibition. Local lore also talked about bootleggers and a stash of treasure buried somewhere along the intricate trails of secret tributaries and estuaries of the Mississippi that only an experienced steam pilot would know about.

"Is that why Autumn picked a boat to get married on? So you'd have to swim ashore to get away?" Joker asked.

Caleb and Matlock started to laugh.

"Don't fucking encourage him," Maverick said, still fussing with his cufflink.

Taylor appeared in the doorway, and my heart went to my throat. She looked stunning.

"Indy asked me to tell you that they're starting in ten minutes." For a moment our gazes locked before her beautiful brown eyes moved over to Maverick. "Wow, don't you scrub up well."

"Yeah, well, I'm twenty seconds away from tearing off this damn shirt and putting on a t-shirt. Whoever invented cufflinks was a sadist."

Taylor stepped into the room. "Here, let me help you."

I watched as she helped Maverick with his cufflinks, my stomach tight with an unfamiliar longing.

"There," she said, once she'd secured them onto each cuff. "You look perfect."

"Perfectly terrified," Joker said.

"Maverick, I love you, buddy, but I think you're just not made for a shirt and tie," Matlock added.

"Don't listen to them, Mav." Taylor gave him an encouraging wink. "You look very handsome!"

Maverick's face softened as he looked at her. "Thanks, T."

She stepped back and gave him a reassuring smile. "Good luck."

I walked over to her.

"You look beautiful," I said, taking her hand and feeling a strange comfort in the feel of her cool fingers tangled with mine.

Fuck.

Bull

I felt like a love-sick teen on prom night. Giddy and full of goddamn butterflies.

And it was crazy. I didn't know what had come over me.

All I knew was that she looked fucking beautiful, and I wanted to lose the night kissing her.

She looked up at me and stars twinkled in her eyes. "You look pretty good yourself."

I leaned down to kiss her. "Ready for your first Kings of Mayhem wedding?"

She grinned. "As ready as I'll ever be."

Ruger joined us, dressed in a suit and tie, his baby son secured in his big arms. Jenna, one of the old ladies, appeared beside him.

"Would you like me to take Will during the ceremony?" she asked.

He shook his head and gave her a wink. "He's right where he needs to be, darlin'."

After nearly losing his wife and son, Ruger wasn't letting them out of his sight.

We followed him out of the room, and I slid my arm around Taylor's waist. The top deck of the River Queen was set up with rows of chairs and a red carpet leading up to an altar. Behind it, the Mississippi glittered in late afternoon light, the sky turning gold and pink as the sun dipped lower.

We took our seat in the second row of chairs, while Maverick, Joker, Matlock, and Caleb walked down the aisle to the small lattice archway that had been erected near the bow of the boat. The heavy perfume of the magnolias and marigolds woven into the latticework filled the warm air, while silk bows draped from the ceiling rippled in the gentle river breeze.

Behind us, a three-piece string band started to play and we swung around. The first bridesmaid to appear was Indy, followed by Chastity, Cassidy, and Honey, all of them in soft pink dresses and clutching white flowers. Then, Autumn appeared on her father's arm, her wild red curls piled on top of her head, her dress a tight sheath of shimmering white silk. As she stepped onto the red carpet, she took one look at the man waiting for her at the altar and she started to cry. I glanced over at Maverick and the six-foot-six tower of muscle with the wild hair and hands so big they could crush you, started to cry right back.

I reached for Taylor's hand, my throat tight with emotion, my pulse rapid, and she sank against me, resting her cheek on my shoulder as she watched Maverick observe his bride walking toward him with tears streaming down his face.

I didn't see much of the ceremony after that because I was lost in the quiet storm taking place inside me. Walls were crumbling. Old emotions were fading to black.

And I was entering a frightening, unfamiliar territory.

After the ceremony, I sat with Ruger on the deck.

Across the room, Taylor sat with the bridesmaids, and Maverick and Autumn.

"She's beautiful," Ruger said.

"Yeah, Maverick has done good," I replied.

He gave me a knowing look. "I'm not talking about Autumn."

I drank a mouthful of bourbon but said nothing.

"Don't do that," he said.

"Do what?"

"Pretend it's not happening."

I took another sip of my bourbon. Crunching ice between my teeth. "I don't know what you're rambling on about."

"You look at her like you're burning her image into your brain."

"Jesus Christ, listen to you," I said, shaking my head.

I hadn't told anyone about my feelings for Taylor.

Unperturbed, Ruger raised an eyebrow at me. "I haven't seen you look at a woman like that in a long time."

I looked down and focused on the amber liquid in my glass. I knew what he was talking about, and it made me curious what he would think if I told him he was right. "What do think about that?"

"I think it's about fucking time." He leaned forward, his elbows resting on his knees. "You have to let her go, man. Hell, you should've done that years ago. You know she wouldn't want you to be alone."

Bull

His words made me think of the random hallway singer singing "Blue Bayou" and grabbing my hands. And a tremendous shiver quaked through my body.

"You know, a crazy thing happened to me when I visited Sybil in the hospital the other day?" I told him about the random hallway singer. "Pretty crazy shit, huh."

"No, it doesn't sound as crazy as you think."

"No?"

He shifted forward in his seat. "I don't know if now is the right time to tell you this."

"Tell me what?" I could see him wrestle with whatever it was he wasn't telling me. "Ruger…"

"When I got shot and I died for those few minutes, I saw Wendy."

"You saw her?"

"And spoke to her." He cleared his throat. "Now I don't know if it was the drugs they had me on, or if it was the chemical changes occurring in a dying brain, who knows, I've given up trying to make sense of it. But what I do know is that I saw Wendy in what was supposed to be my final moments."

I felt my jaw tighten. "And what did she say?"

"She told me to pass on a message to you."

I became very still. "What was it?"

"She said you need to move on."

His words spiraled through me with the force of a tornado.

"You never told me." My voice was edgy. "Why?"

"You would never have believed me."

He was right. I wouldn't have. Hell, I hardly believed what I'd seen and heard myself.

I wasn't a guy who believed in visions and ghosts. And monsters weren't devils hiding under the bed waiting to consume you in your sleep. They were flesh and blood. Men who did bad things. *Very bad things.* I believed in the tangible. The tactile. Not the supernatural.

Yet, here I was, face to face with it.

I couldn't make any sense of it. It went beyond what I believed in. But I was still a fucking human being who could be left standing in front of something he couldn't explain.

I exhaled deeply as I asked, "Can I be real honest with you?"

"Always."

I must be crazy. Or the alcohol was fucking with me. But I needed to admit how I felt to someone.

Fuck, my feelings for Taylor had me wanting to open up like a teenage girl.

"I've spent every day for the last eighteen years missing Wendy. Every morning. Every night. Craving her. Wanting her. Feeling guilty for her death. Dying inside because I couldn't fucking touch her. I would wake up and she would be the first thing I thought of, and for a few seconds she wasn't dead and I had that small moment of respite from the pain. But then I would remember, and all the darkness and guilt, and all the bullshit, would seep back into me again."

Ruger's brows pulled in.

"Fuck, Bull. You've been living this way for almost twenty years?" When I nodded, he shook his head as if it was the craziest thing he'd ever heard. "That's not right, man."

"I know, I know. But then I meet this girl." My eyes honed in on Taylor across the deck, and my heart filled with an unimaginable warmth. "And I don't wake up like that anymore. I don't wake up thinking about the past. About the guilt. I wake up and I'm at peace. Hell, I wake up and I feel fucking happy."

Ruger chuckled. "Then things aren't as casual with Taylor as you thought."

I shook my head and drained my glass. "I don't know what the fuck any of this shit means."

"I do," he said, his voice low. "It means you finally went and did what Wendy has been asking you to do. You've finally found someone else and moved on."

CHAPTER 43

TAYLOR

While Bull was talking to Ruger, I sat with Indy, Chastity, and Honey at one of the tables near the balcony. On the dance floor, Cassidy was lost in her husband, Chance, as they danced slowly to a romantic song. Next to them, Bull's sister Ronnie was slow dancing with her new husband, Ari, and Cool Hand was wrapped around his heavily pregnant wife, Heidi.

"What did you think of your first Kings of Mayhem wedding?" Honey asked me.

"It was really magical."

And it was.

Watching Autumn and Maverick exchange wedding vows had been beautiful. The way they looked at each other, the gentle touches, the soft smiles.

"I really liked it when he gave her the crown pendant." I glanced at all of them. "I notice you all have them too."

"It's a tradition," Chastity explained, her finger toying with the pendant around her neck. "When you marry a king, he gives you his crown."

"It started way back when Hutch Calley gave one to Grandma Sybil," Indy added.

"I like that," I said, sitting back with a smile.

I glanced over at Bull and felt my heart tug with desire. He looked so handsome. So utterly beautiful in his tailored black shirt and black slacks. In his cut, he looked powerful and delectable. But dressed more formally, he was absolutely *mouth-watering*. It was moments like this that made me want so much more with him. That made me wish things were different, that I wasn't hiding a terrible past from him. A past he would find unforgivable.

When Chastity left to feed Will in one of the bedrooms below deck, and Honey snuck off to apparently have sex with Caleb somewhere on the boat, I was left alone with Indy.

"It's a wonder they don't have a thousand babies," Indy laughed as she watched Caleb lift Honey up into his arms and carry her out of view. "I've never seen two people who are more addicted to sex than those two."

She was right. When you were with Caleb and Honey, you could feel their chemistry. It was off the charts.

"You okay? You've gone a little quiet."

"I have?" I asked, trying to sound nonchalant.

"Yeah. Is there something on your mind?"

She must've gotten me at a low point, because all of a sudden, I wanted to confide in her. "You wouldn't understand."

"Try me."

Indy had a presence about her. She was stoic. Stubborn. For the first time in a long time, she made me feel like opening up.

"Have you ever regretted something? Like *really* regretted something to a point that it eats you up inside?"

"Yes."

Yes?

Indy didn't seem the type to regret anything.

"You have?"

"When I was eighteen, I caught Cade in bed with another woman. And when he told me that he didn't know it wasn't me...I didn't believe him. I was so full of anger and grief, and a desperate need to escape from the club and lifestyle, I didn't stop to really listen to him. Didn't stop to really think about what that meant. I learned later, *much later*,

Bull

that he was set up by his father...but at the time I was too selfish and immature to realize that, and so full of doubt about *everything*, so I ran away from him..." She dragged in a deep breath and I could see it in her eyes; her regret ran deep. It was almost comforting to know that someone so confident and stoic as Indy might share the same depths of remorse as I did. It gave me hope. "I turned my back on him when he needed me. And boy, that's a lot of regret to work through right there. If the roles were reversed, he would've done the complete opposite. He would've believed me. He would've found out who was responsible and made them pay. But me...I ran like a coward."

"You were young—"

"—and very stupid." She exhaled deeply. "Now that I know what happened, and what I turned my back on...well, let's just say we've done our fair share of therapy."

I knew what it was like to make a mistake when you were young. And then have to pay for it as an adult. I was living with that every damn day.

"We make mistakes. We're human. We don't always get it right," she said.

"How did you deal with it?"

"First, I needed to know he was okay. He used to see a therapist, a couple of them. He's moved on from all the trauma of the past. Being a part of the MC world exposes you to things that leave deep scars. You have to learn how to process them. And a lot of the time, you have to learn how to live with guilt."

"Have you learned to live with yours?"

"I have. Forgiveness is a powerful thing. Especially when you point it in your own direction." She smiled and it was big and bright. She really was beautiful. In the strange hierarchy of the motorcycle club, she was considered the baby queen next to Ronnie. The other women looked up to her. The men respected her. Yet she seemed so unfazed by it all. She leaned forward and raised a perfect eyebrow at me. "Want to tell me what's on your mind."

Did I?

I had kept my secret for a lifetime. Carried the weight of it on my shoulders for my whole adult life. But sharing it would be a burden, and now wasn't the right time.

"Maybe another time."

Indy wasn't the type to push. But she knew I was hiding something. Something big. But she nodded. "Whenever you're ready."

After Indy excused herself to hit the dance floor with her husband, I slipped away to find a bathroom. I needed a moment away from the music and the celebrations to catch my breath and calm the uneasiness churning in my stomach.

I had come close to telling her my secret.

And that was bad.

Because that move would be a dangerous one, one that could cause me to lose Noah for good.

I found a bathroom on the second floor, and once inside, I stood at the sink and pressed a dampened paper towel to my face.

I was being drawn into the inner sanctum of the club because of Bull and my feelings for him. And the club had opened their arms to me and Noah, and for the first time in my life I felt like we had a family. But I had a secret that told me I wasn't worthy, and I was struggling with the weight of it.

As I turned to leave, I heard someone vomiting in the cubicle.

"Are you okay in there?" I asked.

The toilet flushed and the door opened.

It was the bride.

"Don't mind me," she said with a weak smile as she made her way over to the sink. Our eyes met in the mirror as she started to wash her hands. "Just my luck, morning sickness will turn out to be an all-day sickness."

She was pregnant.

"How far along are you?"

"Almost three months." She stopped washing her hands and braced them on the sink as another wave of nausea rolled through her. "And God help me if the next six months are going to be like this."

She drew in a deep breath

"Does anyone know?"

She shook her head.

"Not even my husband." Her eyes widened a little. "Boy, I don't know if I'll ever get used to saying that. *My husband.*" A big smile spread across her face. "I only found out yesterday. I thought the nausea and headaches were stress from all the crazy wedding plans. Thought I was overdoing it, you know."

"That's amazing news, Autumn. Congratulations."

She sat down on the little bench near the windows. "We were going to wait. I mean, we want to start a family eventually. It's just, we have so many other things planned. Maverick wants a big family, I'm talking, five or six kids. Whereas I didn't think I wanted any until I met him." She blew out a deep breath as another wave of nausea washed over her.

I took out a small bottle of ginger supplements from my purse and handed them to her. "These should help," I said. I grabbed a paper cup from the dispenser on the wall and filled it from the water fountain before handing it to her. "The last time I was on a boat, I got terrible seasickness. I thought it was better to be safe than sorry."

She took one, followed by a gulp of water. "You're a lifesaver, thank you."

As she took another mouthful of water, the light caught the crown pendant around her neck, and I couldn't help but recall the look of absolute affection on Maverick's face when he'd asked her to be his queen and slipped it around her neck.

And for some stupid reason, my heart started to whisper to me about wearing the crown pendant of the president.

But then I realized the absurdity of the concept and frowned.

I was never going to wear Bull's crown.

I pushed the ridiculous thought to the deepest, darkest recesses of my brain, and focused on Autumn as I sat down beside her.

"What do you think Maverick will say about the baby?" I asked.

Her face lit up. "He'll be excited. He comes from a huge family, and I know he was only waiting until I was ready. It's just, I had so many plans, you know."

"I get it. I didn't exactly plan on making Destiny home. But now I'm really pleased we did." I thought of Bull, and a comforting warmth spread through my chest.

"Life is funny, isn't it? Maverick was only ever meant to be a one-night fling. Then it was only supposed to be a casual thing. You know, sex without strings. Then somehow between all the sex and the crazy times, he morphed into the love of my life." She smiled wistfully. "If it's one thing I've learned over the last few years, it's how things aren't as random as they appear to be. Life is more precious than that. Things happen for a reason. Destiny isn't just a mystical concept, and serendipity is a force of nature."

I thought about what she said for a moment.

Her big brown eyes narrowed with a mischievous gleam, and she nudged me with her bare shoulder. "So, you and Bull, huh?"

I was about to deny my feelings for him but stopped. What was the point?

"I really like him."

"Oh, I think it's gone past the liking stage, darlin'. I think that man is head over heels in love with you."

"What? No." I glanced at her. "I mean, do you think?"

She wiped a tiny piece of paper towel from my cheek. "I think you should stop worrying about whatever it is that has that little frown on your face, and start enjoying what is right in front of you. After all, we never know what is going to happen tomorrow. Or if there even will be a tomorrow."

She gave me a wicked smile and brushed her lips to my cheek. "Now, go get that spunky man of yours and enjoy him. Life is too short to do anything else."

When she left the bathroom, I sat a little longer on the bench. Perhaps Autumn was right. Perhaps what really mattered was being in the moment and enjoying right here, right now. That worrying about the past was a waste of time because there was nothing I could do about it. And worrying about tomorrow was pointless because it wasn't guaranteed it would ever come.

Standing up, I decided to take her advice and find Bull. I had lived inside my head for too long, and I didn't want to hide in there anymore.

I was going to find the man who had captured my heart and soul, and the rest of the world could be damned.

Because tonight, my other life didn't exist.

Bull

I was with Bull.
And I was going to savor it while it lasted.

CHAPTER 44

BULL

Just after midnight, the River Queen docked and a hundred drunk and disorderly wedding guests stumbled down the gangway and headed for the clubhouse to keep partying. It would be a party that didn't wind down until after the sun came up.

But I hung back with Taylor.

"Let me take you home," I whispered in her ear.

I didn't want to go back to the clubhouse to party.

I wanted my alone time with my girl.

She looked up at me and I felt the air around us light up with electricity. She nodded and smiled, brushing her lips to mine in response.

Back at my place, we removed our clothes and took our time kissing each other in the small ribbon of moonlight breaking through the window of my bedroom. Fingertips were featherlike, our lips gentle, our tongues needy but savoring every lick, every taste, every delicious tangle.

When our bodies became too tight with longing, I carried her to the bed and lay her down among the pillows where I'd spent many nights fantasizing about her, my body hard, my hand on my cock as I dreamed of her silky body beneath mine. Now she was here, naked and beautiful, her lush red hair spread across the linen as she looked up at me, her chest heaving with anticipation, her eyes gleaming with lust. She parted her firm thighs and I crawled along the length of her, and we both shivered when the slick head of my cock brushed against her warm skin.

With our gazes fused together, I slowly pushed into her and felt an overwhelming rush of emotion move through me. And judging by the look on her face, so did she.

I made love to her slowly. Savoring every touch, every kiss, every inch I stroked in and out of her beautiful body. I couldn't get close enough. Couldn't get deep enough. Every part of me wanted to be joined to her, to be in her, to be a part of her. And the more she moved and mewed beneath me, the more I got lost in her, in the moment, in what was happening. And as my orgasm continued to build, a strange feeling tightened in my chest. A feeling from long ago, awakening inside of me as I made love to her, making promises to her in my head, wanting everything with her.

"Bull..." My name fell from her lips in a soft moan as her eyes closed and her back arched upward. The move sent me deeper into her body, the pleasure almost blinding as her tight pussy sucked my cock, making me drive deeper into the warmth, making me lose my mind.

I gripped the pillow by her head, my body begging me to let go and come. But I didn't want the moment to end. I was high on the feeling, intoxicated by her soft cries of pleasure as she came beneath me, her body writhing, her neck arching, her eyes rolling to the back of her head.

I sealed my mouth over hers, drinking in her moan, my hips rolling and rolling until I couldn't take it anymore.

"What are you doing to me?" I cried into her mouth as light and sound became warped around me. "What have you done to me?"

The walls holding back my orgasm tumbled down, and I crashed into my ecstasy like a tidal wave to the shoreline. I didn't roar. I didn't growl. I didn't cry out. Instead, my eyes found hers and my mouth dropped open, as every cell in my body exploded with pleasure. My heart opened, and a bright light flooded in to fill the chambers, and in that moment, everything was different. I knew it. And so did she.

I collapsed against her, my brain still illuminated in ecstasy but my body soft and spent. I pulled her to me and wrapped my arms around her, savoring her warmth and the silkiness of her naked body pressed into mine.

I closed my eyes, wrapped in the heavenly afterglow of amazing sex.

But before I could descend into a blissful sleep, my eyes jolted open, and a realization ripped through me like lightning.

Jesus Christ, I've fallen in love with her.

CHAPTER 45

TAYLOR

I woke a few hours later to the sound of raindrops hitting the window. I was tangled in the bed sheets, my body soft from sleep, my skin warm with the heat radiating from his big body wrapped around mine.

I wanted to stay like this forever.

With him.

And I smiled because I was happy. Something had happened between us last night. Something magical. Something I never knew existed. I'd felt it as he'd made love to me. Felt it in every touch. Heard it in his moans. Saw it in his eyes and written all over his face.

It was no longer casual.

It wasn't as simple as that.

It wasn't simple at all.

But it was *something*.

He stirred, releasing a low groan as he shifted behind me. His breathing was hot on the nape of my neck. He was waking up. And my body was waking up with him.

When a gentle moan parted my lips, he rolled me onto my back and pushed into me, and we made love again, slowly, *sleepily*, as the rain continued to rattle against the window.

He tangled his hand in my hair and pressed his cheek to mine, his eyes closed as he leisurely stroked into me, whispering in my ear and driving me toward another mind-shattering orgasm.

When we were done, we lay soft and subtle in each other's arms, our limbs tangled, our bodies exhausted.

"I have to go." He pressed a kiss into my hair. "I have to meet someone."

I whimpered my protest.

"I will call you later." His lips brushed my ear. "And I want to spend the night making you moan."

When he left, I drifted back into a deep, satisfied sleep. I didn't need to pick Noah up from Roberta's for another few hours. But just as I started to drift away, my phone started to ring on the bedside table. Heavy and content, I decided to let it go to voicemail. I didn't want to move. I was drunk on orgasms and wanted to drift back into a heavenly sleep.

But thinking it could be Noah, I reached for it.

I felt for it on the nightstand, and pulled it in front of my eyes.

It was a number I didn't recognize.

"Hello..." I said huskily.

"Hello, Taylor." Came a familiar voice. My eyes flicked open and I sat up, a shiver of fear rushing up my spine. "I'm coming to town, and I think it's time you came back to work for me, don't you agree?"

Fear snagged in my chest.

My past had finally caught up with me.

Ten Years Ago

The dress was Givenchy. The shoes Manolo Blahnik. My hair an upstyle of red curls and braiding. Diamonds and rubies dripped from my ears; a matching bracelet wrapped around a gloved wrist. I sipped Cristal from a champagne flute and moved about the room engaging in polite small talk like the well-bred young woman I was pretending to be. Because I was anything but well-bred. I was so far from pedigree, I should need a map to find it. I came from the street. I came from the gutter that stunk of piss and shit.

But tonight, I was playing the role Alex needed me to play.

Tonight, I was a guest at the gala being held in the magnificent mansion of a Supreme Court judge.

And tonight, I was going to blow the mind of the man whose honor we were celebrating.

Senator Gilbert Borntrager.

Multi-millionaire.

Entrepreneur.

Philanthropist.

Notorious womanizer.

And killer.

According to Alex, he was the man of the hour. People adored him for his tireless work with various charities across the country, including the complete funding of a children's orphanage.

He also donated heavily to hospitals and universities, and even had a wing named after him at the local women's hospital.

He was known for his generosity. For his charm and rich, Connecticut style.

What people didn't know—but what Alex did know—was that Gilbert Borntrager had particular tastes when it came to sex. Tastes that ran a lot younger than his sixty-two-year-old wife, Eleanor.

Old Gillie boy liked them younger.

Much younger.

I was barely twenty years old, and according to Alex I was borderline.

But lucky me, he also had a thing for redheads.

I was in the impressive foyer, standing at the foot of a sweeping staircase and beneath a massive crystal chandelier, talking with an ex-district attorney and his insipid, bland daughter, when Borntrager found me.

"I don't believe I've had the pleasure," he said, his gaze sweeping up and down my ball gown and lingering on my naked throat.

The lack of jewelry around my neck and strapless gown were no accident.

Because youth aside, Borntrager also liked to asphyxiate while he fucked, and he paid handsomely to do so.

It wasn't an unusual request. I'd certainly heard of worse. And usually, it was a fetish easily accommodated if you had the money.

But sometimes it went wrong because Old Gillie Boy didn't always know when to stop.

Like the time with his young intern, Polly Malthouse, whose body was pulled out of the Chesapeake Bay following a business trip with Borntrager last November.

According to Borntrager, they shared a meal in the hotel restaurant after a day of meetings. But while he turned in early, she wanted to hit the clubs and bars. She was nineteen and ready to party, and ignored his uncompromising suggestion to stay in. She was an adult, he said. Old enough to make her own decisions while she was off the clock.

When she failed to show up for their flight back to Connecticut the following morning, he called the police.

Three days later, her body was dragged out of the bay. Ruled a homicide, it was still unsolved.

Apparently, there were others. All collateral damage of one rich man's sick urges.

To the outside world, Borntrager was a saint.

But to those who knew his dark side, like Alex did, he was a monster.

"Well, that is something we should remedy," I said seductively, taking a sip of champagne and fixing him with heavy lashes and eyes that spoke of untold pleasure.

"You look young," he stated matter-of-factly, although his eyes flared with excitement. "Barely old enough to drink."

"I'm old enough," I said.

He gave me a stern look. "Why do I feel like you're lying?"

"Okay, you caught me. I'm seventeen." I leaned closer. "But don't tell anybody. I just want to have a good time. It's my first time attending one of these things, and I'm having the best time."

"Your first time?"

"It's also my first trip to DC." I bit down on my lower lip and looked up at him through heavy lashes. "I'm hoping it will include a lot of firsts."

I was eluding to being a virgin and I could tell that it excited him.

But I wasn't a virgin. A man in a dirty flannel shirt and sweatpants

Bull

made sure of that when I was fourteen years old and sleeping under a bridge during a storm. He'd forced himself into me and ripped my innocence from my body as I screamed into the pouring rain.

And any sex since then had been a cold and empty act.

I started to giggle, as if the champagne had gone to my head. A sweet, innocent virgin, in over her head with a suave, worldly senator.

His tongue slid across his lip. A sheen of sweat beaded on his forehead.

"Perhaps we could take this somewhere a little more private," he suggested.

I drained my glass. "I thought you would never ask."

Tonight was worth a fortune, and despite hating what I did, the money was too good to refuse.

Besides, Alex would never stand for me telling him no.

CHAPTER 46

BULL

I hated having to leave her. To untangle my body from the warmth of hers and ride off into a cool, damp day. But I had to meet an informant on the other side of town. Another amoeba who occasionally supplied the Kings with information scraped from the filth of our county. His name was Bug, a small-time criminal who had done the occasional stint over at East Mississippi Correctional. He had his dirty fingers in a lot of pots. A lot of filth. A lot of shit I didn't want to even contemplate.

He lived down a dirt road in a weather-beaten house, with car wrecks and broken kids' toys littering the dead lawn. He had two wives, both of whom he pimped out, and a teenage nanny who liked to drive the wives crazy by strutting around in her tight denim shorts and a tight t-shirt that showed off her flat stomach and generous boobs.

It was a weird setup, but apart from a few calls to Bucky when the wives got to fighting, it was a setup that worked for them.

When I arrived, Bug was sitting on his derelict porch, smoking a cigarette and nursing a black cup of coffee in a glass jar. One of his wives sat next to him, a chubby baby latched onto her gargantuan breast. When I pulled up, he gave her a sharp nod and she disappeared inside.

"Nice to see you made it." Bug's voice was whiny, and when he spoke, his wispy ginger mustache shook like a hairy caterpillar over his thin lips. "Haven't seen you out these parts in a long time, Bull."

I stepped onto the porch and a floorboard groaned beneath my boot. "It's been a while."

He wiped his hands down his dirty t-shirt and offered me one. Reluctantly, I shook it.

"You said on the phone that you had some information."

He ground out his cigarette with his boot. "Had a visitor yesterday, thought you might like to hear what he got to say."

"Go on."

His eyes gleamed greedily. "Like I said on the phone, I got something you need to hear...*but for a price.*"

I pulled a small bag of weed from my back pocket and dropped it on the side table next to him.

Bug grinned, revealing a mouth of tobacco-stained teeth.

"Like I was saying, we had a visitor yesterday. Said he was just visiting for work. Some security detail for a businessman staying just out of town. Said his boss had some business in Destiny. Said he didn't know what the business was about, but he'd overheard some talk about getting revenge on a biker."

As he spoke, a blonde girl in tight denim shorts and a blouse tied at her flat stomach stepped onto the porch from inside the house. When her dark eyes found mine, a seductive smile curled on her dry lips.

"And why would this visitor tell you all of this?" I asked turning back to Bug. "He a friend of yours."

Bug looked sheepish.

"He was visiting with Tammy." He jutted his chin toward the blonde girl who was now leaning against the porch railing. "Got real chatty when he was receiving some horizontal refreshment."

So it wasn't just his wives he pimped out.

I watched as he took another cigarette from behind his ear and lit it.

"This boss have a name?" I asked.

Was it Martel?

My stomach twisted with a sudden expectation.

Could it really be that easy?

"He mentioned a name a few times," came a female voice from behind me. I turned my head. The blonde girl was walking slowly toward me, her eyes hooded, her lips twitching with dark amusement. She circled me, radiating sex and seduction.

"And that name was?"

"Mr. Carisi."

The name rolled off her tongue like silk.

But it wasn't familiar.

"That all he say about his boss?" I asked, ignoring her getting closer to me as she continued to circle. Any minute she was going to pounce. When she slid her hand up my chest, I peeled it off me and took a step back. She was marketing something I wasn't interested in.

Bug licked his thin lips. "You like what you see? I'll do you a good discount. Promise you won't be disappointed."

But I ignored him and focused on the girl.

"Can you tell me anything else?" When she reached for me again, I held her wrist to stop her. "I ain't interested in that, darlin'. Now before I walk away from here feeling like this was a complete waste of my fucking time, can you tell me anything else?"

She narrowed her eyes and wrenched her wrist free.

"Only that his boss had some beef with someone in Destiny."

"Was that someone *me*?"

"He didn't say."

My eyes darted to Bug. "You said he mentioned a biker."

"I did…I mean, I'm sure…didn't you say something about a biker, Tammy?"

"I don't remember on account I was busy getting fucked in the ass at the time."

Realizing they were wasting my time, I glared at Bug. "Next time, don't fucking ring me unless you have something real. Not some fabricated bullshit." I pointed to the bag of weed on the table. "You fucking owe me, and when I come collecting, you better be ready to pay. And I don't mean in fucking pussy!"

Bull

I stormed off the porch to my bike and took off into a breezy morning.

I'd left Taylor's arms for this?

Bug had taken a random piece of information to lure me to his cesspit of a home for a bag of weed, and hoping to make a quick buck on the side by pimping his nanny out to me.

If I wasn't so full of fairy dust from my night with Taylor, I'd be more than pissed, I'd be black with rage.

Riding back to the clubhouse, I pulled over next to a field of corn and called Taylor. She didn't answer the first call, but picked up the second.

"Hey." I couldn't help but smile when I heard her voice. I was looking forward to seeing her and having her beautiful body under mine later. I needed to kiss her sweet lips to get the foul taste of sleaze out of my mouth.

"Hey." Her voice was smoky, like she was still tangled in the warm bed I'd left her in.

"I've got some business back at the clubhouse, but I can wrap it up in a few hours. You want to go out for supper? Or you want to eat in?"

She hesitated. "Yeah, I don't know...I mean...I'm not sure."

There was something strange in her voice.

"I can pick up some takeout and be at your place by six."

"Yeah...I don't know..."

She sounded *off*.

"Babe, is everything okay?"

I heard her hesitate again. "Maybe tonight isn't a good idea."

"You don't want me to come over?"

I heard her swallow thickly as she hesitated. "I've got a bit of a headache."

I looked across at the corn crops swaying in the gentle wind.

"I'm very good with my hands. Scalp massages happen to be my specialty."

She chuckled softly. "That's definitely not your specialty."

"I can do that, too, if you think it will help," I added huskily, knowing exactly what she was talking about.

She laughed again but it faded fast. "Maybe I should have an early night."

"You sure?"

"Yeah, I think…I'm just tired."

She was blowing me off.

She didn't sound tired.

She sounded like she was lying.

Had last night scared her off? She'd seemed fine this morning. So soft and welcoming. Hell, she'd trembled beneath me, moaning my name with pleasure when I'd made her come.

But now…something wasn't quite right.

Was she pulling away from me?

Fuck.

"Are you sure that's it?" I asked, my voice hard.

She hesitated, and it twisted a knot in my chest.

"Sure. Yes. Of course."

She was lying. I could hear it in her voice. I raked my hand through my hair. I knew I should let it go. Get off the phone and see her tomorrow. But the idea that she was pulling away from us fucking killed me.

"Listen, are we okay?" The long pause told me we weren't.

I thought I heard her bite back a sob, but I couldn't be sure. Her voice was small. "I just feel a little unwell tonight. I'll see you tomorrow, okay?"

I nodded, not because of her comment, but because my suspicions were right, something was wrong and she was avoiding me.

I had taken things too far.

Gotten lost in what I felt for her.

And it had frightened her.

Now she was running scared.

Feeling uneasy, I decided to let it go. I wanted to make her mine, but I was fighting an invisible entity. Something I couldn't see. Something she wouldn't share. And if I pushed, she would retreat even further.

"If you change your mind, give me a call, okay?"

Something was wrong with my little bird, and the idea that she

Bull

might regret what was happening between us gutted me.

But I would give her the space she wanted tonight. Then tomorrow, I was going to find out what the fuck had gone wrong.

CHAPTER 47

TAYLOR

After I hung up from Bull, I picked up Noah and took him home. When it got dark, I crawled into bed, feeling heavy with emotion. I knew Bull wanted answers. And he deserved them. But I was afraid once I opened that can of worms it would be the end for us.

I thought about last night and this morning, and my stomach churned with guilt and regret. What we had was magical. But it wasn't real. It *couldn't* be real. And I'd been foolish getting lost in the addictive delirium of it.

I turned restlessly on my bed, finding it hard to relax. Since receiving that phone call my world had turned upside down. *My heart had broken.*

Now, my body ached and my head pounded with anxiety, until I could barely keep my eyes open. I squeezed them shut and let go of my thoughts, allowing my mind to drift away as I sank into a strange, broken twilight sleep.

Sunlight glittered through trees with a dreamy, late afternoon light. We lay on the warm grass, laughing, the perfume of spring magnolias hanging in the air. I loved these moments with Jacob. Loved how we laughed and how at ease we were together.

Bull

Jacob was my very best friend in the whole world. Someone I loved. I didn't need to be anyone but myself with him.

The sound of the car pulling into the driveway drew our attention away from our laughter. I rolled onto my stomach and watched Alex's wife, Victoria, bring her Porsche to a stop, and climb out, her dark bob bouncing as she walked inside. I glanced over at Jacob who was watching her intently.

"Do you love her?" I asked.

His eyes shifted to me. I could see he was going to deny it. But only for a split second. Because then his eyes softened and he looked coy. "How long have you known?"

I thought about the moment I'd found out about my best friend and Victoria. How I'd come home from an early gym class and sat in the garden with a glass of lemonade and my favorite Stephen King book, Dolores Claiborne. How I'd heard the soft moans drift over to me from the pool house. How I'd seen his face buried between Victoria's thighs when I'd peeked in through the side window. How she'd arched her back as he made her come with his tongue.

I sat up. "Are you kidding me? I've known for weeks. You may think you can hide the fact that you're all giddy over a woman, Jacob Campbell, but you can't hide it from me."

His handsome face broke into the boyish grin I was sure won a thousand hearts. "You don't mind?"

I took his hand. "You know how much I love you. I just want you to be happy."

"But what about Alex…"

I shrugged. I loved Alex. But I knew he could be difficult and ruthless. It was no surprise he was onto his fifth wife. I had never seen him be mean to Victoria but I'd heard her sobbing in her room one night when she didn't know I was home. When I'd asked her about it the next day, she had denied it. Said it must've been Emilia, the housekeeper, and then chided me for eavesdropping. When I heard her sobbing a few nights later, I knew better than to bring it up again.

I knew she was unhappy. But it wasn't always like that. In the beginning, she couldn't keep her hands off my godfather. She was always laughing gaily, always touching him with affection. But they all started out like that. All of his wives. I never knew wife one, because she was gone before I came along. But wives two, three, and four, all got sucked into the darkness after a few years of marriage.

Victoria was nice. I liked her. She was much younger than the others. And she always treated me kindly. I figured if Jacob made her happy, then who was I to stop it? I also knew if Alex found out about it, there would be hell to pay. I didn't see the fairness. If Alex was allowed his dalliances, why couldn't Victoria?

"You didn't answer the question," I said, poking him in the ribs.

"Yes. I do."

I laughed at him. "Well, well, well. Jacob's got himself a lady friend," I teased, poking him some more.

"Can you keep a secret?" he asked.

"Haven't I already proved that? I've known about you and Victoria for weeks."

"Good point."

"What's the secret?"

He looked around us, checking to make sure no one was about. He had nothing to worry about. Apart from Victoria inside the house, and a couple of security guards at the end of the driveway, we were alone.

"We're running away together."

I straightened. "You're leaving?"

A weird sensation tightened in the pit of my gut. My best friend was leaving me.

"We need to get away from here."

"But I'll never see you again."

"You'll be okay," he said gently. "You're the toughest person I know."

I looked away. Tears welled in my eyes and it was the strangest feeling. I wasn't a crier. Hell, I wasn't even sure I had all the emotions other people seemed to have. But now, sitting here with my best friend and hearing him tell me he was running away, I felt like crying.

"You could come with us," he said.

I laughed through my sadness. "Yeah, being a third wheel sounds super appealing."

Bull

His smile was weak. "We have to get away from here."

"I know."

"And you and Noah should too."

"And leave all of this," I said, gesturing to the immaculate gardens and the sprawling estate that had been my home for the past eight years.

Jacob's eyes were gentle. "Is Alex still talking about marrying you off to Jean-Paul?"

A tiny coil of anxiety began to unfurl in my stomach at the mention of the arranged marriage between me and Jean-Paul.

He was the eldest son of one of Alex's closest business partners, and recently Alex had gotten the idea in his head that our families should unite in marriage.

But I didn't want to marry him. Hell, I didn't even like Jean-Paul. He walked around like he was the most important thing on God's planet. A gift to women. Rich. Powerful. All because his father was a well-known crime lord.

But Alex knew I would do anything for him and pushed me on the idea.

He assured me that the marriage would be a business arrangement, that it would strengthen ties between the families.

I could handle marrying Jean-Paul if it was a marriage of name only. But there was no way I was letting the arrogant jerk put his hands on me.

"It wouldn't be a real marriage, Jacob. Alex says we'd be married in name only."

"Are you sure about that? I mean, he says that now…"

"What do you mean? If Alex says—"

"He's lying to you, Taylor. Once you're married to Jean-Paul, you will be expected to be his wife in all sense of the word."

I felt a chill trickle down my spine.

"Alex wouldn't expect that."

"He does. He told Victoria that you'd have to learn to be more accommodating to your husband once you were married, whether you liked it or not."

I frowned. Jacob was wrong. Alex wouldn't lie to me.

Jacob looked hesitant. "I know what he makes you do."

My eyes darted to his, and his sudden revelation caused my words to snag in my throat. "You do?"

He nodded. "You don't have to do it, Taylor. He has no right to make you."

"How long have you known?"

"Not until recently. I saw you once—"

"Forget what you saw. Promise me, Jacob." Fear licked at my skin like a hot flame. If Alex knew, he'd kill him. "I don't want you to talk about it."

"You have a choice. You don't have to do that for him—"

"You don't understand."

"He forces you to—"

"Please don't say anymore!"

A wall of unspoken words went up between us.

He knew. And I hated that he knew.

Because now that he knew what I let Alex do to me, he would look at me differently.

The silence between us stretched on for what seemed like eternity.

Then, Jacob chuckled. "We've been best friends for the past three years, and that's the first awkward silence we've ever had."

My laugh was half-hearted. "I suppose so."

"You know what this calls for?"

"No, what?"

He launched at me. Tickling me until we were both rolling on the ground and I was laughing so hard I thought I might pee.

It was Alex's voice breaking into the afternoon air that stopped us. I looked up. He stood across the lawn from us, his dark eyes narrowed, the sleeves of his crisp white shirt rolled up to the elbows.

"You two need to follow me." His voice was as sharp as a knife's edge.

I looked at Jacob and saw the humor leave his face. I didn't know Alex was home. Didn't hear his car. I thought he was still out of town on business.

Not that we had anything to worry about. Alex discouraged me from being friendly with Jacob, but he wouldn't lose his shit over us hanging out. He knew there was nothing between us. In the three years Jacob had been working here, Alex knew we had grown as close as brother and sister.

But something in his voice sent a chill down my spine.

Jacob rose to his feet and helped me to mine. Buying time, I dusted the grass off my legs, then followed him toward the house.

Alex beckoned us over to the pool house.

Jacob and I gave each other a confused look.

Because Alex never went to the pool house...ever.

Something wasn't right.

And it became very apparent when we stepped inside and found Victoria tied to a chair, with two goons standing on each side of her, and Jean-Paul looking cold and intimidating by the window. My eyes shot back to Victoria who was struggling against the ties binding her hands to the chair, the swelling around one of her eyes telling the tale of her last ten minutes with Alex.

Jacob stiffened next to me, his hands fisted at his side. Before he could react, one of the goons grabbed his arms and twisted them behind his back, before shoving him across the room. He pushed Jacob onto another chair and held him there by aiming a gun at him.

Victoria started to cry.

"Alex...?" I looked at my godfather in alarm. Fear prickled at the base of my spine. "What are you doing?"

"What I should've done weeks ago when I found out my gardener was tending more than just the rose bushes. He was tending her bush as well."

Oh hell.

Alex knew about Jacob and Victoria.

His furious gaze locked to mine.

"But I waited to see what you would do. Waited to see where your loyalties lay. I assumed they would keep it from you to begin with, but I knew you were too smart not to figure it out." His black eyes narrowed. "Weeks passed. And nothing. No word from my goddaughter about the gardener and her stepmother. So, that begs the question, did you know?"

Our eyes locked. And I summoned all my strength from everything

I had learned from him. I raised my chin, just slightly, but enough to let him know that I wasn't afraid of him.

"Did you know your friend the gardener was fucking my wife?"

"Yes," I said.

Alex prided himself on keeping a poker face. But his mask slipped momentarily, and I saw the darkness there.

But it wasn't disappointment.

It wasn't anger.

It was psychopathic rage.

He struck me across the face, and the force whipped my head to the side. But it didn't knock me down. Instead, it activated my own rage and an innate instinct for survival. I stalked toward him, but the sound of the goon cocking his pistol at Jacob stopped me.

A smug smile curled on Alex's lip. "There's my girl."

"You don't need to do this." I trembled.

"That's where you're wrong." He removed his gun from his shoulder holster. "Do you know how I've stayed ahead of my enemies for so long? How I've stayed alive with so much bloodletting going on in this business? How I've outlived every one of my rivals who partake in this devil's work?" He leaned in and whispered, "Because I am the devil."

Fear prickled along my skin.

Our eyes were fixed, and I could see the lack of emotion in his. While he could see the alarm in mine.

"You need to let them go," I said calmly, despite my heartbeat pounding in my ears. "Let them disappear. Start something new with someone else. You've done it before."

"Oh, I already have." He smiled but it was cold and lifeless. Then it vanished, and a shadow of evil darkened his face. "But I won't let anyone disrespect me, do you understand? They will pay. Just as you will."

"Please, don't do this," I begged.

Alex didn't look angry. He looked disappointed.

"I want you to remember what role you played in this."

And with that, he walked over to Jacob and put his gun to his temple. "Let it be a lesson to everyone not to cross me."

Bull

My eyes met Jacob's and he started to cry.

"I'm sorry," I mouthed.

When Alex squeezed the trigger and the shot ripped through the afternoon light, I fell to my knees with a ferocious scream ripped straight from my soul.

Jacob fell to the floor, his eyes open and lifeless, his body limp and crumpled.

His soul gone.

I launched upright in bed, shaking and damp with sweat.

For a moment I thought it was another nightmare.

But it wasn't.

Alex had killed Jacob.

My only friend.

And he had done it in front of me as punishment for keeping his wife's affair from him. I had let him down and he saw it as betrayal.

I hadn't allowed myself to think of Jacob in years. *Because it hurt so damn much.*

But apparently, my subconscious thought I needed reminding about who I was dealing with.

Climbing off the bed, I went to the liquor cupboard in the kitchen and removed the bottle of whiskey and a glass. I roughly poured the amber liquid into the glass, spilling it on the counter top and shakily bringing it to my lips.

Desperate to remove the tentacles of my dream from my mind, I knocked back the liquor and enjoyed the burn on the way down.

Jacob's murder had been the beginning of the end for Alex and me.

The man who made me call him *godfather*.

The man I'd looked up to.

The man I'd done terrible things for.

Jacob's terrified face swung before my eyes, so I splashed more whiskey into the glass and knocked it back too.

My godfather was a monster.

And I would never forgive him for what he did.

But it would be easier to hate him if I wasn't just like him.

CHAPTER 48

BULL

I didn't see her until late afternoon the next day when I got back to the clubhouse. I had spent the morning with Ruger and Caleb visiting the Knights of Wrath clubhouse, where we'd sat down with the club's president, Sabre, and discussed the next month's order.

Once our rivals, the Knights were now our allies, as well as our biggest customer. Our arrangement was simple and lucrative for both clubs. The Kings grew the product and they purchased seventy-five percent of it. It was an arrangement that had worked for several years and as a result, our bonds grew stronger.

Sabre was one of the few people I'd reached out to when I'd learned about the hit. He was heavily connected in areas where the Kings had no interests, and with people the Kings had no business with. Like heroin kings and cocaine cartels. He had explored every burrow and ripped up every rock in his world to learn more about the supposed hit.

But he found nothing.

Just as we had.

And the other reliable contacts we had all over the country.

It's what had me convinced that there was no hit out on me.

Gimmel Martel wanted me dead.

Bull

But wasn't using a hired gun to do it.

After our meeting with the Knights, we visited our cannabis fields out by the watermelon fields. It was a massive production overseen by Caleb. Acres of marijuana plants that flew under the radar of the DEA and local law enforcement, thanks to good contacts and a small percent of the profits.

Again, another deal where everyone came out happy.

But I was distracted. I couldn't keep my mind on the task. Because Taylor was pulling away, and I didn't have a fucking clue how to handle it. The more I thought about it, the more I realized something hadn't been right since the night I'd woken up to find her staring out the window. She'd tried to hide the fact that she'd been crying. I didn't press her about it. Instead, I'd taken her pain and doused it in physical pleasure until all she knew was ecstasy.

I knew she was frightened of something but I didn't know what.

And she wasn't about to share it with me.

Now, I'd frightened her off. Because yesterday wasn't just sex. We'd both felt something. Something strong. Something potent.

Something real.

I rang her this morning but she didn't answer. But a little while later, she sent me a message.

I'll see you at the clubhouse this afternoon x

Something was wrong.

And it was fucking crazy, because I was the goddamn president of the biggest MC in the south. I saw and did shit that'd made most men sick to their fucking guts. Hell, I did things most men would turn away from.

Yet, apparently, giving a woman my heart was the most terrifying thing in the world to me. It made me paranoid. It made me fucking *vulnerable.*

And because it was all so new to me, I had no fucking idea how to navigate the feelings I had when I thought about her.

About the possibility she was pulling away.

Instead of being the calm, calculated president who usually

executed every decision with confidence and stoic self-assurance, I felt like a fucking teenager who couldn't control himself.

Leaving the cannabis fields, Ruger and I split up so he could check on Chastity. While Caleb stayed behind.

I rode into the late afternoon sun alone, my heart pounding, my stomach tight.

The first thing I *heard* when I entered the clubhouse was Taylor laughing.

The first thing I *saw*, was her with Randy, laughing like she didn't have a fucking care in the world.

An unfamiliar sensation spread through me like a heatwave, gouging a path through my chest and hitting me like a punch to the heart.

Jealousy.

I wasn't a jealous kind of guy. Jealousy made you weak and, in my world, weak got you dead.

But seeing Taylor laughing so happily with Randy made me more jealous than I'd ever been in my damn life. Because she was pulling away from me, and I didn't know what to do to stop it.

I caught her gaze and her smile faded. She stepped away from Randy, because this woman could read me like a book. With one look she knew there was a bunch of crazy going on inside me. Randy, on the other hand, didn't notice and simply gave me a nod before disappearing into the kitchen.

My eyes met hers.

"I need to see you in my office," I said stiffly.

I thought she was going to fight me, but she didn't. Instead, she dropped in step behind as we walked down the hallway. Once inside my office, she closed the door behind her while I used all my strength not to lose my shit.

"Do you want to fuck him?" I asked like an insane man.

A *stupid, jealous,* insane man.

Her eyes rounded. "Excuse me?"

"Is that why you don't want me anymore? Is that why you're pulling away?"

Taylor straightened and her eyes flared with fire. "Because I'm

Bull

laughing with Randy, now I want to fuck him?" She stalked toward me, her eyes blazing. "Are you fucking kidding me right now?"

"Then why have you pulled away? Why does it feel like I'm…?"

She shoved her hands onto her hips. "Like what?"

"Like I'm fucking losing you," I growled desperately.

"All of this over one night apart? Because I was tired. Why are you being so crazy?"

"Because I'm in love with you, dammit!" I growled.

The L-bomb exploded between us, and she took a step back. My words hung in the air, thick and heavy. My pulse raged in my ears, my chest rising and crashing with anticipation as I waited for her reaction. Of course, I hadn't meant to say that part out loud, but now here we were.

"You love me?"

"No, I love my family and my friends. But I'm fucking *in love* with you."

I couldn't wait a moment longer to touch her. I grabbed her by her hands and pulled her to me, leaning down to plant a hot kiss on her beautiful mouth.

God, I was so in love with her it was driving me insane.

Frustrated at my inability to control all the crazy emotions racing through me, I let her go and stepped back, pushing a hand through my hair. I was in unfamiliar territory and I was fucking up.

"I know I sound like I'm crazy. Fuck, I know I'm *acting* crazy. But the night of the wedding…back at my place…did I imagine it?" I cupped her face and searched her eyes for a sign, needing to know that I hadn't imagined it. "Have I fucked up? Have I gone too fast? Is that why you're pulling away?"

Her eyes softened, and I could see the strain on her face as she pressed her cheek into my palm. She closed her eyes for a moment, as if she was absorbing my touch to her memory.

"No, you haven't fucked up," she said softly. "And you didn't imagine anything because I feel it too…"

Her words slipped away as she opened her eyes, and the moment her gaze landed on mine, her chin quivered.

"Then why won't you tell me what's happening?" I wasn't a man who begged. But I was ready to get on my knees and plead with this goddess to let go of what was holding her back, to beg her to fall for me. Just as I had fallen for her. "Why are you pulling away?"

"I'm not—"

"Then tell me what is wrong. How can I fix this?"

"I just need time…"

"Away from me?"

She pulled away. I could feel her mind racing. It was written all over her beautiful face. Slowly, she lifted her eyes. "I need to tell you something…"

A spark of hope lit up inside me. I was getting through to her.

"You can tell me anything."

"Even if it means you won't feel the same way about me anymore?"

"There's nothing you could say, *little bird*, that would stop me from feeling how I feel about you."

"Oh, there is," she said shakily. She clasped her hands together and let out an unsteady breath. "There is something you need to know about me—"

A sudden knock on the door interrupted her.

I swung around, ready to murder whoever was on the other side.

"Go the fuck away!" I yelled, my hands curling into fists.

"Prez, it's me, Davey, have you seen T, there's no one at the bar and—"

"I swear to God, Davey, if that door opens!"

He paused on the other side of the door, then I heard him chuckle as he walked away, getting the wrong idea. "Horny motherfuckers…"

I turned back to Taylor, but she had taken a step back and I knew I had lost her again. Her walls were back up. She looked at her watch, her brow creased, her teeth grazing her lower lip.

"I have to go. Mindy is watching Noah, and she'll need to get home for supper."

"Taylor…please…" It was impossible to hide the desperation in my voice.

Her eyes softened. "You haven't done anything wrong. This is all on me."

I stood very still. Bracing myself. "Have I lost you?"

She reached for me and brushed her lips over mine and my knees went fucking weak.

"No. But there's things you need to know about me. Things you'll never be able to accept. But I can't tell you here. Not right now. I will call you later and we'll talk."

She walked out of my office and my pounding, dark heart sank. My instincts were buzzing. And my instincts told me this wasn't going to end well.

CHAPTER 49

TAYLOR

I hadn't cried in a long, long time.

When I escaped my past, I promised myself I wouldn't cry over it ever again. It was done. I wasn't that woman anymore.

But seeing the fear in Bull's eyes reminded me that it wasn't true at all.

I was still that woman.

And I had to be. The safety of my brother depended on it.

That left no room for love.

For him.

Especially him.

I was crazy for thinking I could ever be free of my previous life. Who I was. But being with Bull had given me hope. Made me think I could have the life I so badly craved.

I drove home with tears streaming down my cheeks. I knew there was a lot to say to him. That we needed to talk. I was hurting him and it killed me, because my heart ached to tell him how I felt. But I wasn't ready. Because that would mean telling him the truth, and the truth would ruin everything. He said nothing could change the way he felt about me…but he was wrong.

Pain was a dull ache in my chest as I opened my front door, but it

Bull

was quickly replaced with a paralyzing fear when I heard Mindy talking to a familiar voice in the kitchen.

When I entered the room, my breath left me and I felt my knees grow weak.

Mindy looked up from the kitchen table, her smile bright, her eyes twinkling in the light.

"Oh hey, Taylor. Look who showed up!" she said naïvely.

The man with his back to me turned around, and I came face to face with the monster I'd been running from for seven years.

"Tay, Tay," he said, rising to his feet. His arms parted, but when I didn't move, he gave me a hurt look. "What? No hug for daddy?"

After Mindy left, still blissfully unaware about who she had let into my home, I sat down at the table and tried to calm my nerves.

My past was here, and it was about to explode in my face.

"What are you doing here?"

"You haven't seen me since Charleston, and this is the welcome I get?" Alex said.

Twelve months ago, he had turned up at my apartment after seven years.

Just like that.

"Cut the crap, Alex. Why are you here? It wasn't necessary for you to come."

"Of course, it was. I'm growing impatient."

"I need time," I said, my voice shaky.

"Bad news, kid, you don't have any left." He tried to cajole me. "And if you think about confiding in the biker you've been hanging out with..." My eyes darted to him. "Oh yes, I've been watching you, Taylor. I know you've been hanging out with those bikers. At their clubhouse."

"I'm not going to tell anyone anything."

"Oh, I know you won't." He stood up and gave me that cold, psychopathic smile. "Because if you do, you'll never see your brother again."

I stood up so quickly my chair crashed to the floor. "Leave Noah out of this."

"I'm sorry, did I forget to mention that he's gone?" His smirk was cruel. "Oh, don't worry, he's somewhere safe. Your silly little babysitter didn't even notice he was gone. While I distracted the ditzy little girl, Jean-Paul took your boy."

A cold chill shot up my spine. "You're lying."

"Am I?"

Terrified, I tore down the hallway to Noah's room, an overwhelming wave of fear crashing over me when I saw his bedroom was empty.

Alex came up behind me.

"Don't worry. Like I said, he's safe. It'll be good for Noah to have a holiday away from …" He looked around the little apartment with distaste. "The boy deserves more than this, don't you think?"

Inside, I trembled with overwhelming fear, but outwardly, I was rippling with fury.

"If you hurt him, I *will* kill you."

"Oh, he won't be hurt. I find that so unnecessary." He waved the idea off as if it was ridiculous. But then his eyes sharpened. "But you'll never see him again if you don't give me the right decision."

My knees buckled and I had to grab onto the doorknob to hold myself up.

I didn't want to work for Alex anymore, and he knew that.

He stepped closer. "You have one day to give me your answer. Then I take the boy."

When the man who had once been my world disappeared out the front door, I fell to my knees.

Alex had finally caught up to me.

And now my brother was gone.

CHAPTER 50

TAYLOR

If Alex thought I was going to sit back and let him take my brother, then he had another thing coming.

When he left, I waited less than a minute to follow him.

He was hardly difficult to tail. There weren't too many limited-edition Mercedes SUVs in this part of town.

I hung back, careful not to be seen, my stomach churning as I followed him out of Destiny, toward Emerald Lake, a fancy lakeside community where the holiday houses of the rich and infamous dotted the shoreline. Alex pulled into an enormous gated home and disappeared into a garage, the automated door dropping down behind him.

I parked up the street and slipped into the darkness, making my way through shadows and avoiding the light, until I was on the shoreline directly outside of Alex's house. A massive boat was moored on the pier, and the smell of garlic and melted butter drifted across the evening to where I stood watching.

I was hoping to see Noah, but the windows of the lake house were dark. My hands curled into a fist, and I choked back my fear.

I wanted to go in there and confront Alex for everything.

I wanted to yell and scream at him for everything he put me through.

For everything he made me do.

For every lie he made me believe.

Then I wanted to tell him that my debt to him was paid, that I owed him nothing, that I would no longer do what he wanted me to do.

And if he resisted or told me no, then I wanted to put a bullet in him.

But I couldn't. Because I had to be very careful about how I played the next hand.

My life depended on it.

Noah's life depended on it.

With my heart a heavy weight in my chest, I backed away and slipped back into the shadows.

My phone vibrated in my pocket but I waited until I got back to my car before I opened it.

My clients always said you were their favorite.

Resisting the urge to vomit, I quickly messaged him back.

I have your word you won't harm Noah?

I have no intention of doing something so unavoidable.
Do this for me and you are both free. You have my word.

With tears falling down my cheeks, I drove toward Destiny, back to the tiny apartment I shared with my brother, feeling terrified that if I played my cards wrong, I could lose him forever.

When the tears got too much, I pulled over to the side of the road and with my heart breaking, I picked up my phone and dialed Bull's number.

Bull answered on the second ring. "Taylor?"

The sound of his voice tightened the knot in my chest. "Can I see you?"

"Is everything okay?" He sounded sleepy.

Tears welled in my eyes. "I'm sorry about this afternoon…"

"It's okay, baby." I could hear the hint of concern in his deep voice.

"No, it's not. Can I come over?"

"I can come to you. Is Noah in bed?"

My tears breached my lashes and spilled down my cheeks, but I kept my voice steady. "No, he's at a friend's house."

"Then get your sweet ass over here, *little bird*," he whispered huskily.

Twenty minutes later, he answered his door, shirtless and in a pair of sweats sitting low on his hips. When he saw my face, his dark brows pulled in. "Are you okay?"

I went to him and kissed him. Suddenly I wanted this moment to last. I wanted to remember every kiss. Every touch. Every breath with him in it.

Because this was goodbye.

He just didn't know it.

Feeling my desperation, he pulled back.

"Hey, talk to me." His gentle fingers swiped a strand of hair from my face. "Tell me what's going on."

I wish I could.

"I know we need to talk. But not now. Please, I need you."

He frowned. "Why won't you tell me what has you so frightened you can't tell me the truth. Let me help you."

"Because you can't."

"I can protect you from whatever it is you're afraid of."

I shook my head.

No, he couldn't.

I pressed my fingertips into his cheeks and brushed his lips with mine. "Please…" I begged. "We'll talk in the morning. But for now…I need this … please… just make love to me."

I kissed him and he kissed me back. At first it was hesitant, but as it grew in heat, his resistance burned away like embers, and he lifted me up in his big arms, and we both moaned as I wrapped my legs around his hips and he carried me to the bedroom.

On the bed, I straddled him and gently rocked against the hardness in the front of his sweats, and he took my face in his big hands with a moan, kissing me harder.

I wasn't wearing panties beneath my dress. They were on the floor of my car. Because this was why I was here. I wanted this to be my last memory of him.

With a bit of maneuvering, I was able to slide his sweatpants over his narrow hips, and when I sank down on him, he moaned, his head falling back into the pillow as I began to ride him.

"Little bird ..." he breathed, his voice strained, his eyes hooded.

I pulled my dress over my head and he groaned at my nakedness. Reaching up, his tender fingers swept down my throat and across my collarbone, lighting little fires along the way. They left featherlike trails down to my breasts. Every touch tender and meaningful. *Loving.* I gasped, slowly grinding against his pelvis, the friction building in my clit, his big cock filling every inch of me, making me wet, making me moan.

God, he feels good.

The muscles of his firm stomach flexed and clenched into a six-pack as he sat up, and his warm lips found my breasts and sealed over a tight nipple. He licked and sucked, his tongue dragging across my skin until his lips latched onto the other nipple. He hissed in a breath, and his hands slid over me like silk, creating magic with every touch.

I started to cry. I was riding him but he was making love to me with everything he had. His mouth. His tongue. His fingers.

And this was goodbye.

Because tomorrow I would be gone.

Far, far away from here.

A woman running from her past.

A woman running from the law for killing the man who kidnapped her brother and made her do the unthinkable.

Pleasure and heartache were a perfect storm inside me, and despite the chaos in my head, my orgasm was swift. Heartbreak collided with physical pleasure, and tears streamed down my face as I rode the rollercoaster to the top of the ride and freefell into a mind-

Bull

blowing bliss. I closed my eyes and my head tilted back as I came, *loud and unbridled,* under Bull's mesmerized gaze. And for a moment there was nothing but us, and the ecstasy our bodies were taking from each other.

As I came down from my high, I realized my face was wet with tears. I quickly wiped them away, but Bull grabbed my wrist. "Baby…"

I pulled it free and leaned down, smashing my lips to his.

But he pulled back. "Why are you crying?"

He reached over and tucked a strand of hair behind my ear, those magical eyes glittering all over my face, the tenderness in his touch telling me that his feelings ran deep.

His touch broke my heart.

More tears fell down my cheeks, and my emotions spilled out.

"Because you mean everything to me …"

Because this is goodbye and my heart is breaking.

He moaned and kissed me hard, rolling us until I was under his big body, not knowing that this was it for us. He pressed his massive palms to the side of my face and planted kisses against my cheeks, fighting off my tears with his tenderness as his hips began rolling into me again. Slowly and tenderly, *and oh so deeply*, he gave us both mind-shattering climaxes, the length and thickness of him driving us headfirst into blinding ecstasy.

Afterward, we were too spent to speak. Too lost in the haze and the late hour to talk.

"Tomorrow," I whispered.

We fell asleep wrapped in one another, our bodies warm beneath the sheets, our limbs tangled and heavy with contentment, our breathing deep, and soft, and satisfied. But somewhere between midnight and the dark hours before dawn, I whispered my goodbyes to him before I slipped from his warm bed and disappeared into the cold shadows of the morning.

CHAPTER 51

TAYLOR
Eight Years Ago

I stared at myself in the mirror, trying to calm my nerves. My hands shook, and the sting from Alex slapping me across my face was as fresh as the red mark on my cheek. I told myself not to cry, to breathe in deep and keep calm. He had hurt me. Struck me twice before walking away with Jean-Paul, leaving his trusted thugs behind to deal with the carnage. When he was gone, I'd looked over at the two dead bodies lying in pools of blood, their eyes half open but vacant. I'd stared, paralyzed with fear and heartbreak, my brain scrambling to make sense of what'd just happened.

After killing Jacob, Alex had killed Victoria. But he was careful about where the bullet went, considered the trajectory and how far from her temple he needed to hold his gun. Because Alex was no fool. He could dispose of Jacob with little concern, but Victoria was a different story. She was his wife, a permanent fixture in his life, and she would be missed. He needed a plausible reason for her death, and staging a suicide was the best option.

Later tonight, the cops would be called after Alex came home and found his wife dead in the pool house.

I sat in front of my mirror and began fixing the damage so the police officers wouldn't see his handiwork all over my face, while he was at the country club, creating an alibi.

The sudden opening of my bedroom door made me jump, and Jean-Paul walked in. Immediately, the hairs on the back of my neck stood on end. Lately, he'd started to treat me like I was something that belonged to him.

He took one look at me and knew I'd been crying.

"You're crying over him?" he said with disbelief.

"That didn't need to happen," I replied through gritted teeth.

"He betrayed Alex. What did he expect? And Victoria... that whore got what she deserved."

I stood up to face him. "Neither of them deserved to die."

"They showed disrespect."

"But that's not a good enough reason to murder them."

Jean-Paul's cold eyes found mine and he tilted his head to the side suspiciously. "Why are you defending them? You feel something for that boy? Something romantic?"

"No!" Alarm tingled in the base of my spine as he began to walk slowly toward me. I wasn't afraid of Jean-Paul but he was dangerous because he could be so unpredictable. "He was my friend. The only one I had."

"Once we're married, you won't need any friends. I'll be the only friend you need." When he reached me, he slid the back of his fingers down my cheek. "We'll be engaged soon and you won't have time for friends. You will be too busy tending to my needs."

The lust in his eyes churned my stomach. But I bit back my revulsion, determined to show Jean-Paul that he couldn't intimidate me. I had Alex's word. The marriage was a business deal. Nothing more.

"You're forgetting, we'll only be married in name only. I won't be tending to anything of yours."

A snarl curled on Jean-Paul's lips. "You will tend to whatever the hell I tell you to do."

I shivered, remembering Jacob's words.

He's lying to you, Taylor. Once you're married to Jean-Paul, you will be expected to be his wife in every sense of the word.

"You need to leave," I demanded. "I just lost my best friend and you coming in here and speaking like an asshole isn't helping. Get the hell out."

Taking me by surprise, Jean-Paul thrust me up against the wall, one hand on my chest, the other gripping my chin to the point of pain.

"You have a thing for that boy?" He seethed, baring his teeth. "You better not have let him have his way with you, Taylor. Better not have let him take what is going to be mine. I'll know. When I fuck you on our wedding night, I'll know if you've given that sweet pussy of yours to someone else. Alex told me you were pure. If I find out otherwise, I'll punish you in ways that'll make what you just saw look like a walk in the fucking park."

He had no idea what I did for Alex. The things I was forced to do. The men. Or else, he wouldn't have me up against the wall talking about my virginity with his hand wrapped around my throat.

"Get your goddamn hands off me," I seethed.

His eyes dropped to my lips and became hooded. He loosened his grip around my neck, just enough for me to suck in a small breath before he mashed his lips to mine. I gagged and clamped my lips together, twisting my face away from him. But his grip on my chin tightened, making me whimper. And he was getting off on it. I could feel his arousal pressed against my thigh.

"I should just take you now. Take what is mine and be done with you."

He smashed his lips to mine again, forcing his tongue between my lips and into my mouth. I growled and bit down on him, drawing blood and making him more enraged.

"You fucking cunt..." Both hands went around my throat. "You think you can do that to me?"

"Let me go," I gagged.

His arrogant eyes brightened with rage.

"Who the fuck do you think you are?" His hands squeezed tighter." I'm going to drain the life out of you, you traitorous bitch, and then I'm going to fuck your dead body while it's still warm."

"You won't kill me..." I choked out, refusing to let him see how afraid I was. "Alex ... will ... kill ... you."

He scoffed arrogantly, too far gone to see that I was right, too high on inflicting his power over me to see the consequences he would have to face.

"I'll tell Alex I came to console you and you attacked me." His face rippled with the power he felt. He was getting off on choking me to death. "Tell him you lost your mind over your precious pal dying in front of you."

I struggled against him. But his fingers only squeezed harder, cutting off my air supply. I couldn't breathe. My skin grew hot and my brain felt like it was about to pop. Terrified, my hand smacked against the dressing table desperately, knocking over bottles and photo frames as I searched for the only thing that was going to save me from this situation.

Almost at the point of unconsciousness, my hand finally wrapped around the familiar cold steel of my Beretta—the gun I took to jobs with me—and I wasted no time shoving the barrel of it into Jean-Paul's chin.

Fear replaced fury on his face and he let me go. Barely able to keep myself on my feet, I used my hatred for Jean-Paul and the heartbreak of Jacob and Victoria's murders, to keep me upright.

"What the fuck do you think you're doing?" Jean-Paul barked. "Put that gun away before you hurt yourself."

I struggled for breath and felt a wave of dizziness wash over me. But nothing was going to stop me from saying what needed to be said. I fixed him with murderous eyes. "If you ever put your hands on me again, you psychopathic fuck, I will kill you." I released the safety so he knew I wasn't joking. "And you'd better believe I know how to do it."

Jean-Paul retreated. "You'll pay for this."

I exhaled deeply and shot into the wall behind him, just missing his ear.

"That was a warning. I'll put the next one between your eyes."

Jean-Paul fled, and I stumbled across the room to lock the door behind him.

Two days later, Alex sent me to Cabo.

And my life changed forever.

CHAPTER 52

BULL

She's gone.

That was my first thought when I woke up and found the bed empty beside me.

But the bathroom door was closed, and with my mind still anesthetized by sleep, I figured she was in there.

It was early. Outside, the sun had barely reached the sky and the dawn fog still rolled through the streets.

Rolling onto my back, I thought about the woman who had flipped my life on my ass. I thought back to her words last night. *Because you mean everything to me.* And I sank deeper into the pillows, feeling content, feeling in love.

Never in a million fucking years did I think this would happen to me.

That I would fall this hard.

Want someone this much.

But Taylor had changed all of it. And when I thought about her, I found myself grinning like a fucking teenager.

Slowly, last night came back to me in hazy images. Her turning up on my doorstep and wanting me so bad. The emotion in her touch. The need in her kiss.

The tears.

The realization came out of nowhere and hit me like a bolt of lightning.

I sat up with a rush.

Had she been saying goodbye?

I launched out of bed and flung open the bathroom door. The room was empty.

She was gone.

A sharp pain hit me in the gut.

She'd left without a word.

I grabbed my phone off the nightstand and called her. But it went straight to voicemail.

I tried *again and again*, but *again and again* she didn't answer.

Panic unfurled in the base of my spine.

The more I went over last night, the more I was convinced that she was saying goodbye.

Her reluctance to talk.

Her emotion.

Her pulling away from me since the night of Maverick's wedding.

For the fourth time before leaving my house, I tried calling her, but again there was no answer. I climbed on my bike and rode off into the early light to look for her.

By now the morning had woken up, the traffic was heavier and there were more people out on the street. I rode to her apartment and knocked on the door, my gut knotting when there was no answer. I checked the doorknob, it was locked.

Pulling my phone out of my cut, I rang Ruger and asked him if Chastity had heard from Taylor. But she hadn't.

"Everything alright?" he asked.

"No." I looked at my watch. "I got a bad feeling."

"You want me to do something?"

"It might be nothing. I'll get back to you."

Fuck!

Somewhere in the back of my mind a little voice whispered. *He has her.* But I pushed it away. This didn't feel like Martel. Didn't feel like he was involved. Plus, I wasn't convinced there was a hit on me.

Because if he really had a hit out on me, I'd be dead already.

Or else, he needed to get himself another hired gun.

No, this was something else entirely.

This was about her. It was what made her come by my house last night and say goodbye to me with her body.

With alarm twisting in my guts, I broke the door lock and stepped inside.

Three suitcases and a couple of cardboard boxes sat just inside the door, confirming my suspicion that she was leaving. *Running away.* But it looked like she had been interrupted while packing up the apartment.

That little voice whispered in my ear again. *He has her.*

Pulling my gun from my jeans, I moved through the apartment, checking rooms and cupboards. It was quiet. Deathly still. And empty.

Suddenly, Wendy's crumpled body and lifeless eyes swung before me and I faltered, a wave of fear crashing over me. If something had happened to Taylor...

My nostrils flared as I breathed out my fear.

I will rain down hell and fury if they have hurt her.

I gripped my gun, ready to unload my clip into anyone who touched her.

That's when I noticed the file on her desk.

I flicked it open and my heart came to a grinding halt.

What.

The.

Fuck?

The file was thick with surveillance photos.

Surveillance photos of me.

CHAPTER 53

TAYLOR

My front door was ajar.

I pulled the Beretta from my handbag and raised it as I stepped into my apartment, because whoever was inside that door needed to understand who I was, and they needed to understand quickly.

I moved quietly, each step placed carefully, my breath paused, my finger on the trigger. But I faltered when I saw Bull, standing in the middle of the room with his back to me as he looked through the file on my desk. *The file full of information about him.* When he heard me, he swung around, his gun raised high and in my direction.

Just as mine was aimed at him.

Our eyes met across the room, and in that quietly tense moment, I confirmed his suspicions when I didn't lower my weapon.

His eyes darkened and betrayal shimmered across his handsome features as the realization sank into his bones.

For a moment we said nothing. Our eyes said it all.

His: why?

Mine: because I have to.

The air tightened around us.

"How much is he paying you?" His voice was rough.

Mine was tight. "It's not about that. I don't have a choice."

His jaw tightened. Because I had just confirmed it out loud.

"That's bullshit. We always have a choice."

I shook my head. "That's not always true."

His eyes blazed across at me, his jaw tight, his body tense. "Why."

"They have Noah."

He momentarily let his guard slip.

"Who has Noah?" His voice was edged with alarm.

"Alex. Until I get this done."

He didn't move. Not an inch. Not a flicker. *Nothing.* He just stared at me with those beautiful, bright eyes.

And I stared right back, my broken black heart pounding in my ears.

I exhaled and dropped my aim.

It was time to come clean.

After all this time. After all the secrecy. Finally, it was time this ended.

I put my gun on the table and sat down.

Leaning forward, I raked my hands down my face.

This was such a clusterfuck.

I wasn't worried about Bull's gun pointed at my head.

He wasn't about to shoot me, just as much as I wasn't going to shoot him.

But even so, there was a good chance I wouldn't live to see sundown.

Not because of Bull.

Because of Alex. Because I was going to get my brother back, and I was ready to die trying.

"Was any of it true?" Bull's voice was cold, with the hard edge of a knife blade.

I closed my eyes. "Every damn bit."

I felt him pause. Felt my words ripple through his body. Felt him lower his weapon. "You'd better tell me what the fuck is going on, Taylor."

"Where do I even start?"

"Who the fuck are you?"

I exhaled deeply and opened my eyes. "I'm the person who's meant to kill you."

"I figured that part out myself. The photos and the gun were a dead giveaway," he said sharply. "But why you?"

"Because Alex said so."

"Why? I don't even know him."

"No, you don't. But you know his business partner…"

We said the name at the same time.

Gimmel Martel.

He looked away as he absorbed what I was saying, clenching his teeth so his jaw ticked.

I longed to tell him the full story. That my parents didn't die when I was younger like I'd told him. That they were junkie scum who tried selling my virginity to their drug dealer, so I had run away to live on the streets. That Alex had plucked me out of the nightmare of homelessness, and sat me in an ivory tower in the part of town I could only dream about. How at eighteen, after he saved my brother from my mother, I had agreed to do anything for him, and as a result, became his kill girl. How I'd stealthily crawled through the shadows of the seedy underworld taking out whoever he told me to. How the targets were bad men. Every single one of them. Drug dealers. Rival kingpins. Human traffickers. Rapists. Men who had somehow made their way onto his hit list for one reason or another. And how I'd found satisfaction in it. Not because I enjoyed killing, *because I didn't*, but because it made the man I idolized proud of me.

I wanted to tell him how he started to hire me out. A hired killer available for the right price. How, if you needed someone gone, I was an option to make it happen.

A psychopathic night club owner you couldn't forgive for raping your sister and putting her in the hospital for three weeks.

A corrupt senator with a taste for the younger kind who took advantage of your daughter, and who you knew was responsible for her body being found in Chesapeake Bay.

A cruel, corporate playboy who raped and killed your brother in a drug-fueled, sexual rage because he thought he could take whatever he wanted, from whomever he wanted.

How I would lure the target with the promise of sex. But end their life before they could lay a finger on me.

I wanted to tell Bull how I'd had my moment of clarity at the ripe old age of twenty-three years old, when Alex murdered my one and only friend in front of me because he was having an affair with his wife. How the veil had lifted, and I'd seen him for the monster he truly was. But how it was too late for me by then. Because I was already a lethal killing machine.

Bad to the bone.

A monster. Just like him.

And I had to live with it every single day.

I wanted to come clean to Bull. Wanted him to know me, *all of me*, and how remorseful I was for a past I'd never had any control over.

But even now as I lay my cards on the table, I couldn't admit to him just how deep my own venom ran. Because I could already feel him slipping away from me.

I wasn't insane enough to think that our love could survive this. I had accepted that last night when I decided I would kill Alex today. I had accepted it with every tear that fell down my cheeks when we'd made love. With our final touch. Our last kiss.

But standing here now, seeing him and feeling the gulf between us widening, I couldn't find the words.

I hadn't expected to see him today.

I thought I would be gone by now.

But he had figured out that last night was goodbye. And now here he was.

He moved cautiously, taking a step closer. But he said nothing, the cutting silence forcing me to explain at least something.

"I was a runaway when Alex found me on the streets. I'd run away from my parents when I was twelve because they were junkie scum. By the time Alex found me, I was jaded and sick. I'd been beaten. Abused. Raped." Bull's eyebrows drew in and his jaw tightened. "He took a broken fifteen-year-old and spent the next eight years taking advantage of her. Because he could. Because she was so grateful to him, so she never questioned his motives. Never told him no."

I swallowed thickly, feeling the echoes of how I once felt about him.

They were so foreign now, so alien, so wrong. My face stiffened with emotion and remorse.

"It was years before I realized the truth."

"Which was?"

"That he was a psychopath who saw me as nothing more than an opportunity. That he had used me. But by then it was too late. He had already taken my anger and pain, and used it to mold me into what he wanted me to be. And I'd been so desperate to please him, I'd let him." The bleak memories surged forward as if they'd happened only yesterday. "When I realized who he was, I took Noah and we ran. Because he wouldn't let us leave. And if we'd stayed, he would've done the same to Noah as he did to me."

"But he found you?"

"Twelve months ago." I could still feel the fear I felt the night I walked into our apartment and found Alex waiting for us.

"And he sent you here to kill me?"

"No. I was sent here to watch someone. Not to kill anyone."

"Then, what changed?"

"It was a lie from the very beginning. He dangled Noah and my freedom in front of me. Told me all I had to do was be his eyes and ears in Destiny. Report back to him if he ever asked. But he never did. It was a lie. Because the next time I heard from him, he told me I had to …"

"Kill me?"

My voice strangled in my throat. "Yes."

"When did you know he wanted me dead?" Bull's deep voice was clipped.

I looked at him. Watched him swallow deeply. His poker face firmly in place. As was the darkness clouding his eyes.

But I could feel his pain. And it was deep.

"I got a phone call…"

"When?" His voice was sharp.

A thick knot of remorse lodged in my throat. "The day after Maverick and Autumn's wedding."

His face tightened and his jaw popped.

He was thinking about that night on the River Queen after the wedding, and how it wasn't just sex. How we'd admitted our feelings as we made love, losing ourselves in the exquisite touch of each other's body. I could see it written all over his face. It was hurting him. *Deeply*.

I wanted to look away so I didn't have to see the hurt in his eyes. But I wouldn't. Because I did this. I hurt him and I had to face up to it.

"When did you decide you weren't going to kill me?"

"I would never hurt you," I whispered.

"You expect me to believe you were never going to go through with it?"

"Yes."

"Why?"

"I lost the ability to do what I used to do a long time ago. And…" I looked away and let my voice trail off.

"And what?"

"And I could never hurt you." I raised my gaze to meet his. "Because you're the reason I breathe."

CHAPTER 54

BULL

Because you're the reason I breathe.

Her words were like a kick behind the knees.

And they almost brought me down because I desperately wanted to believe her.

"I know this is a lot to take in. But I need you to understand that I never intended for any of this to happen. I couldn't tell you why I was here, or what was going on. Alex told me there would be grave consequences if I did. And he doesn't make idle threats, Bull. He's cruel. He took Noah because I didn't do what I was sent here to do." She shook her head, drawing her brows together. "Plus, I didn't want you to know who I was. Not in the end."

My voice was alien. Cold. Hard. With an edge as sharp as a knife. "Why?"

"Because I love you," she said, and my heart ached for it to be true. But it wasn't. Because this was all a part of the bullshit façade.

"If this is you being in love with me, then I'd hate to see what you're like if you weren't."

She ignored my sarcasm.

"I know it looks bad, and I don't expect you'll believe me. But I fell in love with you. If you believe nothing else, please believe that."

I didn't.

She took a step toward me but then stopped, and for a moment I thought I saw a glimmer of regret on her beautiful face. But then it was gone.

Because she is a cold-blooded killer.

"Am I your first?" I asked, and when she looked away, I knew the answer. *Jesus.* This wasn't a one off. She'd done this before. "How many?"

"Enough."

"Did you make all of them fall in love with you before you put a bullet in them?"

"That's not fair."

My temper snapped.

"Don't talk to me about fairness." I spoke through gritted teeth. "What's not fair is living in darkness for eighteen long, goddamn years, only to finally fall in love with a fucking lie!"

"It's not a lie."

Agony swept through me like wildfire and I gripped my gun. Inside my skull, I was screaming like a madman.

Because you're the reason I breathe.

I wanted to release my pain in a roar. I wanted to fall to my knees and pound the floor until my hands were black and bloody, and so goddamn numb that I couldn't feel anything anymore. I wanted to take her in my arms and kiss her until she fought against me, breathless and wild, and make her tell me *why*. Why did she have to break my fucking heart?

We looked at each other, and the air between us snapped with tension. My heart was wounded and bleeding. But the armor was already beginning to attach itself to the breached walls and harden like cold steel again.

"What happened to Noah?"

I thought about the kid I was growing close to as I sat down at the table next to her, and a weird stalemate settled between us.

"Last night…after I saw you at the clubhouse…when I came home, Alex was waiting for me." Tears glimmered in her eyes. "But he had already taken Noah. Because I hadn't done what he told me to do."

Bull

I thought about her turning up on my doorstep. About the emotion pouring out of her as we'd made love. *The goodbye.* The packed suitcases by the door. She was going to run. But not before she got Noah back.

I glanced around the apartment. "What were you planning to do?"

"I'm going to the lake house where Alex has Noah. I know where it is because I followed him there last night. And I'm going to make him see reason and ask him to let me and Noah go."

"And if he doesn't."

"Then I'm going to kill him."

Jesus Christ. Who the fuck was this woman?

"Either way, I'm going to get Noah back, and we're going to leave town. Start all over again." A tear broke free and spilled down her cheek.

"You're leaving me?"

Another tear spilled down the other cheek as she fought her trembling chin. "Please believe me, it's the best thing I can do for you. After all of this, you deserve better than me."

I shook my head.

"You're going to break my fucking heart...just like that?"

"Only to protect you." She was crying now.

I felt my own emotions overpower me.

"Why didn't you tell me? I could've helped you and Noah. You knew how I felt about you. Fuck, I would've done anything to protect you. *Anything!*"

Before she could answer, the front door opened, and as quick as a whip, we both raised our guns and pointed them at the doorway.

Both our killer instincts were razor sharp.

"Jean-Paul..." Taylor said the name as if it left a sour taste in her mouth.

The man standing in the doorway with his gun pointed at us glared at her.

"Well, well, well, doesn't this look cozy," he said.

"You shouldn't be here," Taylor replied, wiping her wet cheeks.

"Alex begs to differ."

"It's under control."

"Doesn't look like it from where I am standing." He gave me a dark look, but it was Taylor he spoke to. "Are you going to introduce us?"

Taylor didn't take her eyes off me. "Bull, meet Jean-Paul. Jean-Paul, meet Bull."

This was Gimmel Martel's son?

This skinny little runt with the receding hairline?

"Alex wants this done and he wants it done now. He says you're dragging it out, so he sent me down here to check it out. I can see he had reason to be concerned." He looked at me with dark eyes. "Best put that gun down, my friend."

My finger itched on the trigger. I wanted to put a bullet in him. But I had to think about Noah.

"You fool, I had it under control," Taylor said to Jean-Paul, her voice sharp and hard, and completely void of warmth. In seconds she'd changed. She swung her gun away from him, and pointed it at me. "Sorry, Bull. It's nothing personal, I hope you understand."

What.

The.

Fuck.

This woman made my head spin.

I glared at her. "What the fuck are you doing?"

I glanced over at Jean-Paul who was studying her.

"You were right, and I'm too tired to keep up the façade. Anyway, it kind of seems pointless now that Jean-Paul has blown my cover." Her eyes were cold. Her beautiful face expressionless. Her words hard. Her tears dry. "But as much as I hate to admit it, he's right. I've let it drag on too long." She let out a dramatic breath, as if it felt incredible to finally let it all out. "It's time to stop pretending."

"You psychopathic..." my words trailed away.

Jean-Paul was smiling now.

"Where is Noah?" Taylor asked him, although her eyes remained fixed on me.

"He's with Alex."

"At the lake house?"

"Yes."

I saw a small breath of relief escape from her lips.

Bull

"Is he okay?"

"Of course."

"Good." For the first time since she started talking about her brother, she looked at Jean-Paul. "Let's go."

Jean-Paul hesitated, but then lowered his gun and nodded. "I have a car parked down the street."

"Do you have a driver?'

"No. I came alone."

She nodded and walked over to me. Her eyes slipped away from mine as she disarmed me. "Bull, it's time to go."

"You're bringing him?" Jean-Paul asked. "Why not kill him here?"

"Because I want back into the family, and me bringing Bull to your father will ensure it."

Jean-Paul thought about it for a moment, and then nodded. "Okay. But you can do the explaining to Alex. And I'm warning you, he's already pissed that you haven't done it yet. He thinks you've lost your nerve."

"The only thing I've lost is my patience. Now, let's go."

Our eyes met before she ushered me toward the door.

Jean-Paul went first, followed by me with Taylor's gun pressed into my lower back. But as soon as we were out in the hallway, Taylor brushed past me and strode right up to Jean-Paul, knocking him to the ground unconscious.

Very unconscious.

"Help me with him," she said, crouching down and grabbing his ankles.

I admit, I kind of stood there like a confused tool.

"Don't just stand there, help me."

I stared at the woman who only seconds earlier had a gun pressed into my spine.

She looked at me again, and when she saw the emotion on my face, she stood up. "We need to get him inside and then go and get my brother."

"Before I do anything, I want to know what I'm walking into. Will Alex hurt Noah?" I asked.

If he did, I would hunt him down and kill him.

"Not a chance. He's family. And if there is one cardinal rule that Alex lives by, it's that family doesn't hurt family. That's the only reason I'm not dead." Her eyes met mine. Her face stiff with emotion. At least the kid wasn't going to be harmed. "But it doesn't mean he won't take him away so I can never find him."

"Fine." I crouched down and lifted the front of Jean-Paul's shirt. "Let's get this asshole inside your apartment and then pay Alex a visit."

Inside, she disappeared into her bedroom, then returned with something in her hands.

"Here." She threw a set of handcuffs at me. "Put these on him."

I stared at the cuffs. "Why am I even surprised?"

While Taylor shoved a few items into a backpack, I secured the cuffs around Jean-Paul's wrists. He was out cold.

"What are you going to do with him?" I asked.

"We're taking him with us. Alex has my brother. But now I've got Martel's son, and I'm pretty sure he doesn't want him to catch a bullet in his skull."

Her words were cold and sharp, like the edge of a knife blade. And I was still stunned that the woman I thought I knew, *thought I loved*, was even capable of doing such a thing.

I was no saint. But I had thought she was an angel.

Turned out she was just as dark as me.

I didn't know if it scared the hell out of me.

Or if it turned me on.

Either way, I didn't have the time to think about it. We had to get Noah back, and time was running out.

I rose to my feet. "That's the best plan you've got? Swapsies?"

She gave me a pointed look. "It's the *only* one I've got. Unless you have a better one?"

"Not at the moment."

"Then that's the one we're going with."

She crossed the room and removed two bulletproof vests from the closet, throwing one in my direction.

"Really?" I asked, shaking my head. "Your little secret is the gift that just keeps on giving, isn't it?"

"Put it on," she said, already securing hers to her torso.

Bull

I did as she said, and then picked up my gun from the table. Taylor looked from it to me. "That thing is loaded, right?"

I cocked an eyebrow at her.

"Good," she said. "Because you're going to need it."

CHAPTER 55

TAYLOR

Bull drove while I sat in the passenger seat and stared out the window.

I was about to face my past, and it was about time. Because today it ended.

All the fear.

The pain.

All the looking over my shoulder.

I thought back to when the cards were put into play.

After Alex killed Jacob, he sent me to Cabo for a week with one of his bodyguards as protection. I wasn't stupid. David wasn't just there to look after me, he was there to keep an eye on me. And the vacation was a distraction. Alex knew I was cracking. Knew I had seen beneath his mask. He was angry at me. But he wasn't ready to let me go, not while I was still so useful to him. He had invested a lot of time in me, so he sent me away to have a good time, hoping I would forget.

Because seeing your godfather put a bullet in your best friend's head was so easy to forget.

So off to Cabo David and I went.

For five days I used denial as a coping mechanism. I pretended my life was different. I sank into a make-believe world where I didn't kill people for a living, and where the people I loved didn't die.

I lay on the beach and soaked up the sun, drinking enough tequila to make me numb.

I swam in the crystal waters and ate luscious tropical fruit at sunset, followed by more alcohol to make me even more numb.

David was a good vacation buddy. He wasn't a robot like a lot of Alex's men were. Away from the testosterone overload and masculine bravado of Alex's criminal world, he was fun, adventurous, even humorous.

And the fact that he looked like a Greek god, helped me mentally separate him from the suit-wearing, fierce bodyguard he was back at home. On that beach he was someone else. Someone just like me who didn't kill people for Alex.

We had one night together. One hot, sweaty night that meant nothing. But it was fun and exciting, and the orgasms were mind-blowing.

Back home, I felt different. David and I went our separate ways, both of us sure that our one night together could never mean more. Yet, whenever our eyes met across the room, or if we ever passed each other in the hallway or across one of the palatial rooms of Alex's estate, our side glances would linger, and a small smile would tug at our lips. Once, his fingers brushed mine as we passed each other on the steps leading to Alex's office, and the spark was there. A gentle promise that perhaps we were wrong, and there was more to us than just Cabo.

But we never found out.

Two weeks after we returned home, David was killed when a car bomb meant for Alex detonated.

That same night, Alex—*who still hadn't forgiven me for my betrayal*—informed me I was to marry Jean-Paul the following week.

But I was reeling from David's death, and when I fought him, Alex really let his anger reign.

He told me I had given up my rights to decide what I wanted the day I'd climbed into his car as a naïve fifteen-year-old. That he owned me. That I no longer had a choice in anything. *That he made me.*

"I know you made me," I'd bit out at him through gritted teeth. "Because only a monster can make another monster."

"You think I'm a monster?"

"The biggest."

"Oh, Taylor, you haven't seen anything yet. Just keep fighting me and disobeying me, and you'll see what I am *really* capable of."

Right then, I knew I had to go. And I had to take Noah with me.

By the weekend we were gone. Disappearing into the darkness and vanishing for good.

Only it wasn't for good.

Because Alex found us.

Seven years later.

In fact, he'd always known where we were. Always knew what we were doing. What we were up to. Who we were involved with.

And he had waited for the right moment to pounce.

For seven fucking years.

When I arrived home to see him and Jean-Paul standing in my living room after so many years, my heart had almost stopped in my chest. My fears were being realized. They had found us and they were going to take Noah from me as punishment.

But he didn't.

Instead, Alex made me an offer.

For freedom.

"You and Noah are going to move to a place called Destiny, in Mississippi. There you'll slip into the anonymity of the town and move quietly among the community. But you will always have your eyes and ears on one man."

He showed me a photograph of a man he called Bull.

"He is a monster, Taylor. Ruthless. Merciless. He causes a lot of pain and suffering. I need you to watch him."

"Just keep an eye on him?" I asked. Because I was done with the other work Alex had made me do for him, and I had no desire for any more bloodletting. I was still trying to forgive myself for what I had already done.

"Yes," he assured me.

I looked at the photo of Bull again. He looked fierce. Dangerous. "It seems like a lot of effort just to watch someone. Can I ask why?"

Bull

"He is the president of a motorcycle club. Almost untouchable and free to inflict whatever damage he likes on anyone he chooses. We need someone undercover, if you will. If we send men to watch him, he'll know. What he won't see coming is a feisty young woman and her brother who moved to town for a fresh start. Have fun with it. Make up your past. Be who you like. Just don't let them know who you really are, Taylor."

He said the last sentence with the evil cadence of Hannibal Lecter. I wanted to vomit.

Instead, I remained painfully still as I asked, "This isn't about hurting him, right?"

"No. It's about keeping an eye on him and reporting back to us when we contact you." He smiled reassuringly. But it was cold.

"We?" I asked.

"He is of particular interest to my dear friend Gimmel, who simply doesn't want his business interests thwarted by this backwater hillbilly any further." His expression darkened. "This biker scum is a bad man, Taylor. Bad to the bone. But we simply need you to watch him. It couldn't be easier. There's not even a need for you to contact us. We'll reach out to you when we need any information."

"And if I do this, you'll leave me and Noah alone?"

"If you do this for me, Taylor, I will grant you your freedom. I won't call on you again. You and your brother will be free to do as you please."

I hated the plan, but was lured by the idea of no longer running. Of never having to look over my shoulder again. Of Noah and me being safe and free.

"How do I know I can trust you?" I had asked.

"You can't. But you will have to." His eyes had gleamed with the nefarious glint I remembered from long ago. "Because the alternative is much more, how do you say...painful." He turned his back to me to study the photos on the wall, then swung around. "Remember that bodyguard who used to work for me? The good-looking one who died. Now what was his name?"

"David," I bit out. "His name was David."

"Yes, David. What happened to him was such a shame."

In that moment I realized what I had failed to realize all those years ago.

He knew about me and David.

Just like he knew about everything else.

"Did you have David killed to get back at me?" I asked shakily.

His half smile lacked warmth and his eyes were dead.

Evil.

"You think I didn't know about your little affair in Cabo? You think I didn't see the stolen glances and little smiles when you came home from fucking him in Cabo."

"So, you killed him to punish me?"

Our eyes locked, and I saw his hatred for me in them. I was dead to him the moment I had betrayed him.

"I trust that you and I have reached an understanding," he said, ignoring my question, yet confirming that I was right. "That you will comply with my wishes."

I had no choice.

Alex had me over a barrel, and he knew it.

I nodded, hating myself.

"Good!" He nodded to Jean-Paul who handed me an envelope thick with money. "Inside you'll find ten-thousand dollars. It should be enough to help you with your relocation."

I looked away from the envelope and raised my chin defiantly, refusing to take it from Jean-Paul.

"I don't need your money," I said, my pulse pounding in my ears. The only thing I was taking from Alex was my freedom.

There was a dreadful pause before Alex finally threw his head back and laughed. "Finally, there's my feisty little girl! I've been waiting for her to show up."

He indicated for Jean-Paul to put the envelope away, and stepped forward, bringing a frigid, menacing air with him. He looked at me, his dead eyes scrutinizing me for a moment, and inwardly I shook with fear. Because it felt like the devil himself was standing in front of me, reaching in and staining my soul.

But I remained poker-faced. Still as a mouse. Because it would be a cold day in hell before I let Alex see how terrified I was.

Bull

"You have my word," he said finally. Our eyes locked and my face stiffened because I was looking into the eyes of pure evil. Then, just like that, his energy changed and he clapped his hands together. "Now, let's go and eat. I'm famished!"

He forced Noah and me to join him and Jean-Paul for dinner at a local Italian restaurant. He introduced himself to Noah as his godfather, and entertained him with embellished stories about my teenage years, all fabricated and meant purely to win over my brother. And his performance was Oscar-worthy. By the end of the night, Noah was enraptured by him, while I was trying my best not to bring up the meal I had struggled to eat.

I was a strong woman.

But fear should never be underestimated.

It fucks with even the strongest of minds, and it had its hooks firmly lashed into mine.

Later, some people would wonder why I never went to the police. Or the Feds.

Or why I didn't tell Bull.

And my answer would be the honest-to-God truth.

I was terrified of Alex and what he was capable of.

He had friends in powerful places.

Friends from the darkest, nastiest of worlds.

Friends who could inflict your worst nightmare on you with one word from him.

The only person I could trust to take care of this—to protect Noah—was me.

Alex knew I didn't run away from him for me. He knew I ran because I wanted to protect my brother.

Worse, he knew my nightmare was losing Noah, and if I betrayed him again, he would ensure it became my reality.

He drove that point home at the end of the night when he dropped us home. As we said goodnight, he whispered in my ear. "If you breathe a word of this to anybody, especially that cock-sucking biker prick, our deal is off." He stepped back and shifted his gaze to Noah sitting across the room watching TV. "Do we understand each other."

I nodded. My throat knotted with fear.

"Good. I'll be in touch when I need further information."

But they never did reach out for information. The next time I heard from them was the morning after Maverick's wedding. When Alex called me and told me it was time to come back to work for him.

It was the moment I knew I'd been lied to.

I was never in Destiny to keep an eye on Bull like Alex said.

And by the time I realized it, I was in way too deep. I was in love with the man Alex wanted me to destroy.

I never meant to get involved with Bull.

Never meant to run into the back of his van.

Never meant to lose my job and accept his offer of one.

Never meant to fall in love with him.

Of course, when I did, I had planned on telling him about who I was, but not until I had it all figured out in my head.

And I still hadn't done that yet.

Now we sat beside each other like strangers.

With a ridiculous Jean-Paul in the back, dazed and confused.

While my brother was with his godfather, safe but facing an uncertain future.

And I had a mere matter of minutes to figure it all out.

CHAPTER 56

BULL

As I drove, my mind scrambled to put it all together.

A hitman.

A hired gun.

The woman I was in love with was a goddamn assassin.

I had so many unanswered questions, but I couldn't articulate them, so instead of talking to her, a weird, uneasy calm settled between us.

I told myself to focus. To forget about the heartbreak. *The betrayal.* And focus on getting Noah back.

Emerald Lake, where the lake house was located, was an hour's drive out of town, but ten minutes over the county line we were intercepted by Ruger and Cade.

We pulled over on a quiet stretch of road, and bracing myself, I rolled down my window as they walked over.

"What the fuck is going on?" Ruger asked. He glanced over at Taylor, then back to me. "I see you found her."

"How did you know where to find us?"

He held up his phone. "The app on your phone. The one you made us all download the last time you had a hit on you. After your phone call, I knew something wasn't right. So now that we're here, how about you tell me what the fuck is going on."

The four of us drove to a deserted parcel of land, well-hidden from the road, where I explained everything. It didn't go down well. There was yelling. There was tension. There was distrust. And there was a moment where I defended the very person I felt betrayed by, just so my brothers would step back and let us do what we needed to do in order to get Noah back safely.

"I'm not asking you as your president. But we could use your help."

"And what happens to *her* when this is all done?" Ruger asked, looking at Taylor.

She looked at him, her face tight. "You won't ever see me again."

Ruger's eyes shot to mine. "And you're okay with that?"

No, I wasn't fucking okay with it.

I was far from fucking okay with it.

"When we get her brother back, she's free to leave," I said, my voice hard.

Ruger thought for a moment, weighing it all up in his head. Finally, he nodded and said, "Okay, what's the fucking plan?"

Taylor's godfather was holed up in a palatial lake house on a sprawling five-acre block. The plan was for Ruger and Cade to take care of whatever *muscle* Alex might have on the property, while Taylor and I went to look for Noah. We didn't know what we were walking into, but we weren't going in completely blind. Taylor had lived with him for years. She knew how he operated. What security he would have and what they'd be strapping.

"Alex is crazy private, he won't have too many bodyguards," Taylor explained. "Two, maybe three, max."

"He'll have CCTV. It'll be a problem," Cade said.

"There's a blind spot coming up from the lake. I was here last night and again this morning, that's where I was when you came to my apartment. And there's probably more blind spots. This isn't his home. It's a rental. It doesn't appear to have the type of CCTV system he would usually have."

"That works in our favor," Cade said.

"He's more exposed here than anywhere," Taylor added. "He won't be expecting us."

Bull

Ruger and Cade nodded.

"But before we do this...there's something else we need to take care of?" I walked over to her Honda and opened the trunk.

Jean-Paul was awake and protesting about being restrained. But the gag in his mouth muffled it.

"This is Gimmel Martel's son," I said.

"Fucking great," Cade said, shaking his head.

"What the fuck?" Ruger looked at Taylor. "Boy, you're just full of surprises."

I saw Taylor's temper snap. Saw her eyes sharpen. Felt her anger rise above anything else she was feeling.

Ignoring my brothers, she walked over to the trunk of the car and punched Jean-Paul in the face, breaking his nose. "That's for putting your hands on me," she growled. Pain rattled through her knuckles and she shook them. But then she punched him again, this time knocking him out. "And that's for Jacob, you evil fuck!"

A dumb silence fell over all of us.

When she swung around, she looked unapologetic. "You have to believe me when I say he deserved it," she said.

I didn't doubt it. And I hoped one day, I'd find out why.

We dragged the unconscious Jean-Paul and dumped him in one of the gardens surrounding the property. Now that we had Ruger and Cade with us, trading him for Noah seemed like the harder option. The time for negotiations were over. We weren't going to ask for Noah back. We were going to take him.

"Once we get inside, I'll find Alex," Taylor said.

"What happens when you find him?" Ruger asked.

She looked him right in the eye. "I'm going to kill him."

And I could see by the expression on his face, he believed her.

We split up, and while my brothers disappeared, Taylor and I stealthily made our way through a patch of trees toward the back of the lake house. Just as we were about to make a break for the small alleyway leading up to a side entrance, a man stepped out onto the back deck.

Gimmel Martel.

I saw him but Taylor didn't, and I had to pull her back to stop her from breaking our cover. As I grabbed her, we both fell back into the cover of the dense tree line, and collapsed onto the damp soil. For a brief moment I was engulfed in the sweet scent of her, and I couldn't help but breathe her in and lose myself in the perfume that was uniquely her. Brimming with agony, my heart ruptured, and I had to swallow back my pain. She looked up at me, her eyes wide, her lips parted.

I wanted to kiss her. Hold her. Bury my face into the infinite warmth of her smooth throat and clasp her to me so I could feel the gentle beat of her heart.

I wanted to beg her to tell me it wasn't a lie.

But I didn't. Instead, I let her go and shifted my focus to the task at hand.

Because our plan had just changed.

Gimmel Martel was here, only yards away.

And once I got inside the lake house, while Taylor located Alex, I was going to put a bullet in Gimmel.

CHAPTER 57

TAYLOR

Even by Alex's opulent standards, the lake house was over the top. It was a massive brick and wrought-iron monstrosity rising out of the water.

It was impressive.

But it was impractical. It didn't offer him the security he needed, and it was almost too easy to slip inside undetected.

Once inside, Bull let me know he was going to look for Noah, and signaled for me to find Alex.

I found him in the kitchen. He was standing at the massive granite island, chopping tomatoes and onions, the aroma of garlic and Napolitana sauce heavy in the air.

When he looked up and saw me aiming my gun at him, he smirked. "Well, well, well, if it isn't the Little Assassin of the South."

I gripped my gun tighter, hating his taunt.

"Where is Noah?" My voice bit into the cool air of the gleaming white kitchen.

"No need to fret. He's safe."

"He'd better be."

He put his knife down and made a point of taking his time wiping his hands on a dishtowel. "I'm guessing this means you're not coming back to work for me?"

"You guessed right."

"What a shame," he said.

My eyes shifted to the gun sitting on the countertop.

"Don't even think about reaching for that firearm."

His eyes gleamed. "Oh, I wouldn't dream of it. I know what a good marksman you are."

I gritted my teeth. I wasn't going to let him get to me. I wasn't his kill girl anymore.

"Where is Noah?" I asked again.

"He's around here somewhere."

"And Martel? I'm sure he's lurking about."

Alex wasn't about to give up too much information. He waved off the question. "Perhaps."

"You might want to go get him."

He said nothing. Instead, for a moment he was completely still, his black eyes reaching me from across the room. "Why are you doing this, Taylor?"

"Because I am trying to stop a war," I said. "If you do this, Alex, you'll be setting things in motion that you can't possibly stop. You don't want war with the Kings of Mayhem."

Alex raised his eyebrows. "Oh, I don't?"

"No, because it's a war you can't possibly win. And what for? Because Gimmel got his panties in a twist over Bull's refusal to let him run drugs out of Destiny. It's not even your fight!"

I knew Alex was doing this out of loyalty to his long-time business partner. But it was a loyalty that could destroy him and his business empire if he didn't see the dangerous waters he was treading.

"Gimmel is like a brother to me!"

"Gimmel is poison!" I snapped. "He lied about Bull. He's not a monster. He's nothing like he said he is. He is a decent man."

He scoffed. "You sound like a teenage girl with a crush."

Heat flared in my cheeks. And in that moment Alex knew I was in love with Bull, and he started to laugh.

"Well, well, well," he chuckled. "The hitman has fallen in love with the hit."

Bull

He laughed again, and I had an urge to plant a bullet in his smug mouth sooner rather than later.

But then he stopped laughing, and a menacing darkness swept over his face.

"Does he know who you are?" he asked darkly. "Does he know about the men you lured to their deaths with the promise of pussy, only to put a bullet in their brains before they even got a taste?"

Alex was good at finding his enemy's Achilles heel, and he'd just used mine against me. His words jabbed into my conscience. *Shame. Remorse. Guilt.* They spread through me, making me falter, making me weak.

I gritted my teeth. I didn't want to give him the satisfaction of knowing his words got to me. But my emotion was too strong to hold back.

"I was just a child when you turned me into a killer. You made me exactly what I became."

An evil smirk curled on his lips. "It's so much easier to live with your sins when you can blame someone else for them, isn't it, Taylor?"

"It's the truth. You took a broken young woman and made her into a fiend. Made her crave your acceptance and love, only to make her do the unforgivable in order to get it."

"I gave you the kind of life people could only dream of," he growled.

"You made me a monster!" I yelled.

For a moment, I thought I saw a flicker of remorse on his face. But then it was gone and I realized I was wrong. Alex wasn't capable of remorse because he was a psychopath.

"You have nothing to gain from pursuing this, and *everything* to gain from walking away," I said.

Alex shook his head. "I should've known you wouldn't understand the concept of loyalty."

"The Kings of Mayhem will destroy you and everything you've built. I've seen how big they are, Alex. You're outnumbered. Don't do this, don't risk everything for Gimmel. Walk away."

Backed into a corner, an evil glint caught the light in his eyes. "You underestimate me".

"No, you underestimate the Kings of Mayhem."

His eyes darted to the doorway where Bull suddenly appeared. Without warning, he grabbed his gun off the counter and fired it at Bull.

But I fired mine too.

I was quicker.

I was also a better aim.

And I shot Alex.

Right through the heart.

CHAPTER 58

BULL

Alex was dead.

"Are you okay?" I asked Taylor.

She stared at me, wordlessly, as she tried to process what she'd just done.

I looked down at Alex lying dead on the floor, a red stain spreading across the tiles.

Taylor had hit him right in the heart.

"I'm going to find Martel. You get Noah and meet me back at the car."

She nodded but said nothing, too stunned by Alex's death. But as I turned to leave, she stopped me. "Be careful, okay?"

I paused, taking her in, wondering if it was the last time I was going to see her.

She would get Noah to safety. I had no doubt.

But I wasn't so sure Martel was going to go down without a fight.

I moved quietly through the mansion, stealthily, ready to take out anyone who got in my way.

He was close. I could feel him. And I was like a hunter stalking his prey. Every cell in my body alert. Every nerve and fiber buzzing with anticipation. Every step taking me closer to the end game.

This would all be over soon.

I would have my revenge, and Martel would take his place in hell.

A yelp out of place in the silence of the big house drifted down from the stairs winding up to the second story.

Noah.

I increased my pace up the staircase, but stopped when I rounded the corner and found Gimmel Martel waiting for me. He had Noah. One arm was hooked around his neck. The other held a gun aimed at the kid's shoulder.

Fuck.

"I'll shoot him," he warned, pulling Noah closer.

I put my arms up in surrender. "Let the kid go."

"I don't think so."

"It's me you want, not him."

"The kid is staying where he is, now drop it," he demanded, gesturing to the gun in my hand.

I did as he asked, slowly bending down to place the weapon at my feet.

When I straightened, he smiled smugly. "At last."

He was pleased with himself. His lecherous eyes lit up with delight, and his fat jowls reddened with the sudden rise of his heartbeat. He had the upper hand, and he was almost ejaculating with joy.

"At last, indeed," I growled.

He nudged Noah forward until they were standing right in front of me so he could press the muzzle of his gun to my forehead.

I'd had had plenty of guns pointed at me in my lifetime. But the only time one had been pointed at my head was when I had placed the muzzle against my own temple. Back then I had wanted to die. But not today.

I didn't want to die.

I thought about my family and my club. I thought about what my death would mean to them, and what would happen once my body was in the ground and I was no longer around. And then I thought about Taylor and Noah, and what it would mean for me to die before I even had a chance to begin a life with them. I thought about all of the unsaid things. All of the things undone. All of the feelings left unfelt.

Bull

I wasn't done.

I wasn't finished with this life.

There was more to do. More to see. More to feel.

I thought about the last few weeks with Taylor, and felt her satiny skin against mine and the soft silk of her hair against my cheek as I made love to her.

I heard her laughter and saw her smile.

Felt the warmth of her body as she lay next to me, and the tenderness of her touch as she woke me in the early hours to make love.

And then I thought of Noah.

There was so much for me to show him.

So many more *thug moves* to teach him.

"I have prayed for this day," Martel said, an evil glint in his rheumy eyes. "But before I kill you, tell me something…"

"What?"

He pressed his gun deeper into my forehead. "Was it worth it?"

No, it wasn't worth it.

My eyes slid to Noah. He looked terrified.

I'm so sorry, buddy.

"Don't do it in front of the boy."

Glee curled on his ugly lips. "You don't get it, do you? And that was always the problem. So, let me remind you one last time, you cocksucking motherfucker. You don't get to tell me what to do. Do you understand? *You don't get to tell me what to do.*"

Any second now, a bullet was going to turn my world to black.

I had no doubt.

Except, in that moment, Taylor appeared in the doorway, her gun raised, her aim pointed at the man who was seconds away from ending my life. A startled Martel swung the gun in her direction and fired. And in that moment, the woman who had my heart, *who I was so goddamn in love with*, dropped to the floor.

Noah cried out and broke free, and ran over to his sister lying on the floor.

In the confusion, I launched at a distracted Martel and knocked the gun from his hands. I grabbed him and started pounding into him, all the hate and darkness bubbling to the surface and spilling out of me as my fist continued to collide with his face. My revenge took a step backward, letting the fear that he'd just killed the woman I was in love with overpower me, and I lost control.

I was a powder keg of emotion.

Pain and betrayal swirled through me.

Fear and terror that Taylor was dead blinded me with rage.

I was a man possessed. Unable to stop.

I was going to kill him with my bruised and bloody hands.

Until Noah's small voice somehow made its way through the thick waves of darkness in my head.

"Bull," he sobbed. "Taylor needs you."

I looked over at him. And somehow, seeing him kneeling next to his sister made me break through the surface of the black ocean of rage I was drowning in.

If I kept going, Noah's life would change forever. He could never unsee me take Martel's life with my bare hands. He could never unsee the ugliness of murder. Of revenge. *The dark side of me.* It would linger in him for the rest of his life and manifest into nothing good.

In that moment I had to choose. Did I get my revenge on Martel and soak in the satisfaction of his death? Or did I protect Noah from the darkness of watching one man take another man's life?

My need for revenge ran deep and fast through me, like venom in my veins, and every part of the president in me screamed for me to beat the life out of him.

Three months ago, I would've.

Three months ago, I was a different man.

But despite the agony of seeing Taylor wounded on the floor, I broke through the chains of my revenge and pushed it back.

I let Martel go and he fell to the floor.

He would live.

He would wake up broken.

And then he would go to prison.

CHAPTER 59

TAYLOR

Getting shot hurt like a bitch. Even if it was through a bulletproof vest. The Kevlar didn't stop the bullet completely. It rammed into my chest like a goddamn cannon, ripping all the oxygen out of my lungs and making me see a universe of stars as I fell to the floor.

But I was alive.

If I hadn't been wearing one of the vests I'd stolen from Alex's house the night Noah and I had fled, I would be dead. Because the bullet hit me in my breastbone, only inches from my heart.

Paralyzed by pain, I lay on the floor and watched as Bull beat into Martel, his powerful fists pounding into his enemy until he looked like a limp, bloody piece of meat. I tried to call out, but I couldn't breathe. Pain flared in my chest and rattled my lungs. I could see it on Bull's face, he thought I was mortally wounded. I wanted to tell him I was okay, but I was too stunned to say anything.

When Noah cried out, Bull stopped and let Martel collapse to the floor. Dropping to his knees beside me, his eyes were crazed with grief, his face marred with despair.

I tried to tell him with my eyes that I was alive, that I was okay, but when I moved my mouth nothing came out.

He patted me down desperately. "Did the bullet get the vest?"

I looked up into his anxious eyes. I couldn't breathe but I nodded to him. He swallowed thickly, and I could see the relief spread across his face. He loosened the vest and pulled it away so he could survey the damage. He pushed my shirt up and relaxed further when he saw the red bruise already forming on my skin. There was no blood. No mortal wound. Relieved, he sat back and caught his breath.

"Is she going to be okay?" Noah cried.

Bull nodded. "Yeah, kid. It's all over now. You're both safe."

"You need to leave," Bull said.

We were outside, standing in the shadow of a giant oak tree in the garden. Bull had carried me through the house, eager to get Noah away from the carnage inside, and sat me down in a small garden so I could catch my breath.

I glanced over at my brother sitting on the wall of a water fountain at the edge of the driveway.

"What's going to happen?" I asked. I had gotten my breath back, but it still hurt to speak.

"Caleb is on his way. He'll take you and Noah home."

"What about Alex and Martel?"

"I'll fix it. I've already called the sheriff. We'll work something out."

"You called the police?"

"He's been working with the Kings for as long as I can remember. He'll help us clean up this mess."

I thought about Alex lying dead in the kitchen.

We were finally free.

But in my quest for freedom, I had found and lost the man I was crazy in love with. It was tough to accept.

Now he looked at me like he didn't even know me.

His voice was cold and lacked emotion. He stood next to me but felt a world away.

I had lost him.

I thought about last night and how tender he had been with me, and my heart ached, longing to know he still felt the same.

Bull

But he didn't.

I could see it on his face. Hear it in his voice.

"Will you ever be able to forgive me?" I asked before I could stop myself.

He tried to hide it, but his face tightened with inner torment.

"You got what you want, Taylor. You and Noah are free."

"But what about us? Do you think there's any chance we—"

He cut me off. "You need to take Noah home and make sure he forgets all about this."

I wanted to reach for him. To feel his warm skin against mine. To feel his heartbeat against my cheek as he wrapped his strong arms around me.

But those days were gone, and my stomach twisted with the agony of losing him.

"I love you." The words spilled out in a desperate whisper and Bull's expression rippled with longing. With agony.

He paused to look at me. "Take care of your brother."

And with nothing else left to say, he walked away.

CHAPTER 60

TAYLOR

Over the next few days, I hibernated with Noah, desperate to protect him from what he had seen. We talked about it. About what had happened.

Fortunately, he knew very little and never understood the kind of man Alex really was. All he knew was that he spent the night with his godfather, and that his godfather's business associate had done some terrible things to Bull's family, and that Alex had helped.

One day, when he was older, he would learn more about what happened. Who Alex was and the things he had done. A bad man who hurt people, who wasn't the charismatic grandfather he pretended to be.

It also meant he would learn more about me. Who I was. What I had done. But by then, he would have the maturity of mind to understand, and I prayed he would forgive me.

All I could do now was protect him, and hope he had a beautiful childhood.

After a weekend of binging on Netflix and eating junk food, he was itching to go back to school. His world had looked up when Bull had ridden into his life, and he had made a lot of new friends once he had his confidence back and felt accepted by his classmates. Now he couldn't wait to get back to them. I was astounded by how well-adjusted he was in light of what we'd been through.

Whatever happened between me and the club, I wouldn't take him away from Destiny. Not now. He was finally settled. He had friends. Went to birthday parties and sleepovers.

Destiny was our home now.

With or without Bull and the Kings of Mayhem.

I didn't speak to anyone in the days that followed. Chastity rang a few times, but I couldn't face her or the rest of the club, not until I had everything untangled in my head.

The only person I spoke to was Sheriff Buckman who dropped by so I could answer a few more questions. It was a slam dunk, he said. A clear case of self-defense. I wouldn't serve any jail time if I testified in the trial of Gimmel Martel. He said he would live out the rest of his days in a jail cell, and his son wouldn't see the outside of a cell for several decades.

To my surprise, Sheriff Buckman knew what I'd done for Alex. About the paid hits. But he assured me there was no paper trail, no digital footprint or any witnesses to prove any of it. In protecting himself against being associated with any of the killings, Alex had also protected me, to my utter surprise.

"But you know I did them," I said to him, feeling sick to my stomach. "Why aren't you arresting me?"

"I can't prove any of it. This case will be closed within the next few weeks, and you won't face any prosecution. As far as I'm concerned, you did the world a favor." He stood up and tucked his notebook into his pocket. "It's just a pity Bull didn't take out Martel as well. He doesn't deserve the oxygen he's using, and it would've saved me a ton of paperwork."

I knew why Bull didn't kill Martel.

He did it for Noah.

He knew how damaging it would've been for my brother to see it, and my body ached with gratitude. Things could've ended up so much worse, but as it was, Noah was fine and would never have to go through life with the vision of seeing Bull end Gimmel Martel's life.

And I knew what strength it must've taken for Bull to let Martel go.

I just wished he'd let me talk to him, to at least thank him.
But he wasn't taking any of my calls.
We were done.
I realized that now.
And I couldn't blame him.

I didn't know what I was walking into when I turned up at the clubhouse the following Monday. I'd finally spoken to Chastity the night before when she called to make sure I was okay. Ruger had told her everything. When I asked her if anyone else knew, she chuckled softly.

"Oh, honey, MC gossip is faster than lightning. They all knew the very next day."

Which was exactly what I didn't want.

"From what Ruger said, there seems to be a weird understanding among the boys about what you did. Once he explained the situation to them, they understood you were caught between a rock and a hard place. They get it. They'd die for each other. And they're not even bonded by blood." She sighed. "This world of ours is strange."

"Have you heard from Bull?" I asked softly.

She paused. "No. Ruger said he disappeared into his office and told anyone who came close to fuck off. That's my uncle. He retreats like a wounded animal when he's hurt. But that's only because he cares so much and he doesn't know what to do with it. You have to remember, he hasn't loved anyone in almost two decades. Now he's in love with you and…. Well, it didn't turn out how he imagined."

I couldn't swallow because guilt knotted in my throat. There was also a hardness in my gut.

"Chastity?"

"Yeah, honey?"

"Are the girls going to hate me?" I didn't need people to like me. But I wanted them to. Because I'd never had friends like I had with the queens.

The line was silent as Chastity thought for a moment.

Bull

"Show up tomorrow. Own it." She paused. "Just don't run, okay?"

I had no intention of running. Those days were over.

I was going to face the shit.

Show some backbone and explain myself.

I barely got a wink of sleep because the events of the day kept replaying in my head, and Chastity's words kept coming back to haunt me.

He retreats like a wounded animal when he's hurt.

The words swam in and out my nightmares, bringing a sharp, searing pain with them every single time.

By the time I turned up at the clubhouse the next day, I was in knots.

I walked in cautiously, and Randy greeted me with a sharp whistle. "Girl, you've got some lady balls on you, that's for sure," he said, throwing the hand towel over his shoulder.

I shoved my hands in my shorts and let out a rough exhale. "Should I leave?"

He leaned on the bar. "You kidding me? This place is going to be crawling with sweaty, thirsty biker brothers in an hour, who else is going to help me keep them in line?" He gave me a wink. Apart from Chastity, apparently, I had one other friend in the club.

Relieved, I smiled, and he threw the towel at me. "But there's a few people I think you need to talk to before you start."

He nodded toward the booth on the other side of the bar. The queens were here.

"Why do I feel like I'm walking the plank?" I asked nervously.

"Probably because you came here to assassinate their president, and they know it?"

I gave him a wry smile. "Thanks for the awesome pep talk."

I approached the table cautiously. They were all here. Indy. Honey. Cassidy. Chastity. Autumn. Even Ronnie. When I reached them, the talking around the table stopped, and six sets of eyes focused on me.

"Y'all know what happened?"

"Yep," Honey replied.

I looked at each set of eyes and saw the questions there. The sense of betrayal.

"Before I explain myself, I want you to know that I was always real with you guys. That hanging out with you was the first time in a real long time that I felt like I belonged. Your friendships mean the world to me, and I hope that you'll give me the chance to explain." Their silence was deafening, so I continued headfirst into my apology, hoping they would forgive me. "I have a pretty unusual past—"

"Oh, honey, everyone at this table has an unusual past." Indy's dark eyes found mine as she spoke.

"I know, but where I come from..."

Who was I kidding? These ladies weren't going to forgive me. I was ordered to eliminate their president. Their uncle. Their brother. *Their king of Kings.*

I gave her a pointed look.

"I killed people for a living," I said bluntly.

A strange vibe settled across the table.

"Yeah, that probably wins," Honey said, looking uneasy.

"They were bad people. Drug dealers. Gunrunners. But people, nonetheless." I looked around the table. "But I was never going to hurt Bull."

"But you did," Indy said. "Just not with a bullet."

"And if I could change that...please believe me, I would."

"You came into our world to spy on my brother," Ronnie said. "Then you start dating him. Tell me, when exactly did you decide you weren't going to kill him? Before or after you made him fall in love with you?"

Ronnie was going to be tough to crack. She was fiercely protective of her brother.

"I didn't know what my godfather had planned when I came here. I thought it was for surveillance only." The mention of Bull being in love with me made my heart burn with regret. I could still feel his lips against mine as he moaned it into my mouth during our last night together. "Please understand, I only agreed to come here so Noah and I could stop running. It's all I've ever wanted. I never came here to hurt anyone."

"I've heard about enough," Ronnie said, dragging her handbag off the table and standing up so she was eye-level with me. Close up, she

Bull

was fierce. Stepping even closer, her eyes narrowed, blazing with contempt. "My advice to you is to stay the fuck away from me. Do you hear me? I might not be some ruthless, gun-toting gunslinger like you, but I'm as badass as they come, and the only reason you're still standing here now is because my dumbass brother told me if I laid a finger on you he'd—"

"Ronnie!" Bull's voice broke into her outburst, and I swung around to look in the direction of his voice. I hadn't heard him walk in, but there he was, standing with Ruger only yards away, and I realized he must've been here the whole time.

Seeing him tightened the thick knot of regret in my chest. He looked so big and strong, but utterly damaged.

Because of me.

"She saved my life."

His words rippled between us.

"And that's the only reason she's not flat on her ass," Ronnie seethed. "Traitorous bitch!"

"Ronnie..." Bull warned, again.

But her words flowed over me like water and I barely registered them. Because seeing Bull was like a punch in my gut, and I was trembling inside. I ached to go to him, to feel his arms around me, to kiss him until the pain was gone from his heart and he loved me again. But as we stood there, I could tell the gulf between us was wide—almost too wide to cross. His gaze found mine and his chiseled jaw tightened. While all I could do was stare.

"Stay out of my way, traitor."

I turned back to Ronnie, barely aware of what she'd said. Because I was too numb to worry about her. When she walked away, I turned back to Bull. Our eyes locked, and my throat tightened with a cold ache. He wore an unreadable mask. But I could see the turbulence in his eyes. When he turned and walked away, it was too much.

I went after him, down the hallway leading to his office. I called out, but he ignored me until we were alone in the very room where he'd given me some of the best sex of my life.

Fuck me on your desk.

"We need to talk," I said, my voice shaky.

I watched him take a packed backpack from the couch and place it on top of his desk.

"Doesn't seem to be much left to talk about," he said, refusing to look at me as he packed a few things into the backpack.

He wasn't going to make this easy. But I got it. After all, in the MC world a cold shoulder was rare. I was lucky I didn't have a bullet in my skull. I knew the Kings of Mayhem would never harm a woman because it went against everything they valued. But I could be the exception, given my betrayal.

"I can't help who I was in the past," I said. "And you know I had no choice about moving to Destiny."

He opened the top drawer to his desk and removed a notebook, putting it in the breast pocket of his cut. "I do."

"But do you believe that I would never have tried to hurt you."

"Yes."

"Then why won't you look at me, dammit?" I choked out, my chin quivering.

He looked at me, and when his eyes met mine, they were ice cold. "We've been together three months, Taylor. You had three months to tell me!"

"But I couldn't. And you know why I couldn't."

He shook his head and zipped up his backpack. "It would've been nice to know that the woman I was in love with was a cold-blooded killer."

"So, it's okay for you to have killed bad people? But not me? Is that why you don't love me anymore? Because I used to be a hired killer?" I trembled with heartache; my throat tight with emotion. "You told me once, that there was nothing I could say that would change your feelings for me. Is this you telling me you were wrong?"

His barely contained restraint broke, and his backpack fell to the floor with a thud. He stalked toward me, his eyes blazing. A deadly combination of fury and heartache burning off him as he stood over me.

"I couldn't care less how many men you've killed. You and me, we don't live in the real world. Ours is full of darkness and evil, and you do what you gotta do to survive." He moved just an inch closer, but it was enough for me to see his racing pulse pounding in the vein in his neck. "Except lie to the man you're supposed to fucking be in love with."

He was so close and I was intoxicated by his heat. I wanted to reach out and touch him. I felt breathless and dizzy, my own pulse roaring in my ears.

"I *am* in love with you," I whispered.

He stepped back as if my words burned him.

"Sorry, lady, but you have one hell of a way of showing it." He picked up his backpack and threw it over his shoulder.

"Where are you going?" I was terrified I was never going to see him again.

"Away."

"Are you coming back?"

He glared at me. "Unlike some people, I don't get to fucking run away from my problems. I'm the king of fucking kings remember. I have an MC to run."

"Then, when will you be back?"

"When I'm ready."

I started to cry. "Please—"

"What?"

"Tell me how I can make this right." I cried. I went to him but he reared back from my touch. But I couldn't let him walk away, so I reached for him again, and this time he let me. "There has to be a way to make this right."

He looked pained. His face passive but his eyes stormy and anguished. His backpack dropped to the floor again. And with a hiss he pulled me into his rock-hard chest, and I fell like a ragdoll against him.

"How could you fucking do this to me?" he cried suddenly, his face ravaged by turmoil. He dropped his forehead to mine, inhaling deeply as if he was breathing in my very essence. He reached for my jaw. "How could you break down every goddamn wall I had, only to make me want to build new ones?"

"I'm sorry," I sobbed. "But if you give me a chance, I will spend the rest of my life making it up to you."

His grip tightened around my jawbone. His breathing suddenly ragged as his blazing eyes rushed over my face. I could feel his agony, and it was breaking my heart.

"Why, *little bird*?" He moaned desperately. "I fucking loved you. I would have done anything for you."

Loved. Not love.

"I'm sorry—"

He slammed his lips to mine, groaning as his tongue swept into my mouth. I could feel the vibration of it ripple through to my bones. His kiss was desperate. Angry. Heartbroken. His big hands pressed into my cheeks. There was a storm inside of him, raging wild as his mouth dominated mine.

With a moan, he ripped himself away from me.

"You're the best and the worst thing to happen to me," he growled, and then picking up his backpack, stormed out of the room.

I sagged against the wall and slipped to the floor.

He was gone.

And I could only pray it wasn't for good.

CHAPTER 61

TAYLOR

After a week, there was still no sign of him. I switched to autopilot. I climbed out of bed, I got Noah to school and then I went to work.

But the clubhouse wasn't the same with him gone. Nothing was. He was the first thing I thought of in the morning and the last thing when I turned the light out at night.

Everything in between felt empty and gray.

I missed him.

Terribly.

I put one foot in front of the other, but my heart ached and I struggled to smile. I became attached to my phone, always checking it for a message from Bull, and when I was at work, I kept looking over to the door, willing him to walk in.

But he never did. Because he was gone. And I didn't think he was coming back.

After my shifts, I would pick Noah up from school, and sometimes we would hang out at the breakfast counter while he did his homework and talk about his day. Other days, he'd spend the afternoon with his friends, and I would stare out the window and wonder if I was ever going to see Bull again.

At first the Kings were wary of me. But beneath the cool stares and cold shoulders, there was a deep current of understanding. This was the MC world. It was dark. It was dangerous. And it was unpredictable. Things could turn on a dime.

They knew about my past. My parents. What Alex had done. And apparently, Bull had warned them that any attempt for revenge would be met with brutal consequences. They needed to understand that everything was done in an attempt to keep my brother safe, and that at no stage was Bull's life in danger because of me.

It would take time, but they would learn to trust me again.

A second weekend passed without a word from him, and I couldn't stand it any longer.

I approached Ruger. "Please, you have to let me know he's okay."

I didn't know how Ruger felt toward me. Had he forgiven me for the lies?

Did he hate me for hurting his best friend?

He probably thought I had no right asking, but I didn't care. I needed to know he was alright.

Seeing me so distressed, Ruger's face softened and he nodded for me to sit down on the bar stool next to him.

"He's okay." His green eyes sparkled across at me. "He just needs time."

"Do you think he'll ever forgive me?"

He shook his head regretfully. "I don't know."

I took a chance in asking, "Will you?"

Ruger thought for a moment before replying.

"I'm going to tell you something, and I want you to listen carefully because this is a weird fucking situation and I can see how much you're struggling with it. You were caught between a rock and a hard place. I get it. We all do. And if any of us were in the same situation...who knows if we would've done it differently." His brow creased. "I think you're the best thing to ever happen to him."

His unexpected words hit me with so much warmth I wanted to cry.

"You do?"

"You brought him back to life, Taylor. You gave him what none of us could...*hope*. Before you came along, he was stuck in darkness. But

Bull

you changed that. You brought him out of it. You made him happy. Made him love again."

"But he hates me. And I don't blame him."

"He doesn't hate you. He loves you." His gaze met mine. "He's just not sure what to do with that in light of the events that transpired."

His words lingered in me. Hours later, as I spent another evening overcome with longing, they replayed over and over in my mind.

Tonight, Noah was at a sleepover. Despite being a school night, I let him go because he'd suffered two major losses recently.

Pickles.

And now Bull.

I didn't know how to make it up to him. I could barely cope with it myself. Pickles's death had been completely out of my hands, but I was responsible for Bull being gone, and it all wrapped itself around my neck like a giant boa constrictor.

Now I was alone, with a bottle of wine already opened and a storm brewing outside. By late evening, the rain was coming down hard. I could see the glittering needles falling through the illumination from the street light and I was becoming more depressed with every raindrop.

I turned away from the window, fighting tears. I missed him. I missed him desperately.

Taking my glass of wine over to the couch, I curled up in front of the television. But I only stared at the screen. I couldn't absorb anything. All I could do was miss him.

The knock at my front door was so faint, I barely heard it. But it was followed by another one, this time louder. I glanced at the clock. It was a little after nine and I wasn't expecting anyone.

Setting down my glass, I crossed the room and peered through the peephole and immediately, my heart leaped to my throat.

With hurried fingers, I unlocked the door and ripped it open, my pulse hammering in my ears when I saw him standing on my front stoop in the rain.

An overwhelming longing washed over me as he stood across from me.

He was rain-soaked, his sopping t-shirt clinging to his broad chest, and his hair falling in wet tendrils over his forehead.

Speechless, I absorbed the sight of him, wondering for a moment if he was real or if I was somehow imagining this because I was so crazy-lost without him. But he was really here. Standing in front of me. Raindrops rolling down his beautiful face and falling from his parted lips as he panted.

Beside him, his hands were curled into fists.

I whispered his name, but it was swallowed by the storm.

Seeing him cracked open the wound in my chest and poured pain into my already broken heart. I wanted to go to him. To touch him. To hold him. *Kiss him.* But I was terrified he would push me away and tell me he didn't love me anymore.

Neither of us said anything. Instead, we just stared at each other; him, struggling with the emotion coursing through him, and me aching to touch him.

"I told myself I could forget you," he finally called out over the rain. And my stomach dropped to the pit of my stomach. Because he didn't love me anymore and he was here to tell me so.

He shook his head and looked tortured; his brows drawn in by heartache. His fists opened and closed at his sides.

"But I can't fucking get over you. And I don't want to. Because I love you. Do you understand me, *little bird*? I fucking love you!"

I started to cry.

"But if you don't love me...tell me now...because I can't go another minute like this. Because it's killing me, Taylor. It's killing me being without you. And I can't move on until I know how you feel."

With a cry, I ran into his arms and pressed my mouth to his wet lips, kissing him urgently, needing him so desperately, and wanting to ease both of our pain. Rain poured down around us, drenching us as his lips parted and his warm, luscious tongue slipped into my mouth. He shivered against me, his soft moan falling between us as we kissed frantically in the storm.

I pulled away from him only long enough to tell him that I loved him too—that I loved him so much I could barely breathe without him—before finding his mouth again and kissing him like I was dying of thirst and he was my oasis.

"I love you so much," I cried, my tears joining the rain on my cheeks. I buried my face in his drenched chest and he trembled.

When I looked up, I saw his chin shudder with emotion. Rain spilled from his beautiful lips. "I don't want this life if it means it's a life without you. Tell me what you need from me, and it's yours."

It killed me to see him in so much pain.

"You," I cried. "I just need you."

I kissed him and his lips faltered. I felt him hesitate. Felt his need wrestle with his fear.

But then the damn broke, and with a desperate groan, he kissed me back, hard and urgently, his breathing ragged, and with every lick of our tongues, our walls completely fell away.

We tumbled into the living room and it was a blur of limbs ripping off wet clothing before we fell to the floor and Bull covered me with his powerful body. I felt his abs, warm and thick with muscle, sliding against me as he pressed his hips into mine, and the familiarity made me want to cry because I had missed this so damn much.

"God, I missed you," he moaned, as if reading my mind. He slid down my body and lowered his mouth over one nipple, torturously sucking and licking it, before dragging his tongue across my breastbone to repeat the same motion on the other one. "And these breasts..." He let my nipple go and moved lower, dragging his tongue down my ribcage and over the gentle swell of my belly. "It's been torture not being able to have this beautiful body under me." His lips moved over my skin as he spoke. "To touch it. To taste it." He moaned, inhaling my scent as he licked his way past my hip bone. "Tell me this body is mine," he groaned, and I could hear the torment in his smoky voice. "Tell me this body belongs to me." I gripped the plush rug beneath me, and my legs fell open as he moved over the pubic bone.

Two fingers entered me at the same moment his tongue licked through soaking skin. "Tell me this pussy is mine."

I moaned out a yes, but it came out strangled and inaudible.

"Tell me!" he demanded, his fingers sliding in and out of me as he tormented my clit with his tongue. I was soaking wet and I could hear my body pulling at his fingertips.

"Bull..." I moaned out his name, desperate to come.

He lowered his head.

"Tell me your pussy belongs to me. And only me." His tongue flattened across my clit, and I lit up like a skyrocket.

"Yes! Oh God, yes!"

My orgasm crashed through me with indescribable force. With a cry, I arched my back off the floor and threw my hands to his scalp, my fingers tangling wildly in his wet hair.

"That's it, baby," he moaned against my quaking flesh as I came on his mouth. "I've been aching to make you come."

My legs shook, and a serene heat moved slowly through me before I sagged farther into the floor in a boneless heap.

Flushed, I looked up at him, taking in the broad shoulders and chiseled chest as he rose up and knelt back on his knees, his giant cock jutting upward to touch his lower abs.

"Please..." I begged, coming down from my high. "I need you inside me."

It had been weeks since he'd touched me, *loved me*, and I needed him inside me when I came again.

His eyes glimmered with erotic darkness, and I watched with uninhibited wantonness as he took his thick cock in his hands and pressed it to my swollen entrance. I whimpered, trembling as he dragged the engorged head through the sensitive flesh, not knowing how much more I could take.

He fixed his eyes to mine and I could see he was barely keeping control. When he entered me, we both groaned, but then he held himself there, not moving, and it was torture. I needed him to move. Desperately.

"Tell me you're mine," he begged. "Tell me I'm your man."

The lack of movement, the torture, it had me seconds away from another orgasm.

"Yes," I cried. "I'm all yours, Bull. And you're all mine."

He drove his heavy length into me and detonated my hanging climax. I clenched his cock and we came together, clinging to each other as we fell into a blissful oblivion, our bodies tangled and our hearts pounding wildly.

When I came down, I softened against him, relaxing for the first time in weeks.

He was back.

And he was mine.

Later, we showered together, taking our time to lather up one another's bodies, and I soaked up every blissful, soapy touch, savoring every second with him. Because I hadn't forgotten the cold ache or the relentless fog that came with his absence. I knew a world without him in it, and it had left me lifeless and heartbroken.

Now he was home, and I was going to cherish every second.

As we kissed leisurely under the steady stream of warm water, Bull cupped my face in his big hands, his strong fingertips brushing against my jawbone and whispering lightly across my damp skin. And I melted against him, lost in the tenderness of his touch, drunk on the warmth of his kiss and the sweetness of his lips.

And even though it was highly erotic, and despite his erection pressing against my stomach as we kissed and licked, and touched, we did nothing more than lose ourselves in the intimacy of our kissing.

It wasn't until the warm water ran cold that we wrapped ourselves in warm towels and dried off before slipping between the sheets. Immediately, Bull pulled me to his chest and secured me there with his big arms, his body hard and comforting as he wrapped himself around me.

We made love slowly this time. Every touch purposeful. Every moan full of meaning. And in that moment, there was just the two of us, two bodies moving together in the soft glow of a bedside lamp, while a storm continued to rage outside.

Before he came, Bull paused to look down at me, and I was touched by the affection in his eyes.

"I'm all yours, *little bird*. Now and forever. Or for however long you want me."

The look on his face was heartbreaking.

"Forever," I whispered. "I want you for forever."

With the smallest movement of his hips, he started to come, dropping his head with a moan, and I fell in step with him, giving into the rush of ecstasy as it poured into me.

He collapsed against me, the heat of his rapid breath caressing the nook of my neck, the warmth of his big body covering mine.

When our bodies softened and our breathing calmed, I settled into his arms. Looking up into his handsome face, I touched the scruff along his jaw.

"Where have you been?" I asked quietly.

He was quiet for a moment, and I could hear the gentle thump of his heartbeat.

"Riding. Thinking." His fingers absentmindedly traced imaginary lines across the skin of my shoulder. "Riding some more."

"You've been gone so long."

"I needed time."

"What have you been doing?"

His gaze caught mine. "Trying to figure out the best way to ask you to marry me."

CHAPTER 62

TAYLOR

Twelve Months Later

Jesus Christ, the pain was like nothing I'd known.

"You're doing so well, baby."

I grabbed Bull by the t-shirt. "You did this to me…"

Sweat ran down my forehead as another wave of excruciating pain swept through me.

"Well, I hope it was me," he said with that mischievous glint in his eye.

I twisted my hand deeper into his shirt. "Does this look like a time for jokes—" Agony cut me off, and I cried out as two kinds of pain twisted at my insides. "—*goddamn*, it feels like a bowling ball is trying to push its way out of my body!"

When Bull chuckled, I threw him a warning look. The contractions were on top of one another now.

The midwife delivering my baby looked up from between my legs. "Ok, Taylor, I'm going to need you to push."

Taking in a deep breath, I gritted my teeth and pushed for dear life…thankfully, I was rewarded with a strange release.

"We have a head," she said.

I looked at Bull, and relief washed over me like warm water. "We have a head?" And I started to cry when he nodded.

"Yeah, baby. We have a head."

I drew in deep breaths.

"Okay, Taylor. I'm going to need you to push again. I know you're tired. But I need one big push from you, okay. Your baby wants to meet her mama."

With all of my muscles tightened and straining, I pushed, but it was no use. My baby wasn't budging.

"Okay, take a moment to get your breath. Now, I need you to give me another one of those. On a count of three, one…two…three…now push!"

Again, I tried, I pushed as hard as I could, my body clenching, my muscles straining, my eyes squeezed shut, until I couldn't do anymore.

Air burst from me as I let go.

"I can't do this," I cried to Bull, suddenly afraid. I was exhausted. I had nothing left. Fifteen hours of labor had taken its toll, and I was spent.

He clasped a big hand around mine "You can do this, baby. One more push." He tenderly wiped hair from my face and leaned in to press a kiss to my forehead. "My sweet, strong, *little bird*. You're the strongest, fiercest woman I know. You can do this, baby."

I drew in a deep breath and nodded as I let it out in a slow exhale.

"Ready?" the midwife asked.

Another breath.

Another push.

Another cry ripped from deep inside of me, and our daughter came into the world screaming.

I fell back onto the pillows, exhausted, while Bull looked down at me, with a face full of love and affection.

"You did it," he said, his voice touched with emotion. Tears welled in his eyes. "She's fucking beautiful."

The midwife placed our daughter on my chest.

She was perfect.

Eden Western was the most beautiful baby in the world.

Having finally arrived, she released another almighty wail, and I started to cry.

Bull

Bull was in love. He didn't even try to hide his tears. Instead, he leaned forward as they fell down his face, and pressed a quivering kiss to my lips.

"Thank you," he whispered.

I looked at my big bull of a husband, and my heart bloomed with happiness. God had blessed me with so many loves.

Later that day, Maverick brought Noah into the hospital to meet his niece. Excited, he held her securely in his arms and couldn't wipe the grin off his sweet face. He was staying with Maverick and Autumn for a few days, and filled me in on what was happening. Autumn and their baby son, Nalu, were sick and opted to stay home.

Ronnie arrived not long after, her arms filled with a massive bouquet of sunflowers. "Give me a look at my beautiful niece," she said, taking Eden from my arms and cradling her. She looked from my daughter to me, and gave me a wink. "You did good."

Her smile lingered and I knew our relationship was in a good place. She had forgiven me for the lies and the betrayal. We had a fair way to go but I was certain we were going to get there. Because she knew I loved Bull, and she knew I would always stand proudly beside him as his queen.

The afternoon drifted by with other visitors. Cade and Indy came by with River and Bella, whose hand-painted pictures now hung on the wall beside the windows overlooking the river. And afterward, Honey and Caleb came with Cassidy and Chance, both of them bringing all of their kids. Not long after they left, Chastity and Ruger came by with Grandma Sybil and Jury.

By sundown I was exhausted. But I couldn't sleep. I was too damn high on happiness.

It took me hours to convince Bull to go home and get some rest. He fought me. Said he'd sleep when he was dead. Said he didn't want to miss a moment of his daughter's life. He cradled her so long, his arms must've felt like dead weights.

But eventually, even my strong biker king needed his rest. He left when it was very late with the promise to be back in the morning. And as he kissed me goodbye, I was filled with a ferocious love like I'd never known.

Now my daughter lay soundly in my arms, and I let the contentment wrap itself around me.

Life was perfect. Ten months ago, the love of my life had draped his crown pendant around my neck in a wedding ceremony watched over by our friends and family, and members from every chapter of the Kings of Mayhem.

Now we had our beautiful daughter, and my life was finally complete.

I didn't like the girl I used to be. But she'd stepped up when I'd needed her to help me get my brother back, and in doing so, made me realize that instead of running from her, perhaps I could learn to accept her. *Learn to forgive her*. She was a product of her past. While I was a product of my choice. We weren't two separate people like I had tried to convince myself we were. She would always be a part of me, and I needed to accept that so I could move on and heal.

And we both deserved that.

EPILOGUE

BULL

Ten Years Later

Little fingers dug into my scalp, forcing my head upward until I was looking into a pair of big brown eyes.

"Look, Daddy, look at Noah," my five-year-old daughter, Angel, said. She was on my shoulders, wriggling with excitement. My second daughter was adorably enthusiastic. "Look at him up on the stage."

We were at Noah's college graduation. And when I say we, I mean half the outdoor auditorium was full of Kings of Mayhem bikers and their families. We stood at the back of the crowd, respectfully leaving the seating to the other family members because there were more of us than them. Nearly all of the Kings of Mayhem original chapter were there because Noah was a big deal to all of us. Since joining our family a decade ago, he was a permanent fixture at the clubhouse, always studying, always helping out with his nieces and nephews.

Next to me, my wife of ten years snuggled into my chest, her face wet with tears as she watched her brother receiving his college degree.

Shaking the hand of the college dean, Noah started to laugh when the crowd of excited bikers started cheering and whistling with ear-bleeding enthusiasm. He paused for the photographer to take a photo, and then he waved at us, signing *thank you* before walking across the stage to join the other graduates.

"Can you believe it?" Taylor said through her tears. "He's all grown up now."

It was the same thing she said when he graduated high school, and again, when he'd moved into the college dorm. He was a well-adjusted kid who was looking forward to exploring a career in mechatronics.

I had a feeling we were going to see more tears when he eventually moved to New York. Which wasn't too far away. Two weeks ago, a renowned robotics company had offered him a job following his graduation, and the kid had accepted it.

It was just a hunch, but I was pretty sure I was going to see a lot more of New York than I'd ever cared too. I didn't like going too far from Destiny, from my family, and my club. But I was going to miss Noah, a lot. And if I complained about visiting the city later, it would be all bark and no bite because I was going to miss Noah like crazy.

My other daughter, ten-year-old, Eden, was walking toward us with her eleven-year-old cousin, Will. They were born exactly twelve months apart, almost down to the hour, and were best friends. Where you found Eden, you found Will.

Walking beside them, was Axel, my son. At seven years old, he was my very own mini-me, right down to the bright blue eyes, but thankfully without my acute color blindness. He also had a shock of dark hair and the cutest damn dimples you ever saw on a kid.

"You guys ready to party?" I asked.

"Yay! Party! Party! Party!" Angel cried, wriggling on my shoulders again.

Back at the clubhouse, we held a mammoth celebration for Noah and his classmates. He was a popular kid on campus, and he and his friends filled the lawn of the Kings of Mayhem compound as they celebrated their graduation.

While Cade and Caleb fought over how to barbecue steaks on the grill, I sat back and watched the celebrations.

Across the lawn, a band belted out Led Zeppelin and Creedence Clearwater Revival songs.

The compound was full. Humming with life and celebrations. Beer

Bull

kegs were flowing and the aroma of barbecue filled the sunny afternoon air.

On the makeshift dance floor, Grandma Sybil was tearing it up with Yale and Animal, while Cade's teenage son, River, danced with one of Noah's college friends, clearly smitten with the older girl.

Everyone was having a good time.

Me, I took the time to reflect.

A lot had happened in the last ten years.

Peace had settled in our world. And while a lot of our rivals had fallen, it had been a time of great prosperity for the Kings of Mayhem. There was more time for celebration. There was more time for family. And there was little need for the bloodletting of years prior.

The last ten years had also been the happiest of my life. My beautiful wife gave me two daughters and a son, and I can't begin to explain the feeling. Once upon a time, I thought I was going to die alone. Now our home was filled with childhood activity, brother and sister fights, and so much fucking contentment I hated to think back to a time before them. My life had turned on its axis when I'd met Taylor, and it'd spun on its ass when I became a father, skyrocketing me into a strange and terrifying world. And I was so fucking grateful for all of it.

My family wasn't the only one that grew. My nephews and niece had more children of their own, and Autumn and Maverick had the six kids he always wanted.

Old ladies came and went. Randy found marital happiness with the girl who replaced Taylor behind the bar, and now he and his wife ran the bar together. While Matlock made good on his promise and married Danni Deepthroat.

Red also found his other half when he took a baking class at the local cooking school. He fell crazy in love with a sweet girl called Amy who fell as equally crazy in love with him.

And Joker, our resident funny man, found serious happiness with our local librarian.

Tiffani disappeared from the clubhouse. Finally got tired of the non-committal cock sucking and deep dicking. She married some mechanic she met over in Humphrey, and moved away. Last I heard she was in Vegas working as a showgirl.

Vader and Roberta remarried after spending more and more time together with their kids, and realizing some old feelings never died. They even had another kid. A boy they named Anakin. And Hawke and Davey both decided having an old lady around wasn't such a bad thing, and both took the plunge for a second time.

But with the good came the bad. We lost Griffin, Garrett Calley's older brother, when he finally succumbed to his muscular dystrophy after a valiant fight. And a few years later, we lost our fire bug, Nitro, when one of his side jobs went wrong and he was caught in an explosion.

But the good far outweighed the bad.

It had been a good decade.

Hell, it had been a great decade.

Gimmel Martel died in prison, three months into a life sentence. Shivved by an inmate who didn't appreciate his treatment of underage girls on the outside. The Feds had a field day pulling apart his tattered empire. Within the year of our encounter at the lake house, barely a scrap of his existence was left behind.

Jean-Paul didn't live for much longer than his father. He was found dead in the prison laundry with severe head trauma only weeks later. Not surprisingly, no one saw anything, so no one was charged.

Seeking some space from the celebrations, I took a moment in my office. I sat down in my chair and looked around the room where so much had taken place over the years.

War had been waged in this room. But love had also conquered.

"I was wondering where you disappeared to," came a soft, familiar voice.

I looked up to see my gorgeous wife standing in the doorway, looking every inch as delicious as the first day I'd laid my eyes on her. We had a good marriage. Hell, we had a *hot* marriage. I was obsessed with my queen. Every inch of her. And even after a decade, I found it hard to keep my hands off her.

"Just taking a moment, is all," I said, looking around the office. "Things are changing so fast, aren't they?"

"You're not getting all sentimental on me, are you, Bull Western?"

Bull

I offered her a half smile. She was right. It seemed the older I got, the more nostalgic I became.

My wife gently closed the door behind her, locking it.

"You know, the first time you fucked me was in this very room," she said, seductively moving toward me, her fingers slowly undoing the buttons of her blouse.

"How can I forget?" I raised an eyebrow. "You told me to fuck you on my desk."

She chuckled. "How very straightforward of me."

"It's one of the things that made me like you so much."

She smiled wickedly and let her blouse drop open, exposing a pair of perfect, naked breasts underneath. After ten years and three children, her body was softer and curvier, and still as sexy as fuck.

"Was there anything else that made you like me so much?" she asked, shimmying out of her skirt and stepping out of her panties until she was completely naked.

My cock roared to life behind my zipper. "You know you drove me insane for weeks."

She gave me a wicked smile. "Is that a fact?"

"You know how much I wanted you."

"What about now?" She climbed on my lap and slid her legs on either side of me. She gasped feeling the size of me through my pants. "Fuck, baby, you're hard already."

"What can I say? I'm a fucking sucker for my naked wife."

She started to rock against my lap, sending a bolt of pleasure along my thick shaft. Moaning, she lowered her head to kiss me and then pulled back, a soft whisper on her luscious lips. "I think you'd better fuck me on your desk now to refresh my memory."

We separated long enough for me to get naked before I scooped her up and set her down on my desk and did exactly as my queen asked.

Afterward, as we dressed and she curled up on my lap, she nestled her head into my chest and smiled.

"Our life is good," she whispered.

"It is."

"I mean, it was hard at first. We both lost people. Both faced diversities. But somehow we found each other and it stuck."

"And they've been the best years of my life."

She chuckled.

"What's so funny?" I asked.

"If there were two people who should never have found what we have, it was us." She smiled softly. "Why do you think it worked out for us?"

I pressed my lips to her hair and held her closer to me. "It's because I was made for you, and you were always going to be the love of my life."

THE END

Bull

KINGS OF MAYHEM MC PLAYLIST

The Fire Down Below
Bob Seger & The Silver Bullet Band

Only One Too (Pull Club Mix) ... this version is outta this world!!
Jewel

Only One Too
Jewel

Where Are You Now?
Inglorious

So Am I
Ava Max

Can't You See
The Marshall Tucker Band

Thousand Eyes
Lia Ices

Penny Dee

Unskinny Bop
Poison

Smooth
Car Stereo Wars

Born to Be Wild
Steppenwolf

Put Your Curse on Me
Stonefield

Mary Had A Little Lamb
Stevie Ray Vaughan

Holy Diver
Dio

Red Cold River
Breaking Benjamin

Cocaine
Eric Clapton

Cowboy
Kid Rock

Hunter
RIAYA feat. John Mark McMillan

Long Cool Woman (In A Black Dress)
The Hollies

Bull

Burnin'
Black Stone Cherry

Oh Darlin' What Have I Done
The White Buffalo

Penny Dee

CONNECT WITH ME ONLINE

Check these links for more books from Penny Dee.

READER GROUP

For more mayhem join by FB readers group:
Penny's Queens of Mayhem
www.facebook.com/groups/604941899983066/

NEWSLETTER

https://bit.ly/364AFvo

WEBSITE

http://www.pennydeebooks.com/

INSTAGRAM

@pennydeeromance

BOOKBUB

http://www.bookbub.com/authors/penny-dee

Bull

EMAIL
penny@pennydeebooks.com

FACEBOOK
http://www.facebook.com/pennydeebooks/

ABOUT THE AUTHOR

Penny Dee writes contemporary romance about rock stars, bikers, hockey players and everyone in-between. Her stories bring the suspense, the feels and a whole lot of heat.

She found her happily ever after with an Australian hottie who she met on a blind date.

Printed in Great Britain
by Amazon